A DEEP DECEIT

Hilary Bonner is a former showbusiness editor of the *Mail on Sunday* and the *Daily Mirror*. She now lives in Somerset, and continues to work as a freelance journalist, covering film, television and theatre. She is the author of four previous novels, *The Cruelty of Morning*, *A Fancy to Kill For*, *A Passion So Deadly* and *For Death Comes Softly*.

Praise for Hilary Bonner

'Welcome to a sharp new talent in crime writing'
Daily Express

'A compelling thriller that skilfully weaves together passion and tragedy with sinister obsession'
Company

'A great murder mysetery' *Daily Mail*

'A stormy, steamy thriller that keeps you turning the pages from minute one' *Daily Star*

'A fast-paced thriller with sex, drugs and convincing showbiz detail' *Sunday Mirror*

'I was caught on page one by this mesmerising thriller and raced through it in a single sitting . . . a dark, erotic thriller, Robert Goddard with sex' Sarah Broadhurst, *The Bookseller*

Also by Hilary Bonner

FICTION

The Cruelty of Morning
A Fancy to Kill For
A Passion So Deadly
For Death Comes Softly

NON-FICTION

Heartbeat – The Real Life Story
Benny – A Biography of Benny Hill
René and Me (with Gorden Kaye)
Journeyman (with Clive Gunnell)

HILARY BONNER

A DEEP
DECEIT

ARROW

Published in the United Kingdom in 2001 by
Arrow Books

1 3 5 7 9 10 8 6 4 2

First published in the United Kingdom in 2000 by William Heinemann

Arrow Books Limited
Random House UK Limited
20 Vauxhall Bridge Road, London, SW1V 2SA

Random House Australia (Pty) Limited
20 Alfred Street, Milsons Point, Sydney, New South Wales 2061,
Australia

Random House New Zealand Limited
18 Poland Road, Glenfield
Auckland 10, New Zealand

Random House (Pty) Limited
Endulini, 5a Jubilee Road, Parktown 2193, South Africa

Random House Group Limited Reg. No. 954009

www.randomhouse.co.uk

A CIP catalogue record for this book is available from the
British Library

Papers used by Random House UK Limited are natural, recyclable
products made from wood grown in sustainable forests. The
manufacturing processes conform to the environmental regulations of
the country of origin

ISBN 0 09 928092 2

Typeset in Plantin by SX Composing DTP, Rayleigh, Essex
Printed and bound in Germany by
Elsnerdruck, Berlin

For Lynne Drew

With thanks to:

Dr Paul Nathan, Dr John Griffin, Dr Arden Tomison, Home Office Pathologist Dr Hugh White, Barry Sullivan LL.B, Detective Sergeant Pat Pitts and Detective Constable Phil Diss of the Devon and Cornwall Constabulary, Chief Superintendent Steve Livings and Detective Sergeant Frank Waghorn of the Avon and Somerset Constabulary (again), the staff of St Ives Archive Centre, Library and Tourist Office, and the people of Cornwall and Key West who remain among the last great individuals in life and provided much of the inspiration for this book.

I am so very grateful to them all.

Smooth runs the water where the brook is deep
And in his simple show he harbours treason
The fox barks not when he would steal a lamb;
No, no, my sovereign, Gloucester is a man
Unsounded yet, and full of deep deceit.

William Shakespeare
Henry VI, Part Two, Act 3

One

The first blow split my lip and loosened my front teeth. I tasted the salt of my own blood filling my mouth. Somehow I managed to turn and run from the bedroom out on to the landing but I wasn't nearly fast enough. He was after me at once. The second blow flattened my nose. I felt the bone turn into mush and more warm blood spurt from my torn nostrils. The next blow sliced my face open and cracked a cheekbone. Pain filled my head. I fell heavily on to the floor, clutching at my ruined face, struggling to catch my breath, desperate to escape.

He stood above me, quite calm it seemed. Then he drew back his right leg and kicked me with all his might. He was wearing leather lace-up shoes with hard toes, the heavy old-fashioned kind. The kick caught me fully in the ribs with such force that I was half lifted off the ground and sent spiralling crazily down the stairs. I bounced my way down, stair by stair, the sharp edges digging into my already shattered rib cage, my arms and legs twisting impossibly beneath me, and landed with a sickening thump at the bottom.

My wrist felt broken and I had twisted my ankle so badly that I knew, without trying, I would not be able to walk.

I was aware of him standing at the top of the stairs. Quite still, silently watching.

Tears mingled with the blood running down my smashed face. I half crawled, half dragged myself across the hall, and reached out with my one good arm in an attempt to open the front door. I grasped the handle and managed somehow to turn it, but the door didn't budge. I assumed it must be locked. In defeat, I slumped into a heap again.

Suddenly I realised he must have come down the stairs. He had an ability to move very quietly, uncannily so, even at the height of his furies. He was like a cat stalking his prey and I could feel his shadow looming over me. I could hear the rasp of his breath. I whimpered. I hated myself for my weakness but I had no defence against him. I didn't look up. I couldn't bear to look up. I knew what I would see.

Instead, I summoned my strength to make my tortured way into the dining room, still half crawling, half dragging myself using my one good arm.

I made it to the table and crawled underneath. I curled myself into a tight ball, desperate not to be hurt any more, hearing the tread of his feet as he followed me, without hurry, into the room. I knew that he had been drinking heavily again, alcohol and his abuse always went together, and maybe this slowed him a little, but there was, in any case, no urgency for him. He had total command of my very existence.

He rested one hand on the table top and I could hear his fingers drumming. Tap tap tap, tappity tap. A rhythmic drumming. Then, quite abruptly, he lifted the table and tipped it so that it turned on to its side and I was revealed cowering there on the polished wooden floor, a frightened, whimpering thing.

2

I was certain I was going to die. There had been other terrible frightening times. But this was the worst, the very worst.

I could not run and I could not fight him. He was physically indomitable. It was not that he was a particularly big or strong man. It was more that his rages were so violent they gave him an almost unnatural power. And, of course, he believed he was God on Earth. Really, he did.

He stood above me, laughing. There was a hammer in his right hand, a heavy lump hammer which I didn't remember seeing before. It occurred to me that maybe he had acquired it specifically to kill me. He carried it loosely, letting it swing with his arm as if it were a cricket bat. He was still laughing. This really is the end, I thought. He could crush my skull with one blow from that. Eventually he raised his right arm. My terrified gaze rose with him, following the arc of the hammer, and I could no longer avoid looking into his face. My eyes were drawn there as if by a magnetic force.

Except, of course, that he had no face. I knew that already. But the shock of seeing it was always just as great as the first time. That was what I dreaded most of all, more even than the very worst of the violence. The horror of his facelessness was somehow greater than the pain he inflicted. I gazed into the empty black hole where his face should have been, and I could not look away. My eyes were riveted on the awful nothingness of him . . .

I heard myself screaming – terrible, frantic, piercing screams. And then it was all over.

*

I woke in Carl's arms, as I always did. I woke to the soothing sound of his lovely gentle voice and he held me close to him, even though I was a screaming, hysterical thing, pummelling his broad chest with my fists, kicking out desperately.

Slowly my hysteria lessened. Eventually I stopped punching and kicking, but it was a while before I could stop screaming. It always was.

'Shh, shh, my darling,' he soothed, in that soft American accent I had fallen in love with all those years before. 'It's all right, Suzanne,' he said. 'You're at home with me. It was just a dream, honey. Everything's fine. I won't let anybody hurt you.'

As I listened to his reassurances I felt the awful tension drift from my body. The pain had been so real. Cautiously I touched my lip and my nose. They were both undamaged. I was not bleeding. I did not have cracked ribs, a broken wrist or a twisted ankle, but I checked each part of my body carefully, just as I did every time.

Carl stroked my hair, then my face with one hand, and kept the other arm wrapped round me. He knew so well how to calm me.

The tears still poured down my face. He touched them, tenderly, and then he kissed them, still whispering reassurance. It was several minutes before I was able to stop crying. Carl carried on kissing my eyes and stroking me.

He knew my nightmares as well as I did. He was so vividly aware of them that it was almost as if he too suffered what I suffered. Sometimes I could feel his body trembling as he comforted me. He understood completely how to help me recover, how to help us both recover.

4

He would not try to make love to me, he never did at these times, because he knew as well as I did myself that I just couldn't, much as I adored him, not then. At any other time I responded to Carl's touch with the same loving arousal that he had first excited in me almost seven years previously. I loved him to pieces and we were blissfully happy together. Our home was a tiny cottage high above St Ives harbour and I had grown to love the little Cornish seaside town almost as much as I loved Carl.

Yet I could not stop the nightmares. Nothing could. Not even Carl. He could help me overcome them, but he could not stop them happening. At first I had been afraid to go to bed and had worn myself out pacing our tiny house, unable to bear the thought of sleep. They were not so frequent now. In the last year there had been just five. And always I prayed, as I knew Carl did, that this one would be the last.

'Will they ever stop?' I asked him for the umpteenth time. They were my first coherent words. They were invariably my first coherent words.

'One day,' he whispered, his lips very close to my ear. 'One day, I promise you.'

He was so kind. I knew he would not let himself sleep now. He never did. He realised that I needed him awake and loving me. And he knew that for at least the next week, maybe two weeks, the fear would be all around me again. And that some nights I would not dare to sleep. He would stay up with me until exhaustion overcame me. He always did.

He was my rock.

Two

Often, when I was trying to get over a nightmare I would make myself think happy thoughts. Try to remember the good times.

The very best memory of all was the day I first met Carl, the day everything changed. The day I began to believe that maybe, just maybe, I would find happiness.

I was crying when he first appeared by my side, almost by magic. I was desperate and so badly needed someone I could trust and lean upon. Then, out of nowhere, along came Carl.

I had gone to the Isabella Garden in Richmond Park because I needed to be alone. I was twenty years old. I had been married at eighteen, and I was desperately unhappy.

I was orphaned when I was just a toddler and my grandmother brought me up. It was a very sheltered childhood, unhealthily so, I suppose, although I had not known that at the time. Gran even contrived to teach me at home through most of what should have been my school years – and that suited me just fine. My one brief spell at primary school had been torture. Indeed, I never learned to cope with much of the world outside the home I shared with Gran.

I was certainly totally ill prepared for marriage so young – particularly to a strong, domineering man who turned out to have none of the kindness about him that Gran had always shown me, and which I had somehow expected to receive automatically from someone I was to share my life with. Instead, he turned out to be both cruel and violent.

Gran was long dead by the time I met Carl, and I felt completely alone in the world. Even though I was only twenty, I honestly believed that my life was over, that I would be forever trapped in a vicious, loveless marriage.

The Isabella was one of my hiding places, one of my sanctuaries. It's famous for its wonderful shows of spring shrubs, when the blooming rhododendrons and azaleas and camellias display themselves in all their blazing multicoloured glory. The autumn can also be glorious there, but not the winter. And this was a particularly unpleasant December Wednesday, cold, damp and relentlessly grey. But even so, I was grateful for the peace of the place.

I sat by a murky-looking pond weeping silently, and I thought I had the garden more or less to myself. Even the ducks seemed to have found somewhere more pleasantly hospitable. I was certainly not aware that there was another person nearby as I perched on an old, dead, moss-covered tree trunk, oblivious to its soggy wetness, lost in my own misery.

He must have approached very quietly because he was standing quite close to me before I noticed him. My head was bowed. My eyes were filled with tears. I saw his feet first, clad in Wellington boots. Then a hand reached out to me, offering a red-spotted handkerchief, the kind I had only seen before in films tied round a cowboy's neck.

He didn't startle me. There was nothing threatening about his presence and somehow I knew that immediately.

I looked up at him, seeing his face for the first time. It was a broad, unevenly featured face, but nevertheless quite pleasing. He had a big craggy chin, a reddish complexion emphasised by his cropped pale-blond hair, a wide, full-lipped mouth and the brightest, kindest blue eyes I had ever seen. But then, it was a long time since I had known any kindness at all.

I was aware at once of the gentleness in him. And there was concern in those blue eyes too, concern for a stranger. He had the look of someone who knew what pain was when he saw it.

He did not say anything at first, just continued to hold that spotted handkerchief in front of me. Eventually I took it, blew my nose and did my best to dry my eyes.

Only then did he speak, with that slight stammer which, I would learn later, occurred just when he was nervous. 'A-are are you all r-right?'

I didn't answer. It was, after all, pretty obvious that I wasn't all right.

He shook his head and made a kind of tutting sound. 'S-sorry, silly question,' he said.

'It's OK,' I replied. 'I'll be fine in a minute.'

He stood silently for a while as I sniffed inelegantly into his handkerchief, struggling desperately to stem the tears and regain control. 'I'm s-sorry,' he said again. 'Would you like me to leave you? I d-don't want to intrude?'

He took a couple of steps backwards towards the pond, without looking where he was going. His left foot sank deeply into the thick, gooey mud around the

8

edge of the water. He stumbled and for a moment I thought he was going to fall, then he recovered himself and shrugged his shoulders. 'Typical,' he said.

He was unsure of himself, and hesitant and clumsy in his movements, but there was humour in his eyes. And even at that moment he managed to coax a smile out of me.

Immediately he grinned back. I reckoned he was in his early thirties, maybe twelve or thirteen years my senior, but in spite of the lines etched quite deeply round his mouth and across his forehead the grin was a boyish one. He positively beamed at me and his mouth stretched so wide that it seemed as if his face might crack. His teeth were perfect: bright, white and wonderfully even. His accent had already told me that he was American. I didn't know much of the world, but I had read somewhere that being American and having good teeth went together. Involuntarily I felt my own smile widen.

'That's b-better,' he remarked. He ran the fingers of one hand through his stubbly blond hair, stepped towards me again and reached out with the other for his handkerchief. 'Finished with that?' he asked.

I glanced at the now damp and soiled piece of cotton with horror. 'I can't give you it back in that state. . .' I began.

'It doesn't matter,' he murmured, interrupting me. He took the handkerchief, put it back in his pocket and sat down next to me on the moss-covered tree trunk.

Although I had barely noticed its cold wetness until then, suddenly I was concerned for him. He wasn't wearing a long coat like me, just a short leather jacket over blue jeans.

'The moss is sodden,' I warned.

'Oh right.' He glanced down at the tree trunk beneath him as if seeing it for the first time, then jumped to his feet, pulling at his jeans, which were already very wet and had stuck to him. 'Y-yuk,' he stammered.

Somewhat to my surprise, I burst out laughing. I could barely remember when I had last laughed.

As though reading my mind, he said: 'You have a lovely laugh, you should try it m-more often.'

It was gone three o'clock and the day was starting to grow even colder and more unpleasant. All too soon it would be dark. That's England in December for you. He shivered and thrust his hands into the pockets of his jacket. He had big, capable hands, scrubbed scrupulously clean but rough-skinned and battered-looking, the kind of hands that were accustomed to working for their living.

'Horrible weather,' I remarked, falling back in true English fashion on the safest conversation topic of them all.

He nodded.

I was suddenly curious about him. 'It's really ghastly, so what brought you here today?' I asked.

He removed his right hand from his jacket pocket and I saw that he was clutching a small sketch pad and a pencil. 'Just l-looking for a few ideas,' he said.

'You're an artist?' I enquired.

'Trying to be,' he said easily.

I took the pad from him, surprisingly forward for me back then, and leafed through it. He was being modest. Books and painting were my one solace in life. The ultimate escape. Along with exploring the parks and gardens of west London, they were all that made life worth living for me. If I wasn't at the Isabella or Kew Gardens, or strolling through the grounds of Chiswick House, whenever I could get out of the house for long enough I would be browsing in one of the local libraries or a bookshop or wandering around an art gallery just staring and dreaming. It was almost like running away. One way and another books and paintings were everything to me, and I was pretty sure that this stranger's drawings were exceptionally good.

His sketches of the cowering shrubs and skeletal trees of winter were bleak and angular, only vaguely representational and totally individual.

'These are wonderful,' I said.

I glanced at him, open admiration in my eyes.

He blushed. He had the kind of complexion which colours easily. I found that endearing. I blushed easily too, and hated it, so I felt for him. He shuffled his feet nervously and put his hands back in his pockets. 'You enjoy looking at drawings and paintings?' he queried.

I nodded.

'Anything in particular?'

It was my turn to hesitate. I wasn't used to talking about art. My husband and I did not have those kinds of conversations. In fact, we didn't have any kind of conversation at all. He told me what to do and I did it. Anything in order not to provoke those outbursts of rage I was so afraid of.

'Oh, everything really . . .' I began.

He was smiling at me encouragingly but I was sure I must sound pathetic. I strove to explain. 'I go to galleries when I can, but mostly I've only been able to look at books. I get them from the library and I've tried to gain a sense of how painting and sculpture has

11

developed. Somebody in almost every period has made some kind of gigantic leap forward, haven't they? Leonardo da Vinci broke every rule in the book during the Renaissance. But who could have dreamed that one day we would have the Impressionists and the Cubists? There's so much that's wonderful. And it's all led to what modern painters are trying to do today, and it's just so exciting . . .'

I paused. I seemed to have progressed from stupefied silence to verbal diarrhoea. But he was looking at me as if he was fascinated by what I was saying.

'You like abstracts then?'

I nodded.

'That's what I try to do, well mostly. These are inclined to be my bread and butter.' He patted the pocket containing his sketches. 'It's the use of colour and shape that intrigues me. You see, you're right about every generation making a leap forward. You wouldn't think any artist could still produce something new, something original. But we can. Well, some can. The best ones.'

I noticed that he had stopped stammering.

He spoke with quiet enthusiasm, his voice a slow drawl, gentle as his eyes. 'Have you seen the Kandinsky exhibition at the Royal Academy?' he asked suddenly.

I shook my head. It was hard for me to get away for long enough to visit any central London galleries, and in any case I rarely had money of my own for fares and admission fees.

'But you know him, you know Kandinsky?' he persisted.

'Oh yes. Wassily Kandinsky. He was so ahead of his

12

time it's difficult to believe that he's been dead for over half a century. I think he was an absolute genius.'

He nodded his agreement. 'Of course he was and you must see the exhibition. You really must. No book can do justice to the scale and the drama of Kandinsky. Look, I'll take you. I'd love to take you, I really would . . .'

I was startled. 'You don't know anything about me,' I blurted out suddenly. 'I can't go anywhere with you.'

'N-no, of course not. I'm s-sorry.' He backed off at once. And I noticed that the stammer was back.

I could feel the tears pricking again. I looked away.

'I kn-know that you need a friend,' he said hesitantly.

I suppose I wore my pain like a cloak in those days. His voice was even more quiet and gentle. I couldn't stop myself shedding just a few more tears.

He reached out and touched my cheek, very lightly. 'Are you s-sure you couldn't come, it wouldn't take long, we c-could go on the Tube.'

Hesitant he might have been, but he wasn't giving up easily. I was later to learn that was very much part of the man. He didn't give up – not on anything or anyone that he cared about. None the less, what he was suggesting, such a small thing, was quite impossible.

I shook my head.

'Well, look, perhaps we could m-meet here again and just talk. C-could you come tomorrow afternoon?'

'I don't know.' He obviously realised that I was not free to do as I pleased. He did not, however, ask if I was married. Instead he just said, with that boyish grin: 'O-or the next day?'

13

'Well, perhaps,' I heard myself reply, thinking that I must be quite mad. Didn't I have enough troubles?

'I'll be here,' he told me firmly, without even a hint of a stammer.

He walked with me through the garden and up the path to the car park where I had left my bicycle chained to a post. My bike was about the only thing I owned that I valued. It made it possible for me to escape at least sometimes from the horrible reality of my life. About the nearest I ever got to any feeling of freedom was when I cycled through Richmond Park to the Isabella, or down by the river, or to any other of my special haunts.

I sought out peace and tranquillity. And the few snatched hours I managed to steal in these places were precious to me.

It was extraordinary to have met someone who I felt understood that, and so much else about me, even though we were still strangers. Carl said very little that first time, but walked close by my side. Silent. Calm. It felt good, somehow, from the beginning.

He watched me as I unchained my bicycle – a bright red mountain bike, my last present from Gran. It had been state of the art when she had given it to me and I was still very proud of it. I kept it spotlessly clean and shiny.

'I could give you a lift in my van,' he said eventually. 'The bike will fit in the back, I think.'

I replied far too quickly. 'No,' I said at once, and my voice was much louder and sharper than I had intended.

He held up both hands, palms towards me. 'No, o-of course not. I'm s-sorry . . .'

I battled to recover myself. The thought of arriving home loaded into a strange van sent me into a panic. It also made me remember how dangerous it would be for me even to consider seeing this man again.

Swiftly I clambered aboard my bike and set off. 'The day after tomorrow,' I called over my shoulder. 'I don't think I can make it after all.'

I could barely see his face. He was already in the distance and in any case I had to watch the road. He did not shout after me. But I was aware of him standing there, staring silently at my retreating back.

I did not return to the Isabella two days later. I wanted to, but I did not dare. I didn't visit the garden for almost three weeks – although almost every day I thought about my gentle American stranger.

Eventually I did go back there, telling myself there was nothing unusual in this. After all, the garden was one of my special places and I was certainly not going there in the hope of meeting the stranger again.

But as I wandered through the garden I was somehow led to the same tree trunk and I did vaguely wonder if he would be there. It was a silly thought and I knew it. I gave myself a telling off as I sat down on the old broken tree and threw a few pieces of stale bread at the ducks.

The sun was shining for once, in spite of the time of year. Christmas was just a couple of days away, but the cares of a world, which seemed to me then to be such a grim, desolate place rested heavily on my shoulders. I was deeply unhappy and I didn't know what to do about it.

Then suddenly he was by my side. Silently, as before. I looked up at him. The gentle eyes. The broad, ruddy face. The short blond hair that looked a bit like a scrubby crop of discoloured grass. I had so frequently seen that face inside my head since our one and only meeting. I thought I was behaving like a fool. For a few seconds neither of us spoke.

He crouched down in front of me. 'I-I'm s-so g-glad you've c-come,' he said, his stammer the worst I had so far known it.

'Yes.' I studied him. 'I wondered if you might be here . . .' It wasn't like me to give so much away.

'I've b-been here every afternoon since we met,' he replied. His eyes were earnest. He was still hesitant and yet obviously so determined. I found that mix in him quite captivating, and would continue to do so throughout all our years together.

'I've been w-worried about you.'

It was such a strange thing to say to someone you barely know, yet I was quite certain that he was telling the truth. He wasn't playing a game. Carl never played games with other people's emotions and somehow I realised that even then.

Tentatively he stretched forward and took my hand in his. His touch was as gentle as his voice and his eyes. Something happened inside me. I half reached out for him, not believing what I was doing. He shuffled around, so that he could sit on the tree trunk next to me, then wrapped his free arm round me. I leaned into him and let the tears come as never before.

I cried my heart out in the middle of the Isabella Garden that sunny December afternoon as Carl held me. When I could cry no more he took his handkerchief from his pocket and handed it to me, just as he had the first time.

I half expected him to run. I think I would have

done if I had been confronted by such a hysterical woman. 'God, I'm sorry,' I said eventually.

He grinned that crooked boyish grin. 'If we're going to be friends I think we should make a pact to stop apologising to each other.'

Friends? Even that still seemed barely possible.

'You don't know . . . you still don't know anything . . .' I stuttered.

'I know that I want to h-help you, to stop you being so sad. I don't know why, but I do.'

I felt his arm tighten around me.

'I c-can, you know,' he murmured. 'I c-can stop you being so sad.'

The extraordinary thing was that even then, at the height of my misery, I did not really doubt him. I could not see how any other life would ever be possible, yet at last there was hope.

It does happen. People do meet and instantly fall in love. And sometimes they stay in love. That meeting was almost seven years before the threats started. And Carl and I had lived together, an inseparable pair, for more than six of those years – a modern miracle, perhaps. But for me Carl had a way of making miracles happen. He did indeed stop my sadness. And I never felt safer than when I lay in his arms.

All I needed to make my life perfect was for the nightmares to go away. And I had to believe that one day they would.

Three

I had gone almost six months without a nightmare when it happened. That was the longest gap ever since Carl and I had arrived in St Ives. Maybe the moment had come, I had told myself, maybe there would be no more. I dared not think about it, but I did allow myself to hope.

I had even begun to make some kind of life for myself outside the tightly contained nest of my home with Carl. One of the most famous schools of modern artists had evolved in St Ives, painters and sculptors drawn by a light so pure that you could wake up thinking the sun was shining outside even on a rainy day. It was the home of Barbara Hepworth and Peter Lanyon, Patrick Heron, and Terry Frost, and a host of others whom I had only known of through reading about them and looking at their work in books. It was all of this which had attracted Carl to the town and for me it was as if all these wonderful artists leaped from the pages I had pored over so avidly and came alive. As I walked the streets I could feel these artistic giants walking with me. Their work was suddenly within my grasp. The Tate Gallery, a huge, white, angular building towering somewhat monstrously above the town, displays some of their paintings and sculptures with an almost clinical efficiency, but the pioneer spirit that inspired these men and women and brought them international fame is in the very air that you breathe in St Ives. At Barbara Hepworth's house, you can see the piece of stone she was working on when she died so tragically, her tools alongside it just as she had left them. St Ives is full of magic.

I went regularly to the library just as I had done in London, to learn more about the town and the county that Carl and I had adopted. If St Ives is steeped in history, Cornwall is a mysterious county of legend and ghosts, martyrs and heroes. I was fascinated by it and, as usual, I immersed myself in the past as much as the present. It was in the library, a splendid old Victorian building on Fore Street, that, sitting engrossed at one end of a long table, I first began to read the story of John Payne, mayor of St Ives, who had been a leader of the last great Cornish uprising in 1548, when the Cornish had refused to accept the new Common Prayer Book in English. As many as 6000 Cornishmen were believed to have died in battle and John Payne was one of those later executed.

I decided this was a man both Carl and I should know more about, and added the book to the selection I planned to take home with me that day.

'He built his own gallows, you know,' said the young assistant librarian in a soft Cornish voice, as I presented the John Payne book at the counter to be stamped out.

'So I gather.'

'Anyway. Good choice.' She handed the book back to me along with the other three I had picked. 'Everyone English should know about John Payne and the Prayer Book Rebellion. If they'd printed a Cornish Prayer Book, like they did a Welsh one, or if

John Payne and his lads had won we might all still be speaking Cornish around here.'

I smiled at the allusion to Cornwall and England being separate countries. There was a twinkle in the girl's eye, but I never quite knew whether the Cornish were joking or not when they made comments like that. Usually not, I suspected.

'What makes you so sure I'm not Cornish anyway?' I asked.

'You wouldn't need to read about John Payne at your age if you were,' she replied with a big smile. She was, I realised, a strikingly pretty girl and had the kind of self-confidence that I could never even imagine aspiring to.

'My name's Mariette,' she went on and held out her hand in a rather old-fashioned gesture. I took it and shook.

'Suzanne,' I said and not a lot more. I wasn't used to making friends. I didn't have any, really, and never had. Only Carl.

I had seen Mariette before, of course. She had been working at the library for about six months I thought, and she had checked out books for me before, but we had never embarked on any kind of conversation, however brief. I had noticed, though, that she always seemed bright and cheery, and did not appear to have a care in the world. I envied Mariette and all who were like her more than they could ever realise, and when she began to seek me out regularly I am sure that she had no idea how much it meant to me.

I remember vividly the first time we went for morning coffee together.

'Do you like cappuccino?' she had asked me.

'Oh yes,' I said. Carl had introduced me to cappuccino and espresso as he had to so many things. Conversation over fine coffee had not figured much in my life before I met him.

'Come on, then, I'm due a break,' she said. 'They do great cappuccino at that new place round the corner.'

Mariette grabbed her coat and we hurried out of the library. 'I haven't got long,' she said. 'Let's make the most of it.'

Mariette had lots of very dark curly hair, which bounced when she walked – the kind of hair I had always envied. Mine was straight and lank, and a sort of mousy nothing colour.

'What are you staring at?' she asked as she pushed open the double doors of a little coffee bar, which seemed really quite trendy for St Ives.

'Y-your hair,' I confessed haltingly. 'I've always wanted hair like that.'

I thought I sounded fairly pathetic, but if I did, Mariette gave no sign. 'Oh, we all want the hair we haven't got,' she responded with a giggle. 'I'd love to have smooth, straight hair like yours, get sick to death of all these curls all over the place.' She glanced thoughtfully at me. 'Maybe you could do with some nice blond highlights, though,' she ventured.

I think my jaw dropped. The idea of dyeing my hair, and peroxide blond at that, had never occurred to me. And I was a long way off being ready for it. I would just have to put up with the bland nothingness of my mousy hair, which, I have to admit, I did think rather suited the bland nothingness of the rest of me.

I was such an average sort of person; average

height, average build, average-looking in every way. When I stood in front of a mirror I saw nothing remotely memorable. Brownish-grey eyes, regular features, a neat mouth, a small, snubby nose. I knew that my eyes were bright and my complexion clear and healthy-looking, but when Carl told me I was pretty I didn't really believe him. Probably because nobody but Carl had ever said such a thing to me, and he loved me, so I assumed that he judged everything about me differently from the rest of mankind.

Mariette guided me to a glass-topped table in a corner by the window and as soon as we sat down she took a packet of cigarettes out of her bag. 'Been dying for a fag all morning,' she muttered as she lit up, drew in a deep, joyful breath and offered me the packet.

I shook my head. Carl didn't approve of smoking. He was strongly anti drugs of any kind and although he enjoyed an occasional drink, particularly a pint or two of beer in one of St Ives's many pubs, he loathed blatant drunkenness. Carl never liked to be out of control nor to see others so, apparently a legacy of his childhood. Carl had had an unconventional upbringing, mostly in Key West in Florida, the only son of parents whom he described, without a deal of affection, as the last great hippies.

A handsome young waiter came and took our order. He and Mariette obviously knew each other. He spoke with a strong French accent and seemed to enjoy saying her name, fussing around our table rather more than might really have been necessary. He had quite long wavy brown hair, which he was constantly brushing out of his eyes, and tufts of brown hair sprouted at the open neck of his spotless white shirt.

Mariette flirted with him outrageously. I was fascinated. I didn't even know how to flirt. Her eyes followed the waiter as he moved around the room. 'I think he's got the cutest bum in Cornwall!' she said, making a little sucking noise with her teeth.

I glanced at her in some alarm.

She giggled, something she did a lot. 'Sorry, forgot you were an old married woman,' she said.

It wasn't that really, though. It was just that I wasn't used to girl talk and certainly not Mariette's brand of it. It would not have occurred to me to comment on the condition of a man's bum. I had never sat chatting with a girlfriend talking about men, and had no idea how to join in.

Mariette was unfazed by my reaction. She was a few years younger than me, shorter and with a slight plumpness which might one day spoil her looks. But not for a long time. At twenty-two or twenty-three she was merely voluptuous. She was quite stunning in every way, with big brown eyes and that curly hair so black you could hardly believe the colour was natural, although somehow you knew it was. Her skin was pale and creamy, and her lips full and pink. Like me, she wore very little make-up, but I suspected that our reasons were rather different. She didn't need make-up and jolly well knew it. I just didn't have a clue how to go about putting on anything beyond a dash of mascara, a smear of foundation and a smudge of lipstick.

'Do you know,' she said, 'I've not had it since New Year's Eve.'

I nearly choked on my cappuccino. 'Oh,' I

remarked lamely.

'Yeah,' Mariette continued conversationally. 'Went to a party with my Micky and all he did was get fruity with this tart from Truro. So I pulled her bloke – not that he was up to much. But then my Micky has the cheek to get all sanctimonious and chuck me up.'

The French waiter reappeared, to ask smilingly if there was anything else we would like.

'Tell you later, darling,' said Mariette shamelessly. The waiter's smile widened. When he eventually carried our empty coffee cups back to the kitchen Mariette's eyes followed his retreating bum. 'What I couldn't do with that,' she murmured.

I was staggered. But I found myself giggling along with her. For me even such inconsequential events were an adventure, and I could not wait to get home and tell Carl about my new friend – although I did leave out our conversations concerning the merits of the waiter's bum and the state of Mariette's sex life.

As coffee breaks with Mariette became a weekly occurrence I began to relax and even join in the cheeky chat. Our gossipy sessions were a great novelty to me because Carl and I were always so totally immersed in each other that we had never felt the need to mix much with anyone from outside. In any case, we only felt really safe with each other. I even wondered if my new friendship with Mariette might cause him any anxiety, but he gave no indication that it did.

I was however finding myself drawn towards a lifestyle very different from anything I had ever experienced. Mariette's independence seemed so appealing to me. Exciting even!

Although I had never handled money and was daunted by the vague prospect of ever doing so – Carl had always dealt with all of that, as had somebody throughout my life – I began to fantasise about earning some money of my own. I wondered if I might be able to get a job in the town, perhaps just part time. Anything that would allow me to stand on my own two feet at last, albeit just a little. And one day I mentioned it to Mariette in the library.

'Good idea, I'll ask around and see what's going,' she replied easily.

She had, of course, no idea what a monumental step it would be for me.

I was thoughtful when I left the library and began to walk up the steep cobbled streets towards our little cottage. One way and another, the idea of a job was becoming more and more appealing. It was early July and the sun was warm on my back. As I walked, dodging the holidaymakers, I could see the glow of the bay through gaps between the higgledy-piggledy mish-mash of buildings. The sight never failed to lift me, and I had at last begun to feel so strong and well, and unusually untroubled, that I decided to talk over my job idea with Carl.

Over our usual snack lunch of bits and pieces grabbed from the fridge, I mentioned as casually as I could manage that perhaps I might like to find a job one of these days, to have some kind of commitment outside our home.

Carl was eating an orange and struggling not to let the juice run down his chin. He was one of those people who always seemed to have a problem eating without dribbling or dropping something. I used to think it must be to do with the shape of his mouth and it always made me want to laugh, particularly watching him try to be so careful. Eventually he wiped the back of his hand across his mouth, and then rubbed both his hands down the sides of the paint-spattered blue cotton smock he always wore when he was working. He stared at me thoughtfully before he spoke. 'It's not so easy, you know, Suzanne,' he said. 'You've never worked; I think you would find it very stressful.'

I supposed that he was right and didn't push the point.

I slept soundly and nightmare free yet again that night and woke soon after dawn to another quite glorious summer morning. Through the bedroom window I could see the sun rising over the bay. It was the kind of morning which defied you to be anything other than happy and optimistic. One of these days, I thought, I will build a life of my own, like Mariette, I really will.

Carl, almost always an early riser, was already up and about, and I could smell that he had made fresh coffee. I tripped down the stairs, my head buzzing with all my ideas.

'You look like you're in a good mood,' he remarked with a grin.

'I am,' I said, and kissed him lightly on the cheek.

'Right then,' he responded. 'It's a glorious day. Shall we drive out of town a bit and take a walk along the coastal path? It's still very early, shouldn't be too many grockles about yet.'

I nodded enthusiastically, gulped down a cup of coffee, nibbled at a slice of bread and honey, then followed Carl out of the door.

His old red van was parked just around the corner

on the brow of the hill. It was pretty battered but, even so, as we approached it we noticed that there were fresh scratches right down the side nearest to us.

'Goddamn it,' exclaimed Carl, reaching out to touch the damage. 'I thought they only did this to Mercs and Beamers.'

I smiled. I was still in a good mood. Neither Carl nor I were exactly car proud. We couldn't afford anything much to be proud of, for a start.

Then Carl stood back and studied the scratches more carefully.

'It's some kind of graffiti, isn't it?' he muttered, half to himself. 'Some kind of writing, I think, but very difficult to read.'

He narrowed his eyes and half squinted at the marks.

'"Know, Know, Know . . . something." I'm not sure. What do you make of it, Suzanne?'

'"Know the truth",' I read aloud, suddenly seeing most of the badly formed letters on the van quite clearly.

I glanced at Carl.

He was frowning by then. Concentrating hard.

'"I know the truth",' he said quietly.

Then he turned to look at me. We stared at each other for a few seconds. It felt like a very long time.

'Kids,' he said eventually. 'Damned stupid kids.'

'Of course,' I agreed. 'Must be kids. What else?'

We climbed into the van, drove out a few miles on the road heading south towards Land's End, parked in a lay-by just outside Zennor and found our way on to a part of the famous coastal path which runs all the way from Minehead on the north coast of Devon, right down around the bottom end of Cornwall and up the south coast to Portland Bill in Dorset.

The sun was still shining brightly. There wasn't a cloud in the sky. The sea was that kind of aquamarine blue that is so rarely seen off the British Isles.

And yet somehow the day was not quite as glorious for Carl and I as it had been such a short time ago.

We only walked for an hour of so. Our hearts were not in it. As soon as we returned to the cottage Carl went into his studio – then just a makeshift lean-to in the backyard but with plenty of good natural light – and began to paint. Not one of the wonderful abstracts which were his pride and joy, but a cosy seaside scene of the kind that were our bread and butter.

I sat quietly on a stool and watched him as I so often did, even though my mind kept wandering. I had somehow lost the desire to go off job-hunting.

Carl could paint the chocolate box pictures, as we called them, blindfold. Sometimes he used pastels and watercolour, but more often he worked in oils because oil paintings fetched the best prices. Carl was a highly accomplished oil painter, very skilled in all the technicalities of producing just the right colour and texture, but that morning his progress was slow. His brush did not sweep across the canvas with anything like its usual assured flourish.

The light was almost too bright. The studio, which had a glass roof, caught rather too much morning sun on a day like this, and it could be blinding for an artist. I knew that Carl preferred the pure light of a more wintry day. He was sweating, too. Every possible window was open but it was hot in the small conservatory-like building. In the winter it was extremely cold, of course, but Carl never seemed to notice.

He worked on a tall easel and stood with one leg bent and balanced on a footstool so that he could lean his palette on his knee. His big wooden paintbox was on the table to one side, every tube and jar meticulously laid out. Carl was a very ordered painter. The studio was never untidy, not at all the way I had always imagined an artist's studio would be. Carl said he couldn't work in a mess. Occasionally he took a break from layering on the paint to step back and study the all too familiar scene taking form on his canvas – a fishing smack in the foreground of St Ives bay, a vividly setting sun behind.

The painting was as technically excellent as ever, but I knew how much the subject bored him.

'Do you know how many sunsets over St Ives I've painted since we came to live here, Suzanne?' he asked, as he paused to drink a mug of coffee I had made for him.

I shook my head.

'Neither do I.' He grinned. 'If I counted them I think I really would go mad.'

He gave me a peck on the cheek and went back to work. About an hour or so later, as he squeezed some crimson paint on to his palette the tube split open and dollops of the bright-red goo spurted on to the canvas.

Carl rarely swore. 'Bugger it!' he said, dabbing at the canvas with an oily cloth. Then he put down his palette, stepped away from his easel and turned to face me. 'This is silly,' he said, 'I can't concentrate. Come on, we're going out.'

He led me into the town, stopping in Fore Street at Warren's pasty shop for what we reckoned were the best oggies in town and then at an off-licence for a bottle of wine, before marching me up the hill. I knew where he was taking me. We both loved the Barbara Hepworth museum, set in the white-painted cottage in the little narrow street leading up from the harbour, which had been the famous sculptor's home. It wasn't like the Tate Gallery down the road, all antiseptic and don't touch and blaring out that awful ever-so-British establishment message that most of us aren't really good enough to appreciate art.

In Barbara Hepworth's place you can sit on a bench eating your lunch while children crawl through the convoluted holes of her huge garden sculptures and her workshop remains exactly as it was the very last time she had used it, even down to the discarded smock and the half-finished carvings.

The garden was bathed in warm sunshine that morning. It's not a big garden, but mature trees and shrubs give plenty of shade and variety, and provide a wonderful backdrop for the Hepworth sculptures. We sat on our favourite south-facing bench in its sheltered spot backing on to the garden wall alongside the white-painted hut where Barbara used to sleep sometimes on balmy summer nights. Her bed is still there.

The wine was a chilled bottle of Sancerre – a real extravagance by our standards. Usually we only drank wine on our rare nights out at a local restaurant. Carl opened the bottle carefully, keeping it in its brown paper bag and turning his back to the garden. Drinking in public places, apart from licensed premises, is not allowed in St Ives any more, a legacy of too many afternoon boozers, particularly during the holiday season, spilling out on to the streets outside pubs like the Sloop and causing drunken mayhem. However, with a little discretion quiet drinkers like Carl and me could still wash down a summer picnic with something more interesting than lemonade.

Carl poured generous measures into two paper cups and raised his in a familiar toast. 'To us,' he said. 'And most of all to you, my Lady of the Harbour.'

He often called me that. It had a special significance for us. He leaned very close and whispered in my ear. The birds were singing. There was a child playing contentedly just a yard or two from our feet, intent on climbing through every possible shape in Barbara's largest work, which is the centrepiece of the Hepworth garden, dominating the small central lawn. The towering green bronze *Foursquare*, fifteen feet high, has a magnetic attraction for small children and I had already learned enough about the artist to know that she would have liked nothing better than to have watched this one at play amidst her work.

A couple of tourists, clutching guidebooks and talking in loud American accents, wandered by. Yet I was barely aware of anything except the closeness of the man I loved. It was always like that. Carl and I had no children, of course, and had agreed that we should have none, the way things were. Naturally I hoped that one day it would be possible to have

31

Carl's child, but I was still very young and we already had so much together. He made me happy and he made me laugh.

He took a bite of his pasty and several chunks of meat and potato fell into his lap. I really had never understood how so meticulous a man could have such a job getting food into his mouth without dropping it and in spite of the tension we both felt that day I found myself giggling.

He brushed the bits of food off his trousers, sat up very straight and pretended to drop the entire pasty. I giggled all the more.

'God, I wish I was Little Miss Perfect like you,' he said.

I kissed his cheek. Somehow or other he had managed to get flakes of pastry on it.

He grinned at me and spoke with his mouth full: 'Nothing is going to hurt us, Suzanne. Nothing. We're going to stay just as happy as we are now, always . . .'

I let his words wash over me.

Nonetheless, the damage had been done, somewhere deep inside. Hand in hand we walked home in the mid-afternoon. We paused by the Market House, now the town hall, outside which John Payne was hanged in 1549, the place of his execution marked by a bronze and marble tablet. The sight always made me shiver. The story went that the St Ives Mayor had been entertaining the provost marshal, whose job was to pacify the rebellious county of Cornwall, in the George and Dragon inn, when he was asked to have gallows erected by the time the meal was over. He did so without question and afterwards obediently escorted the provost marshal to the scaffold.

The provost then asked if the construction was strong enough and, upon being assured that it certainly was, turned to John Payne: 'Well, then get up speedily for they are prepared for you.'

'I hope,' answered the mayor, 'you mean not as you speak.'

'In faith,' said the provost, 'there is no remedy for you have been a busy rebel.'

I heard my own voice recite those words verbatim from the book about the Prayer Book Rebellion that I had borrowed from the library. And I was aware of Carl staring at me.

'A cheerful little tale,' he said.

I smiled wanly. 'Have we built our own gallows, Carl?' I asked.

'Suzanne, stop it,' he said and for once he was very serious, without a trace of teasing banter in his voice. 'Everything is going to be absolutely fine. I wish you wouldn't be so morbid.'

The ghosts of St Ives felt very close that day. Just across Market Place was the little old-fashioned gentlemen's outfitters where successive proprietors had reported seeing a ghost in the form of a pair of disembodied legs wearing wide blue trousers.

Funny things, ghost stories: one day they'll make you laugh and another your flesh will crawl. This was one of the flesh-crawling days.

'The ghosts of our own pasts are always with us, like the poor,' I said.

Carl managed a dry laugh.

'Where do you get these sayings, Suzanne?'

I shrugged. 'I think I made that one up,' I said.

Carl flung an arm round my shoulders and pulled me close to him. 'C'mon, let's go home,' he said, the usual gentle teasing note back in his voice. 'Ghosts aren't allowed in Rose Cottage. I've banned them.'

We both knew that could never be quite true. Carl had been as disturbed as me by the curious damage to our van. I was well aware of that in spite of his gallant attempts to conceal his unease. As we carried on walking up the hill the sun continued to blaze, casting deep, dark shadows in the narrow streets. In one of those places where I knew there was a convenient gap between the buildings I turned to look back over the rooftops to the sea. A figure disappeared abruptly into a doorway. For a moment I wondered if someone was following us. I gave myself a silent dressing down for being paranoid. The water in St Ives bay still shimmered silver and gold, but my heart was no longer singing. All the old fears had invaded me again. I tried desperately to snap out of it, but I couldn't quite.

'Right, I'll cook supper,' said Carl when we arrived home. 'Now tell me what would be madame's fancy, then get out of my kitchen.'

As a rule I loved him cooking for me. He was a good cook and had the knack of turning our meals together into an event, but that night I somehow didn't want him to.

'I'll cook,' I said. 'It will give me something to do . . .'

He didn't press the point. He knew what I meant. I was hoping that being busy would stop me from dwelling on matters I preferred to forget. We had somehow not got around to buying any fresh food so I made spaghetti bolognaise with tins of minced meat

34

and tomatoes. We always had plenty of garlic and onions. Too late I realised that there was no fresh parmesan in the fridge. Neither of us liked the dried-up powdered stuff you can buy in drums, so we had none of that to use as an emergency stand-in either. One way and another it was not the best spag-bog I had ever made, but if Carl noticed he gave no sign.

'Right, I'll wash up, then how about an early night?' he suggested after we had finished eating.

I knew he wanted to make love to me, and I had no intention of rejecting him, even though I did not think it would work – not for me, at any rate. And it didn't. I couldn't concentrate. I derived some comfort from his closeness, I could never fail to do that, and from the familiar intimacy when he took me into the bathroom, as he always did afterwards, and we washed together beneath the shower. But later I was afraid to sleep. Carl was as gentle and under-standing as ever. Yet, for hours after he had gone to sleep, I lay wide awake, trying not to toss and turn so much that I disturbed him.

I felt quite sure that when I did sleep I would have a nightmare. Such premonitions were not unusual, however much I fought against them, and almost always came true. This night was no exception. I was aware that maybe I half brought it on myself, but there seemed nothing I could do about it and the vivid detail was so overwhelming that I had no awareness that I was dreaming, that I was in fact asleep.

Instead I was caught in a terrible biting reality which took over my whole being. I felt the pain, smelled the blood, sensed the pleasure that came first and hated myself for it.

His arms were around me, his lips seeking mine, then kissing and nibbling my ears, my neck, my breasts. Methodically, efficiently.

The warm glow of arousal became a burning at the very core of me. He entered me, gently but forcefully pushing himself deep deep into me, as far as possible into the essence of my body.

My eyes were tightly closed, as if the lids were glued together and I could not open them. It did not matter. This was not really lovemaking, just clinically executed sex. But that did not matter either. The physical sensation was everything, all that existed.

The tingling sensation inside me rose and rose until the moment of climax burst upon me and I could feel great waves of pleasure rushing through my body. Then – it was always then, at that moment, at the beginning of my coming – he hit me.

I felt the flat of his left palm smash into the side of my face with a force so great that it almost broke my jaw. My cries of pleasure turned into screams of pain as with his other hand he made a fist and punched me full in the chest, the belly and then again the face, all the time pushing himself into me.

The gentle nibbling and kissing turned into a cruel biting and my breasts started to bleed, but there could be no escape until he had reached his climax. Always it was like that, he would raise himself triumphantly from me and eventually the blows would stop.

But then came the worst moment. Just like in all these terrible dreams, the moment I dreaded more than the pain that was so real, more than the blood and the brutality. The moment when I could eventually open my eyes, when I could not stop them opening, in fact, and I had to see again the black hole where his face should be.

That was the moment when my screams reached their loudest, that was the moment when Carl coaxed me into some kind of wakefulness and for the umpteenth time held me tight while I hit and kicked out at him as he willed me to be still, so patiently, so tenderly calming me.

'The dreams will go away, one day they will,' he said. 'I'll make them, my darling, I'll make them.'

I lay in his arms still weeping, trembling. So many times he had told me that. So many times I had wanted it to be true. And this time I really had thought it could have happened. 'They had gone away, I believed they might have gone away for good,' I sobbed. 'It was the van. It was just so horrid. I can't help feeling that it was a message . . .'

'I know, honey,' he whispered. 'I was so afraid that would bring it all back. But try not to worry, my darling. It must have been kids. It cannot really be a threat to us. It just can't . . .'

Somehow he gentled me so much that I actually managed a few minutes' fitful sleep before morning.

Perhaps the sleep helped. One way and another I didn't feel quite as bad the next morning as I had expected. The nightmare remained vivid enough. I could always remember every detail when I woke up, that was one of the worst aspects of it, but it was another bright sunny day.

Unusually, I got up before Carl. I made tea and took him a cup in bed, just as he was waking.

There was anxiety in his eyes as I leaned over him

37

and kissed his forehead, but he could always sense my state of mind, my mood. I knew he recognised that I was really quite calm considering what I had been through in the night.

Later that day, Carl bought a can of red spray paint and some fine sandpaper and did a pretty good job of removing all but a trace of the words crudely scratched on to the van.

It was a great tribute to him and, I suppose, to the power of our love that I was able to return quite quickly to some kind of normality. I think I even convinced myself that the words on our old van really had been nothing other than meaningless vandalism.

Four

Another four months passed without a nightmare and much of the old day-to-day happiness and contentment returned. Carl's and my life together was simple and intimate, our pleasures thoroughly unsophisticated. He had his work. I had my pride in his work. We never tired of exploring the beautiful county that was our home. We liked to walk together along the clifftops and beaches, and inland through the woods and meadows, particularly in the spring when we sought out the special places where the bluebells and the daffodils and primroses carpeted the ground. We had our shared love of fine art, we enjoyed cooking and eating good food together and we delighted in each other's company. We laughed a lot. Carl could always make me laugh. We were so comfortable together.

It was surprisingly easy to forget our suspicions that something sinister lay behind the damage to the van. And in spite of that this four-month gap was the second longest period I had been without a nightmare since our arrival in St Ives.

However, I abandoned the idea of applying for a job. Instead I buried myself in the familiarly safe cocoon of my life with Carl. Once again the world outside us seemed full of danger.

My friendship with Mariette developed over the summer, which, in spite of such a promising start, had generally been cooler than usual for St Ives. Occasionally I joined her for a lunchtime snack in a café or, on the brighter days, sandwiches eaten sitting on the sea wall dodging gulls and tourists, both of which could be infuriating.

It was the summer of the total eclipse. Carl and I watched it together from St Ives Head, the rocky piece of land jutting out to sea to the south of the harbour and always known to the locals as 'The Island' because that is what it looks like from most parts of the town, although it is in fact joined to the mainland by a wide, grass-covered causeway.

We were disappointed in the weather, of course. Both the day before and the day after the eclipse were gloriously sunny, but not that special Wednesday. We woke up to a damp, murky morning, but nonetheless set off to the island good and early, in order to secure a prime cliff-edge spot. There we stood, along with hundreds of other disappointed eclipse watchers, feeling vaguely ridiculous as we stared glumly at a completely cloud-laden sky. Then, minutes before totality, the clouds parted and there, quite clearly revealed, was a crescent of sun, the rest of it covered by the moon. It was stunning, and by then, unexpected. The gathered crowd collectively gasped. Then there was an outbreak of clapping. Then a sort of communal rustling sound as we all obediently reached for our special eclipse glasses. Then almost everyone gathered on the island began to laugh. The partially eclipsed sun, although clearly visible, was still covered in a film of light cloud. Through our black safety glasses all any of us could see was a reflection of our own faces.

The atmosphere was extraordinary, quite carnival-like. But when the moment of totality came the laughter stopped abruptly. All of us had been prepared for a couple of minutes of darkness in the middle of the day; we knew well enough what was going to happen, but when it happened it was still a shock.

I clasped Carl's hand tightly. We did not speak. Nobody spoke. The enormity of the moment was overwhelming. The lights of St Ives switched on and above the town a display of fireworks flashed across the blackness. It was weird. At first there was silence and then the sky filled with hysterical seagulls. Confused and bewildered, they went absolutely mad, wheeling and screeching in their hundreds. As the sky began to lighten so their cries became less frenzied. The birds understood that something extraordinary had happened, every bit as much as the humans had.

I pulled my jacket closer around me. The temperature had dropped dramatically during the eclipse, just as it does at night, but it wasn't only that which had chilled me and made me shiver. In the modern air-conditioned world it is easy sometimes to forget the sheer might of nature. I don't think anything has ever reminded me quite as much of the insignificance of the human race as watching the eclipse of the sun on that dull August morning. And to be watching from the heart of Cornwall, this ancient county steeped in legend and mystery, added an extra indefinable magic to the whole experience.

I clutched Carl's hand even more tightly, feeling the tears welling. I can't quite explain why I had been so moved, but there it was.

'I could murder a pint,' said Carl.

I swung to look at him. He was totally po-faced.

'You Philistine,' I said. 'Have you no soul? That was just amazing, wasn't it?'

'Was it?' he enquired guilelessly.

I made a threatening gesture with the palm of my right hand. I knew he was joking, but even so . . .

Carl relented. 'Yes, it was amazing,' he said, his face softening. 'Of course it was. Makes all our problems seem so unimportant, doesn't it?'

I knew exactly what he meant. And I just hoped that our problems would indeed prove to be unimportant.

One way and another the eclipse was the high spot of an indifferent summer, which turned gradually into a mild but exceptionally wet early autumn. During the torrential rain which drenched the south west through almost all of September the roof in our lean-to kitchen sprang a leak again. Carl tried to patch it as best he could. Our absentee landlord hadn't raised our rent for almost three years and we didn't want to jog his memory.

Carl finished several of the abstracts I considered to be quite brilliant. He had taken to using oil pastels rather than paint. They didn't fetch the price of oil paintings, but he could complete them much more quickly and in any case I knew that he enjoyed the medium. Also, the speed with which he could produce in pastels gave his work a spontaneity, which I thought added a distinctive sharpness.

One evening I made pumpkin soup, one of his favourite dishes. I served the soup in deep round bowls, its vivid yellowish-red colour streaked with cream and dotted with chopped chives. Carl enthused as much about the look of it as the taste and as soon as he had finished eating disappeared into his studio, for once telling me not to follow him because he wanted to surprise me. Only three or four hours later he emerged with a splendid three-foot-square painting of my pumpkin soup. On it he had written 'For Suzanne.' It was the most wonderful present I had ever been given. The next day he framed it for me. We hung it in the dining room and it seemed to transform the room. It remains to this day my favourite of all Carl's paintings, not least for the spirit in which it was painted and given to me.

This was a prolific period for Carl. There was another piece, in brilliant primary colours, which I also thought particularly impressive. It consisted of a striking series of interlocking circular shapes, each one sharply defined in itself and yet also blending to be part of another. He called it *Balloons*.

One afternoon, exceptionally dry and bright for November, we walked together to the Logan Gallery, the little shop up the hill that sold most of Carl's work for him, taking with us *Balloons* and two other recent paintings. The owner, Will Jones, was a quietly spoken former schoolteacher with a real eye, Carl always said. Will had taught art for many years and dreamed of one day becoming a full-time painter himself. That dream never came true. Will said he guessed he'd never been quite good enough, although Carl and I didn't believe he meant it. Artists never did. I had grown to understand that most unsuccessful painters were convinced the only reason they weren't as big as Picasso was that there had been a conspiracy against them. But if Will had that bitterness inside him, at least he didn't show it.

Indeed, he insisted that having his own gallery was a good second best for him.

He greeted us warmly as he always did, unfolding himself from his chair as we entered the shop and stretching out his arms in welcome. He was exceptionally tall, about six foot five, and spent most of his time in old St Ives ducking to avoid smashing his head – somewhat protected though it was by a thick, almost bouffant halo of silver hair – against doorways and low ceilings.

He kissed me rather theatrically on both cheeks and his arms quickly wound themselves round my waist. I well was aware that Will grasped every opportunity to touch me with considerable enthusiasm. I wished he wouldn't, but he didn't mean any harm. He was just a tactile sort of person. Sometimes I quite enjoyed the attention, to tell the truth, and he never really took liberties. He looked a bit like Peter O'Toole with big hair, had a penchant for velvet jackets and capes, and was certainly the most unlikely shopkeeper. I suppose he reckoned he could at least look like an artist, although I always thought he resembled an actor playing the part.

He was, however, physically overwhelming, partly because of his size and partly because of his personality. The bear-hug in which he grasped me took the breath from my body.

'Will, be careful,' I admonished him.

He backed off at once. 'Sorry, darling, just *so* pleased to see you,' he cried and winked at me in that way he had, which demonstrated that he wasn't in the least bit sorry and would actually like to hug me again.

I nearly always accompanied Carl to the Logan

Gallery because I enjoyed looking around and I liked chatting to Will. He was the kind of man who accepted you for what you were and didn't ask too many personal questions. I even liked the name he had chosen for his much loved gallery – Logan, after the famous Logan Rock, a sixty-five-ton hunk of granite balanced impossibly on a clifftop at Treen right down at the bottom end of Cornwall not far from Land's End.

'As wondrous a piece of natural sculpture as you'll ever be lucky enough to encounter,' was Will's opinion of the Logan Rock. And you had to warm to a man who could see the world like that. He was a true romantic, right enough, and I liked romantics.

Will took the three wrapped paintings from Carl, but at first merely put them to one side unopened. 'Coffee?' he enquired. This was part of the ritual.

While Will busied himself with the kettle in the little back room, Carl and I studied the work of the opposition, as it were. There was a small Clive Gunnell bronze called *Windows* – an abstract of intertwining ovals, their inner curves finished in a beautiful green patina – which I particularly admired, but Carl and I weren't into buying other people's art. Sadly, we could not afford to.

'Turn it round,' instructed Will, when he returned to the gallery and noticed me studying the Gunnell. The bronze was mounted and balanced on a plinth, which allowed it to be rotated. Slowly I turned it a full circle.

'See, it looks right from every angle,' said Will. 'You should be able to do that with any piece of work that is truly sculptural. And if you can't, then

45

whatever it is and whoever it's by, it's too one-dimensional and not really a sculpture at all.'

Will had a habit of always having to know more than you did and a rather condescending way of lecturing in a schoolmasterly fashion, but he did know his business, there was no doubt about that, which was why Carl had so much respect for him.

Only when we were sipping our coffee from brightly coloured mugs did Will start to unwrap Carl's paintings. Then he propped them one by one against a wall and stood back, hands on hips, head thrown back, legs akimbo. A flamboyant pose.

The first he looked at was *Balloons*, black-edged and framed in white wood – Carl did all his own framing; he said he had no intention of sharing his meagre profits with anybody else. *Balloons* was a large painting, slightly more than three foot square, just a little bigger than my *Pumpkin Soup*. Its vibrant colour and dramatic shapes seemed to dominate the gallery. I reckoned it was the finest piece of work in the room – apart from the Gunnell bronze, perhaps.

Will was silent for what seemed a lifetime. 'You get better with every canvas, Carl,' he said eventually.

Carl beamed. I glowed. We both respected Will's opinion enormously – don't take my description of him to suggest that we regarded him as a figure of fun, because we didn't. Rather, we considered him a true eccentric, but also a true expert.

The other two paintings, smaller but equally original and striking, also met with the gallery owner's approval.

'You'll take them all?' queried Carl anxiously. He knew that his abstracts weren't easy to sell.

'Of course I'll take them,' said Will. 'I just wish I

could sell them for what they're really worth, that's all.'

Carl and I knew exactly what he meant. Art is a world of great contrasts, like show business really. Those at the top of the tree are mega-earning superstars and those at the bottom barely make a living at all – particularly if they try to be original.

Carl's name was not well known and two or three hundred pounds was the most that Will could ever ask for one of his paintings – even those large abstracts he sweated blood over. Not a lot for something Carl had worked on over several weeks.

Nonetheless we left the gallery in high spirits.

'How about a little celebration in the Sloop?' Carl asked, clutching my hand and swinging both our arms. I happily agreed and we began to amble down to the harbour.

Although for various deep-seated reasons neither Carl nor I approved of excessive drinking – we had each in different ways seen the damage it can do – we both liked pubs. Carl had the fascination common among Americans for English pubs and I think we both saw public houses as somewhere we could enjoy a certain conviviality without involvement. Mind you, perhaps to ensure we didn't get too involved, once a week was about the limit of our pub-going, more often than not at a lunchtime rather than the heavier evening session. However, the promise of a decent sale changed things.

It was late afternoon, almost five o'clock. The day had been quite glorious and the setting sun glowed amber and orange. Carl actively disliked going down to St Ives harbour or to the beaches during the tourist season when the place was overrun with people. He had made an exception for the eclipse, partly because I had been so determined that we should watch it from the waterside, but normally he preferred to remain in our little bit of town, up on the hill and way back from the harbour and the beaches, which stayed much the same throughout the year. I wasn't quite so fussy, but he did have a point. I remembered my noisy summer lunchtime visits to the seafront with Mariette and thought how there was just no comparison with the joy of being down by the waterside on a fine, holidaymaker-free, November day like this one. In the quiet off-season times Carl and I loved to walk together along the beach at low tide and, indeed, to visit the Sloop, which was one of the places we avoided in high season because it was always packed with tourists.

As we approached the famous old waterside inn, a familiar figure emerged through the pub doors and began to totter somewhat unsteadily towards us.

'Oh, no,' muttered Carl. 'I really can't stand that woman.'

'At least she's leaving,' I said in his ear.

'Whisky must have run out,' Carl responded uncharitably.

We both half stopped in our tracks, wondering if we could turn round and escape notice, but by this time Fenella Austen was already upon us. In some ways I was less concerned by this than Carl, because in the six years we had lived in the town Fenella, still widely regarded as the matriarch of the local artistic community even though her fortunes as a painter and sculptor had fallen dramatically in recent years, had totally failed to recognise my existence. I was actually quite relieved by this since, although I tried not to let on to Carl in case he thought I really was a complete and utter wimp, the bloody woman scared me to death – particularly when she was drunk, which seemed to be most of the time nowadays.

Fenella walked straight up to Carl, ignoring me as usual, and flung her arms round him, possibly to ensure she remained upright. Nonetheless it annoyed me.

'And so how's our new bright young thing,' she bellowed, slurring her words only slightly. Fenella had only one level of speech – full volume.

'Fenella, I'm neither new nor young, I'm forty years old, I've lived in St Ives for six years and, although you and I may think I'm bright, the rest of the art world is showing no sign of catching on,' said Carl in a tone of exaggerated patience.

Fennella was probably only in her late fifties but had been playing the part of cynical elder for many years, certainly ever since we had moved to Cornwall. She leered at Carl. Maybe it was supposed to be a smile, I really didn't know. She carried with her a strong stench of beer and whisky, and her hair looked as if it could do with a wash. She dyed it a mid-brown colour but not nearly often enough. A grimy yellowish grey displayed itself in a two-inch wedge at the roots. Come to think of it, her face looked as if it could do with a wash too. She wore heavy black eye make-up which had become badly smudged. Her skin was pale and blotchy. I suppose you had to admit it was all a bit of a shame, really, because Fenella still had striking dark-brown eyes and the remains of what must once have been a formidable high-cheeked bone structure. We had seen a sharp deterioration in her looks even in the few years we had been in St Ives.

The local perception was that she was killing herself with drink. She also smoked like a chimney and if one didn't get her before her time it seemed inevitable that the other would.

'You're just a lad to me, Carl, sweetheart,' continued Fenella in that deep, throaty voice which was the product of her sixty-fag-a-day habit.

She was, as usual, overplaying her hand – literally as well as metaphorically, as it happened. Her right hand had closed itself around Carl's left buttock. I watched as her fingers squeezed him.

He winced and removed the offending hand smartly from its target. 'If I did that to you it would be sexual harassment,' he said, lightly but unwisely.

'Harass away, darling,' invited Fenella, as Carl managed to manoeuvre his way past her. 'I can hardly wait . . .'

Having lost her support she staggered dangerously and for one lovely moment I thought she was going to fall over. She didn't, of course.

'Don't turn her down for me, Carl,' I whispered in his ear as we hurried along the promenade to the steps.

'D-do me a favour,' muttered Carl. The slight stammer meant that the woman had definitely got to him. Certainly he was no longer amused. I suppose you couldn't blame him. She was a pest.

He took my hand as we jumped from the quite high bottom step on to the beach. The tide was out and the sun had almost dropped from the sky and hovered deeply golden now, glowing the last of its fire just above the horizon, bathing the entire bay in a truly wonderful light. I was a Londoner born and bred but I had grown to feel a sense of belonging in Cornwall greater than anything I had known before. Its past and its present both suited me. I liked to imagine the harbour in the great days of pilchard fishing when the whole town was kept alive by its one industry. The huge shoals of pilchards that used regularly to frequent the north Cornwall coast in the autumn, were caught by net in shallow water, a process known as seining. Great mountains of the small silvery fish would be dumped on the harbour side, then salted in big wooden tubs and exported to the Mediterranean in sailing ships. I could see the scenes so clearly: the men on their boats emptying their nets and on shore women, children, the elderly, picking up the fish, sorting them, carrying them to the salt vats, everyone involved in gathering this extraordinary autumn harvest. Maybe I romanticised it inside my head, but I couldn't help it. Neither could I help being enthralled by the tales of the wreckers and smugglers whose wild exploits form such a part of Cornish history. St Ives had relied almost entirely on its tourist industry for decades but, in my opinion anyway, the old fishing port had not to lost its unique character, its special magic.

I gazed out to sea, blinking against that last brilliant fire of the sun. The light in St Ives is almost always special, which is why artists still flock there, but that day it somehow seemed more spectacular than ever.

Switching my gaze briefly inland, I saw Fenella Austen disappear into the narrow streets of the town, no doubt to pester somebody else.

'Let's forget the b-bloody woman,' said Carl.

'Too right,' I replied. 'Stand still.'

I used his shoulder to lean against as I removed my shoes and socks, something I almost always did on the beach unless the weather was really bitterly cold. I loved the feel of the coarse damp sand against my bare feet. I dug my heels in and curled up my toes.

Carl grinned at me. 'Come along, Robinson,' he said and he grasped my hand and led me along the beach at a trot.

Laughing together, the way we did so much of the time, we eventually slowed to a walk and spent several dreamy minutes enjoying the sunset and looking at the boats before we decided to double back and have that drink as intended in the Sloop.

A few days later, right out of the blue, Mariette invited me to her house for what she described as a 'girls' night in'. 'A good gossip and a few drinks,' she said. 'Bring a bottle.'

I was quite excited. In spite of everything it seemed that I was beginning to exist as an individual. It felt as if I were being invited into some kind of inner circle.

Carl seemed pleased for me too, although, as we were meeting well after dark at 7 p.m., he insisted that he walk me to Mariette's house and pick me up later, and he cautioned me to take care when he left me at the door of her cottage at the top end of Fore Street, just a few minutes walk from the library.

'Don't be silly.' I smiled at him and he had the grace to look a bit sheepish before grinning back at me.

Mariette still lived with her mother. The first surprise came in the narrow hallway of their cottage, two-bedroomed, I knew, but not an awful lot bigger than ours, which was so cluttered you could hardly make your way through. The walls were lined on either side with shelves packed with brassware. Loads of the stuff.

'Front door was open one day and a party of tourists just walked straight in; they thought the place was a shop,' murmured Mariette smilingly. 'You ain't seen nothing yet,' she continued as she led the way into the small lace-curtained front room.

More pieces of brass were everywhere, horse brasses, brass weights, plates, jugs, candlesticks and a vast assortment of ornaments ranging from a Madonna and Child to a range of animals including cats, dogs, pigs and rabbits.

'She's got about 4000 pieces,' said Mariette, gesturing me to a chintz-covered armchair. 'Cleans 'em in rotation and it takes her an hour and a half every day.'

'Amazing,' I said. It was the best I could come up with.

'Now you know the Cornish are barking,' Mariette giggled.

I did not meet Mrs Brenda Powell that evening. Apparently the deal was that she steered clear of her daughter's girls' nights, even though it was Mrs Powell, apparently, who had diligently supplied sandwiches, cheese and biscuits, and homemade cake for the occasion. Mariette appeared to have her mother, whom I knew to be a widow, pretty well trained it seemed to me. Certainly being installed in her own front room – with, I was told, Mrs Powell busily cleaning brass in the kitchen next door – did not cramp Mariette's usual style, nor that of her three friends, none of whom I had met before, which made me quite nervous. The gossip was as raunchy as I had begun to become accustomed to – only this time there were five young women swapping stories of their sexual adventures. Well, four, actually. I had very little to say, although I found that I thoroughly enjoyed listening to the tales of their exploits.

'Suzanne's all right, adored by a man who will do *anything* to make her happy.' Mariette put a hugely suggestive emphasis on the word 'anything'. I tried not to look embarrassed.

'He's coming to get you, I'll bet,' she added.

Hesitantly I agreed that he was.

'Good, we'll all get a chance to have a look,' she said. I had yet to introduce Carl to her.

'No, he told me he'd wait outside,' I replied innocently.

'Really,' remarked Mariette, and glanced at her watch. It was about ten minutes before the time I had agreed to meet him.

'And no doubt he's there already. He doesn't take chances with our Suze!'

The entire group then crowded around the bay window and began to peek through the net curtains in order to get a glimpse of Carl as he waited for me in the street.

'Is that him?' cried Mariette. I peered around her and was just in time to see the back of a male figure disappearing round the corner. At that moment Carl appeared from the other direction and propped himself against the street lamp outside.

'No, that's him, there,' I said somewhat unnecessarily.

'Oh, doesn't he look nice,' said Mariette in a rather soppy voice. 'God, I'm jealous.'

I manoeuvred myself so that I too could get a good view of him. He did look nice. That was the only word for Carl really, that and kind. He was not startlingly handsome, or startlingly anything for that matter, just nice, kind, solid, reliable and funny. And I did love him so.

'Invite him in, go on, just for a moment, oh, go on.'

The entire throng encouraged me. I stepped briskly outside into the cool night air and, quite out of character, asked Carl if he would come in and meet the girls. Even the words sounded strange as I spoke them.

Carl looked terrified. His stammer made an appearance again. 'I d-don't think so, Suzanne, p-p-please, I'd rather not . . .'

He could not escape, though. Mariette and her friends were apparently not prepared to wait indoors for long. When I did not return swiftly with Carl alongside, all four of them followed me out into the street, surrounded Carl and insisted on being introduced. He blushed, his already ruddy face turning absolutely crimson, and I found it as endearing as I had that very first time in Richmond Park.

'He really is very very nice,' whispered Mariette in my ear as we finally said our farewells.

Carl hurried me up the hill. I think he was sweating. 'Good G-God, Suzanne, I felt like a prize bull,' he said.

'You are a prize bull, my love,' I replied.

He laughed, albeit a little uncertainly.

'Mariette says she's jealous,' I went on. 'I reckon it's because she thinks you'll do *anything* for me.'

I put a suggestive emphasis on the word 'anything' in just the way Mariette had done.

Carl looked slightly aghast. 'Did she say that too?'

I nodded.

'Do women really talk like that about men?'

I chuckled. He didn't know the half of it. 'Apparently,' I said.

'Just don't ever throw me to the w-wolves again, that's all,' he admonished, still with just a hint of nervous stammer. But he was smiling when he said it.

Those truly were a happy few months. Nothing at all happened to cause Carl or I any anxiety. The van incident became ancient history. I really did get a taste of the normality I craved.

Mariette had alternate Saturdays off from the library and one weekend she persuaded me to go on a shopping expedition to Penzance with her. Actually, I didn't take much persuading, but I wasn't sure what Carl would make of it. I knew he was anxious about my friendship with Mariette, even though he passed little comment, so I didn't tell him about the trip until the night before Mariette and I were due to take the little train from the station just by Porthminster Beach.

He was fine about it though. 'Don't ever think I don't want you to enjoy yourself, Suzanne, because I do, in every possible way,' he said. 'Just remember that you don't know Mariette that well, won't you.'

I knew what he was saying. In a funny kind of way it felt as if I knew Mariette very well indeed, but I didn't of course, nor could I. Carl was just reminding me to be cautious and I knew that he was quite right to do so. That was how it was with us.

Of course, then I had to ask him for some money. Apart from my nightmares, which were lessening, money was our sole problem. We managed, but only just, and as I spent more time with Mariette I was increasingly embarrassed by having to rely on Carl for every penny. That had been one of the reasons why I had liked the idea of getting a job.

Carl, though, was as generous as ever. He swiftly produced fifty pounds from somewhere. I had few halfway decent clothes and I badly needed some new ones. Fifty pounds would not go very far, but for us it was a lot of money. I thanked him with enthusiasm.

'Don't spend it all at once,' he responded with a twinkle.

I set off cheerily to meet Mariette at the station the next morning.

She eyed the calf-length skirt, cotton print blouse and cardigan I was wearing – more or less the best clothes I possessed – with a distinct lack of enthusiasm. 'What you need is a complete make-over, my girl,' she said.

I didn't even know what a make-over was.

She led me through the crowds at Penzance to a shop called, rather appropriately I suppose, New Look. The prices, the lowest on the High Street, Mariette said, were, it seemed, the greatest attraction – that and a manic adherence to all the latest fashion fads. But every garment looked to me about three sizes too small and skimpy for any normal person.

'Rubbish,' said Mariette. 'You're slim enough and at least we might find something here which looks as if it should be worn by someone in their twenties, rather than a ninety-year-old woman.'

I retreated, wounded and beaten, and very soon, I'm not quite sure exactly how, found myself buying a bright-orange suit with a daringly short skirt. At least I thought it was pretty daring. In fact, even as I handed over a considerable chunk of my fifty pounds, I wasn't sure I should be buying it at all. 'Don't you think it looks, well, you know, a bit tarty?' I enquired hesitantly.

'Yes,' said Mariette. 'Great, isn't it.'

I was then persuaded to buy a pair of ridiculously high platform shoes, but I balked at Mariette's next suggestion.

'No, I am not dyeing my hair,' I told her firmly. 'Absolutely not.'

'I didn't say dye it, I said have a few blond highlights,' she responded in a wheedling tone of voice.

I stood my ground.

'Well, what about a nice trendy haircut then? I've got a friend who's a hairdresser who'll give you a great cheap cut.'

I couldn't even remember if I'd ever been to a hairdresser in my life. Gran had always cut my hair when I was a child. In adulthood I had let it grow long and straight, just occasionally trimming the ends myself in front of a mirror. But I was a woman, albeit one who had missed out on so much, and I was sorely tempted. Eventually, against my better judgement, I allowed myself to be persuaded.

An hour later I was sitting in a leather chair at the extraordinarily named Fair-dos salon, while Mariette's friend, a striking redhead called Chrissy, snipped away alarmingly, and Mariette set to work on my make-up. I was beyond protesting by then.

Two hours later I gazed in the mirror at a different human being.

My hair was several inches shorter, layered and gelled so that it kind of stuck out round my face. Hard to describe, but I had to agree with Mariette that it did seem to suit me. My lips were more or less the same colour as my new suit, I appeared to have had a cheekbone transplant and my eyes looked about two sizes larger than they had before.

'Go on,' said Mariette. 'Put on the new suit and shoes, and let's have a look at you.'

Obediently – I was thoroughly enjoying myself by then, by the way – I took my carrier bags into the loo and changed into my new outfit. When I emerged, teetering a little unsteadily on my platforms, Chrissy and Mariette both applauded, and Mariette emitted a loud and vulgar wolf whistle.

'Why don't you keep it on,' she suggested.

I lurched back into the real word. I had a feeling it was not a good idea to confront Carl so unexpectedly with my total transformation. 'I don't think so,' I said.

'Go on,' encouraged Mariette, apparently reading my mind. 'There's not a man in the world who wouldn't be bowled over. Carl'll love it, you'll see.'

The three of us trailed off to a nearby pub and shared a bottle of white wine. I felt sure everybody would stare at me in my new orange suit, but of course nobody did. Given some courage by this and the wine, probably, I finally agreed to keep the outfit on. I should have known better.

Carl called down to me from our upstairs room when I arrived home.

'Don't come down, I'll come up,' I called back.

'I've something to show you.'

But as I started to clump up the stairs I tripped over my strange new shoes and almost fell backwards. I recovered myself without injury, but not without making a terrific noise. By the time I reached the top of the stairs Carl was standing there looking at me.

I was still on a bit of a high. I smiled and threw my arms open wide. 'What do you think?' I asked, doing a kind of twirl for him.

He didn't show any anger. He didn't shout. He didn't say I looked like a tart. He didn't say anything like that. He just looked disappointed and a bit sad. 'I think you look like somebody else,' he said eventually.

'You d-don't like it?' I stuttered.

'What's to like?' he asked mildly. 'I can barely recognise you.'

I felt terrible. I went straight downstairs to the bathroom, kicked off the silly shoes and scrubbed every vestige of make-up off my face. I combed down my hair and flattened it against my head, making it look as long and as much the way it had before as possible. Then I took off the tarty orange suit and let it fall carelessly on to the floor. There were a pair of jeans and a sweater in the airing cupboard. I put them on and went back upstairs to Carl.

He smiled at me and touched my cheek. 'That's better,' he said. 'I know who you are again now. It's you I love, Suzanne. Not some creature created by your friend Mariette.'

And that was that. He hadn't liked Mariette's make-over, that was for sure, but he didn't create a fuss. Indeed, by the time we went to bed that night it was almost as if it hadn't happened.

I was just sorry I had wasted so much money on the orange suit. And, of course, I never wore it again.

One way or another, I really had more or less forgotten our vandalised van when two days after my unfortunate shopping expedition, a letter arrived.

The words and letters were cut out of a newspaper. The message was stark and chilling. 'I SAW YOU TOGETHER LAST NIGHT. I WATCHED YOU IN BED. HOW LONG DO YOU THINK THIS CAN GO ON? HOW LONG CAN YOU LIVE A LIE? FACE THE TRUTH, SUZANNE.'

The post had arrived while Carl was in the bathroom. There were three pieces of mail, one obviously junk, the electricity bill and the offending letter. The address was carefully printed using letters from one of those stencil kits you can buy in Smith's, and although with the benefit of hindsight it did look a bit odd, I did not initially study it very closely and no particular warning bells rang as I put the mail on the rickety old dining-room table and sat myself down to open it.

My shock was total. My cup of tea grew cold at my side as I stared dumbly at the letter on the table before me. This was nothing like the scratched words on our van, which surely could have been the work of kids. Someone out there was definitely threatening us. Or, more particularly, me. It was quite terrifying seeing my name there on the page. 'FACE THE TRUTH, SUZANNE', made my blood run cold.

My first instinct, of course, was to shout for Carl, but then, for once, I decided it was my place to protect him. I wouldn't show it to him, wouldn't give him more to worry about. When I heard his footsteps on the stairs I slipped the letter quickly back into its envelope and stuffed it into the pocket of my jeans. Then I forced myself to appear bright and normal as Carl ruffled my hair in passing – if he minded it being so much shorter he never passed comment – and went into our tiny kitchen to pour himself his breakfast coffee.

He was particularly buoyant and energetic that morning, the way he always was on those good days when he couldn't wait to get to work. Encouraged by Will's reaction to the paintings we had delivered to him, in particular *Balloons*, he was working on another even bigger abstract inspired by the kind of shapes we saw daily on the yachts out in the bay. Carl liked best of all to use the things he saw in our everyday life in St Ives in an innovative way. He soon retreated into his studio, humming something indecipherable. It was probably his great favourite, Leonard Cohen, but you couldn't really tell. Carl was a hopeless singer, quite incapable of carrying a tune. His attempts did invariably make me smile, though.

But that morning I felt I had little to smile about. When I was sure Carl was safely engrossed in his work I took the envelope from my pocket and looked at it again without opening it. I told myself that what I should do was to rip the thing to shreds, dump it in the bin and force myself not to think about it. But for some reason I couldn't bring myself to throw it away. Instead, I hid it in the cupboard under the stairs, tucking it into a crack in a bit of old broken brickwork.

The day passed slowly for me, although Carl was

in his element. He barely emerged from the studio. I made him some egg sandwiches for lunch but he seemed almost unaware of my existence when I took them to him.

'It's good, Carl,' I told him, peering over his shoulders. The colours were more muted than *Balloons*, but the shapes even more clearly defined and dramatic.

'Mm,' was his distracted reply. He ate one of the sandwiches when I actually placed it in his hand and ignored the rest. That was how it was when he was working well. Normally I would have thoroughly enjoyed watching him work like this, but on that day I didn't even attempt to. I was completely preoccupied too, but not happily so. I just wandered aimlessly about the house. I thought about going to the library but I wasn't up to any banter with Mariette. I hadn't seen her since our shopping expedition and I knew she would want to know all about Carl's reaction, which I did not want to discuss.

Later I cooked dinner for Carl and tried to chat normally while we ate but did not succeed very well. It was only because he was having one of his work-obsessed days, his mind totally focused on his latest painting, that he was not aware of my unease. Usually he was acutely tuned in to my moods.

In bed I dared not sleep. Indeed, I had been dreading bedtime all day. When I heard Carl's steady breathing and became aware of the stillness in his body that indicated he was asleep, I climbed out of bed, went downstairs, made coffee and paced the house all night, determined to stay awake, convinced it was the only way to keep the demons at bay – just as I had done when it all began.

I also kept peeping through the curtains at the alleyway outside. 'I saw you together last night, I watched you in bed.' Was somebody really watching us like that? I never saw any sign of it. Nonetheless the very idea made me feel sick.

In the morning, before Carl woke, I climbed back into bed beside him and allowed him to assume that I had been there sleeping all night long.

I continued to do this for three nights. During the day it was a struggle to keep my eyes open. In contrast, Carl was working so hard that he fell asleep as soon as his head hit the pillow. On the third day he finished the painting that had so engrossed him.

It was almost as if he awoke from a period of half-consciousness. I knew he was seeing me clearly for the first time in three days and became aware of him watching me acutely. At first I denied there was anything wrong, but he was not convinced.

'You really don't look well,' he told me anxiously. 'Are you sure you feel all right?'

'I'm fine,' I said. 'Really, I am.'

Again and again I tried to reassure him, but it was the wrong way round for us and I was not very effective in my new role. The way I looked didn't help, either.

'Suzanne, you look worn out. You haven't been sleeping, have you?'

I knew I had bags beneath my eyes and that I looked drawn and tired. Three nights without sleep is not something many of us can survive without showing the unmistakable signs of exhaustion. 'I'll sleep tonight,' I told him obliquely. 'I'm sure of it . . .'

I didn't, of course. I still couldn't trust myself. And some time during that fourth night after the arrival of the letter, as I stood quietly by the picture window looking down over the rooftops at the harbour lights, afraid even to sit in case I fell asleep and entered my terrible nightmare world, I became aware of Carl standing beside me.

He reached out for me and I could no longer hold back the tears.

'Tell me, my love, tell me what's wrong,' he coaxed. 'Something has happened. Please tell me.'

I could no longer resist. I had tried to be strong, but I had no strength without Carl. I had always been weak. I had thought that maybe I would become stronger with the years but it seemed it was not to be.

I gave in. I took him to the cupboard under the stairs, groped about until I found the crack in the brickwork and removed the letter I had so ineffectually tried to hide from him.

He looked very grim as he read it, then threw it angrily on to the floor. 'You're completely exhausted, aren't you.'

I just nodded.

'You've been refusing to let yourself sleep. You can't go on like that. You'll make yourself ill.'

He led me upstairs, helped me undress, pulled back the duvet and made me lie down on the bed. Then he lay down beside me and wrapped his arms round me, giving me comfort the way he always did, the way only he could. 'Nobody can see us, not in here, we're quite private, you know that, really.'

As usual, he had read my mind. More than anything I hated the thought of someone watching us when we were together in bed, the way that awful letter had suggested. Of course it couldn't be true. I held on to Carl tightly.

Why didn't you tell me?' he asked quietly.

'I suppose I didn't want it to be real,' I replied.

He kissed the top of my head, my face, my throat, my neck. 'I'm going to make it go away,' he told me. 'It won't be real for long. Nothing is going to hurt you, how many times must I tell you . . .'

I could not stay awake, then. The need to sleep overcame me. The unwelcome visitor could be kept at bay no longer.

I slept until early afternoon the next day. Carl had worked yet another of his miracles and I somehow managed it without dreaming – or certainly without any of the horror dreams.

He was sitting in our old wicker rocking chair watching me when I finally opened my eyes.

Nobody who has not suffered the kind of nightmares that have plagued me could ever understand quite how I felt at that moment. Nobody who hasn't endured total debilitating exhaustion and yet fought off sleep as if it were his or her worst enemy, even though only sleep can bring relief, can know what it is like to have given in and to have survived a night of rest to wake in peace.

Suddenly the demons had retreated a little again. I was beginning to realise that they would probably never leave me, but the world did not look as bleak as it had the previous day.

'Are you feeling any better?' he asked.

I told him I was and even managed a wan smile.

'I will find out who is doing this,' he said. 'And I will stop it.'

I believed him because I always believed him. Carl had never let me down in the whole of our life together.

He made me boiled eggs and toasted soldiers from good local bread spread thickly with Cornish butter, and I sat up in bed and ate.

'Do you feel strong enough to talk about it?' he asked, pouring me a second mug of coffee.

I nodded.

Together we tried to think of anyone who could have sent us the letter. There was no one we could realistically suspect, certainly nobody from our new life together. We never got close enough to anybody for them to learn much about us, let alone to discover the past.

Mariette was the nearest I had to a friend, but even she was only barely a friend. You share your life with your true friends, and I couldn't do that.

Nonetheless Carl asked me if I was sure about Mariette.

I shrugged. 'What's to be sure of?' I asked. 'I like her company. I like listening to her stories. But she knows nothing about us.'

'She told you she was jealous of us, of you. People do strange things out of jealousy.'

'Oh, she wasn't serious. Mariette has men like other people have hot dinners. She has nothing to be jealous of.'

'Are you sure?' asked Carl again. 'From what you've told me, Mariette's love life consists of a series of one-night stands. I think she has a lot to be jealous of us about.' He touched my hand gently.

I shrugged again. 'In any case, I've never told her anything about our lives before we came here,' I said.

Carl nodded. 'Well, all right, I suppose it couldn't be her, really.'

I shook my head. 'Anyway, she's too nice,' I said.

'People can have more than one side to them,' muttered Carl.

'You don't,' I said.

'Yes I do,' he replied. 'It's just that you bring out the best in me.'

I smiled. 'In any case, it just can't be Mariette,' I insisted.

'No, I suppose not,' Carl agreed. 'But who, then?'

'Let's list the people we know.'

It wasn't a very long list: Will at the gallery, our neighbours, our local fishmonger who for some reason looked after us particularly well, the boss of our favourite restaurant, a couple of local shopkeepers, the dreaded Fenella and the others we knew vaguely from the pub scene.

'That old hag Fenella is capable of anything, I reckon,' said Carl with feeling.

But we both knew the truth well enough. Apart from any other considerations, everyone on our rather pathetic list had one thing in common: they knew absolutely nothing about Carl and me and our past. They had no motive that we could possibly imagine and no knowledge to harm us with.

'It has to be someone from before, that's the only logical answer,' said Carl.

I shrugged again. 'But there isn't anybody, is there?'

When we came to live in St Ives, Carl and I had discarded our old lives like a pair of worn-out shoes. For so long now there had just been each other. There was nobody left from the past, not for either of us. There could not be.

We were sitting together at the table in our single downstairs room. Carl walked to the window, which looked into the narrow alleyway outside. Only the upstairs room, that bit higher up, had the wonderful sea view over the rooftops.

'I don't know what to do,' he said softly, almost as if he was talking to himself. I was not used to uncertainty in Carl. He always seemed so strong.

'The police?' I suggested tentatively.

'I don't think so,' he said. 'Do you?'

I shook my head. The last thing either of us wanted to do was to answer a load of questions from the police.

We were both silent for a moment, then Carl turned away from the window. He sat down beside me again and put his arm round me. I could tell that his moment of indecision was over. He seemed right back to his normal strong self. 'It's you and me, girl,' he said in his lovely slow drawl. 'You and me against the world. That's the way it's always been and that's the way it always will be – which is just fine by me. We don't need anyone else, not now, not ever.'

He kissed me and I managed a smile.

'C'mon,' he instructed suddenly. 'Let's conduct our own investigation.'

He led me down the hill through the town to the Logan Gallery.

'For goodness' sake, Carl, you don't suspect Will, do you?' I asked.

Carl shook his head. 'He knows everybody, doesn't he? We need all the help we can get.'

I understood what Carl was up to. He wanted to

do something, however potentially fruitless, rather than just sit around waiting for another letter, heaven forbid, to arrive.

Will greeted me with the usual bear-hug. I pushed him away more abruptly than normal and noticed a fleeting expression of hurt surprise in his eyes, but he quickly recovered and offered us coffee. Carl had no time for it that day. He didn't mess about. He produced the letter at once and handed it to the gallery boss.

Will glanced at it quickly. He looked absolutely shocked and appeared to be momentarily rendered speechless.

'Any ideas? Somebody scratched the same sort of stuff on the van, as well,' Carl explained.

Will just shook his head. 'Why have you shown me this? What does it mean?' he enquired.

'I haven't the faintest idea what it means, but it's upset Suzanne terribly and it's not doing me a great deal of good either,' replied Carl.

Will nodded. 'I'm not surprised,' he said.

'Look, Will, I have to find out who's doing this.'

'Have you been to the police?'

Carl shook his head. 'I reckon I should be able to sort it out. Look at the postmark. Penzance. It's somebody local.'

Will studied the letter and the envelope. 'Words cut out of a newspaper. I thought that only happened on TV,' he remarked.

'That's what Carl said,' I told him.

'It's got to be somebody with a screw loose,' said Carl.

Will gave a short laugh. 'That's half the artistic community of St Ives,' he said.

Carl reached out for the letter. Will put his hand on my arm.

'Try not to fret, Suzanne,' he said. 'I hate to think of you being upset.'

I smiled wanly.

Carl put the letter back in his jacket pocket. 'Well, if you think of anything – or anyone – give us a shout,' he said.

'I can't imagine who it could be,' responded Will. 'I know you get all sorts of petty jealousies in a town like this, particularly among the artists, but I've never heard of anything like this before. What could the writer possibly know, anyway?'

Carl shrugged. Neither of us had any more to say.

I thanked Will and steered Carl towards the door. As an afterthought I turned back to Will. 'Do you want to come to supper at the weekend?' I asked.

Will was one of the few people we entertained. Apart from enjoying his company, it was the nearest Carl and I would ever get to networking, but we didn't often formally invite him. Usually he just sort of turned up on the doorstep and we did our best to entertain him for a couple of hours.

Will's face brightened at once. 'Love to.'

Outside the gallery I took Carl's hand. 'C'mon, let's go home,' I said.

Carl shook his head. 'I want to go to the Sloop, ask around,' he told me.

'Are you sure, Carl?' I asked him. 'It's a dangerous thing to do, you know.'

He put a hand on each of my shoulders and rested his face against mine. 'I know. I just hate doing nothing,' he said.

I was well aware of that. 'Sometimes it's the best

71

thing there is,' I told him. 'And the hardest . . .'

'I know,' he said again.

I grasped his arm. 'Let's go home, Carl,' I coaxed. 'Let's leave it.'

And to my immense relief he agreed. For the time being.

Five

I relied totally on Carl. I was used to relying on people. That's how I came to be trapped in my terrible marriage. I had not been brought up to have either a mind or a life of my own.

My parents were killed in a car crash when I was three years old. I had gone to live with my widowed grandmother. At the time I was happy enough. Indeed, in many ways a child couldn't have been better cared for.

I had no brothers and sisters and no uncles or aunts that I knew of. Gran tried to be all of those things to me and succeeded pretty damn well, by and large.

There were drawbacks. Gran was definitely over-protective. She always wanted to shelter me from the real world, but that suited me perfectly because I was a timid child, introverted and unsure of myself. I never tried to break out of the comforting cocoon Gran created around us both.

Even at an early age I suffered from shocking night-mares. There was a recurring one in which terrible pictures used to fly around inside my head of bloody flesh and dismembered limbs. I used to wake in the night screaming, but it seemed I had good reason to.

As I grew older I learned how I had been strapped into my seat in the back of my father's car when an out-of-control juggernaut had collided with us and crushed the entire front of the vehicle. My parents died instantly, their bodies broken and squashed beneath the tremendous weight of the huge lorry. Extraordinarily, the rear of the car was barely damaged and I escaped virtually without injury, but in severe shock. I was told later that I did not speak for several weeks, although I never had any memory of that nor – at least in my conscious mind – of the accident itself. I think my body's defence mechanisms had clicked effectively into action. However, I had witnessed it all, seen my parents' lives so violently torn from them, and Gran was always quite certain that it had been imprinted on my subconscious and had irrevocably affected the way I was. She believed in things like that, did Gran. And, of course, she was probably right.

For years she slept in the same room as me because of my bad dreams and when I had a nightmare she comforted me just as Carl was to do years later.

She used to sing hymns to me, of all things. Often Christmas carols, whatever the time of year, because so many of them were so gentle and soothing, she said. 'Silent Night' was a great favourite. Well, it could have been a lot worse. She might have treated me to regular renditions of 'Abide with Me'.

One way or another, I was neither mentally nor physically strong. I had a weak chest and suffered from chronic bronchitis, a complaint that was to plague me into adulthood until I moved to St Ives. Cornwall, with its slightly warmer climate and wonderful fresh sea air, proved to be good for me in every way and I had suffered only a handful of minor chest infections in the six years I had been there. But throughout my childhood I had been a sickly, mixed up kid who caught every bug going and was afraid of

74

everything that moved. Gran was always reluctant for me to mix too much with other children. She had been a schoolteacher by trade in her younger days and her years within Britain's education system had left her with a pretty dismal opinion of it. Certainly, when I reached the age of five, she was most reluctant for me to attend school.

'Schools reduce all children to the level of the lowest common denominator, both academically and behaviourally,' she would pontificate.

Gran had a way of speaking that defied contradiction. Like most of our family she was a small woman, slightly built, but she had a presence which defied her stature. Her ex-pupils, the more devoted of whom visited us occasionally, told stories of how she would walk into class, write on the blackboard that she had a sore throat and did not intend to speak, and still conduct a lesson, using written instructions and keeping a class of otherwise unruly children working away in perfect order by virtue of little more than a slight frown or a raising of the eyebrow.

She was an old-fashioned sort of person, my Gran. She wore twinsets, tweed skirts with their hems well below the knee and flat lace-up shoes. Her hair, which I believe had been the same iron-grey colour from her early thirties, was held in a neat bun and I don't think she ever wore make-up, not even a dusting of face powder or a hint of lipstick. Although a Londoner born and bred, she had married a Devonian, also a schoolteacher, and had taught most of her working life in a school in the little market town of Crediton. Her name was Mrs Theresa Eddie and one of her old pupils told me that, with the wonderfully convoluted logic of children, a nickname had been chosen for her deriving from combining her initial and her last name – Teddie, West Country slang for potato. Gran then became known as Spud – a name that creates the impression of a certain vulgarity and could not have been less appropriate, which doubtless added to its attraction.

Gran did not have a vulgar bone in her body. She was well-spoken and well-mannered, and expected all around her to be the same. In addition, everything about her was ordered, including her memory. She had quite an intellect and I used to imagine as a child that she had a filing cabinet of some kind in her brain from which she could extract almost any piece of information at will.

Nowadays I suppose you might think of her as a kind of computer on legs. She rarely showed emotion, that was for certain, and she never lost control.

I thought she was indomitable. She was certainly not to be trifled with and she was fiercely independent. She did not doubt for one second that her opinion of the negative effect of formal schooling, reached with so much first-hand knowledge, was correct and she did not expect to be challenged on this. For two terms she kept me at home, without anyone in the state education system seeming to notice, and quite effectively taught me the rudiments of reading, writing and arithmetic, and a lot more besides.

But eventually the authorities caught up with us and an inspector called. Gran fed him tea poured from a silver tea pot into china cups. The teaspoons were also silver and the sugar came in lumps. I was stood in the middle of the living room, all dark-brown furniture and dark-cream walls adorned with those kinds of Victorian reproduction paintings that have each matured to the same indecipherable murkiness, and asked to recite my multiplication tables, the alphabet, and various rhymes and homilies I had already learned by heart. So well rehearsed was I that I managed to do so without faltering and Gran rested triumphantly back in her brown velvet armchair.

Whether or not the inspector was impressed by my performance we never discovered. He certainly was not dissuaded from his course of ensuring that I was sent to school. The weight of the law came down upon us, and even Gran had to give in to the inevitable so I was duly despatched to our local state primary school. By this time I was thoroughly terrified of the prospect and from the start the horrors of school lived up to all my expectations. I shall never forget my first day at St Justin's, a soulless red-brick building just a couple of streets away from where Gran and I lived. The other children in my class had already been together for two terms and I was an outsider in more ways than one. I was convinced that I wouldn't fit in and I was right.

I was undersized and painfully thin, and not only did all the other five- and six-year-old children seem to be years older than me already, they were also much bigger. Although there was no uniform at St Justin's, Gran had kitted me out in a grey gymslip, which flapped around the calves of my legs. Ever sensible and practical, she had allowed plenty of room for growth. I also wore old-fashioned black lace-up shoes and ankle socks. The other children all had on brightly coloured sweaters and shirts, tracksuits, jeans and sneakers. Even I realised that I stood out like something off the pages of *Billy Bunter*.

There is always a leader, at every stage and in every walk of life. And all too often, I did not learn until much later, the leader is whoever is most inappropriate. At St Justin's the leader of the pack was a staggeringly precocious six-year-old called Janet Postings and she took it upon herself to make my life a misery from the moment I arrived.

Thanks to Gran I could already read and write better than any of the other girls and boys in my class, but this did not seem to work in my favour. In fact, just the opposite. I was asked to read aloud on my first morning.

'Let's see what you can do,' said the teacher. Reading aloud was no problem for me. That was the way Gran taught. And the book was actually similar to the reading material I was already used to. I read clearly and fluently, the way Gran had always insisted upon, and when I finished I was all too aware that the entire class were staring at me. And they weren't very friendly.

The trouble started at morning break. Janet Postings broke off from whatever activity she and a small group were involved in at one end of the playground and ran across to where I had sat down alone on a wooden bench, eating the apple Gran had provided me with.

'Do you want to join in our game?' she asked. Janet Postings was fair-haired, blue-eyed and very pretty. In fact, she looked quite angelic. And I had yet to discover that looks can be very deceptive, particularly in children.

My hearted lifted. 'Oh, yes,' I said eagerly.

'Well, you can't,' she replied. 'It's my game and I don't like you. I think you're a show-off.'

I felt my face turn crimson. How often over the years I was to loathe myself for blushing so easily. That was just the beginning. It seemed that if Janet Postings didn't like you at St Justin's, then neither did anyone else.

My hair was long and straight, and tied back in bunches. A constant leisure activity for the rest of the class was to pull at them. It's the kind of damn silly thing you read and hear about in schools, and you think it probably doesn't really happen because it's too stupid – even for five- and six-year-olds – but it happened to me, that's all I can say.

In addition, my books and gym kit would go missing, and I would find things broken and dirty. Then I would get into trouble with Gran, who would lecture me on how I should look after my belongings. Somehow, I could never tell her what was really happening.

On one occasion a group of girls, who had apparently been lurking in a gateway waiting for me to pass by, jumped on me as I walked home. They snatched my satchel and emptied my books into a puddle.

There were sixteen girls and thirteen boys in my class. Funnily enough, the boys weren't really a problem. They just used to ignore me. It was the girls who seemed to hate me. I suppose it was a classic case of habitual bullying, but nobody seemed even to recognise that as a problem in schools in those days. I had no idea why I was picked on so relentlessly. I certainly did nothing to provoke it, or I thought I didn't, and I had no ability whatsoever to deal with it. I just could not cope with other children in any way.

I retreated into myself. I kept my eyes cast

downwards and hardly spoke at all, except to the teachers and then only when spoken to. They seemed to notice nothing amiss, even though I think I can honestly say that during my time at St Justin's I added absolutely nothing to the learning Gran had already instilled in me.

My nightmares grew worse and took on whole new dimensions. Sometimes I was chased by hordes of chanting children who cornered me and then, just as they were about to pounce upon me, turned into howling, teeth-baring wolves.

Things reached a crisis one day after I had endured this daily torture at St Justin's for almost a year. Every day after each playtime, at morning break, lunch and afternoon break, each class had to line up in alphabetical order on a raised platform alongside the north wall of the school building to wait to be collected by their teacher. My surname was Adams then, so, inevitably, I was always at the front of the line and it seemed to greatly amuse those behind me to push me off the platform until our teacher arrived. They were a clever lot, St Justin's Class Two. They never shoved hard enough to hurt me, just sufficiently to ensure that I repeatedly had to half jump off the platform and then clamber back up again.

For almost a year, three times a day, I endured this. Finally I cracked. Even wimps and natural-born victims have a breaking point. Perhaps especially wimps and victims. Pushed off once too often, I ran to the back of the line, wrapped my arms round my head, leaned my body forward and charged. I did it well, finding a strength I did not know I had. The worm really turned. I was, I suppose, beyond fear by then. Twenty-eight small bodies went flying and landed in a crying, screaming heap. There were no broken bones or other serious injuries, but plenty of grazed and bleeding arms and legs, bumped heads and even, I believe, a chipped tooth or two. It was a totally chaotic scene and, for just a moment or two, I remember being quite pleased with myself.

Then the trouble started. I was sent immediately to the headmistress, having been unceremoniously shopped by my dear little friends who certainly did not share my tendency to be tongue-tied. She gave me a corker of a telling off, which reduced me to tears. I knew none of it was fair but, as ever, could not find the words to explain myself. Ultimately the head told me to wait in the corridor outside her office. I was still standing there snivelling when Gran arrived two hours later, having been summoned to the school.

Gran had to walk past me on her way into the headmistress's office. I was a complete wreck by then, of course, and I saw the corners of Gran's mouth turn down and a flash of anger in her eyes. At first I thought she was angry with me, which she probably was, but she seemed to be even more angry with the school.

She was, of course, as calm and controlled as ever. She told me to stop crying, that she was there and that everything was going to be all right – typical Gran, never emotional but always strong and reassuring. Then she took me by the hand and led me back into the headmistress's office.

She listened in silence while the headmistress ranted for some time about my 'appalling behaviour', but did not seem to be overly impressed.

'And you think that gives you the right to leave a

six-year-old child to cry alone in a corridor, do you?' she asked eventually in an icy tone.

Gran really was my champion, bless her.

'She has to learn her lesson; what she did was very dangerous,' said the headmistress. 'Somebody could have been badly hurt.'

'I think it would be best if I took her home for a few days, don't you?' enquired Gran, but in a firm tone of voice, which made it clear she was not really interested in the headmistress's opinion, but was merely telling her what she intended to do.

Gran had spoken and there was little more discussion. But it was already the end of the school day when we left together after what would turn out to be my last appearance at St Justin's. Pupils were waiting outside for buses and parents as Gran led me out through the big wrought-iron gates. 'Straight back, eyes forward,' she murmured.

I did my best to comply. Because I was with Gran, none of the other children dared approach me, but I was aware of dozens of pairs of eyes staring at me. And I knew that I had blushed bright crimson as I always did when nervous or embarrassed.

At home, Gran tried to get me to tell her exactly what had happened and why. I still could not find the words. She was not pleased with me, of course, but she was more disbelieving than anything else. Gran knew well enough that the last thing I had was an aggressive nature. Maybe her years as a schoolteacher had given her some insight into the behaviour of children, which the staff of St Justin's did not seem to share.

Gran had never stopped battling with the local authorities in order to do what she thought was best for me, but after that incident she doubled her efforts.

'This child must be taught at home,' she wrote to the local director of education. 'She is a disturbed and physically weak child, quite unable to cope with the rigours of day-to-day life in a school and all the rough and tumble that entails.'

She was, of course, quite right. But what never occurred to Gran, I am sure, and what I did not consider until many years later, was just how much I had become the child that she had made me.

The same schools inspector eventually returned to re-evaluate the situation.

'Look at her,' commanded Gran, 'and tell me that child should be sent back to school.'

I stood trembling before them both, desperately trying not to cry. I had never been confident but when I had been confronted by the inspector previously I had certainly not been afraid. This time I was terrified of him, of all strangers, and of being forced to go back to the school that had caused me so much misery.

I don't know how much he noticed the difference in me, or whether it was just that Gran was such a formidable woman, but she won the day. A few weeks later she was given official permission to teach me at home and I never did return to school following the incident of the platform.

Over the years we were inspected regularly by education officers from the local authority, but academically Gran's education of me could not be faulted. I might have more or less missed almost a year of learning because of my inability to function at St Justin's, but under Gran's tuition I quickly caught up. Throughout my schooling with her I was at a much higher standard in almost all subjects, particularly English Literature and History, than the average for my age. And I will always be grateful to Gran for nurturing my love of books. Nor did she totally neglect the more practical side of my education, teaching me to cook, to sew and to type.

Gran studied public examination syllabuses and I studied with Gran. I re-entered the public domain only to take my GCSE examinations at the nearest state secondary school. I effortlessly passed all the arts subjects with high grades and managed to scrape through maths. Only in the sciences did Gran's teaching perhaps not quite pass muster and of course there had been little or no opportunity for practical experiments.

My upbringing was about as sheltered as you could possibly get, I suppose. Yet I was happy enough – except during my time at St Justin's – if only, maybe, because I knew no better. Gran saw it as her mission in life to look after me and I always liked being looked after.

I accepted that I needed looking after much more than most children. Indeed, I accepted, as I grew older, that I would always need looking after. I never seemed to have the ability to make decisions for myself. I read newspapers and watched TV – our small portable set, which was a reluctant concession from Gran who did not really approve but eventually gave in to my pleas for one on the grounds that there was so much to be learned from it – and as I grew into adolescence realised that I was reaching an age when many young people chose to rebel. I had no such desire. I was contented with my lot. I would not have known how to rebel, or whom to rebel against. Gran was the kindest, cleverest woman in the world, I thought, and I felt so safe with her.

Gran and I had few friends and rarely went out, except to church on Sundays and a fellowship meeting once a week. Gran was very religious and I naturally grew up accepting her standards and beliefs. I certainly never questioned her simplistic conviction that God was as real as she and I were. I think she actually did believe in an old bearded guru sitting on a cloud somewhere up in the sky.

About the only outside influence we had came from the little chapel we were members of, not far from our Hounslow home. Gran was strictly chapel, predictably unimpressed by the pomp and ceremony of the Catholic church and even the Church of England. The pastor was a tall, handsome, rather aloof man called Robert Foster. Gran adored him. He was the only person she had ever met, she told me, who knew the Bible better than she did – and that included an awful lot of clergymen, Gran said.

I was eighteen and had just taken my A levels – English, History, and Art – when I began to realise that Gran was not well. She looked tired all the time and seemed to be in some pain. Eventually she went to the doctor, something that didn't happen often in our house. Gran usually reckoned that an aspirin and an early night were a cure for almost anything. When she came home after her visit to the surgery – I had not been allowed to accompany her, which was rare because Gran and I usually went everywhere together – she seemed anxious and distracted.

I tried to find out what was wrong but she wouldn't tell me. The Reverend Foster came to the house, and he and Gran spent more than an hour closeted together. Eventually she came out of the dining room where they had been talking behind closed doors and told me she had something to say.

It seemed she was dying of cancer.

I could barely take it in. Gran was my world. I knew nothing else. Selfishly, perhaps, I didn't think at first in terms of her pain or even of my own loss. I thought at once only about how I would survive. I simply did not know how to cope without her. But I might have known she would have thought of that.

'You're my biggest worry, child,' she told me. 'My only worry. I am happy to go to my Maker, I've always tried to serve Him and I don't doubt His promise of eternal life,' she announced predictably. 'But you, girl. You need looking after . . .'

Gran paused and the Reverend Foster stepped forward.

'Robert has agreed to take you on,' said Gran, clutching the clergyman by the arm and sounding as if she were talking about an old horse or a broken-down motor car rather than a teenage girl. 'Robert needs a wife and I'm sure you'll make him a good one. I know he's twenty-odd years older than you, but I think you will be helped by the stability of an older man.'

I remember gazing at the pair of them in amazement. The whole thing was such a shock. 'B-b-but, we barely know each other,' I stuttered.

The Reverend Foster stepped forward and positioned himself directly in front of me. He placed one big hand firmly on each of my shoulders and peered down at me. His eyes, staring directly into mine, were a piercing blue and I was aware of them having an almost hypnotic effect. 'We will have a lifetime to get to know each other, my dear,' he said.

His voice was pleasingly soft, but I knew from his sermons from the pulpit that it was not always so.

I glanced uncertainly at Gran. 'I don't know, I-it's j-just so much to take in,' I stammered.

Gran tried to smile reassuringly. She looked so ill and weary. 'I don't know what else to do,' she said, and she spoke very quietly and slowly. 'I just feel sure it's for the best.'

I trusted Gran with my life. She seemed to have no doubts. I don't remember either her or Robert Foster being all that interested in what I thought of the plans they had made for me and I went along with them. I seemed to have no choice. I don't think I really thought about the magnitude of what I was doing. I had no sense of committing myself to another person for the rest of my life.

Our brief courtship was barely worthy of the name. I only saw Robert Foster when he came to the house and Gran was usually with us. He never took me out anywhere, or introduced me to his friends or family. He did present me with an engagement ring, a single diamond in a narrow gold band, which I thought was rather lovely, and sometimes he brought flowers, although I was never entirely sure whether they were meant for me or for Gran. Everything between us was stiffly formal and distant.

We were married within two months. Gran didn't have long to live and her last wish was to be at the wedding. This was held at Robert's church, of course, with his bishop officiating. Gran and I had almost no friends or family worth mentioning, but half the congregation were there to see the pastor wed. I got through the day in a kind of a daze. My wedding dress, traditional ivory white, had been hired for the occasion. Two little blue-eyed blond girls I did not know at all, but who reminded me disconcertingly of Janet Postings and appeared to be of almost exactly matching height and colouring, were my bridesmaids. They had been drafted in from the Sunday School.

'I'm just so proud and happy,' Gran croaked.

Even her voice was fading. I suppose that was all I cared about, really, making Gran happy and I hadn't thought much beyond that. For myself I felt nothing, really, just a great emptiness.

Among strangers and wearing somebody else's dress I married a stranger. Robert Foster and I had barely been alone together. I had never had even the most casual and innocent boyfriend. I barely knew what to expect even of our wedding night – Gran had been an excellent tutor of Shakespeare, the Magna Carta and trigonometry but, predictably enough, sex education had not featured on her curriculum – let alone our life together.

I just knew that this marriage was what Gran wanted, that she thought it was the right thing to do and she had never let me down. But, of course, she had a blind spot when it came to Christianity and those who represented it. She honestly thought she could do no better thing on earth than to marry off her awkward unworldly granddaughter to a clergyman – and, more than that, the pastor of her own chapel.

The truth was that she had never really looked beyond the pulpit at the man himself. And, slavishly following her wishes as I always had done, neither did I until it was too late.

Gran died within six months of the wedding and after that there was no one in the world for me to turn to apart from my new husband.

And he turned out to be a monster wearing a dog collar.

I dread to think what might have happened to me were it not for Carl.

Six

I could not travel. I certainly could not go abroad. I had never been abroad in my life. I did not even have a passport.

But Carl used to take me with him to his homeland. Through his wonderful stories I felt as if I had toured the Florida Keys, driven over the Seven-mile Bridge, drunk in the bars of Key West, visited Hemingway's house, ridden the Conch Train, basked in the tropical sun and even danced in the streets after dark in the hazy hippieland of Carl's childhood.

Carl had such a wonderful way of bringing it all to life.

He told me stories of how he grew up with the smell of oil paint in his nostrils. From when he was a very little boy he used to sit at his father's feet as he painted and was allowed to visit the studios of many of the other painters, including Eugene Otto, who became perhaps Key West's first really well-known painter.

Carl's childhood sounded so exciting to me, although I knew it had not actually been a very happy one. His father had never achieved the success he hoped for as an artist and as a result – or that was his excuse, Carl used to say – had consoled himself with drink and drugs. As time passed the days spent painting were increasingly replaced by days passed in a drunken drugged haze.

'What about your mother?' I had asked him once as we sat together in the little public garden on the cliffside off the road to Hale, where a splendid Barbara Hepworth bronze stands proudly before the backdrop of what must be one of the most beautiful sea views in the world.

Carl's eyes grew wistful. But he just shrugged. 'In the beginning she often used to join in. I suppose it was fun to start with, that's how it is with drugs, isn't it? She smoked dope, but I never saw her do anything else, not like him . . .' Carl shuddered. 'Anyway, it meant I had plenty of time to myself . . .'

Indeed, from what I could gather the young Carl was more or less ignored by both his parents most of the time. He ran free in the streets, learning to cook and fend for himself from an early age, and even, when things got really bad, how to hustle and beg from tourists.

'I was good at that,' he told me, smiling.

'I'm surprised you didn't turn into a druggie yourself.'

Carl was as reasonable and logical as ever. 'I suppose you go one way or the other,' he replied quietly. 'I've known people who regularly smoke dope and even do coke who are just fine. It wasn't like that with my folks, that's all . . .'

He didn't mind telling me tales of the folklore and history of Key West, in fact, I think he positively enjoyed doing so, but when it came to confiding in me about his family that was about as far as he ever went. There was a lot of pain there for Carl.

None the less I knew this unique and crazy city, closer to Havana than Miami, shrouded in history and mystery just like Cornwall, still held a place in his heart, otherwise he could not have made it so special for me.

'Cayo Hueso,' he whispered to me. 'Island of Bones. That's what Key West was first known as. They reckon the Caloosa Indians used it as a burial ground. From a cemetery to a playground for presidents, that's Key West. Built by fishermen, poets and pirates, sailors, soldiers, rum runners and treasure salvagers . . .'

'Treasure salvagers,' I interrupted him. 'Is that American-speak for wreckers?'

He grinned. 'I guess.'

The more he told me about Key West, on the southernmost tip of America, the more it reminded me of Cornwall, on the southernmost tip of Britain.

'I know,' he agreed. 'I think it's what drew me here, from the moment I came to the UK I knew I wanted to end up here. I can't explain, just something about this county . . .' He paused. 'The people are the same, you know, I swear it.'

I laughed. That could be going too far, I reckoned.

'No, I mean it,' he said. 'There's the artists and the deadbeats, of course, plenty of those in both places. But Key West folk, they're different from other Americans, like the Cornish are different. In 1982 Key West declared independence, you know, founded the Conch Republic, created a flag. They celebrate their own Independence Day every year.'

It was my turn to laugh. 'A joke, I assume,' I said.

'Maybe,' said Carl. 'But don't tell me the Cornish wouldn't be quite capable of doing something like that.'

I had to admit he was probably right. In any case I loved his stories, and I pretended to myself that one day I would be able to go there and see it all for myself, with Carl by my side. I did have good dreams as well as the unspeakably bad ones and Key West often featured in the good ones.

I would picture myself standing on Mallory Dock at sundown, along with the jugglers, mime artists, musicians and the dancing, jostling crowds Carl told me gathered there every evening to celebrate. I imagined myself holding Carl's hand and drinking exotic cocktails while we watched the sun sink into the Caribbean sea just eighty miles away from Cuba.

I knew why Carl had left his homeland and why he felt he could never go back, but I also realised how much he still missed it. Carl had been married before and his wife had left him for another man. I could not understand how anyone could leave so loving and caring a person as Carl, and I knew that this betrayal still broke his heart. It was, he said, the reason he had sought a new life in a new country.

Simple, straightforward and a big overreaction, some might think. But Carl was like that. I knew well enough the extent of his loyalty, the lengths to which he would go for someone he loved. He would naturally expect that kind of commitment the other way round and for it to last for ever. I knew that was what he expected from me, and it was what I wanted to give him.

Although Carl was so strong in so many ways there was also an insecure side to him, which I believed stemmed from all that had happened to him before our time together. I understood that all right. Few of us can ever truly escape from our own pasts. And how I wished that I could escape from mine.

But Carl had given me a new life, and six years I

could look back on with joy. I loved him with all of my heart and mind, and I really would not have known what to do without him there to guide me. Among the sweetest of my memories was the moment when we arrived in St Ives together for the first time. It was a beautiful late-September night and he had driven straight to the harbour. We parked the van and walked to the waterside. The moon had been high and bright, and the sky full of stars. The tide was low and several of the boats moored there had bottomed out and lay crookedly on the sand basin, their masts creating a crazy pattern of angular shadows.

It was almost midnight and St Ives was already asleep. Momentarily the moon was covered by a passing cloud and the sky turned black as coal. I was used to the bustle of London where darkness never really falls and the silence overwhelmed me. Indeed, the sense of peace was such that it felt as if we might be the only two people awake in the whole world.

I breathed in the smell of the sea. You could taste the salt in the air. A slight breeze was blowing inland. It made the hairs on my arms and the back of my neck stand up and sent a shiver down my spine.

'My Lady of the Harbour,' Carl whispered in my ear.

He put his arm round me and I snuggled up to him, unsure of what was going to come next but happy just to be with him.

'This is the start of our new life,' he murmured. 'Tomorrow we will find ourselves a new home.'

As ever, whatever Carl promised seemed to come true.

We slept in his old van, which he had driven all the way from London, wrapped a duvet round ourselves and huddled as close together as we could get on seats divided by a gear lever. We would have been more comfortable stretched out in the back, but the van was stuffed full of our various possessions – mostly things belonging to Carl, like all his painting gear and completed paintings. I had brought little from my previous life except a few clothes – but there was my red bicycle, Gran's bike, of which I was so proud.

The next day we bought the local newspapers so that we could study the property pages and toured the estate agents.

Rose Cottage, on a hill at the back of the town just off the beginning of the main road out to Penzance, was the second place we saw. Whatever roses it might originally have taken its name from had long gone. It didn't even have a garden. The front of the granite-built cottage, its highly suspect roof stained with lichen, veered steeply upwards directly from a narrow cobbled alleyway. The front door led straight into a small, dark living room. Another door, open on our arrival, led into a poky kitchen and through the glazed kitchen door at the rear we could see that there was just a tiny backyard, enhanced only by a washing line and a dustbin rather than the blooming display of roses we had allowed ourselves to hope for. This was not a two-up-two-down. This was a one-up-one-down, with a lean-to bathroom and kitchen tagged on downstairs. The window of the downstairs living room directly faced the living room of the cottage opposite, no more than five feet away. No wonder the rather grimy net curtains looked as if they remained perpetually drawn.

At first glance Rose Cottage, although quite picturesque in its way, did not appear to be a very attractive proposition at all. I had already discovered that this was fairly predictable. Landlords of the better St Ives properties are inclined to prefer to plug in to the lucrative summer market rather than settle for the much lower weekly rent of an all-year-round let.

Carl and I glumly took in the grubby two-seater sofa, an elderly gate-legged table and a collection of four odd dining chairs, about all the room would take, before allowing ourselves, without enthusiasm, to be led up the rickety staircase in one corner.

It was then that everything began to change. Rose Cottage's only bedroom boasted two windows, a large picture window at the front, which just cleared the roof of the cottage opposite and below – such was the steep slope of the hill on which they were both built.

The view over rooftops took in the whole of St Ives bay. I felt my breath catch in my throat. It was late afternoon on a bright, sunny day. The cottage faced west and we could see the sun glowing orange and beginning to fall into the sea. The only outlook from the window at the back of the room, which I realised must face east, was the blank wall of the cottage above – but there was space enough in between to retain the sense of privacy and, I felt sure, to allow the morning sun to stream in. Also, the room seemed slightly larger than the one below. I couldn't quite work out how but the estate agent explained that old St Ives had been built in such a higgledy-piggledy fashion that buildings often more or less slot into each other.

The town is not badly planned, it was just never planned at all. The reason for the tangled network of alleyways often leading to dead ends, occasional outcrops of rock, unexplained bulges in walls, and ancient cottages displaying impossible curves and angles, is simply that the early builders put a house anywhere they could find a location. Then the later builders filled in the gaps.

Maybe all this added to the magic, for Rose Cottage certainly cast some kind of a spell over Carl and me. I could feel him clutching my hand tightly. We did not speak. Instead, we allowed ourselves to be taken downstairs again, shown the kind of bathroom in which it would clearly be quite possible to sit on the toilet, wash your feet in the undersized bath and brush your teeth at the same time, then out through a tatty little lean-to kitchen into the yard. And there was the clincher.

Alongside the wall, which divided the tiny cottage from the property next door and to the right, somebody had built another lean-to, a curious makeshift construction made up of a brick base with steel panels above, framing a line of ill-fitting windows, its roof of corrugated iron punctuated by large glass skylights, which probably stood where there had once perhaps been flower beds. It was not very big – quite long, maybe fifteen or sixteen feet, but no more than six feet wide – and should in no way be confused with a modern double-glazed conservatory. Indeed you could almost see the gaps around some of the sadly deficient glazing through which the wind would surely whistle on chilly winter days. However, to both Carl and me the place practically screamed '*Studio*'. Its glass-panelled roof sloped directly towards the clear north light that artists so love and it was big enough, surely, for just one painter to work in. Particularly if he were organised and tidy, and Carl was both. Extremely so. I had seen that in London where he had worked in just a corner of a flat, which comprised only one big room. If he made a mess he cleared it up at once, his paints and brushes were kept in meticulous order in a large mahogany box, and his work was always scrupulously catalogued and neatly stored. I glanced at him. I could almost see him erecting his easel in his head.

We needed no discussion. Rose Cottage had sold itself to us. And the good news was that we could move in straight away. Indeed, when Carl offered to pay a month's rent as deposit and three months' in advance, the need for references no longer seemed to apply and Rose Cottage was ours. Carl had already told me that cash was not an immediate problem. He had brought with him from London a leather document case, in which he had habitually kept whatever money he had earned and managed to save, which had been concealed beneath the floorboards of his flat. He did not trust banks, he had explained to me.

We drove the van up the hill from the car park by the harbour where we had parked it, and caused traffic chaos when we had to block the road in order to unload. Rose Cottage seemed pretty well perfect to us and we had rented it ever since from an absentee landlord apparently quite content to receive a regular small income from tenants who gave him no bother.

That was the beginning. And at first almost all its promise, all of our dreams, were realised.

The first six years of our life together passed uneventfully and, by and large, were remarkably content. The early memories in particular were such happy ones, because they had brought with them a sense of peace and a degree of loving companionship that I had never thought possible.

You can't deny your own past, of course, not to yourself, anyway. But Carl and I succeeded in settling into Rose Cottage so easily and completely that it was almost as if the place had been built specially for us – which Carl insisted it had been, albeit 200 years or so earlier.

The cottage had everything we wanted. We bought a futon sofa and turned the glorious upstairs room into a kind of bedsit. We found some wonderful old pale-gold curtains in a charity shop, which we hung in the dull downstairs room that we used as a dining room in the evenings, when we could pull the curtains and mask the room's ugliness with candlelight.

The studio in the backyard suited Carl perfectly. We even discovered, when trying to brighten up the shabby little kitchen by replacing the decaying brown linoleum that covered the floor with a dazzlingly colourful material, that there was a small, apparently forgotten, cellar below. Its entrance was protected by a piece of old stone right by the sink, which had at first seemed no different from the rest of the floor but which had given a slightly hollow ring when Carl had tapped the new floor covering in place. He had been delighted when he succeeded in prising up the stone with a crowbar to reveal a seven-foot-square cellar, which gave him an excellent hiding place for his cash earnings and also somewhere to store completed paintings. I had been pleased too, because, having both a vivid imagination and a love of history, I immediately conjured up an image of our cellar housing stashes of illicit contraband brought there by Cornish smugglers.

Mostly we led a very quiet life, our love for each other all that really mattered to either of us, and even the arrival of the letter did not alter that. Not to begin with. We were determined, at the end of that fateful year, that Christmas would not be spoiled. We enjoyed special occasions. We celebrated alone, as was our habit in most things, with roast pheasant and a bottle of good claret, after spending a jolly – and mercifully Fenella-Austen-free – lunchtime hour in the Sloop.

By the end of January both Carl and I had almost begun to dare to believe that perhaps both the van incident and the letter had not really meant anything. Certainly I had still somehow managed to keep any further nightmares at bay. But the peace I so hoped we had found was shattered when, one dark and cold morning, the postman brought another letter.

I suppose I had been kidding myself that there wouldn't be any more. That it had ended as abruptly as it had begun. After all, two months had elapsed since the first letter arrived so to receive one again, just like that, was a greater shock than ever. This time the message was not only devastating but also devastatingly appropriate. 'YOU CANNOT HIDE FROM THE TRUTH ANY MORE', it said.

Carl and I both tried to pretend to the other that we were able to take it in our stride, but I knew deep down that neither of us was as calm as we pretended to be.

Seven

'This can't go on,' I told Carl the next day. 'I think we should go to the police. We're both living my nightmare now. Anything would be better than that . . .'

He looked at me as if I had slapped his face. 'No!' he said emphatically. 'No. I cannot risk losing you.'

I sighed. I was no longer a frightened twenty-year-old girl. Nowadays I was a frightened twenty-seven-year-old woman. Nothing had changed, really, except that I was beginning to believe that nobody could run for ever.

Carl cuddled me and told me stories, as he always did when he knew I was upset. He told me again about growing up in Key West in the Sixties and early Seventies when the artists and writers were there with a vengeance, and the whole place existed in a cloud of scented smoke from marijuana and joss sticks, and he as a small boy used to go hunting for clams on the beach accompanied by a chorus of songs from guitar-playing hippies.

Sometimes he made his growing up sound forsaken and lonely. It depended on his mood, I knew that. Sometimes he resented the haze of drugs and booze, which had engulfed his parents to the extent where they could hardly be bothered with their only son. Sometimes he romanticised it all. This was one of those days. He was trying to lift me, of course. 'Did I ever tell you about Crabman Killenny?' he asked.

I shook my head.

'They called him Crabman because he could sing the crabs off the beach.'

I laughed.

'No, really, every night he'd go to the beach and sing to the sunset. His voice was so bad even the crabs couldn't stand it. A great procession of them would make their way across the sand and up into the streets. All we kids used to go and watch. We reckoned they'd rather be squashed underneath the Conch Train than listen to old Crabman Killenny singing.'

'Yuk,' I said. And I laughed again dutifully.

'No truly, I saw it with my own eyes.'

And Carl stared at me, arms outstretched, hands palms up, a picture of offended innocence.

Nobody could make me forget pain like Carl. He was just so easy to be with somehow. I loved his gentle sense of humour. He had a way of jollying me out of myself. It didn't quite work on this occasion though, and the tranquillity of our day-to-day existence never quite returned. Any chance of that was wrecked by a series of three or four nightmares, brought on, I knew all too well, by the letters.

Carl and I still didn't have a clue who might be responsible. For a start, there was no one whom we could possibly imagine knew anything about us that might lead him or her to behave in such a way.

'Who could hate us that much?' I asked Carl one Sunday morning.

He shrugged. 'I wish I knew, Suzanne. The most hateful person I know around here is that damned Fenella Austen.'

It wasn't the first time he had mentioned her name

and I wished he wouldn't. There was no logic in focusing on Fenella and I told him so.

'But what if we've got it wrong; what if we're being threatened because of something that has happened here in St Ives? Maybe Fenella resents us, resents me. You know what artists can be like. I sell better than she does nowadays.'

'Carl, you're not exactly Damien Hirst, thank God. We barely get by. And there is absolutely nothing about either of us since we've been in St Ives that anybody could use against us, you know that.'

Carl grunted his agreement. But he seemed to be totally preoccupied, perhaps even obsessed, with finding the letter writer. And it was that, probably, which led him to behave later that day in a rather hot-headed manner, which was quite out of character.

I understood that Carl could not bear anything that threatened our lives together. But I had had no idea of his intentions when he suggested we visited the Sloop, and indeed, still do not know for certain that he had actually intended to do what he did.

I was trying not to think about our problems when we walked down to the pub at lunchtime. It was a wet and blustery February day, and there were virtually no holidaymakers around. The bar was jam-packed full of locals, most of whom we knew at least a little and who knew us.

I might have guessed that, one way or another, something was going to break soon. Although Carl did not have nightmares, he seemed possibly to be more disturbed by the anonymous campaign against us than I was. He insisted that he was upset only because he knew what it was doing to me, that he wasn't worried himself, but I knew very well just how on edge he was all the time.

We shrugged off our wet coats and propped our umbrellas in a corner among a pile of them, which were already steaming gently. Predictably enough, Fenella Austen was at the bar holding court. She did the rounds of all the pubs in St Ives, but recently seemed to have been using the Sloop more than any other, much to the irritation of Carl and me who had a big soft spot for the place. Equally predictably, she was already well oiled even though it was only just one o'clock. As Carl approached the bar to buy our first round of drinks she paused in mid flow, took a deep draught from her glass, which was filled almost to the brim with a substance that looked suspiciously like only very slightly diluted whisky, and put her free arm round his waist.

'Ah, my favourite boy wonder,' she drawled, her voice dripping with sarcasm.

At first Carl did quite well. He gave her a small, icy smile. 'Some boy,' he said mildly.

Then, as ever, her hand slipped down to his backside, which she squeezed in her customary familiar manner. The bloody woman seemed to have a fixation with Carl's bottom and I suspected he was not in the mood to put up with it. I was right. There was a brief moment of calm before the storm and I found myself wondering if it was much the same kind of thing as Mariette and her waiter's bum. Just as I was deciding that there really was no comparison all hell broke loose.

'You are a p-poisonous old woman and if you d-don't take your hand away from my a-arse I'll stuff it up your own,' I heard Carl say.

I could hardly miss it. He shouted at the top of his voice. Carl hardly ever raised his voice, hardly ever swore and was never crude or uncouth. I had never even heard him say 'arse' before. The stammer, which occurred only very rarely by then and under extreme stress, somehow made his outburst all the more devastating. I was flabbergasted. The silence was suddenly deafening. All eyes were on Carl and Fenella. Apart from anything else, taking on Fenella was unheard of. She had not achieved her almost legendary status in St Ives without good reason.

Slowly she put her drink down on the bar and turned to face Carl directly, quite deliberately keeping her left hand on his bottom, so that her face was just inches from his although a little above. Fenella was exceptionally tall, particularly for a woman of her age. She was well over six foot and on that Sunday morning was wearing high-heeled shoes. Carl had to peer up to look her in the eye. 'You silly little man,' she said eventually and for her quite quietly, and certainly very calmly.

Then and only then did she remove her hand from Carl's bum, swing back round on her heels and return her attention to her glass of whisky. Not a bad performance for someone who was definitely at least half cut, I remember thinking.

There was a strangled giggle or two here and there but conversation had started to begin again when it became apparent that Carl was not going to be dismissed so lightly. 'I said you were a p-poisonous old woman,' he yelled and this time there was almost a note of hysteria in his voice. 'Poisonous, as in p-poison pen.'

With a weary sigh Fenella turned towards him

again. 'What the fuck are you talking about?' she asked, her voice only very slightly slurred.

'You know d-damned well what I'm talking about,' said Carl, still yelling.

'Really,' countered Fenella, who sounded dangerously calm. 'Well, then, why not at least enlighten the rest of the bar. I'm sure everyone else is bewildered even if I, allegedly, am not.'

'She's been sending poison pen letters to me and my wife,' shouted Carl.

Fenella raised her eyebrows. 'And what did I say in these letters, pray?' she asked.

'You know what you s-said,' he told her.

'Now let me think,' replied Fenella and tapped a finger against her pursed lips as if she were musing. 'I know. Perhaps it was something devastatingly truthful like how you are a no-talent no-hoper married to a silly bitch with no personality?'

The words were devastating. Her voice was one of polite enquiry. I tried to stop Carl taking this any further, but it was too late. He rose to the bait. 'You're a vicious old has-been,' he bellowed at her. 'You're jealous of me and Suzanne, that's why you're doing this to us . . .'

A collective gasp echoed around the bar. I knew that Carl had gone too far.

The barman, hearing the danger signals, came belting round from the lounge bar just in time to see Fenella throw her whisky in Carl's face. She was not even pretending to be calm now. 'Don't you ever speak to me like that,' she stormed. 'This is my bar in my town and I want you out of it.'

Carl began to wipe whisky from his face with the back of one hand. God knows what might have

106

happened next but I didn't wait to find out. I knew I had to be decisive for once in my life. I grabbed Carl by both hands and, pulling with all my strength, dragged him towards the door.

His legs started to move in the right direction before he became aware of what was happening. Nonetheless he opened his mouth to protest.

'Don't argue; for once do as I say,' I commanded. 'We're leaving.'

Suddenly overcome by the scene, perhaps, he complied almost meekly.

When I got him outside I realised, or rather the driving rain made us both realise, that we had left our coats and umbrellas in the bar. Cornish weather is not always as benign as summer visitors think. The weeks since Christmas had been bleak. On this occasion the wind and rain were blowing directly inshore, carrying with them an icy saltiness that chilled to the bone. A particularly vicious gust caught us full in the face, quite taking my breath away. 'Just don't move,' I managed to gasp to Carl, as I dashed inside to fetch protection from the foul weather.

By the time we had pulled on our coats and abandoned even the thought of trying to erect our umbrellas, I had gone off the idea of a lunchtime drink completely.

Unfortunately, Carl had not.

'Let's go up to the Union,' he said, brushing aside my protests.

'Just don't go accusing anybody else, will you?'

'I'm not a c-complete damned fool, Suzanne,' he snapped, still stammering slightly.

'Then why are you behaving like one?' I heard myself counter before I had time to think.

It was about as near as we had ever got to a quarrel. Certainly my sharp answer, every bit as uncharacteristic as Carl's outburst in the pub, had stopped him dead in his tracks. 'Is that what you think?' he asked.

I turned to look at him directly, his shoulders hunched against the wind and rain, his hair sodden, droplets of water running off his nose and chin, the expression in his eyes full of concern. Everything Carl did was governed by his huge capacity for love and loyalty. I knew that, and adored him for it, but I decided not to capitulate. I had gone this far, I would have to see it through. 'Yes, I do,' I said. 'You're not a fool, Carl, anything but. You have just behaved like one, though.'

He stared at me for a second or two, then his face broke into a grin. 'You're right, of course. It's just that I am so worried and we had to meet that goddamned woman, didn't we. She really gets under my skin.'

'I noticed,' I said with feeling.

We had reached the Union by then, a comfortable little pub away from the sea front. Carl managed a smile in answer to my slightly acid response as he stepped to one side and quite flamboyantly ushered me into the bar.

At first I thought things were looking up. Old Dan Nash was ensconced in a corner and, quite unlike the dreaded Fenella, Carl and I were always pleased to see him. He was one of our favourite characters, one of the last of the pilchard fishermen St Ives used to be full of before the fish stopped coming. Dan's stories of the good old days were always worth listening to and invariably beautifully told in his low Cornish burr, which added great charm and even a kind of authority to his tales.

On this day, though, he seemed agitated and at first uncommunicative, barely responding to our greetings.

'What's wrong with old Dan, then?' Carl asked the barmaid as he ordered a pint of bitter for himself and a glass of white wine for me.

'Reckons he's seen the Lady with the Lantern,' replied the girl, raising her eyes heavenwards. 'Silly old fool; think he's losing his marbles . . .'

'I 'eard that,' said a voice from the corner. There was certainly nothing wrong with Dan's hearing.

The girl, a new face behind the bar as far as I was concerned although Carl seemed to know her, didn't appear to care that the old man had heard her being so unkindly rude about him. She shrugged her shoulders and headed for the other bar.

'Don't worry, Dan,' said Carl. 'That one's too young and stupid to have any marbles to lose in the first place.'

Dan chuckled his appreciation and gestured for us to join him. 'I did see the Lady, though,' he insisted. 'Clear as I can see the pair of you.'

Now I was vaguely aware, from my reading of local books and archives, of the legend of the Lady with the Lantern and I wasn't entirely sure that it was a story we wanted to hear that day. But Carl, probably thinking we were in for a good yarn that might make us forget our troubles, had already sat down on the wooden bench alongside Dan. One of the really nice things about Carl was what a good listener he was and the way he always had time for people. Normally I too was more than happy to listen to the old fishermen's tales, and ultimately, in spite of my reluctance, I felt I had little choice but to join the pair of them.

'There was a shipwreck, you see,' Dan began. 'Oh, two, three hundred year ago. A big ship driven on to thigee rocks beyond the island . . .'

He paused and gestured vaguely in the direction of St Ives Head.

'Many of 'em on board perished right away and as the wreck began to disintegrate still more of 'em was swept into the sea. 'Twas a filthy, dirty night. The waves came in right over thigee harbour wall and the wind was blawing a gale – bit like today, only one of the worst storms in 'istory, they say. Nonetheless some brave St Ives lads went to the rescue. Fishermen, they was, and they manned their boat and rowed out to the stricken ship. It weren't possible to get alongside but they approached as near as they dared and, using a rope strung between the two vessels, managed to rescue several sailors.

'Then a woman appeared on the capsizing deck of the wrecked ship. 'Er seemed to be weak with fear and was supported by a group of sailors, but she clutched a child tightly in 'er arms, which she refused to pass over to any of the sailors while the fishermen attempted to rope her to safety, even though they entreated her to. Eventually, with the ship approaching its death throes, 'er was lowered into the water still holding on to thigee child. 'Owever, as the fishermen dragged 'er through the raging sea she fainted and let go 'er grip on 'er child, which was lost.

'The Lady was successfully pulled into the boat and delivered to the safety of dry land where 'er regained consciousness all right. But when 'er learned of the fate of 'er child she lost the will to live and died within hours.

''Er was buried in the churchyard over yonder, but shortly afterwards was seen to cross over the churchyard wall on to the beach and walk out to the island.

'There she spent hours an' hours searching them terrible rocks before eventually returning to 'er grave.

'And 'er's never given up, 'asn't the Lady. 'Er still does it to this day, you see. And when the nights be stormy or particularly dark, like they've bin all bleddy week, 'er carries a lantern . . .'

Dan paused, looking agitated again. 'I saw 'er last night,' he said. 'Saw 'er making her way across thigee beach and off to the island, awful big sea there was an' all, but 'er never takes no heed of that, just carries on looking for that child, searching, waving that lantern every which way . . .'

Dan lifted his pint of Guinness to his lips and I noticed that his hand was shaking. 'Something mighty bad's going to happen,' he insisted. 'It always does when you see the Lady. There'll be a disaster, 'tis fate, nought you can do about it.'

He stared at us, his eyes wide with horror. I felt a shiver run down my spine. Carl was very still beside me.

'Look at thigee weather,' continued Dan, gesturing through the steamed-up window. The howl of the wind and the dashing assault of the rain could be heard clearly enough inside the bar. ''Twill not abate now till 'tis 'appened, whatever 'tis . . .' His voice tailed off.

'Take no notice.' The voice from behind us breaking the spell belonged to Rob Partridge, a local policeman who spent most of his off-duty hours in one or other of St Ives's many hostelries. Not a man to be impressed with Cornish legend, the orange-haired Partridge's only real interests in life were reputed to be beer and horse-racing. 'Bleddy load of tosh. I've told you before, Dan, about frightening the horses . . .'

Carl and I were barely listening. Somehow the Union no longer seemed so cosy and welcoming. Without having to discuss it we emptied our glasses and stood up.

'Load of tosh, you know,' said Rob again as we left. He leaned unsteadily our way and breathed beer over us. We were not particularly reassured. Rob Partridge was not a man who inspired confidence in any direction. In fact, in spite of his uniform, he was regarded as a bit of a joke in the town.

'Of course,' said Carl.

We barely spoke as we trudged up the hill towards Rose Cottage and that was very unusual for us. I knew Carl wasn't quite back to normal. It might seem trivial but I suspected that the Lady with the Lamp story was still preying on his mind. He was strongly inclined to be superstitious. He believed in omens; he said he had been brought up to. He had his paints and his brushes all arranged in a certain order and if anybody ever changed anything he was convinced it was unlucky. I knew better than to touch anything, but once Will had visited us and, before Carl or I realised what he was doing, had idly moved some brushes around while chatting in the studio.

As soon as Will left, Carl had plastered a thick layer of paint right over the top of the painting he had been working on. 'I may as well start over again,' he had said and I was never quite sure if he was being melodramatic or if, quite simply, he was just dissatisfied with his work.

As soon as we were indoors Carl disappeared straight upstairs. I went into the kitchen to heat soup and make toast. Maybe some warming food would make us both feel better. The torrential rain had found its way through the roof again, and water was leaking steadily, forming an already quite substantial puddle on the floor. The sight depressed me further. I mopped up the worst of it, stuck a bucket under the leak and turned my back on it. I poured the soup into big mugs, put them on a tray along with a plate of hot buttered toast and followed Carl upstairs.

He was sitting in one of our two window armchairs. I sat myself in the other and passed him a steaming mug. 'The Lady with the Lantern, the bad fortune is supposed to happen to the one who sees her,' I said eventually.

'Really,' said Carl. 'Why did you turn so pale, then?'

I shrugged. 'Sometimes I think Cornwall does it to you. I do love it here, you know that. But the place is full of ghost stories. As if we don't have enough of our own . . .'

I shivered again. The window was so steamed up and the cloud so thick and low that you could barely see our wonderful view over the harbour. The rain continued ferociously and the sound of it driving against the window-panes was almost like the rat-a-tat-tat of a machine-gun.

Carl didn't speak again. For once he didn't seem to have any words of comfort.

'We mustn't let it get to us, not any of it,' I said stoically.

With what appeared to be a considerable effort of will, he found his voice then. 'I know, and I'm sorry, Suzanne, I just can't bear to think of our happiness, our life together being wrecked by some sicko who's trying to destroy us.'

'We've just got to get through this,' I consoled. 'We don't even really know what any of it means, do we?'

'I suppose not,' he replied in an unconvinced sort of way.

'And you really can't bounce around the town accusing people like you did Fenella Austen,' I remonstrated.

He sighed. 'I know. I've never liked that woman, though.'

'That doesn't mean she's writing us threatening letters, or that she scratched the van.'

'She's capable of it, I'm sure.'

'Maybe. But I'm not certain it would be her style. She hasn't got the subtlety.'

Carl almost glowered at me. 'Subtlety. You call those letters subtle?'

'More subtle than throwing insults at a living, local legend in front of half of St Ives,' I commented.

He smiled wryly. 'I suppose you're right,' he acknowledges. 'I know you're right, I've already admitted that.'

'Carl, I thought the idea was that we would always keep a low profile, that we didn't want to be noticed too much, didn't want to get involved . . .' I let the words tail off.

He smiled again, in a rather more relaxed way this time. 'Never again, I promise.'

He held out his hand. I took it. I felt his fingers squeezing mine.

'I'll tell you this, though, Suzanne,' he continued, and his voice sounded strong and determined again. 'I won't have you hurt by anyone.'

For the first time in my life with Carl I found myself afraid. Not *of* him, of course, but *for* him and what he might do to protect me.

I had to convince him that I could cope, that I was not being destroyed by what was happening to us. So I had somehow to keep the nightmares at bay, because I could not conceal what they did to me.

The only way I survived at that time was by burying my head in the sand. I didn't have one-hundred-per-cent success, of course, but I was surprised to find just how well I seemed able to cope once I had put my mind to it. It was a bit like pulling the blankets back over your head on those mornings when you really feel unable to face the world. It seemed to come to me quite naturally – maybe that was my background.

One way and another I managed another two-and-a-half-month spell without a nightmare. In spite of Dan Nash's insistence on the meaning behind his sighting of the Lady with the Lantern, the storms, which indeed raged throughout most of February, did eventually subside without any major disaster hitting either us or, in fact, anyone we knew in the town. Life returned to some kind of normality. We did not go back to the Sloop, preferring the Union or the Golden Lion, or almost any of the others now that Fenella Austen seemed to have turned the old waterside inn into 'her bar'.

Only one or two of those who witnessed Carl's outburst and his reference to poison pen letters even mentioned it to us again and we made light of it, both of us muttering something about a joke that had gone wrong and been misunderstood.

Mariette heard about it, of course, and I spun her a yarn about an old friend of Carl's who had thought he was being funny. I wasn't quite sure she believed me, but she seemed to accept it.

St Ives seemed to forget quickly, but we never quite could. Shopping in the town one day, we saw Fenella coming towards us and I dragged a reluctant Carl into a store in order to avoid her.

He was quite angry with me.

'You owe her an apology, Carl, you know that,' I remonstrated.

'Well, I'll be damned if she's getting one and I'll be damned if I'll skulk around town because of her,' he snapped.

He could admit to me that he had been wrong to accuse Fenella in such a manner, but he certainly wasn't going to admit it to her, it seemed. He could be very stubborn, could Carl.

When I was out and about on my own I kept my eyes well peeled for Fenella and managed to dodge her successfully for weeks on end. I was more embarrassed than anything else but I also knew I was no match for her in the verbals department. I would never willingly take on the likes of Fenella Austen.

The idea of getting a job had gone completely out of my mind right from the moment our van had been vandalised, but as Carl buried himself in his work – that had always been his main way of dealing with our problems – my lurking desire for some kind of outside activity rose to the surface again. And one beautiful early April day, when the sun was shining brightly and every patch of garden in the town seemed to be ablaze with daffodils, my spirits were so uplifted that I was moved to mention to Mariette that if ever there was an opening at the library I would be interested. After all, following a winter that had been unusually bleak for Cornwall, it seemed as if the whole world were being reborn, so why shouldn't I be too?

'Sooner than you think,' she replied. It transpired that the young man who had the most junior job was employed only on a temporary basis and was soon leaving to go to university.

I decided I would again mention to Carl the possibility of my taking a job and I would do it that very evening, probably over supper. But just as we were about to dish up the pan-fried dabs Carl had bought from our lovely fishmonger, while I had been at the library chatting to Mariette, there was a knocking on the front door.

'Bound to be Will, probably inviting himself to dinner again,' remarked Carl in an unconcerned kind of way. 'It's OK, there's plenty for him . . .' We were used to Will turning up unexpectedly, after all we had no telephone, nor had we ever found any real need for one.

I opened the front door and, as Carl had predicted, there stood Will. Nonetheless, I had not the slightest intention of inviting him in, in spite of what Carl had said. I really wanted to talk to Carl alone before it was once more too late.

Will waved a bottle at me. 'Pink champagne, how about that?' he announced. 'Won it in a raffle. Thought maybe I could persuade you both to share it with me?'

He grinned at me confidently. Too confidently. I was vaguely irritated by his presumption. 'I'm sorry,

Will, we were just sitting down to supper and we really do need to be on our own tonight,' I heard myself say. If he hadn't irritated me and if I hadn't been so intent on talking to Carl, I might have been a little more gracious.

The grin froze on Will's face. For a moment he looked dumbfounded. Well, we always made him welcome. But his features quickly relaxed. 'Of course,' he said. 'Don't worry about it. I was just passing. Another time, aye?'

'Yes, as ever. Another time.'

He gave a kind of half-salute with his free hand and turned away.

I felt guilty then. 'Sorry, Will, you don't mind, do you? Just bad timing tonight, really . . .' My voice tailed off.

'No problem,' called Will over his shoulder. ''Course I understand. I'll keep the champagne for the next time you pop round to the gallery. How's that?'

I muttered my agreement at his retreating back and closed the front door.

Carl was just putting a big platter of dabs on the table. 'Why did you turn him away?' he asked mildly. 'I told you there was plenty. I thought you liked Will.'

'I do, but he does take liberties,' I said, perhaps a little grumpily. 'In any case, there's something I want to tell you.'

'OK.' He gestured me to sit down and help myself. 'Fire away.'

'You know I mentioned once before that I liked the idea of getting a job?' I began tentatively as I ladled a dab on to my plate.

He nodded but did not say anything.

'Actually there's one going in the library,' I went on. 'Mariette seems to think I could get it if I wanted . . .'

I didn't quite finish all that I had intended to say and there seemed to be a long silence before Carl replied. 'Well, I think that's a wonderful idea,' he said.

My heart soared. If, upon reflection, his smile was strained, I did not notice it at first. I just knew I was beginning to really yearn for outside stimuli. But before I could tell him how delighted I was with his reaction, Carl started to speak again. 'I'm just so sorry that it's not possible,' he said very quietly.

It was almost like a slap in the face. 'What do you mean?' I asked him haltingly.

'Suzanne, you know very well it won't be possible,' he repeated.

'I don't. Why not? Carl, please, oh please, Carl.' I heard myself imploring him.

'Suzanne, how can you have a job?' he asked. 'You'd never cope and you don't even have a National Insurance number . . .'

Worse than that, I realised I didn't even quite know what a National Insurance number was.

Carl put down the forkful of dab he was about to put in his mouth, reached out with his hand to squeeze mine, and said again how sorry he was. He leaned across the table and kissed me gently on the end of my nose. For once I found him patronising more than anything else.

'It's not the end of the world, my Lady of the Harbour,' he coaxed. 'Anyway, aren't I enough for you any more?'

119

His voice was gentle and teasing. Nonetheless, I heard myself reply very seriously and very honestly, putting into words thoughts I had never mentioned to him before: 'Sometimes I do want more, Carl, yes I do.' I touched his face with one hand in order to soften the blow of my words. 'I just want a job and friends, the normal things, the ordinary things . . .'

Then I saw the pain flash across his eyes, this man who had given me a whole fresh start in life, a new identity. And fear. Maybe even fear. Carl, too, could be afraid, I knew that, although he seemed to have only one fear, really: the fear of anything disrupting our love and our life.

I could not hurt him. 'It's OK, Carl,' I said, before he even spoke again. 'I know you are right. I suppose I always knew it wouldn't really be possible. Maybe one day, aye?'

Carl smiled and kissed me again. This time on the mouth. 'Yes, darling,' he whispered. 'One day.'

I knew he didn't mean it, though. And sometimes I wondered how long you could keep a secret.

A couple of days later Carl decided he would make bouillabaisse for supper and we paid a visit to our favourite local fishmonger. Steve was a young man with film star good-looks, totally incongruous in a fishmonger's apron yet apparently enviably content in his work, who somehow contrived to be quite passionate about fish and frequently waxed lyrical about his product.

True to form he produced a monk-fish which he proclaimed to be particularly splendid. 'Just look at the shine on that,' he enthused. 'You'll not get a healthier looking fish than that one . . .'

'Steve, I think I should point out that the fish is dead,' Carl interrupted dryly.

'Good Lord!' countered Steve. 'So it is.'

On the way home we dropped in at the Logan Gallery to visit Will Jones and find out how the sales of Carl's paintings were going.

I was anxious about visiting Will for the first time since I had turned him away from Rose Cottage, but to my great relief, he was as friendly as ever to both of us. He didn't seem to be harbouring any grudge at all and our visit to the gallery really cheered Carl up, because we learned that his paintings were selling exceptionally well. So well, in fact, that Carl invited Will to share the bouillabaisse with us that night as a kind of thank-you.

As ever, on the rare occasions when we actually invited him to our house, Will accepted with alacrity. He was something of a loner and I used to think that sometimes he might be lonely too, but neither Carl nor I knew much about his private life. We were always made very welcome at the gallery and occasionally Will entertained us, invariably most generously, at a local restaurant, but we had never been invited to his clifftop bungalow home out on the Penzance Road. We knew that he lived alone and he had told us that he had never been married. If he had a special woman friend nobody in the town knew of it. Indeed, Will seemed not to make friends easily and I always thought that one reason the three of us were so comfortable with each other was because none of us wanted to probe. I had once ventured to Carl that maybe Will was gay. Carl had laughed and asked me if I had never noticed the way the gallery owner looked at me. Nonetheless I was not entirely convinced.

Anyway, I was glad Carl had invited him partly because it eradicated my remaining guilt about the pink champagne incident, and I welcomed any diversion that might help take our minds off our worries.

The rest of the afternoon passed pleasantly enough. Carl spent an hour or two framing his latest painting and I made a pretence of helping him. As usual, more than anything I just watched. Carl was so deft with his hands that it was a pleasure to watch him choose just the right colour and weight of framing material, and angle the beading so absolutely perfectly. When he had finished he started work on the bouillabaisse.

By the time Will arrived just before seven the whole cottage was full of an aroma of garlicky fish.

'Delicious,' Will said as he sniffed his appreciation and handed me a bottle of rather good white wine. We ate around the table in the downstairs room, curtains drawn and candlelit as usual in order to disguise its dinginess. But we had rigged up a single spotlight on the wall, which effectively illuminated my *Pumpkin Soup* painting.

Supper was excellent.

'This bouillabaisse is as good as I've had in any restaurant,' remarked Will.

'What do you mean "as good as",' countered Carl. 'How about "far better", or "much superior" or something else along those lines . . .'

'Why are great chefs always so arrogant, Will?' I asked.

He shrugged his shoulders. 'What, Carl arrogant? A talented painter, a brilliant cook and he's got you,

Suzanne? What on earth has the man got to be arrogant about?'

'And I'm stinking rich,' said Carl, waving his arm around the dimly lit little room. 'How do you like my mansion?'

Will grinned and put a hand over one of mine, which was resting on the table. 'You two have quite enough riches,' he said. 'I would swap everything I possess, the gallery, the car, my house, for what you have . . .'

He spoke lightly enough and his tone was as theatrical as ever, but we had noticed before that Will was inclined to become a bit hyperbolic after a few glasses of wine.

Carl invariably responded with the easy teasing banter which came so easily to him. 'That can be arranged, Will,' he said. 'When do you want to move in? I think you may have to raise the ceilings, though, and God knows how you'll get on with my old van.'

Will laughed and said that he had forgotten about the van, and the offer was withdrawn.

Very occasionally, particularly if Carl had sold some paintings at a good price, we would go out to supper in a little fish restaurant just a few doors away from our home.

This was a real treat for us, and I was delighted when, later in the week having had such an exceptional run of sales, Carl suggested we celebrate with a meal out in our favourite restaurant.

I washed my hair, trying desperately to blow-dry a little bounce into its lank flatness which was emphasised by then by my half-grown-out layered haircut, and we both put on our smartest clothes – we

123

didn't need to, but we enjoyed dressing up every now and again. I even considered risking the orange suit, tucked away at the back of my wardrobe – I hadn't quite been able to bring myself to throw it out – but thought better of it. In the end I settled for the familiar and safe calf-length skirt, cotton print blouse and a jacket.

The Inn Plaice, in spite of its appalling name, was anything but and, because it was in a back street away from the seafront, had to rely on the quality of its food rather than a stunning location with which to tempt diners. Its proprietor, Pete Trevellian, the younger son of a family of fishermen, behaved more as if he were hosting a dinner party for friends in his house than running a restaurant, but Pete had a good set-up. His fish, mostly supplied direct from his family's fishing boats, was good and fresh, and his father and brothers were able to make a better living than many fishermen in the area partly because of the family restaurant outlet. The Inn Plaice had a big local following and, unlike many eating houses in the town, which relied almost entirely on the seasonal tourist trade, was able to remain open all the year round.

Pete greeted us, as he did most of his regulars, with a complimentary glass of wine. But once we were settled at our table with menus Carl suddenly announced that he had forgotten a quick errand he must run, and jumped up and left before I had time to protest. He was gone for several minutes and, just as I was beginning to wonder where on earth he had got to, he returned clutching a bunch of daffodils. 'For you with my love,' he said. 'Supermarket special, I'm afraid – should have thought of it earlier, shouldn't I?'

124

I shook my head and thanked him profusely. Another of the many things I loved about Carl was his spontaneity. It was typical of him to be sitting at a restaurant table, think about buying me flowers, and just rush off and get some. I was as knocked out by my slightly tired-looking daffs as I would have been by a bouquet of orchids.

Carl ordered more wine. We then turned our attention to the menu and chose crab chowder followed by an assortment of grilled local fish served with a side dish of Pete's irresistibly crunchy chips, and fresh fruit salad with clotted cream for dessert.

In the end we got through two bottles of wine, as well as Pete's initial glasses, an unusually large amount for us, but it just turned into one of those sort of evenings. As we said our goodbyes and set out on the short walk home I realised that I was definitely slightly tipsy. I made a concentrated effort to walk straight as Carl could be a bit stiff about drinking to excess, but he seemed easygoing enough that night. After all it was he who had ordered the deadly second bottle and I fancied he might not be stone-cold sober himself. I leaned against him heavily as we turned, perhaps both of us swaying slightly, into the cobbled alley that led to Rose Cottage.

I could see from the light of the street lamp on the corner that there was something strange about our front door. It seemed to have shiny red marks all over it, standing out starkly against the faded, pale-blue paint. I caught my breath. I could feel Carl stiffen beside me. Both instantly sober, we covered the last few yards to the cottage in silence. The shiny red marks were writing, as I think we had both immediately suspected, although we could not see to read what had been scrawled across the door to our home until we were directly in front of it: 'YOU CANNOT ESCAPE – I'M WATCHING.'

The words were roughly scrawled in thick daubs of bright-red gloss paint which had run and dripped down the wooden panels. I reached out and touched a particularly shiny patch. It was still wet. My hand came away smeared with red. I stared at it. The dripping red paint looked like blood. I felt my vision blur.

Carl's grip on my arm tightened.

I wanted to cry out, but my voice temporarily deserted me.

Carl found his all right. He bellowed his anger into the cold night air. 'Son of a bitch!' he shouted at the top of his voice. And immediately he began to scrub at the paint with his free hand and the sleeve of his good overcoat. I didn't try to stop him. After a few seconds he seemed to pull himself together and stopped the frantic rubbing. 'We don't even have to look at this,' he muttered, his earlier flash of near hysteria apparently under control.

Swiftly he unlocked the front door and together we climbed the stairs to bed. The joy of our evening out had been destroyed.

We didn't say much. There wasn't much to say. But I knew what would happen that night, knew it with dreadful clarity, and so, I am sure, did Carl. I did not have the energy nor the determination to pace the house and keep myself awake, so I just gave in to the promise of misery. Maybe I hoped that the alcohol I had consumed would give me some kind of bizarre protection as I slept. It didn't.

That night the nightmare was the very worst of all. The blood had seen to that. For that is what I saw on my front door, blood, not paint. And it was blood, I knew all too well, that I was going to see inside my head. Always.

At breakfast the next morning, I finally gave voice to most of what I was thinking. 'The reality may be that we just can't hide any more,' I told Carl sombrely.

'Maybe,' he said. 'Not here, anyway. Maybe we can't stay here any longer. I think the time has come to move on. What do you say?'

I was numbed by his words. 'This is our home,' I protested. 'I don't want to move from here, I really don't.'

'Anywhere we are together would be our home,' he countered. 'That's all that matters isn't it?'

I nodded. I didn't know quite what to say.

'Let's give it a few days, see if anything else happens,' I managed eventually.

But I knew what I truly felt. Not only did I not *want* to run again, I was not *going* to run again. The running was over. I also knew I could not expect any more from Carl. He had done too much already to protect me. I suspected that he was drained of energy. I was not going to be a victim any more, not of nightmares nor superstitions nor anonymous threats. I reckoned it was up to me to sort out our lives once and for all, to remove the fear that had always been there in its different ways for both of us.

That afternoon, while Carl was working, I slipped out of the house. I had to creep away stealthily because Carl would never have allowed me to do what I was planning. He loved me too much and I knew only too well how great was his fear of losing me. But I had had enough. It had all gone on far too long.

I found an inner strength I did not know I had. On tiptoe I left the cottage, opening and shutting the old front door with the greatest of care. I was afraid, but my steps were determined as I walked along our little cobbled lane and into the network of narrow streets that led down the hill from our cottage to the harbour, the place that had always been so special to us.

I wanted to be there alone just once more before it all changed, perhaps for ever. Before I took our futures into frightening unknown territory beyond the point of no return.

This was where Carl had given me my new name. 'You're Suzanne from now on,' he had told me softly. 'Suzanne – my Lady of the Harbour.'

And as I walked alone along the harbour side, inside my head I could hear him singing to me softly from the Leonard Cohen song of the Sixties that he so loved and from which he had named me Suzanne, the song that had been so much a part of his growing up, a growing up so utterly different from my own sheltered childhood:

> And the sun pours down like honey
> On our lady of the harbour
> And she shows you where to look
> Among the garbage and the flowers
> There are heroes in the seaweed
> There are children in the morning
> They are leaning out for love
> They will lean that way for ever

I turned away from the quayside and headed towards the police station.

Eight

I was certain it would be a relief to rid myself of the burden I had carried for so long. And as I walked through the Cornish seaside town I had grown to love so much, on my way to confront the past at last, irrevocably, my thoughts turned, as they so often did, to how it had begun.

Poor Gran. All she had ever wanted was to protect me, to do her best for me. When she arranged for me to marry Robert Foster she believed she had found somebody who would love and continue to protect me just as she had done. And, of course, it did not occur to her to doubt a man of God.

Until well after the wedding I suppose I never doubted him either. I was bewildered, but not afraid. I had never had reason to be afraid of those close to me – I suppose there had only ever been Gran, really, and I expected, as a matter of course, kindness from both a husband and a clergyman. The fact that I had barely ever been alone with Robert did not particularly concern me at the time. Maybe I thought that was normal for a bride and I suppose it had been once in a bygone age. I read a lot of Jane Austen in those days and had always suspected that I might have been more at home in her time than my own. I told myself that what was happening to me was all rather romantic. I knew Robert Foster only in the way Gran presented him to me – as an intelligent and apparently kindly man, a cleric respected and revered by his congregation. But I quickly found out how wrong I was – certainly about his kindness.

When we were married in Robert's church, with what seemed like the entire congregation gathered there, I did feel some of Gran's pride in spite of the sense of unreality about it all. The music was rousing, people said I looked beautiful. There was something splendid about the occasion and, unused to being the centre of attention, I found I quite liked it.

My wedding night – spent in the rectory that was to be my home because Robert did not have time for a honeymoon – was painful and difficult. I knew so little about sex and had had no experience. It went without saying that I was a virgin. I hadn't even known exactly what would happen – or how, but Robert had been patient as he could, and had allowed me to take my time, and I suppose I had expected pain. It was not until much later that I learned that, had there been more love, more arousal, rather than a clinical kind of forbearance, I might have experienced no pain at all.

After the wedding he was always busy during the day. And I realised early on that while he undoubtedly worked hard he also drank heavily, although he contrived only very rarely to appear even slightly drunk and never in public. He managed to maintain the façade of being the perfect chapel cleric in an order strongly opposed to alcohol. Extra-ordinary, really. I had even heard him preach from the pulpit about the evils of drink. Maybe he believed what he said, I don't know. In a curious kind of way he had good reason to, he must have known what it did to him. Maybe that gave him a crisis of conscience

– although he gave no sign of having any kind of conscience at all. I certainly believed in the evils of drink by the time Robert Foster had finished with me.

Unlike most clergymen, he preferred me not to get involved in his church-work, explaining to his congregation that I was not strong enough to be a traditional pastor's wife. Instead, I stayed in the big, ugly old Victorian manse that was our home, twiddling my thumbs and cooking his evening meal. After that he continued working or reading in his study while I sat alone in the living room. Then he would summon me to bed – and that truly was the way it was. There was always a coldness about Robert. He never expressed any love towards me, never showed any warmth, but he was an ardent and accomplished lover, and our lovemaking was at first the high point of my long dull days. To begin with, briefly, he had indeed been a surprisingly good lover, technically at any rate. He knew how to excite a woman if he cared to do so. On a good night his knowledge and expertise even made up, at least partially, for his eternal coldness. I learned to relax my body and to switch off my mind against the emotional emptiness I was somehow so aware of, in spite of my inexperience, and to enjoy the sheer physical sensation.

Eventually I achieved my first orgasm and I think that was when I maybe even began to fall in love with Robert a little. I had no way of knowing that there could ever be more. For his part he seemed to take almost a kind of pride in bringing me so easily to a climax. He once told me he thought it was what gave man the most power of all over woman.

But after Gran died things began to change for the

worse. Towards the end of her life Robert allowed me to bring her into the manse and nurse her there. Looking back, I think Gran was one of the few people in the world Robert might have been genuinely fond of – if he was indeed capable at all of any depth of human feeling. Anyway, I was grateful to him for that if nothing else. Gran was weak and terribly sick in the flesh but indomitable in the mind to the end. I loved her to pieces and so hated to see her suffer, but took comfort that I was with her, which I knew would be all that she would wish for, and that she remained without any fear of death. Looking after her filled my days, but they seemed all the more empty when Gran finally left us. And it was then that the true brutality of the man I had married began to show itself.

Gran had been dead for about three weeks when Robert hit me for the first time. It was in bed. And what he did seemed to me to be the ultimate cruelty. I had yet to learn that it was merely the beginning.

It was just like the nightmare that had continued to plague me, except that I could see his face all right and the cruel glint in his eye. We had sex as we did almost every night and although I suspected from his clumsy movements, a certain slowness in his speech and a slight glaze to his eyes that he had been drinking particularly heavily, as ever it did not affect his sexual appetite nor his ability to function. He knew where to touch me, how to excite me, how to make me cry out for more, but he did so, as always, in the cold, detached but efficient way that I had grown used to, almost as if he were conducting a biological experiment. On this terrible night he brought me to orgasm and, as I felt the pleasure overwhelm me, he suddenly raised his right hand and hit me hard across

133

the mouth. The dream had always kept it so vivid for me, my lip cut open, tasting my own blood, then being punched in the chest, my body reeling in confusion.

Years had passed, my life had changed beyond recognition, yet as I turned my back on the harbour I loved so much, the seagulls wheeling above my head, I could still feel the dreadful pain and the humiliation of it.

He had grasped my right arm and forced it back on the pillows at an angle so agonising that I believed my wrist would break. All the time I was aware of his excitement rising to a level beyond anything I had felt in him before. He kept on hitting me as he began to come and I had instinctively known that it was the most extreme orgasm he had ever had with me. By the time he had finished I felt like a punchbag.

In the morning it was as if it had never happened. He made no comment about my bruised and cut face except to suggest that I did not go out until my appearance had improved. His manner indicated that I was to blame, although he did not say so. Indeed, I wondered if it was in some way my fault. I was in total shock and I had no one to turn to. I had no friends. The nearest to that were the people I knew within the church and Robert was the head of our church, the man they all respected and looked up to.

For several weeks life went on just the way it had before. I already knew about bad dreams, and I came almost to think of that one brutal outburst as just a nightmare. The sex continued in just the same way it always had, except that I never again reached an orgasm with Robert, although I frequently pretended in order to appease him.

It was almost two months before he attacked me again. This time it was before demanding to have sex with me, almost as if it were some kind of foreplay.

As Robert's drinking became more and more excessive – I discovered that there were bottles of alcohol, usually vodka, hidden in every room of our house – his physical abuse settled into a pattern. His worst drinking sessions were in bouts that lasted four or five days and occurred maybe every three weeks or so. It was amazing that he managed to continue to function so effectively, both at work and in bed, during those times, but he did. And it was then that he was at his most violent. However, he never again hit me in the face. Appearances are important for a clergyman, I suppose.

I had nowhere else to go and no money. I knew that Gran had left me everything including the house that had been our home but Robert had handled the settlement of the will and I had simply signed all the papers he put before me. That is the way I had been used to leading my life. I had never even had my own bank account. Most of our household bills were settled by Robert on account and the only money I ever had were the few pounds a week he handed me in cash.

Yet I planned and plotted ways to leave him. I even rang up a hostel for battered wives, which I had read about in the local paper, but I couldn't quite bring myself to run to them. Then, a couple of weeks after I made that call, the telephone bill arrived. Routine itemising of calls had just begun. I had not given a thought to my panicky call becoming a matter of record and, although Robert was a meticulous man, pedantic about detail, I had no idea that he had taken to checking up on me.

That night he gave me the worst beating of all.

He told me he knew whom I had been phoning. He punched and kicked me until I begged for mercy, although I accepted by now he was capable of none. It was extraordinary to sit in the chapel on Sundays and listen to him preaching. He was a charismatic man. I think many of his congregation regarded him as a kind of stand-in for God. How could I tell them that to me he had become a devil?

I heard a rib crack as he kicked me. I heard it go almost before I felt the sharp searing pain. Afterwards he bound me tightly around the middle with strips torn from a sheet, and told me that the ache as my ribs healed would remind me of what would happen again and again if I ever betrayed him.

'If you leave me I will find you,' he said. 'I will find you and I will bring the wrath of God upon you.'

Looking back, I think he was mad, I just didn't realise it then. I believed every word he said, every threat he made.

And it was about three weeks after that particularly vicious attack that I met Carl in the Isabella Garden. All too often Robert was working, and drinking, at home in the manse. I was confined to barracks then, always fearing that something, almost anything, might spark one of his dreadful rages. But two afternoons a week he devoted to parish visits and on a third he took Bible classes in the chapel. It quickly became a habit that on those occasions I would meet Carl.

I lived for those afternoons. Often we met in the Isabella; all through that first winter after I had first encountered him, we regularly shivered together in the beautiful little wooded park. We never did make the Kandinsky exhibition at the Academy, but occasionally we visited local art galleries, or Kew Gardens, or went for a walk along the riverside. Cafés, restaurants and pubs seemed far too dangerous. Wherever we went I was always terrified that we would be seen together and that someone would tell Robert. My husband was well known in the area. That went with his job.

It was six months before I let Carl take me back to the small flat he rented off the Sheen Road. I had told him already about Robert and what he did to me. I suppose I had needed to and the release helped me to bear it. Carl begged me to leave my marriage, but it was not that easy. I didn't know how to run. Since the death of my parents, and I could barely even remember them, I had only really known two people well before Carl – my gran and Robert – and they had both overwhelmed my entire being. Also my fear of Robert remained as great as ever. I believed that he would find me wherever I went. And I believed him capable of far greater violence than he had so far inflicted on me. I believed him capable of anything.

The first time I went to Carl's flat – one large room in which he ate, slept, cooked and painted, with just a bathroom tagged on, but light and airy and beautifully kept – he fussed over me wonderfully, treated me to a lovely tea he had prepared and eventually kissed me, just once, and for the first time on the lips. That was all. Then he took me home, dropping me off a few streets away from the manse where I had left my bike chained to some railings.

The second time we made love. It began when he played me the song for the first time. The song 'Suzanne'. It was then that he had first told me about his hippie parents and how little time they had for him when he was a kid, and that his earliest memory was of this one song, a classic from another age, a Sixties leftover, played again and again, a crackly LP on a not very good record player.

Suzanne takes you down to her place near the river
You can hear the boats go by
You can spend the night beside her
And you know that she's half crazy
But that's why you want to be there . . .

I had never even heard Leonard Cohen before. I wasn't sure what I made of him at first.

Carl chuckled. 'You're in good company,' he said. 'I can only barely sing in tune myself and when I was in college they told me that was why I loved Cohen.'

None the less there was something mesmerising about the moody Sixties singer. And strangely soothing, too.

When Carl unfolded the sofa, which doubled as his bed, and we lay down together, it seemed like the most natural thing in the world. It was a beautiful June afternoon and the sun poured in through the big bay window, embracing us in its brilliant warmth.

He undressed me very slowly and his eyes filled with tears when he saw my bruises. My body was almost always covered with them. I had got used to it. Carl was distraught. I think that was when I first began really to love him. He covered my poor battered body with kisses. I had never known such tenderness. My gran had loved me and been kind to me, but never tender. Robert did not know the meaning of the word except from the pulpit. Maybe I thought that all men were at best coldly efficient in bed and at worst brutal. My only experience was with the monster I had married. Carl was so gentle.

He stroked me and kissed me in every secret place, and all the while he whispered softly and repeatedly the chorus of 'Suzanne':

And you want to travel with her
And you want to travel blind
And you know that she will trust you
For you've touched her perfect body with your mind.

I am English. I was entranced, but also vaguely embarrassed. 'I don't think my body is very perfect,' I murmured.

'It is to me,' he said. And he was deadly serious. Indeed, it seemed as if there was not a square inch of me that he did not touch lightly with his fingers or brush with his lips. And all the time his eyes were fixed upon me in wonderment, as if I were some kind of work of art, as if he truly did find me quite perfect.

I had never wanted to reject him, but I had not been sure that I would be able to respond. I did, though. When he slipped into me I felt my own desire rise to meet his almost instantly. He brought me to orgasm on that very first occasion and afterwards we cried in each other's arms. Then he led me into his tiny bathroom and we stood under the shower together while he washed me and then himself, just as he always would throughout our life together. I found it extraordinarily moving.

Robert did not seem to suspect anything. Perhaps he was too stupefied by drink. Certainly as long as I cleaned his house, was present to cook his meals and meekly allowed him to violate my body, he didn't seem to care what I did. Once I had slept with Carl the loveless violent sex with Robert became all the more abhorrent to me. I was twenty-one years old then. My adulthood was only just beginning and yet I felt I was trapped for ever. The beatings, too, seemed worse now that I had someone who appeared to feel them as much as I did.

There came a time when I decided that I would, could, take no more.

Nine

St Ives police station is a small, ugly, modern building which was once a Health Centre.

Although I had lived in the town for so long, I had thankfully had no dealings with the police, unless you counted the occasional pub meeting with Constable Partridge, and it took me some time to find the station. I knew it was somewhere around Royal Square, but so well is it concealed in a dead-end alley behind the Western Hotel and the Royal Cinema that I had to ask a shopkeeper for directions. You have to be actually on your way up the alley before you can see the only POLICE sign I noticed in the area. Indeed, I had heard Rob Partridge say that the reason crime figures in St Ives reamined so low was that hardly anybody could find the nick in order to report an offence.

I stood and studied the police station for a minute or two, perhaps deliberately delaying what I planned to do. It looked as if it might originally have been painted white, although you could no longer be too sure, and it was covered with an excessive number of drainpipes. It was not a very imposing sort of place in which to embark on the momentous course of action I intended. However, I summoned the remains of my courage and walked in – only to be confronted by a second anticlimax. The front office area appeared to be completely empty. I began to look around for a bell to ring, but after a few moment a plump, white-haired man wearing a grey uniform I did not recognise emerged from an office behind the counter.

He had a clipboard in his hand upon which was secured some kind of official-looking form, which he continued to study as he walked towards me. 'Yes?' he enquired without a deal of interest, barely looking up from his reading.

At first I couldn't get any words out.

'Yes?' he said again, just a touch impatiently.

I blurted it out then. 'I've come to report a murder,' I said. My voice sounded very loud.

The man in the grey uniform put down his clipboard very slowly and leaned forward on the counter. He contrived to raise one eyebrow, something I have always found physically impossible. But his expression smacked more of disbelief than shock or alarm. I had once read somewhere that in the UK you are considerably more likely to be struck by lightning than to be murdered. And St Ives, mercifully, is hardly an acknowledged hotbed of crime.

Anyway, whatever he may have been thinking, the man said nothing. The silence in the little lobby was unbearable for me. I had to break it. Right away. 'I've come to report a murder,' I repeated. My voice was even louder.

'I see,' he said. He stared at me.

I stared back. 'I've killed my husband.'

I don't know how I got the words out. I know that I half screamed them.

I was suddenly desperate to tell my story, for someone, anyone, to listen.

The grey-uniformed man continued to stare at me

long and hard. He did not seem particularly affected by what I had told him. 'And when would that have been, then, madam?' he enquired politely.

'Oh, almost seven years ago.'

'I see,' he said again, and he stroked his chin in a world-weary sort of gesture.

'It was a long time ago but I can't go on hiding so I thought I would come here and confess, and then . . .'

The telephone rang in the rear office from which the man had just emerged. He raised one hand in a silencing gesture, interrupting my babbling, and promptly retreated to answer it, leaving me stranded in mid sentence. His white hair looked greasy and so did his skin. Maybe his excessive weight made him sweat a lot. He did not fill me with confidence. My big confession was beginning to turn into a total anticlimax.

I could hear him talking into the phone for two or three minutes while I stood alone in the small outer reception area, twitching. I was impatient to get on with it and on the verge of becoming quite overwrought. It seemed an extraordinarily long time before he eventually finished his call and returned to me. The attention he then gave me remained grudging. 'I'm just a civilian desk clerk, madam,' he told me in a flat tone of voice. 'Perhaps you'd take a seat in the interview room there and I'll get someone to see you as soon as possible.'

I opened my mouth to protest. I wasn't sure that I could wait. I needed to get this over with. The desk clerk waved impatiently at an open door opposite the counter. I could see a table inside it and a couple of simple wooden chairs. Meekly I did as I was told, making my way into the windowless little room and sitting down as bidden, but leaving the door open so that I could still hear clearly enough anything that happened outside.

The clerk retreated to his rear office yet again, but a telephone rang once more before he had even attempted to contact anyone to deal with me.

He seemed so unconcerned. I was a murderer. That was my dreadful secret. And all these years I had had to live with it. Now I had finally revealed the truth, but nobody seemed to care very much. It was weird.

The clerk took another seemingly interminable call and it was some minutes later that he finally dialled what I assumed was an internal number and asked for Detective Sergeant Perry. 'I have a woman here who says she killed her husband,' he reported bluntly, but his tone was lightly ironic and the emphasis heavily on the word 'says'.

I don't know quite what I had expected – to be clapped immediately into handcuffs and thrown behind bars, perhaps – but I certainly hadn't imagined anything like this.

Another five minutes or so passed before a young woman emerged through the locked door, which presumably led in to the police station proper. She called 'All right, Ben, I'll take it from here' across the front desk, presumably to the grey-uniformed clerk yet again invisibly installed in the back office and marched straight into the interview room. 'Hi, I'm Detective Sergeant Julie Perry,' she introduced herself cheerily, holding out her right hand in greeting.

She was taller than average, maybe five foot ten, very fair, slim and fit-looking. She had the kind of face that made you quite sure she laughed a lot. Her lips turned up at the corners and although her skin was smooth and clear, apart from a light dusting of freckles, there were just hints of crinkly little laughter lines around her mouth and greenish-grey eyes. She looked as if she were about the same age as me and yet she seemed so capable, so sure of herself, so wise even. Certainly streetwise, whatever that was. Instinctively I envied her. I know that I gazed at her wide-eyed for a moment, barely hearing what she was saying to me.

She smiled reassuringly. I had not expected that kind of response either. 'Pretty grim in here, isn't it?' she remarked conversationally. 'We can do a bit better if you'd like to come upstairs.'

She escorted me to a second interview room, which at least had a window and was also equipped with a double tape-recorder. She then asked if I would like coffee and departed to fetch it herself, returning with two mugs and a pocket full of sugar packets. 'Instant, I'm afraid,' she said, smiling apologetically. 'But it's better than nothing.'

She leaned back in her chair, stirred sugar into her coffee and even took the time to indulge in a little bit of small talk about the weather and how splendid St Ives could be out of season, before encouraging me to get to the point of my visit.

I think we were partly waiting to be joined by another officer. I was horrified when Rob Partridge walked in and I think he was a bit shocked to see me sitting there.

Rob sat down without comment and I didn't say anything either. I could have done without the presence of anyone I knew or who knew me, even as slight and casual as was my acquaintance with PC

145

Partridge, but I supposed such things were inescapable in a small town and it wasn't going to make any difference at all in the long run.

DS Perry switched on the tape-recorder and began to ask me questions. Gradually it had all become rather formal and I struggled to control my nerves, which were jangling madly, but Julie Perry was quietly sympathetic in her approach and not at all what I had imagined. Not that I was very clear what I had imagined, if anything. Apart from Rob, who had never seemed to count until that moment, I had never even met a police officer before.

'Why don't you tell me the whole story, beginning at the beginning,' she advised.

That was easier said than done, of course. It was a long time since I had put any of it into words. Carl and I never talked about it any more, you see. I am not sure that we ever did talk about it, really. Not after the day it happened. There had not been much to say, not after what we had done.

I believed I had as many good reasons as anybody had ever had to kill a man. None the less I was a murderer, something I'd never been able to come to terms with. Something I had never wanted to even think about, let alone discuss.

I didn't even know quite where the beginning was. DS Perry was sitting opposite me across a small table and she studied me appraisingly. I could feel the panic rising in me. The room was not particularly warm but little beads of sweat were forming on my forehead and my armpits felt sticky. 'I had to come because of the threats,' I said. 'Somebody else knows what I did. I just want to tell the truth now, to get it over with . . .'

Rob Partridge remained silent. He had yet to say a word.

DS Perry stood up and walked across to the window, standing with her back to me as if she were looking out of it into the street below. 'Take your time,' she said.

I struggled for control, overcome with the enormity of what I was about to do.

All I could do, I reckoned, was to try to tell it the way I relived it again and again inside my head, sometimes during the day and sometimes at night within the awfulness of my dreams.

And I did so, as calmly and clearly as I could manage.

I woke that terrible morning as I so often had after Robert had attacked me, cowering afraid in some corner of the house to which I had crept once his rage was spent. On this occasion I was in the bathroom, curled up on the bath mat. My body ached and throbbed as usual. Sometimes in the deep silence of the night or of early morning I could hear Robert snoring, as he often did when he slumped into a drunken stupor. This time I heard nothing except the birds singing outside. I glanced through the window. It was already daylight. A fine drizzle was falling and there must have been a light breeze. I could see that the branches of the big old chestnut tree, which was as tall as our house, were swaying gently. The leaves were just beginning to turn the colours of autumn. It seemed strange that these things could be as normal when I was somehow starkly aware that nothing else was. I had a severe headache. Gingerly I touched my forehead with one hand. There was a bump on it the size of a hen's egg. With equal caution I stretched myself. I felt so sore. I pushed aside the towel I had used to cover myself and as I did so saw with horror that it was covered with bloodstains. I looked at my hands. There was blood on them. I was naked beneath the towel. There were smears of blood all over my body. My heart lurched. I pulled myself to my feet and peered anxiously at the bathroom mirror. There was blood on my face.

I could feel the panic rising inside me. I examined myself to see where the blood might have come from. I was battered and bruised as usual, but I did not seem to be cut.

I unlocked the bathroom door, which I had locked in a pathetic attempt to keep Robert out should he have furiously pursued me as he sometimes did, made my way along the landing and went into the bedroom I shared with Robert. The heavy dark curtains at the window were drawn close. I could just see the shape of him lying in bed and he seemed to be deeply asleep. Certainly he was not moving. Cautiously I crept across the room and pulled back a curtain, just a little way – enough to allow in a narrow shaft of morning light.

Then I turned round.

Robert lay in a sodden mess of congealed blood. The pillow and the duvet were drenched in it. For just a few seconds I was frozen to the spot, the horror of it too great to take in. I made myself approach the bed and pull back the covers.

Robert's body was a mass of blood. I forced myself to look at his face. Blood had stuck to it like thick paint. His eyes were wide open, accusing, his mouth gaped and was full of thick blood.

I didn't scream. I don't think my throat would have functioned. Fear, panic, horror, all overwhelmed me. I stepped back from the bed and made my way backwards, still facing the bed and the dreadful corpse that lay in it, until I reached the door. I did not want to look at Robert any more, but I could not tear my eyes away. Only when I had retreated on to the landing and closed the bedroom door behind me, shutting out the terrible image, did I turn round. Then I began to run, throwing myself down the stairs two and three at a time. For once, and in spite of the shock and horror of it, I knew exactly what I was going to do.

I hurried into the kitchen and used the phone there to call Carl.

It was before seven. He answered sleepily.

'Carl, thank God,' I said.

He recognised my voice, of course. But I knew how strange I must sound. 'Please, Carl, please, come over here, come quickly. Please.'

I wasn't crying. I didn't have the energy for that. I felt totally drained and I knew that I must have sounded it.

'What's happened?' he asked. 'What's wrong, honey? Whatever is wrong?'

I wouldn't tell him. I couldn't. Not over the phone. I couldn't find the words for what had happened, for what I had done. I have always thought that he probably half guessed.

Carl knew where I lived well enough, he had often dropped me and my bicycle off close by, although of course he had never been to the house. He was with me within thirty minutes. I was sitting in one of the upright chairs at the kitchen table, still naked, still covered with blood when I heard the doorbell ring. I stumbled out into the hallway. I didn't even check that it was Carl outside before I opened the door and afterwards I often wondered what would have happened had it been someone else.

He looked at me in silence for what seemed like an endless stretch of time, before he seemed able to react. I heard him draw in his breath in a shocked gasp. Then he pushed me back into the hall, stepped swiftly inside the house himself and closed the front door behind us.

I had still not covered myself. I was not functioning at all. I just stood there before him naked, bruised, bloody and shivering. But I had not realised how bitterly cold I was until he touched me and I felt the warmth of his arms enfolding me. I began to tremble then. My whole body was shaking.

I leaned against him heavily. 'He's in the bedroom,' I said in a very small voice.

Carl nodded. He asked no questions. If he hadn't guessed before he certainly had then. He took off the raincoat he was wearing and wrapped it round me.

The door to the kitchen was ajar. Carl led me back there and sat me in a chair, making sure I was sitting up straight, almost as if he was afraid I might fall over. Then he went upstairs.

I expect he was only out of the kitchen for a couple of minutes but it seemed like for ever. Everything appeared to happen in a kind of slow motion that morning.

When he reappeared he was carrying a heavily bloodstained knife.

I began to remember, then – as much as I ever

150

remembered any of it. It began when I decided that the next time Robert beat me I would be ready for him. Most of Robert's attacks occurred in the bedroom, happened in bed, in some horrible way linked for him with the act of sex. I could not take any more. And I could imagine only one way to escape my tormentor and that was to destroy him. I think he had made me half mad with pain and fear. I sought out the sharpest and most lethal knife in the house, my four-inch Kitchen Devil, with its point like a needle, which I used for peeling vegetables, and tucked it under the mattress of the bed I shared with the husband I had grown to hate and fear so much.

I did not tell Carl what I had done because I did not want him to share my burden of guilt. But inevitably he eventually had to. Because, of course, it was to Carl I turned at once after the deed was done.

I still could not believe that I had actually used the knife, but I knew I must have done.

The night I killed him, Robert had found the knife under the mattress where I had hidden it. He had taunted me with it, grabbed me round the neck and shaken me as he asked me very softly what I planned to do with it.

And as I sat trembling at the kitchen table, when I put my hand to my throat I could still feel the angry weals he had left there. No wonder my voice was so strange and hoarse.

Robert had been horribly angry and had beaten me more viciously than ever. I knew that at some stage he had punched me so hard that he had knocked me off the bed. I thought I must have hit my head on the bedside table, or on something, and been concussed for a few moments, because after that everything was shadowy. Perhaps Robert had been afraid that he had finally gone too far. Perhaps he had backed off, then, allowing me to grab the knife and use it on him. I could still see and feel the hot sticky blood spurting out of him, hitting me full in the face.

I had some vague recollection of eventually crawling off, maybe only half conscious, to the sanctuary of the bathroom, but that was all. The rest was a blank.

Carl sat down next to me and put the bloodstained knife on the table in front of us.

'Oh my God,' I said. 'What have I done?'

'You know what you've done, don't you,' he said gently.

I nodded, staring at him. Of course I knew. I just didn't want it to be true. 'I've killed Robert, I've stabbed him to death,' I responded simply.

'Yes,' he said and his voice was very solemn. 'We've got to leave now. Quickly.'

I started to cry, then, and the tears brought some relief, but not as much as his presence, his calm strength.

'Nobody is ever going to hurt you again,' he said.

He took me upstairs to the bathroom, stood me in the shower and washed me. He found clean towels in the airing cupboard and dried me with them. Then he fetched me some clothes from the bedroom – I could not go in there again – and dressed me.

When I was clean, dry and fully clothed, at last I began to feel marginally better. 'Shouldn't we telephone the police?' I asked in a fairly half-hearted manner. From the start that never seemed a very attractive proposition.

'Oh darling,' he soothed, putting his arms round

152

me again. 'Do you think you have the strength to deal with all that?'

I hesitated. 'I s-suppose not,' I stammered.

'Honey, at the very best you would need to face a trial and would have to plead guilty to manslaughter,' he went on. 'But it could be worse than that. You could well be charged with murder. You must accept that. You stabbed your husband repeatedly. He was a clergyman. Respected. Popular. I know what you did was in self-defence and that you acted out of desperation, that you were frantic, beside yourself, not responsible. Of course I know that. But who else is going to believe it? That is what you have to ask yourself.'

His words soothed me the way they invariably did. I was sure he must be right. He was always right.

'You and I know that you destroyed a monster,' said Carl. 'I'm not going to let that destroy us.'

Carl had driven over in his old red van.

'The transport's not up to much, but it's good enough, I reckon, to take us plumb away from here, someplace new. We are just going to leave the past behind us.'

Nothing could have seemed more attractive at that moment. Carl packed a small bag for me, just clothes. I didn't care what I left behind as long as I could get out of that house, and away from Robert's body and all the dreadful memories, as quickly a possible.

I was in a kind of dream as we left the manse, but Gran's bike, the only possession I really cared about, stood in the hallway and as we passed it I asked Carl if there would be room to take it with us.

'Of course,' he said. 'Anything you want . . .'

Later I regretted that I had not taken the few books

I owned and valued, including several that Gran had given me and written messages in, but at the time I did not care about anything except getting away.

Carl wheeled the bike out to his van and I took the key from where it lived on a hook in the hallway and, out of habit, locked the front door of the manse.

First we drove to Carl's Sheen Road flat and he asked me to stay there while he visited a couple of local galleries which had sold some of his work and owed him money. 'We're going to need all we can get,' he said, 'and you'll be quite safe. Nobody knows you are here. Nobody even knows we know each other, do they?'

I said I certainly hoped that was so.

He was only gone for a couple of hours, but it seemed much longer. When he finally returned he began to load the van with what possessions he wanted to take with him, mainly his painting gear. He also prised up a floorboard and removed an old leather document case. 'Cash,' he said. 'I'm not into banks. I only deal in cash and I stash away what I can. I collected three hundred-odd quid this morning. We should have enough now to last us till we get settled.'

One way and another it was almost mid afternoon before we clambered back aboard the van and embarked irrevocably on our Great Escape. I remember that I did not even ask Carl where we were going. I didn't care as long as it was away from my past and my terrible crime. I was vaguely aware, as we ploughed through the slow moving traffic of the Sheen Road, down through Mortlake, over Chiswick Bridge, along a short stretch of the A4 and on to the M4, that we must be heading west.

'We're going to Cornwall,' Carl announced. 'St

Ives. It's the place for a painter. Don't worry, honey. As long as I have my paints I can provide for us.'

Of course I hadn't given the practical side of what we were doing a thought. I had never had to think about that sort of thing, not even with Robert. The drizzling rain continued through most of our journey and even though it was warm in the van I sat shivering by Carl's side all the way to Cornwall.

We stopped once at a motorway service station just outside Exeter to get petrol and Carl tried to persuade me to have something to eat. I couldn't face food.

Soon after we passed into Cornwall the van slew violently to the left. Carl regained control only with difficulty and we slowed to an ungainly halt by the roadside. The offside rear tyre had burst.

In order to change the wheel we had to take almost everything out of the back of the van. Strangely enough, the sheer physical effort involved made me feel a little better. Carl was not the most mechanically minded man in the world, but eventually he managed to complete the task – I was no help, that was for certain, I couldn't even drive let alone change a wheel – and we trundled on our way again.

The old van was not capable of any high speed and so it was that we did not reach St Ives until almost midnight. The rain stopped just before we entered the town, and the night was clear and moonlit by then. I remember being captivated by the little sea-side resort right from the start. Carl drove straight to the waterside and we parked illegally alongside the old sea wall, reasoning that nobody would bother us at that time of night. We clambered gratefully out of the van, leaned against the wall and gazed out to sea. The silence was devastating and the water, reflecting the moonlight, had seemed so still. I sensed that peace was within my grasp at last.

'My Lady of the Harbour . . .' I could still hear Carl's words . . .

'And that was nearly seven years ago?' queried Sergeant Perry, somewhere in the distance. Her voice almost startled me. I had gone into a kind of trance. I seemed to have a habit of doing this, come to think of it. I suppose all that stuff about us travelling to St Ives was irrelevant, really. It had just carried on naturally for me, part of my dreadful story.

I nodded.

'A long time to carry such a thing around with you,' she said.

I nodded again.

Six and a half years of hiding, I thought. Six and a half years of fear. I had been so happy with Carl, but the past had always lurked and now, despite my uncertainty about what might happen next, I did feel that a weight had been lifted from my shoulders. I hoped Carl wouldn't be too angry with me, but suddenly there had been no choice.

I took a deep breath, returning sharply inside my head to the present. Carl would be frantic with worry. I rarely went out alone at all, except to the library, and never without telling him where I was going and when I would be back. I had been gone for over two hours.

I didn't know what would happen to me, but I suppose I expected to be arrested. 'Could somebody contact my husband,' I asked.

'We already have,' said DS Perry.

I could only imagine how shocked he must have been. But I was still sure I had done the right thing.

The DS suggested that I wait a moment while her colleagues completed some enquiries they were making and she left me alone with a stunned-looking Rob Partridge. After a couple of minutes a uniformed constable came in and told Rob he was wanted on the phone. Rob retreated with obvious relief and the constable positioned himself by the door like a sentry. I assumed that DS Perry and the others were checking up on me and my story.

I wondered what prison would be like. From the moment I decided to make my confession I had been in no doubt whatsoever that I would go to jail. I saw no alternative. I didn't relish the prospect, but I doubted it could be any worse than what I had endured with the man I had eventually killed.

I just hoped that Carl would not feel too betrayed, and that one day he and I would have a future and would be able to live a normal life. Throughout whatever came before that it would be the dream of a future with Carl that would keep me going.

I was beginning to become aware that normality was something I had never experienced.

Ten

The biggest shock was still to come.

'Why don't you go home now and someone will call round to see you in a day or two,' said Sergeant Perry when she eventually returned.

I looked at her in amazement. 'You can't just be letting me go, surely,' I said. 'I murdered my husband; I killed Robert Foster.'

'I don't think so,' she replied.

I couldn't believe my ears. 'But I did!'

'We have done quite a bit of checking already; we've been on to the Metropolitan Police and they have no record at all of the murder you have reported,' she continued calmly.

I was staggered. 'W-What does that mean?' I stammered.

'I think it means you couldn't have killed your husband,' she said quietly.

'But I did,' I responded. 'I stabbed him to death. I can still see the blood. He was lying dead in a pool of blood . . .'

'Mrs Peters, we have been round to see your present husband. I told you that. He's here now, waiting for you. And he's very upset. He has explained to us all about your terrible nightmares . . .'

'This is not a nightmare, it happened!' I said. I was suddenly very angry. Anger was new to me. Fear and pain I understood well enough, but not anger.

'Mrs Peters,' the sergeant went on patiently, 'the Reverend Robert Foster was not murdered.'

'B-But he's dead, isn't he?' I cried.

'I believe so,' said the sergeant. 'But I don't know the details. We will look into it more, of course. However, I see no reason to detain you.'

'How did he die then, if I didn't stab him? How?'

'We don't know yet. The Met are looking into it and will be sending us a full report.'

'So how can you be sure that he wasn't murdered? He was. He was. With my kitchen knife.'

I realised I probably sounded absurd. I could hear the note of hysteria in my voice. Surely never had anyone tried harder to get themselves arrested on a murder charge.

'There was never a murder investigation, that's how we know,' continued the sergeant. 'Surely there would have been if a man had been found stabbed? That can hardly be natural causes, can it? You must see that.'

I saw all right. DS Perry was barely concentrating on me at all any more. I suspected she just thought I was one of those people unable to differentiate between what was real and what was not.

She could be forgiven, I suppose. My head was reeling. I could feel a dull ache beginning in my temples. 'What about all the threats, those awful letters I got and the paint daubed on our front door?' I asked.

She nodded. 'We'll look into that too. You thought you were being threatened because somebody knew you had killed your husband. Well, it seems that cannot be so. Can you think of anything else that might lie behind these anonymous threats?'

I shook my head numbly. I really didn't know what was going on any more.

'Well, let's take it a step at a time then, shall we, Mrs Peters?' said the sergeant, quite incomprehensibly I thought.

The hysteria took a grip of me for a moment or two. 'It's not Mrs Peters,' I yelled at her. 'I'm still Mrs Foster. I'm not married to Carl. We couldn't possibly have got married, we would have been found out. It's not even Suzanne. I had to take a new name because of what I'd done. I've been living a lie . . .'

'It's not an offence to change your name, women commonly use the name of a man they live with but have not married. I assumed you preferred to be called Mrs Peters.' The sergeant sighed. 'Look, we will get back to you, you can rely on that. Meanwhile go home, get some rest . . .'

She just wanted to be rid of me, I suspected. Everyone thought I was weak, even the police. Too weak and confused to be a murderer apparently.

She led me into the interview room in the reception area where I had first been installed. Carl was waiting there, sitting on one of the plain wooden chairs. His eyes were red-rimmed. The strain was also apparent in the tight little lines round his mouth. But if he was angry with me he didn't show it.

His eyes lit up when I walked in, the way they always did when he saw me, and he even managed half a smile as he stood up and wrapped an arm rather awkwardly round me, just as he had on that fateful morning so long ago.

'You can take her home now, Mr Peters,' said the sergeant, carefully not calling me by any name at all.

Carl did not need a second bidding. 'Let's go,

honey,' he muttered, and bundled me outside.

When we were in the car park he gently turned me to face him. 'My darling,' he said. 'Why on earth did you go to the police? Haven't I told you often enough that I will look after you. It's dangerous for us to involve anyone in our lives, you know that – let alone the police.'

'But . . . but they said there was no murder,' I stuttered. 'I don't understand . . .'

'They'll f-f-find out the truth eventually, they're b-bound too,' he hissed through clenched teeth, the strain of it all making him stammer.

I shuddered. Just a while ago I had been so sure of myself – nervous to the point of being afraid, but quite certain I was doing the right thing. Now I didn't even know what the right thing was any more. DS Perry had made it fairly clear that she thought I was a raving nutter. The front desk clerk had seemed to assume that even before I'd really got going with my story. They certainly appeared to believe, just like Carl and my gran, that I was congenitally unable to cope with the practicalities of life, to sort anything out for myself.

'Don't worry, honey, just don't worry about anything,' soothed Carl as he steered me through the narrow streets back to Rose Cottage. Sometimes he really did behave as if I were stupid. How could I possibly not worry, for goodness' sake?

Then, as bad luck would have it, we saw the rear end of Fenella Austen disappearing round the corner by the library. I had been hoping that Carl wouldn't notice her, neither of us needed any further agitation, but of course he did. I felt him stiffen beside me and he muttered something under his breath, so softly that I couldn't quite catch the words. I could guess, though. Carl still distrusted Fenella.

'Carl, you know she can't be the one, there's no logic to thinking that,' I said quietly.

'Somebody sent those letters and plastered paint over our door. Somebody had a go at our van, tried to drive us out of our minds.'

'Yes, and we don't have a clue who it was, not a clue.'

His arm was still across my shoulders and he drew me closer to him. 'I suppose you're right,' he muttered eventually.

'You know I'm right,' I replied.

He gave a kind of grumpy snort. 'I just know that without the threats none of this would have happened. You felt beleaguered, hunted. That's why you went to the police.'

'Maybe,' I said. 'But I think I might have wanted to do that eventually anyway. I did tell you, try to warn you about how I feel. I'm tired of hiding, Carl, sick of it.'

'So you haven't been happy with me all these years; you've been living a lie, have you?' he enquired abruptly in a flat voice and removed his arm from my shoulder.

'Of course I've been happy with you,' I cried. And that was the truth, for certain. 'We've both been living a kind of lie, but not with each other, never that.'

He put his arm round me again and kissed my cheek. 'There you are, then,' he said. 'If it hadn't been for those goddamned letters and all the other stuff we'd still be happy. Wouldn't we?'

I had to agree, reluctantly. 'In a way we would, I suppose,' I said. 'But there has to be more to life than what we have allowed ourselves . . .'

'Of course we would still have been happy,' interrupted Carl heartily, as if he hadn't been listening to me at all. 'That's all that changed it. I just wish I really did know who sent them. There'd be another murder then.'

He set me thinking again. 'But the police say there wasn't one in the first place . . .' I began.

'You're confused. They'll find out, they're bound to find out.'

We were almost at the cottage by then, the funny little house that had been our haven for so long.

'It'll be all right, Suzanne, it's just got to be,' he whispered into my ear as he unlocked our front door.

Inside the house I could not settle.

Carl busied himself in the kitchen cooking supper, but everything seemed different. I had known that what I did that afternoon would change our lives irrevocably, but what had actually happened was nothing like anything I had imagined.

I had foreseen being charged with murder, being arrested and locked up at once in a police cell. It had never occurred to me that I might be told there had been no crime committed and sent home. I just couldn't get my head around it and, for once, Carl wasn't helping.

He seemed intent on carrying on as if nothing had happened. Perhaps it was all he knew how to do for the moment. Whatever his motivation, I found it really irritating.

He was clutching a small saucepan when he came to me as I stood by the dining-room table scraping at some wax, which had fallen on to the polished wood

163

from a candle. It wasn't that I cared a jot for the table at that moment – it was in any case the same rather shabby gate-legged one, which had been in the house when we first moved in – just that I was looking for something to do with my hands.

'Now, taste this,' Carl instructed abruptly, thrusting a wooden spoon under my nose.

I wanted to tell him to go way and leave me alone. I didn't, of course.

'It's a new sauce for pasta – crabmeat and clam,' he continued, almost prodding me with the dripping spoon. 'Fresh clams, naturally. Steve dropped them round earlier . . .'

Eventually I obediently complied, stuck out my tongue and licked at the spoon.

'What do you think?' he asked, as if my opinion of his blessed pasta sauce were his only anxiety in all the world.

'Lovely,' I said flatly. I really couldn't have cared less.

If he realised this he wasn't showing it. 'Is there enough garlic?'

I nodded. I really didn't want to know.

'Good. Now, I put some Cajun spices in. It's not too hot, is it?'

I shook my head.

'But can you spot my special secret ingredient?'

I couldn't carry on with this nonsense. 'No, Carl, I can't,' I snapped. 'I have other things on my mind. Don't you understand that.'

He hung his head like a schoolboy chastised by his teacher. I was never irritated by Carl. He wasn't used to this kind of outburst from me, but I couldn't help it. Couldn't withdraw it, either. I just wanted time to think. But Carl seemed intent on not giving me that.

He retreated, wounded, to the kitchen but returned within minutes clutching two glasses. 'Cooking sherry, there was only this little drop left in the bottle after I made the sauce,' he said. 'I want to propose a toast.'

I didn't really want a drink, but I took one nonetheless.

'To our future,' said Carl stoutly, raising his glass to mine.

It was not like Carl to be so insensitive. At that moment I couldn't sort out the present, let alone the future, and I was staggered that he did not seem to have any understanding of this. As for the past, well, I was plain bewildered.

I took a reluctant sip. It might have been me, but I thought the stuff tasted quite disgusting. As soon as he returned to the kitchen, saying it was time to put on the pasta, I took the opportunity to get as far away from him as was possible in our little house.

I went upstairs, stood by our beautiful picture window and gazed blankly out over the bay. For once the spectacular view gave me no pleasure. In fact, I barely saw it, to be honest.

I kept thinking about my surreal experience at the police station. It didn't make any sense. I felt I had been fobbed off, dismissed as being of no conse-quence like some kind of prankster. I half wondered that they hadn't accused me of wasting police time, such had been the attitude of DS Perry.

There were so many unanswered questions I should have asked and didn't. The Devon and Cornwall Constabulary weren't really interested, that was the truth of it, or they would not have let me leave without having received a full report from the Metropolitan Police. Perhaps Carl was right to treat me as if I were stupid. I certainly felt it, as well as everything else. I wanted to go back to the police station and demand that they find out at once exactly what the Met believed had happened in my Hounslow manse home seven years previously. And I might have done so, too, were it not for Carl. As it was, I could not face the confrontation with him that I knew such a course of action would bring about. So I just stood there in a vaguely trancelike state.

Because of that, maybe, I did not notice anyone in the street outside before the doorbell rang.

I heard Carl shout 'just a minute', followed by a muffled curse as he dropped something in the kitchen and then his heavy footsteps as he made his way across our little dining room to the front door.

'Hallo, there, brought you some good news,' said a familiar voice from the alleyway outside.

'Right,' said Carl, making no move to invite the caller in.

'Yes,' the voice continued. Will Jones, no doubt about that.

There was a pause.

Then Will, obviously puzzled by the absence of Carl's usual hospitality, spoke again. 'Aren't you going to invite me in, then?'

'Of course,' said Carl unenthusiastically and I could hear a shuffle as he stepped aside, then Will's footsteps, followed by the slight bang and click of the door closing.

No wonder Will sounded puzzled. We both liked him but his occasional unexpected visits to our little home were welcome for more reasons than that. He had only ever been turned away once before, the night of the pink champagne, and I think he had understood that I had always felt a bit guilty about that. Apart from anything else, he usually brought with him an envelope full of money when he called. Will knew how broke Carl and I almost invariably were and was in the habit of passing on the cash to Carl almost immediately after he sold a painting. A call from Will usually meant a sale, so he was nearly always a welcome visitor.

'Where's Suzanne?' he asked. If Carl was in the house it was unusual for me not to be there with him, particularly in the evening, and Will knew that.

'She's upstairs,' said Carl.

Will must have made a move as if he were intending to climb the staircase – after all, he knew well enough that we more or less lived in our airy top room with its stunning picture window and that was where we usually entertained him when he brought us 'good news' – because I heard Carl tell him not to go upstairs.

'She's in a bit of a state, you see,' he muttered by way of explanation.

'What's wrong, Carl, can I help at all?' enquired Will predictably. He was the kind of man who always seemed to want to help if he could. Mind you, I just wished he'd go away and I suspected Carl felt the same. There are times when the last thing you want is someone else's help. And Will could be very persistent in his attentions to us.

Very quietly I made my way to the top of the staircase. There was a bend in it, and if you were both silent and careful you could squat there and watch what was going on below through the banisters without being spotted. Why is it that overhearing yourself being talked about is always so irresistible? Even in my confused and depressed state of mind I wanted to know exactly what Carl was going to say about me and how Will would react.

At first Carl just sighed. For a moment I thought he might try to pass it off and show Will the door. But he didn't. After a few seconds he gestured to Will to sit down and joined him on one of the old upright chairs round the table.

'It's this hate campaign against us, if that's what it is . . .' Carl began.

I saw Will's expression change, a kind of shadow fall across his face. He did not speak, just sat waiting for Carl to continue, which he eventually did.

'I knew she'd be upset, but I never thought she'd be quite so bad. I think it was the nightmares. She thinks they're never going to go away, not now these letters and all the rest of it have started . . .'

'What nightmares?' asked Will.

Carl hesitated. 'Oh, she's always had them,' he said eventually. 'Since childhood. But I think she thought they had finished. The threats brought them back, worse than ever.'

'I didn't know. Poor Suzanne,' said Will and I was touched by the concern in his voice.

'She went to the police today,' Carl continued.

Will appeared to be almost as anxious as Carl. 'What did they say?'

'About the letters, you mean?'

Will really did sound puzzled then. 'Yes, of course, the letters. What else?' he asked.

Carl blinked rapidly. 'Of course,' he repeated quickly. 'The letters and the other threats. It's what they're referring to, that's what's worrying us.'

Will looked and sounded surprised now. 'You know what they're about then, do you?'

Carl nodded.

'Are you sure?' asked Will.

'We're sure all right,' said Carl.

Will half looked as if he might say more, but he didn't. Neither did Carl speak for a bit. I didn't see that it really mattered whether he told Will any more of it anyway, and half hoped that he would. The whole world was going to know soon enough, I assumed, so we might as well get it over with. There wasn't really a secret any longer, was there?

However, Carl just drew in a deep breath, as if making a great effort to pull himself together. 'Look, Will, thanks for coming round, but I'm afraid we're just not very sociable today,' he said then. 'I need to be alone with Suzanne. I'm sorry. We're both upset.'

Will stared at him for a moment or two. 'Why don't you let me go up and talk to her for a minute. I'm sure I could help,' he said.

My heart sank. I didn't want to have to talk to anyone.

Thankfully, Carl dissuaded him. 'I don't think so, Will. I think she would really like to be on her own for a while.'

'Of course.' Will stood up at once as if he were about to leave, then reached into his pocket and brought out one of the brown envelopes we were invariably so grateful to receive. 'I nearly forgot. Sold two of your landscapes last week,' he said.

Carl muttered his thanks and escorted Will towards the door.

'Give Suzanne my love, then.'

Carl nodded as Will stepped outside. On the doorstep he turned and put a big hand on Carl's arm. 'I'm so sorry about all this. Tell her, won't you?' he said quietly.

'I know you are, Will, thank you, and of course I'll tell her.'

He went back into the kitchen. He must have guessed I had been listening, even if not watching, but he didn't look up as he passed the bottom of the staircase.

There was silence for a few minutes more and then Carl called me to eat my supper. Obediently I trotted downstairs and sat at the table.

'You heard Will, I expect,' he said casually.

I nodded my assent. He didn't say any more. He had spread a white cloth over the old table and put a small vase containing a few flowers in the centre. A candle stood next to it, its flame flickering palely. Strange when all that is normal becomes suddenly abnormal. I had experienced that sensation before.

I think the pasta was very good, Carl's cooking was usually excellent, but I barely remember eating it and did so only because I thought it would be the easiest option. I couldn't stand the thought of Carl making a fuss. At first we ate in silence. I really did feel drained. In any case there was only one thing I wanted to talk to him about and he had made it quite clear that he did not want to talk about it at all.

There was fresh pineapple and local Cornish ice cream for dessert. While we were eating it the candle flickered more dramatically and blew out. The only light in the room then was from the single spotlight aimed at my *Pumpkin Soup* painting, and suddenly it seemed quite harsh and unforgiving. I thought Carl had probably opened the small kitchen window while he was cooking – he often did. He must have been more preoccupied than he was letting on because he made no move to relight the candle, which was unlike him.

When the meal was over I made one last attempt to question him about his recollections of Robert's death but he still didn't want to talk about it.

'You saw Robert, didn't you, bleeding from the knife wounds, from where I'd stabbed him . . .' I began.

'Go to bed and I'll bring you up a hot drink.'

'Carl, I do not understand what the police are saying to me. I really need to get to the bottom of it. Don't you, Carl? Don't you want that too?' I persisted lamely.

'The less we have to do with the police or any other officials in our lives the better,' he replied obliquely. 'We've always agreed on that, haven't we?'

I nodded. 'But things are different now, Carl, this can't go on.'

Carl looked weary. 'Honey, why don't you go to bed?' he asked again. 'We're both tired. There's nothing we can do about the cops until they've completed their silly investigation. There can only be one result. You and I know the truth and so, soon enough, slow as they seem to be, will the Devon and Cornwall Constabulary. That's what I'm afraid of. It'll spoil everything, won't it?

'But right now, why don't you just go to bed. Things will look brighter and clearer in the morning. They always do, don't they?'

I nodded in a resigned sort of way. But I didn't really think so, not in this case.

'Go on, I'll make you some creamy cocoa,' Carl encouraged.

Again I meekly obeyed him, from habit, I suppose, as much as anything. And in the end I was actually quite happy to do as he said. My brain was in turmoil. I was bewildered. I longed for oblivion.

I climbed the funny old staircase, proceeded to unfold the futon sofa and turn it into our double bed, a task I had performed so many times in this house. I opened the old seaman's chest in which we kept our bedding, removed the duvet, bottom sheet and pillows, and flung them on the futon in a tangled lump.

Downstairs I could hear Carl moving about. He would clear up meticulously before he brought me the promised hot drink. That was in his nature. Crisis or no crisis, I had no doubt that all the dishes would be washed and put away, and both kitchen and dining room restored to perfect order. I had often thought that it was a good job I had been brought up by Gran to be tidy, because I couldn't imagine Carl being able to live with someone who wasn't.

I turned on the bedside radio in the hope of being able to listen to something restful and beautiful, which might calm me, but it was on CD mode and, predictably, the strains of Leonard Cohen filled the room. I wasn't in the mood. I switched it on to radio, fiddling with the dial until I found Classic FM. Something I vaguely recognised as being Mozart, although I couldn't have said what, was playing. It was both gentle and beautiful but I doubted anything would have done much to improve my distraught state of mind.

With a great effort of will I unfolded the bottom

sheet and spread it over the futon, placed the pillows neatly side by side and shook the duvet into some semblance of order.

I really needed comfort so I sought out a pair of Carl's heavy cotton pyjamas, warm and cosy, and engulfed myself in them. Then I climbed into the bed and pulled the cover up to my neck. It was all so familiar, so comfortable, but it gave me no solace at all.

I just lay there, wide awake and fretting, until I heard Carl go through his nightly routine of checking that both front and back doors were locked, then returning to check them both again as he almost always seemed to, and eventually his footsteps on the stairs. He put a steaming mug of cocoa on the floor next to my side of the bed and sat down alongside me.

He kissed me on the end of my nose. 'I bet you've got my pyjamas on tonight,' he said. He knew me so well. I allowed him to tug the duvet back an inch or two. 'You have too. I really fancy you in my jim-jams, do you know that,' he went on.

I forced a smile. I didn't think I could face sex.

'It's all right,' he said, gently stroking my hair and reading my mind as usual. 'I just want you to sleep well tonight, that's all. Now drink your cocoa before it gets cold.'

He passed me the mug. It was my favourite, with a reproduction of Monet's *Westminster Bridge over the Thames* all round it. It reminded me of long Thames-side walks with Gran when I was a child. I took a series of deep drafts and after a bit I did start to feel much more calm and relaxed. My eyelids began to droop. My last memory that night was of Carl smiling at me, his face misting over before my eyes.

The next thing I was aware of was him shaking my shoulder gently, trying to wake me. Eventually and reluctantly I opened my eyes and blinked in the glare of daylight. Another glorious April day, it seemed. The sun was streaming in the window and I was vaguely aware that it was quite high in the sky. I glanced at the clock on the bedside table. It was 11.15 a.m. I tried to raise myself off the bed. My limbs felt leaden and my head was still muzzy.

'You've had a good long sleep,' said Carl. 'Time to wake up now.'

'I can't believe it,' I said. 'I must have slept for over twelve hours.'

'Good thing too,' he said. 'Just what you needed.'

'I suppose so.' I shook my head tentatively. It felt a bit as if it belonged to somebody else. 'I don't feel all that hot this morning though.'

'You soon will,' he assured me. 'This is going to be one of the good days.'

I smiled wanly. The memory of all the events of the previous day was already vivid in spite of my slight wooziness and, in the circumstances, I thought it unlikely that this new day could be much of an improvement.

'Dress now, sweetheart,' he told me. 'Wear something warm. Don't be long.'

Unquestioningly, I did as he bade me, maybe out of habit, maybe because I didn't have the energy to resist. I pulled on jeans, a T-shirt and a big, thick sweater on top. Then I went downstairs. He had made tea and laid a light breakfast on the dining-room table.

I found to my surprise that I was ravenously hungry.

He watched with open delight as I demolished a brimming bowl of cornflakes, downed three large mugs of tea and consumed several slices of toast and honey. 'Good, that will get your strength up,' he told me.

'Yes, and I guess I'm going to need to be strong,' I remarked wryly.

'You certainly are,' he said. 'I'm going to spirit you away. I'm taking you somewhere nobody can find us.'

Eleven

I didn't think that was what I wanted. Not any more. But I always did what Carl said. Doing what somebody else told me to had always been a habit for me and old habits die hard. In any case I did not seem able to think clearly. Everything appeared blurred.

I let him help me outside and down the alleyway to where the van was parked in the street leading steeply down to the harbour. We were just pulling away when Detective Sergeant Perry arrived.

She was slowing down, obviously looking for a parking space, when she spotted us and flashed her lights. Carl said 'Damn!' loudly. He didn't stop the van.

I looked at him, startled. He just hit the accelerator and carried on driving, swerving around the policewoman's car. I hadn't wanted him to do that. Whatever the police had to say I felt I was ready for it, even if Carl didn't agree.

I turned and peered out of the back window. DS Perry's car was facing the wrong way. I wondered if she would try to turn and follow us, but she did not seem to be attempting to do so.

'I want to talk to her, Carl,' I said. 'Please go back.'

He shook his head and carried on driving, swinging the car around the twisting streets of St Ives.

'Carl, I need to hear what she has found out,' I said. 'I want to know what the police have discovered about Robert. I have to.'

'You know already,' he said abruptly. 'And I expect they know now, too.'

I really didn't understand any of it.

'They're bound to know the truth by now,' he muttered.

'I'm beginning to wonder if I do.'

'How can you not?' asked Carl. 'You were there. You were responsible, and me too, for what we did afterwards.'

He looked frightened and I had never seen Carl afraid before. That had always been my prerogative.

'Whatever the truth, we can't keep running, Carl,' I insisted. 'I don't want to run any more . . .'

He took one hand off the steering wheel and put it on my knee. 'Honey,' he said. 'What choice do we have? What choice have we ever had?'

I started to argue with him. I had virtually never argued with him before. Not seriously, anyway. 'The choice is to go back to the police station, carry through what I've begun . . .'

'No,' he interrupted. His voice very sharp.

'You're wrong, Carl, I'm sure of it. This has to end, for both of us.'

I could see that he didn't like me speaking out like this, making a stand against him. He shot a glance at me sideways. He really did look angry now.

But when he spoke again he was my usual kind, gentle Carl. 'I only ever want to do the best for you. You trust me, don't you?'

I nodded. Of course I trusted him.

'I don't want you to be forced into anything, that's all,' he went on. 'Just do it my way one more time, just for a bit . . .'

The sun was still shining and my head still felt muzzy. We were on the open road now, the B road which wends its way along the north coast via Zennor and St Just towards Land's End. It twists and turns its way through miles of scrubby moorland. Even the main highway, the A30, is of such a low standard right down in the foot of Cornwall that the locals always said it would not have been given A status anywhere else in the UK. Carl and I had a record at home, that we'd bought second-hand from a market, of West Country folk singer Cyril Tawney singing 'Second-hand City', a song about Plymouth, which contains the line 'hanging on to England like Lucifer's tail' – and Plymouth wasn't even quite in Cornwall. We passed a great many familiar places and sights we had learned about from books and then explored in the van and on foot. The beautiful cliff-edge home of the painter Patrick Heron, one of Carl's heroes, the remains of old tin mines, flocks of rough sheep, occasional ponies. I descended into a kind of trance again, only half aware.

I didn't have the strength to argue with Carl any more. It was very warm in the van, and eventually I found the muzziness inside my head overwhelming me and I drifted off into a fitful dozing sleep.

I was woken when the vehicle began to bump and swerve. I opened my eyes and could see that we were on a narrow, winding, uneven track leading straight through a rough moor-land area.

It looked vaguely familiar. Then I realised that just off the track was a small tucked-away bluebell wood, which Carl and I had discovered in the early days of exploring the countryside around our home and had since visited several times. It was April. There would still be bluebells in bloom.

'Are we going for a walk, Carl?' I asked, feeling even more bewildered.

He smiled tightly. 'Not exactly,' he answered.

In fact we drove right past the entrance to the wood. I had not previously been so far along the track. It became progressively more uneven, until it was barely any kind of thoroughfare at all, just an expanse of rocky outcrop and mud.

'Where are we going?' I enquired. I wasn't alarmed, just tired.

'You'll see,' he replied.

Eventually we came across a deserted old shed alongside a disused quarry, which seemed to be in the middle of nowhere. Carl drove straight into the quarry down a precariously steep slope and parked the van in the middle of a covert of tangled scrubby bushes. And he did so in such a way that I felt sure it was not the first time he had been to this place. He climbed out from the driver's seat, walked around to the passenger side and helped me out. I still felt woozy and leaned on him heavily as he assisted me up the steep incline to the shed, which was granite-built and quite solid-looking in spite of its obvious state of neglect. Its windows were boarded up, a heavy wooden door, firmly shut, to one side. The place did not look as if anyone had been near it in years.

'Come on, we'll be safe here,' said Carl. 'Nobody will find us.'

I glanced back down into the quarry where we had left the van. It was totally concealed. I tried one more time to reason with Carl. 'But why, Carl?' I asked. 'I want to be found. Honestly I do. I keep telling you, I don't want to hide for the rest of my life . . .'

'Trust me, honey,' he answered. 'Like you've always done. It won't be for ever, just till I can find out exactly what the police know.'

He produced a key and unlocked the big, rusty-looking padlock, which was attached to the heavy wooden door. The lock turned surprisingly smoothly and the door opened easily, although it looked as if it had been wedged shut and unused for years. Obliquely I thought that both lock and hinges must have been oiled quite recently.

I glanced at Carl in surprise.

'I stumbled across this place by accident one day,' he said. 'The padlock was in place, but it wasn't locked. I went to that old ironmonger's in Penzance to get a key for it, oiled it and put it back on. All I had to do was make sure that I kept the shed looking the same from the outside as it has done since it was abandoned God knows how many years ago. But inside – well, see for yourself.'

We were still standing in the doorway. Carl took a torch out of his pocket and shone it inside, steering me into the shed and closing the door behind us. I could see two camp beds, a Primus stove, a Calor gas heater, a couple of straight-backed wooden chairs and an old table. There was a new-looking sleeping bag on each bed. My eyes questioned him.

'I had to have somewhere for us to go, for us to hide, just in case,' he said. 'Particularly after the threats started . . .'

'You've been planning this . . .' I began and knew that the shock was clear in my voice.

'I hoped we'd never need it,' he said quickly.

'Why didn't you tell me about it, show me the place, ask me what I thought?'

I was quite disturbed by what was happening.

'I didn't want to worry you more than you were already, with the letters and everything,' he said.

'Carl, I'm worried about being here.'

'Don't be,' he instructed. 'It won't be for long, I promise. Everything will be just fine.'

He led me to one of the chairs and I obediently sat on it. My legs and my head still felt rather as if they belonged to someone else.

'I'll make us some tea.' He lit an oil lamp and some candles before switching off the torch. There appeared to be no natural light.

I sat in silence watching as he busied himself with the Primus stove and a kettle. I could not fight the fuzziness inside my head and for a moment or two I could think of nothing more to say.

He brought two steaming mugs to the table and put one into my hand.

'So what are we doing here?' I asked then.

'Taking stock, buying time,' he replied stoutly.

'Carl, we're hiding and this time we're really hiding, like rats in a hole.'

Carl reached over and touched my face. 'Don't be melodramatic,' he said.

'Carl!' I waved a hand vaguely at the dimly lit hut. 'I'm hardly being melodramatic. Look at the place.'

I shivered. The shed felt cold and damp. It was, after all, still only quite early in April. The sun outside might have been bright and warm that day but there was a thoroughly unpleasant chill inside this old disused building. I dreaded to think what it would be like to sleep here, to spend a night here, maybe several nights, and found it hard to grasp that it really was Carl's plan to do so.

'It's not so bad,' I heard him say stubbornly. 'And it's only for a little while. I'll think of something, you'll see.'

'This isn't what I want, Carl.' I pushed the point, determined not to be overruled by him. 'I want to face up to things, sort things out. Why don't we do that? It would be for the best, I'm absolutely sure of it.'

He sighed.

'You don't know the full story . . .' he began haltingly.

'Then tell me, for goodness' sake,' I said.

'No, I can't. I just want to protect you, that's all.'

'Oh, Carl, I'm not a child.'

He looked startled. 'Drink your tea,' he said. 'It'll make you feel better.'

I opened my mouth to tell him not to be absurd, but I picked up the mug and swallowed instead. The tea was hot and sweet. Maybe it would at least revive me a little and help clear my head.

It seemed to do just the opposite. I struggled even to keep my eyes open. After a bit I was vaguely aware of Carl helping me to one of the camp beds, then there was only blackness. He was singing to me softly when I woke.

I hoisted myself on to an elbow. I realised I was lying in a sleeping bag with blankets piled on top. Nonetheless my teeth were chattering with the cold. And the bedding felt damp.

Carl was sitting on the floor by the bed tinkering with the gas heater. But his eyes were on me. His voice seemed to come from a distance as he sang, repeating one verse over and over again. Eventually, even in my thoroughly befuddled condition, the words became clear to me.

Your master took you travelling
At least that's what you said
And now do you come back
To bring your prisoner wine and bread?

I struggled to focus on him. He leaned towards me and began to stroke and kiss me, gentle and caring as always.

'That's me, my darling, I am your prisoner,' he told me.

His eyes seemed very bright even though the room was so dimly lit. I had no idea whether it was night or day, although I thought that the wood which covered what had once been windows had been only roughly fitted and that, were it day I would be able to see at least some chinks of light.

Carl was still talking. 'I couldn't let them take you away from me, Suzanne. I couldn't let you go. I have to keep you with me so that I can look after you.'

His face looked strangely contorted in the candlelight, or perhaps that was the fuzziness in my head. For a moment I could hardly remember where we were. And I didn't like it much when I did remember.

I tried to pull myself upright, to get up off the bed, and Carl did not attempt to prevent me doing so, but I could not stand properly. When I fell backwards, however, he caught me and laid me safely down into the musty pillows.

'There my darling, there,' he soothed. 'You're just not strong. You never have been. You have to let me look after you, you must . . .'

'Carl, you're not looking after me. You know I have a weak chest. I'm so cold.'

183

'I know honey, I can't get this damned heater to work, that's the problem. But I will, I promise you, then we'll be really cosy . . .'

I fell asleep again. I don't know for how long. When I woke for the second time my head was much clearer, but it ached. The hut seemed colder and danker than ever. My chest was really starting to hurt.

I was still lying on the camp bed. Carl was sitting next to me looking anxious, the gas heater still in pieces between his legs. There was a slightly glazed expression in his eyes that I couldn't quite recognise. Then it dawned on me. It was desperation. I stared at him. The kindness was still there, the usual concern, the caring. I could see that in his eyes too. But I had so many questions. I really didn't understand what he was doing.

'What are we doing Carl, why do we have to stay here?' I asked, for what seemed like the umpteenth time.

'I'm looking after you,' he replied doggedly. 'Just like I always have.'

I saw that he had made more tea. He fetched me a mug, dodging all my questions.

'Later,' my darling. 'Have some tea, then I'll make you some breakfast.'

'B-but,' I began to protest.

'Drink your tea,' said Carl again, as if he were my nanny, not my lover, the man I had shared my life with for almost seven years. But then, he was always like that with me. I had encouraged him to be so, I supposed. I had needed that. Needed to be looked after as much as he had needed to look after me.

I drank my tea. First, I would do what he wanted, as I always did. Then, afterwards, I would insist that he told me what was going on.

But there was no afterwards. Soon, there was only the blackness again.

I don't know how long I was out for that time, but when I came round, or woke, or whatever, I did not open my eyes properly. Instead I squinted out of one half-open slit. Carl was sitting on a chair by the bed watching me. I had never thought it strange that he liked to watch me sleep, that he would sit for hours just looking at me while I slept. I was used to that kind of attention, that kind of obsessive care. I had been brought up to it.

He seemed to have given up trying to fix the gas heater. He was wearing a thick sweater, a fleece, a sheepskin coat and a woolly hat – just about all the winter clothes he possessed on top of each other in layers. I noticed that he had unzipped the second sleeping bag and covered me with that too. I was still terribly cold.

I studied him through my half-open eye again. Was it a kind of madness I could see in him? I didn't know.

I decided to show some courage. I forced myself into a sitting position and, before he could speak or make a move towards me, I demanded: 'Have you been drugging me, Carl?'

He looked pained and shook his head. 'Of course not, honey. I just gave you something to make you sleep, to soothe away your troubles, that's all. I've not drugged you, no, that's not it at all.'

He knelt down on the floor beside me and rested his head in my lap. 'I'd never hurt you, never, you know that,' he said in that gentle, soothing drawl that had always captivated me.

'Carl, you *are* hurting me. I don't want to be here. And I'm freezing. It's damp in here. I really don't feel well.'

I began to cough. It was not a deliberate ploy to prove my point. With my tendency towards bronchitis I didn't have to pretend anything, not in those conditions. I felt terrible. In the six and a half years that I had lived by the seaside in St Ives I had suffered, by my standards, from only the mildest of chest infections, certainly nothing serious enough even to necessitate consulting a doctor, which had been all for the best as neither Carl nor I was registered with one. This was different. My childhood memories of chronic bronchitis remained vivid; and I feared that I was in for a serious bout.

'I'm so sorry,' he said, all concern. 'Look, I'll heat some soup for you and then I'll have another go at that damned heater . . .'

I watched him open a tin and pour the contents into a saucepan. The Primus stove was already alight. I assumed he had left it on in the hope that it might heat the room a little. It hadn't succeeded. Eventually he handed me a steaming mug of soup. And I suddenly knew with devastating clarity that I must not drink it. But I did not know quite how to avoid doing so until he turned his back on me and bent over the dismembered gas heater again.

The camp bed was in a corner of the hut. The concrete floor was rough and uneven and in places had cracked and crumbled away. I simply emptied the contents of my mug into the corner so that the hot liquid ran down the wall and under the bed, hoping that it would somehow seep away, or congeal there, and not trickle out anywhere that he might see it. When Carl looked round at me I continued to appear to sip from the mug and then, when I thought I could reasonably have drunk it all, I pretended to become drowsy and to lapse into deep sleep again.

After a while I was aware of him moving around the room. He snuffed out all but one candle and then lay down on the second camp bed. I listened to the sound of his breathing, which eventually settled into the deep, even pattern I knew so well. He was definitely asleep.

As quietly as I could I crawled out of bed and went to the door. There were two big bolts, which had been pushed across. I struggled to pull them back. I still felt weak and they did not move easily or silently. I was sure I would wake him – and I did.

He was beside me swiftly, his arms around me, still gentle, still caring. But when he spoke his stammer had reappeared with a vengeance. He had real trouble getting the words out. And I knew that was a bad sign.

'My d-darling, my darling,' he said. 'Y-you mustn't l-leave me, you know that, you must n-n-never l-leave me . . .'

I had not thought I could ever be scared of Carl, but suddenly I was very frightened indeed. He was not my prisoner, I was his. There was no doubt about that. I screamed at him: 'Let me go, let me go.'

I even shouted for help, although I was sure there would be nobody nearby to hear me.

He tried to quieten me in the way he always had during my terrible dreams, but I would not be quiet.

Eventually he pushed my head back and forced

something liquid into my mouth. I choked on it, trying not to swallow, but he closed my mouth and stroked my throat and eventually, of course, I did swallow.

Soon the blackness came again.

Twelve

The next time I regained consciousness I did not seem able to stir at all. I could open my eyes but my arms and legs felt paralysed.

I tried to lift just a foot or a hand, but nothing would move. At first I thought it was maybe because I was so groggy. Then I began to panic. Although my eyes were open and I was awake after a fashion, I could not focus properly. I was in a state of considerable confusion in which the only stark reality was the sensation of paralysis. The panic began really to take a grip. Finally the burning pains in my wrists and ankles as I struggled to move my arms and legs told me what was really wrong.

I was tied to the framework of the camp bed.

Once I realised this my panic changed direction but it did not lessen. I wrenched myself upwards. The ropes cut searingly into my skin. I started to scream.

I could hear Carl's voice making soothing sounds. His face was very close to mine. He was leaning on the flimsy camp bed holding it down, staring at me as usual, his eyes full of concern.

The shed, with its windows boarded fast, was only dimly lit from a couple of flickering candles and my focus was still a little bleary, but I was able to see clearly enough now. Although perhaps I had yet to grasp the full meaning of it all.

Carl reached out and stroked my hair. 'Shush,

sweetheart,' he soothed, the way he always did. 'Look, I've got the gas heater going. I told you I'd make it warm and cosy in here . . .'

I suppose the temperature in the damp old building had risen a little, but I was still shivering with the cold. My forehead was burning though. The shakes were hard to control. I wondered vaguely whether I had a fever.

Carl was still talking, his voice a kind of drone, saying the same things again, the same things over and over in different ways. '. . . It's just that I can't let you go, I can't be without you. I can't let them take you away. I had to make sure you would stay with me, so that I could protect you always. I would kill myself if I let any harm befall you. You know that, don't you? You know I'd never hurt you, only take care of you. That's all I ever want to do . . .'

This was worse than any of my nightmares. In many ways this was more dreadful than anything Robert had done to me, because I loved and trusted Carl so much. I felt betrayed. The man I adored had tied me up and was holding me prisoner. He had kidnapped me. And although I was still puzzled by so much of it, there were things I seemed able to see with sudden clarity.

I had a sudden terrible thought. 'You sent the letters, you did it all, didn't you, Carl?' I whispered through lips that felt dry and chapped. 'You sent those awful letters; you daubed that message on the cottage door. It was you.'

The accusation clearly shook him. 'No, darling, don't even say it. Why would I do something like that?'

'To bind me to you,' I said. 'Just as these ropes tie

me to the bed. To keep me your prisoner.'

'You shouldn't even think such awful things,' he said quietly. 'You're confused, honey. Try to get some rest.'

I stopped struggling, and lay back against the pillow. I knew he was lying, that he had done it. All at once I felt almost devastatingly calm. It seemed that nothing worse could ever happen to me than this. Surely there could be nothing more horrible than a betrayal of this magnitude. For a moment or two I was overcome by a coughing fit, the palms of my hands were clammy, but when I finally managed to stop, I tried again. 'Carl, I keep telling you, don't you think you're hurting me now?'

He had been kneeling next to the bed, hanging on to it. He sank back on his heels, then, and released his grasp. He continued to stare at me for a moment or two longer, then he buried his head in his hands. 'I'm keeping you safe, my darling,' he muttered through his fingers. 'That's all, keeping you safe . . .'

He was babbling. And still stammering. 'I l-love you, Suzanne. I'm the one who saved you. I will always p-protect you . . .'

There was more, too, an endless stream of protestations of devotion, which suddenly seemed so meaningless.

I did not take my eyes off him. Neither did I struggle any more. I realised there was no point. I shut his voice out of my head and started to think back over the various threats and the way they were worded, and of the night that our front door was daubed with the red paint. The more I thought the more it made sense that Carl had damaged his own van, written the letters, Carl himself had been responsible for the shocking message in blood red, Carl was behind all the sinister threats we had received.

'You did it, Carl, I'm sure of it,' I said eventually. 'I've been thinking about the night we got home from the Inn Plaice and found the door had been painted – you left the restaurant, allegedly to get me flowers. You were gone a long time, plenty of time to paint the door . . .'

He continued to squat there, his face buried in his hands. Then he started to moan. It was the eeriest sound, an endless low wail of a noise.

'Why, Carl, why did you do it?'

He stopped moaning and spoke then, but only through the fingers still covering his face. 'I've d-done nothing,' he said. 'Nothing except try to remind you of how dangerous the outside world is for you, that's all.'

'You never intended to let me stop having the nightmares, did you?' I continued flatly. 'You might have lost control of me then.'

It was as if he had not heard me. 'You've always understood, you see,' he said. 'Understood how much we n-needed each other.'

He took his hands away from his face, swung his body forward and kneeled by the side of the bed again, leaning close so that his face, illuminated by a candle on the box serving as a makeshift table, was closer than ever, just an inch or two away from mine. 'I had to g-get you away. I know, you see, I know things you don't. Sometimes it's right to r-r-run away and if you wait, well, that's when terrible things happen,' he whispered. 'I didn't mean to frighten you, sweetheart.'

I was frightened, though, frightened of Carl. It was extraordinary.

'Let me go, please let me go,' I pleaded.

'We have to be t-together,' he said flatly. 'We always have to be together. You must see that, you always used to. I have to keep you safe, away from d-danger.'

I continued to struggle to control the trembling, which was threatening to engulf my body from head to foot, unsure whether it was caused by the cold, by fever or by fear, or maybe all three.

I did not want him to see just how terribly frightened I was.

'Carl, you must know we can't hide for ever,' I said eventually.

'Suzanne, we have hidden for almost seven years,' he countered. 'We were happy, weren't we, content in our little cottage in St Ives. Even though we were hiding it didn't feel as if we were, did it? We would still be there if you hadn't decided to go the police.'

He muttered the last few words through clenched teeth and without a hint of a stammer. I had not realised before quite how angry I must have made him.

I was extremely uncomfortable, as I was hardly able to move at all. I coughed again and the ropes dug into my wrists and ankles. I wasn't quite as cold as I had been, but the shivering continued and the pain in my chest was becoming more severe. It seemed inevitable that I was developing bronchitis. Then I realised abruptly that there was an additional reason for my discomfort. I needed to go to the lavatory. And I told Carl so.

He barely reacted. Just looked uncertain.

'For goodness' sake untie me, Carl,' I said.

He still did nothing.

'Do you want me to lie in my own filth?' I asked. 'Is that what we've come to?'

He shook his head then, and began to untie the ropes fastening me to the bed.

I sat up and rubbed my sore wrists and ankles, making sure that he saw the red weals that had formed in my flesh. He winced. I tried to stand up and nearly fell backwards. I had lost the circulation in my legs. I could barely stay upright.

At once Carl's strong arms were round me. I leaned heavily on to him, grabbing his shoulder. I had no choice. It was that or fall over. He helped me to the portable chemical loo in one corner – another disturbing indication of how carefully he must have planned for this – and made as if he were going to help me to pull down my trousers.

I glowered at him. 'Turn your back, I can manage,' I ordered.

He did so at once. But I could see his shoulders slump. The intimacy between us had always been such that I would not previously have asked him to turn away during even such a personal activity as having a wee.

When I had finished and had rearranged my clothes I moved quickly and sat down on one of the wooden chairs.

He stood close by, loosely holding the ropes with which I had been tied in his left hand. 'Do you want to sit there or do you want to lie down on the bed again?' he asked me.

'I'll stay here,' I said.

'On the chair or on the bed, up to you, but I'm

going to tie you wherever you are,' he warned. There was a catch in his voice.

'For goodness' sake, Carl, I'm not going anywhere,' I said.

'But you tried to, didn't you?' he said. 'You tried to run away from me. I'm afraid you are going to come to harm. I can't let that happen. I have to keep you here.'

'I don't like being locked up, and I certainly don't like being tied up.'

'It's for your own good,' he said. 'I promise you, my darling. Everything that I have done is for you.'

He began to tie my arms to the back of the chair. I knew that in his youth in Key West, Carl had learned to sail and had crewed for the tourist boats. I suspected, although I didn't know because I had never been on a boat of any kind in my life, that the knots he used were nautical ones. I didn't protest any more. There wasn't any point.

Carl's voice was high-pitched and unnatural-sounding. His face glowed white in the candlelight. His eyes were very bright.

I had little idea what time of day it was or how long I had been in the shed with Carl. As I had earlier suspected, I could see daylight outside through the cracks around the boarded-up window, but other than that day and night blended into one.

Carl provided me with food and hot drinks at regular intervals.

I refused to eat or drink anything he gave me. 'Do you think I'm a fool?' I asked. 'I'm not going to let you drug me again. I'm really not.'

He looked hurt. 'I didn't drug you, not the way you

mean, not really, I've told you that,' he protested.

I ignored him.

'Look, please eat, I haven't touched the food, honestly,' he went on. 'In any case it was only a sleeping draft to keep you calm, nothing more.'

But I couldn't believe a word he said any longer.

Eventually he opened a large plastic container of water, placed two clear plastic beakers on the box that served as a table and filled them. I was still sitting on the chair, my legs tied and just one arm free.

'Take one,' he instructed. I did not move.

'For goodness' sake, take one,' he repeated. His voice was slightly louder and he sounded quite exasperated.

I took one.

'Right,' he said. He picked up the other one and drank from it. 'There, now have a drink,' he said. 'You're going to be ill otherwise.'

I shook my head and put the beaker down on the box again.

He sighed, picked up the remaining beaker and drank from it briefly. 'Now will you drink.'

I shook my head again. I suppose I was being stubborn for the sake of it. I really had had enough.

So had Carl, apparently. 'For God's sake, Suzanne,' he shouted. And he kicked the box so that the beaker of water flew in the air and spilled its contents over the floor, and the box shot across the room and clattered into the metal frame of one of the camp beds.

Somewhere outside a dog barked.

Carl ran to a window and tried to peer through a narrow crack in the boarding that covered it. Apparently he saw nothing to cause him any additional anxiety. After a minute or so he turned away from the window. Once again I could see his face quite clearly in the candlelight. There were dark shadows under his eyes. His mouth was a tight line. Strange to think how often I had kissed that mouth. Shoulders hunched, he walked across the room and carefully replaced the box he had kicked in an upright position. Then he straightened the camp bed.

I thought I heard the dog bark again, but I wasn't quite sure. Perhaps it was my imagination, wishful thinking that somebody was going to stumble across us here in this hidden place and I would be freed, released from the clutches of the man I had until so very recently wanted only to be with for ever.

Carl was listening too. He stood with his head slightly on one side. Suddenly I was sure that I wasn't imagining the sound of the dog barking and that it was more than one dog. I think Carl realised the same thing at almost exactly the same moment. He looked frightened and bewildered. He did not move. It was as if he were frozen to the spot.

Before either of us had time to work out what was going on there was a loud bang. The door burst open, torn off its hinges by some sort of battering ram expertly wielded by two large uniformed policemen.

More uniformed police stormed in, several of them armed. Three of them pounced on Carl and two more were quickly by my side reassuring me. From then on everything seemed to happen very fast.

DS Perry appeared and swiftly untied my bonds. I tried to sit up, but my limbs still felt leaden and I collapsed back on to the pillows.

'Take it steady,' said Julie Perry. 'We've got an ambulance outside.'

One of the policemen holding Carl addressed him very loudly and clearly, as if making quite sure that he understood. 'Carl Peters,' he said. 'I am arresting you on suspicion of abduction . . .'

Carl let out a cry, almost as if somebody had hit him. 'Abduction? I haven't abducted anyone. Suzanne is my wife. She's mine. I brought her here to protect her. She came with me willingly, I didn't abduct her . . . how could I . . . tell them, Suzanne, tell them . . .'

The words poured out of him. He was almost screaming by the time he had finished. The police bundled him off as quickly as they could. I didn't say anything. I had nothing to say.

Thirteen

They didn't explain it all to me, not then. Although Detective Sergeant Perry did tell me how they came to find us. Curious rather than alarmed – Carl and I were, after all, two adults not wanted for any crime – she had talked to Mariette after we disappeared, and asked her if she knew any favourite haunts of ours, places we liked to visit, anywhere we might be. For some reason, perhaps because it was still the season, Mariette had mentioned the hidden-away bluebell wood, which I remembered telling her of when she had asked me questions about my life with Carl. But Mariette had been unable to give precise directions and in any case it had not necessarily been relevant. But then, apparently, a courting couple had heard my screams the night I tried to escape and had reported the incident to the police. When DS Perry learned about this, luckily for me she began to put two and two together.

Carl and I had both regarded the area around the bluebell wood, and certainly the old quarry further along the track where the hut was, as being very remote, but in fact nowhere is far from civilisation in Cornwall. And apparently the rough track both of us had only previously driven along during the day became something of a lovers' lane at night.

I suppose I was relieved. I was also confused – Carl had been right about that – and my physical condition only added to my distress. I was suddenly over-whelmed by a coughing fit. DS Perry passed me a paper tissue and I coughed dark phlegm into it. It even hurt to breathe. But in spite of feeling so ill – my chest infection was definitely getting worse – my mind was in turmoil.

I had an absolute corker of a headache. I was only vaguely aware of being carried out of the hut and loaded into the waiting ambulance. Even cocooned in blankets, I still couldn't stop shivering. The para-medic who rode in the back with me listened to my chest, took my temperature and looked anxious. But I remained more worried about all that had happened than I was about my physical state. They drove me to hospital in Penzance where I was wheeled into Casualty. I did not have to wait long before being seen by a young, white-coated doctor.

'You're suffering from severe shock,' he said almost at once.

I didn't need a medical diagnosis to know that. And I reckoned I was still woozy from whatever drugs Carl had fed me.

'I also think you may have chronic bronchitis,' the doctor went on.

I managed a wan smile. 'I'm used to it,' I said. 'It's OK.'

He gave me a look that indicated he wasn't quite sure about that. 'Better have you in for a couple of days,' he said.

In spite of my protests that I would be absolutely fine I was admitted with surprising alacrity for the National Health Service and tucked into bed. Warm and safe at last, I could feel myself drifting off almost at once. I don't know whether it was the after effects of the drugs Carl had fed me or some sort of defence mechanism. All I knew was that I wanted to sleep for ever. But I wouldn't let myself. I was determined to stay awake until someone explained to me exactly what had really happened all those years ago in Hounslow when Robert Foster had died. I was sure it held the key to everything that had happened, to all that Carl had done.

A nurse brought me some medication but certainly I did not intend to swallow any more drugs. 'I'm not taking anything,' I announced.

'Just to make you sleep, and some antibiotics for the chest infection.'

Little did she know how hard I was fighting to keep awake. 'I don't want anything to make me sleep. I don't want to sleep at all until someone explains things to me.'

The nurse sighed and said she'd fetch the ward sister.

'All right,' said the ward sister and sighed too. 'There's a Sergeant Perry outside. I'll bring her in.'

I made a big effort and propped myself up on the pillows. My chest felt as if it was being crushed beneath a double-decker bus. I tried to ignore it.

After a couple of minutes the curtains around my bed were pulled slightly to one side and Sergeant Perry stuck her head round. 'The Führer says I've got five minutes,' she announced with a smile.

I didn't smile back. I felt much more ill than I was revealing to anyone, but that paled into insignificance compared with my mental state.

I had to know the truth about Robert. I had found my husband covered with blood. I had killed him. I must have killed him. Carl had been determined that

201

we still had to hide, horrifically determined, prepared to go to almost any lengths, it seemed. Yet the police had already told me that Robert had not been murdered. I was beginning to wonder if it was me who was going mad.

'Just tell me everything you know, please,' I said.

Sergeant Perry glanced instinctively at her watch, then took a closer look at me. I could see the anxiety in her eyes. I knew I was beginning to sweat and I had given up trying to control my shakes.

'Please,' I said again. 'I have to know. For a start, if my husband Robert Foster wasn't murdered, what did happen to him?'

Sergeant Perry was still standing at the foot of my bed. As if making a decision she came over and sat down on the chair next to me. 'Robert Foster died of natural causes,' she said expressionlessly.

I looked at her askance. 'How could he have done?' I asked. 'I saw all the blood, I got it all over me . . .'

I stopped. I still didn't want to think about it, even after all these years. That had always been one of the problems. I couldn't face the thought that I had stabbed a man to death, not even a man I hated so much, and with such good reason. When I had confessed at the police station I had, I suppose, hoped in some silly kind of way that, whatever happened to me, I wouldn't have to confront Robert's death again. I had confessed to killing him and that would be that. I knew well enough, now, that whatever the truth, it wasn't going to be as simple as that. I had to concentrate, to try to remember.

'I went into the bedroom and saw him lying there in his own blood,' I went on. 'I have never been able to remember exactly what happened in the night. Like I told you before. I have just always assumed that when I got the chance I got hold of the knife and used it on him. What else could I have thought? There was nobody other than me who could have killed him, nobody else was in the house until I called Carl. I am absolutely sure Robert was dead before Carl arrived. And all that blood – he had to have died a violent death.'

DS Perry shook her head. 'No,' she said. 'Well, not in the way you mean, anyway.'

I opened my mouth to speak and all that came out was another fit of coughing. It came from deep inside me and I felt as if my body was tearing apart. I held a tissue to my mouth and tried not to let DS Perry see the black phlegm that I spat into it.

'How did he die, then, how could he have died?' I asked quietly when I was finally able.

'Did you know that your husband had sclerosis of the liver?' the policewoman asked.

I shook my head, amazed. Although I don't know quite why I should have been surprised. I had known so little about Robert, really. For a start I had never known why he had wanted to hurt me so much.

'He was an alcoholic, you must have known that,' she went on.

I half nodded. I suppose I had realised that he was an alcoholic. I must have known, although I never thought of it in those terms. Just that he drank vast quantities of alcohol, and the more he drank the more violent and dangerous he became.

'He was a minister in the Chapel of the Advent. They are opposed to alcohol. He wasn't supposed to drink at all,' I said. 'But he did, constantly.'

'That kind is often the worst, but you'd know that more than me, I expect.'

I nodded again. I didn't want to talk about the terrible beatings I had suffered from a drunken Robert. I just hoped that one day I would be able to forget them.

'Sclerosis of the liver is a vicious illness,' the police sergeant went on. 'One of the most extreme results is haematemesis – when the liver ceases to function so drastically that blood leaks into the stomach where it becomes a potentially lethal irritant. The victim vomits blood, vast quantities of it.' She paused. 'Your husband died of chronic blood loss . . . caused by his sclerosis. He was not murdered. You did not kill him and neither did anyone else.'

'B-but when I came to in the bathroom in the morning I was covered with blood, Robert's blood. How did it get all over me if I didn't kill him?'

Julie Perry shrugged. 'I've been thinking about that. You used the phrase "came to". Almost certainly you'd been knocked out. I reckon Robert Foster must have started haemorrhaging blood while he was beating you. That's how you got his blood on you. You had concussion, you didn't know what was happening. You just crawled off to hide in the bathroom as soon as you got the chance.'

'Carl always said I had killed him,' I said quietly. 'He let me believe it . . . he showed me the knife covered with Robert's blood . . .'

Sergeant Perry nodded. 'Yes, I realise that,' she said.

Carl had not been half hysterical. Carl hadn't been beaten unconscious in the night. He had seen Robert lying naked on the bed. Surely he must have realised that there were no stab wounds in his body. Was this another of his tricks, like the threatening letters?

'So did Carl deliberately deceive me, then, for all those years?' I asked, thinking aloud.

Julie Perry shrugged again. 'Hard to tell. Not necessarily. He found the knife, he saw the blood, just like you did . . .'

I struggled to make sense of it. Carl was always so cool and calm, even under extreme stress. The kind of man who double-checked everything – even a blood-covered body for stab wounds.

I felt as if my ribcage was about to cave in. I wanted to cough, but I wasn't capable.

'Look, there's more, something else . . .' I heard DS Perry say somewhere in the distance.

Most clearly I could hear my own breathing. It was coming in desperate wheezing gasps. I suspected DS Perry could hear it too.

'I tell you what, why don't you rest,' she said, not for the first time sounding like all the others who had tried to protect me throughout my life. 'Let me talk to you tomorrow.'

'No,' I said, surprisingly firmly for me in any situation and particularly when I felt so ill that I was having difficulty even in breathing let alone speaking. 'I want to know now,' I croaked.

She looked at me for a moment or two as if appraising both my physical and mental state. Then she sighed. 'We have been checking out Carl in the States. Something happened there a long time ago too . . .'

I wanted to know so much and yet in spite of my entreaties for her to continue I was beginning to have serious trouble concentrating on what she was saying.

My chest hurt more than I could ever remember, more even than it had during the severe bronchial attacks of my childhood. My forehead was burning, and by then I was wet with sweat.

I finally managed a cough and it was as if some kind of barrier inside me burst open. I was engulfed in a coughing fit much more violent than any that had preceded it. At first black phlegm dribbled out of my mouth and then I began to cough up blood. Suddenly I was very frightened indeed. It felt as if my ribs had finally caved in on to my vital organs.

I was vaguely aware of DS Perry jumping to her feet and crying out. Then I think I must have passed out.

I didn't know a lot about what happened next or for some time afterwards. I was vaguely aware of being moved out of my bed and on to a trolley again, and of being trundled off to the intensive care unit. At some time, somewhere, I know I heard the words 'pneumonia, Mrs Peters.' That was about it. Nothing meant much, really, except the overwhelming desire to stay alive. Instinctively, somewhere inside my head, I knew I truly was that ill.

The act of breathing became a terrible agonising struggle. The pain grasped me round my middle like a particularly vicious straitjacket. At some stage I remember shadowy people forcing some kind of tube down my throat, and trying to fight them off and not being able to. Most of the rest of it remains a blank – a bit like so much of the night when Robert died.

I was later to learn that I had bilateral pneumonia, which then turned to pleurisy. This meant that not only were both my lungs infected but also the lining of my chest wall. I spent several days in intensive care on a ventilator and it was getting on for two weeks before I returned properly to the world.

By then an awful lot had happened.

I was back on the ward, stupor-like most of the time, when I woke from a fitful sleep to find Mariette sitting by my bed.

'They said you were a lot better, but I didn't want to wake you,' she told me with a small smile. 'You do look better, I must say.'

I was puzzled. 'What do you mean? Have you been to see me before?' I asked.

She nodded. 'A couple of times, you know, when I could,' she said.

I was touched. I needed a friend. One thing about being as ill as I had been is that you don't have time to think about anything except your physical misery. I was starting to think again, beginning to remember, and Carl filled my jumbled thoughts. Carl had not been to see me. Of course not. He had been arrested.

'I suppose you know what's happened?' I enquired of Mariette.

'More or less,' she replied. 'It's the talk of the town, the kidnap and everything.'

I managed a small smile myself. 'It wasn't really a kidnap,' I stated.

'Sounded like one to me,' she said. 'Who'd have thought that of your Carl?'

'I still don't understand it.'

'No. And you thought you'd murdered your first husband, as if you'd be capable of anything like that.'

'Good God, does everyone know about that too?'

'You know St Ives. Some of it was in the papers,

207

don't know where the rest of it came from. Mind you, they always say the nick leaks like a sieve . . .'

Mariette was kind and attentive, and completely unjudgemental. I had somehow always known so much about her life, but she had never known anything of mine. If she was shocked by anything she had learned she did not show it. But, unsurprisingly perhaps in the circumstances, she did not really know what to say to me.

At one point she started to say speak, then seemed to change her mind. 'There was talk of something that happened in America, too, but, oh, it's sure to be only rumour . . .'

'What, Mariette? DS Perry mentioned something about America, just before I collapsed.'

Mariette grasped the opportunity with which I had presented her. 'Then it's DS Perry you should be talking to, not me. I should know better than even to start repeating the gossip of St Ives. It's invariably a load of old nonsense.'

I could tell she didn't really believe that, but she wasn't saying any more. She could be very stubborn when she wanted, could Mariette. She left pretty quickly then, and I asked a passing nurse for a telephone.

After waiting fruitlessly for at least half an hour I asked another nurse. Then I fell asleep. When I woke up there was still no sign of a telephone.

Ultimately it was nearly the end of the day before one of those cumbersome trolleys was brought to me. Strange, with all the modern technology available, that nothing has changed in most NHS hospitals in this respect for several decades.

I called Directory Enquiries to get the number of

the police station, dialled it and asked for DS Perry. She wasn't there.

'She's away,' I was told. I was pretty sure it was the same desk clerk I had spoken to when I went there.

I gave my name, mentioned Carl's, said it was urgent and asked if there was anywhere else I could speak to her.

'Not sure about that,' said the clerk. He seemed about as interested and dynamic as he had the first time I had encountered him.

'I don't even know where Carl is,' I muttered vaguely.

'He's been remanded in custody, abduction is a serious offence, Mrs Peters,' said the clerk and that was about as informative as he was going to be. 'I can get PC Partridge to call you, if you like. He's about the only one around today.'

I groaned inwardly. I didn't have a lot of confidence in PC Partridge. I also left a message for DS Perry and ultimately the promise of a call-back from one or other of them was what I had to settle for. I explained that it might be difficult for anyone to get through to me in hospital and asked that they keep insisting. The clerk muttered something inaudible.

I waited all that late afternoon and evening, and the next morning, before impatience got the better of me and I called again. I still reached a brick wall. This time I talked to an uninterested female voice.

'DS Perry is still away, I'm afraid.'

I asked for PC Partridge again.

'He's in court today.'

'Can you get a message to him? I called yesterday but he hasn't got back to me . . .'

'Did you leave a message for him then?'

'Yes.'

'Well, he's sure to have got it.'

'But I haven't heard from him.'

'He'll call when he can, I'm sure. You're in hospital you say? Not always easy to get through, is it?'

'You can say that again,' I said with feeling. 'Look, I want to talk to someone about my husband Carl Peters. Can you help.'

'I'm afraid not. You could try Penzance. I believe it's being dealt with from there now.'

'But I was told PC Partridge could help me.'

'I'm sure he probably can. He did work on the case with DS Perry.'

I stifled an impatient sigh. 'Please give him another message. I really do need to speak to him urgently.'

I got nowhere. But I still felt too weak to put up much of a fight. All I could do was lie back in my hospital bed and carry on waiting for Rob Partridge to call.

That afternoon there was a bit of a diversion. Will Jones paid me a visit, bringing with him a beautiful book about Patrick Heron, which I received gratefully. I was still in a bit of a daze but, in spite of my befuddled and anxious state, it was good to have company, to chat for a bit.

At first we made a rather strained kind of small talk, but it was better than nothing. As with Mariette's visit, it was good just to think that someone cared enough to come calling.

At one point, after quite a long silence, Will enquired if I had any money on me. Typically, I hadn't even thought about it. And the answer was that I didn't have a penny. Will took his wallet from his pocket and handed me two twenty-pound notes. 'I owe you more, I've sold some of Carl's paintings,' he said. 'I'll work out how much by the time you get out of here . . .'

I thanked him. The money should have gone to Carl, I supposed. There was another vaguely uncomfortable silence. Then Will began to ask me a lot of questions, most of which I either could not or did not wish to answer.

'So he just sort of went off the rails, really?' he muttered.

I nodded.

'What pushed him, do you know?'

I sighed. Not sure whether I wanted to talk like this or not. 'Fear, more than anything,' I said. 'Fear of losing me. Fear of what might happen to us.'

'And you thought all this time that you'd killed your husband?'

'Absolutely,' I confirmed.

'And you both thought that was what the letters and the rest of it referred to?'

'Oh, the letters, yes, of course . . .'

I hadn't thought about any of that for a while. I had had other things on my mind, like being imprisoned against my will by the man I loved, and fighting off critical bouts of pneumonia and pleurisy. 'Well, I thought that, but not Carl, of course,' I went on. 'Carl sent the letters, I'm sure of that now.'

Will looked startled. 'Did he admit it?'

'I think so,' I wasn't quite sure, come to think of it. 'What does it matter anyway, after all that has happened?'

'No, I suppose not. So Carl really has turned into a villain, hasn't he?'

He was right enough, of course, but I still didn't like to hear it.

'Fancy letting you think you'd killed someone all these years . . .'

'We don't know that for sure,' I managed to protest, clutching at straws, maybe.

Will gave me that look of his, which he switched on when he was demonstrating just how much cleverer he was than you. Fond as I was of him, it never failed to irritate me. 'Well, of course, you must believe what you want to believe, Suzanne,' he began. Then he was interrupted by a large nurse bearing a thermometer, which she placed uncompromisingly in my mouth. Which might have been all for the best.

The thermometer was still there when Will left.

'I'll pop round when you're home,' he had said before he departed.

I tried to mutter something and reached for the thermometer. The large nurse tapped my hand reprovingly. And in my condition I didn't have the strength to argue, even had I not had a thermometer wedged between my lips.

Fourteen

I had to see him. And I had to know the worst.

You could not share all that I had shared with Carl and not want to see a man who you thought you had known so well, yet whom perhaps you hadn't known at all.

I discharged myself from hospital early the next morning. Nobody had phoned me back from the police, and I couldn't wait any longer. I somehow felt sure that if I could just get myself to St Ives police station I could sort everything out. I walked to Penzance railway station and caught the next train back to the little seaside town where Carl and I had been so happy for so long. At St Ives I made my way along the beach to the harbour, breathing in the sea air, taking strength from its fresh saltiness, before turning into the town and up through the network of steep streets to the hidden-away police station. I arrived there just after 9 a.m., out of breath and wondering if I had done a bit too much walking, but determined to get some answers. I was hoping, of course, that DS Perry would be back from wherever she had been over the two previous days. At least she seemed to have some idea what was going on. But even to be able to see Rob Partridge would be a result. I craved some kind of familiarity.

It seemed a lifetime had passed since, resolved to

rid myself of my long-carried burden, I had first approached the ugly, dirty white building

The desk clerk greeted me with his customary lack of enthusiasm. Did they only have one clerk, or was I just lucky, I wondered glumly. He was, however, a little more communicative than in the past. He told me that DS Perry was in Plymouth and would be there for some time. Apparently there had been a particularly unpleasant murder of a young girl. That was why she hadn't responded to my phone calls.

I was still feeling very poorly and becoming aware that maybe I should have stayed in hospital at least another couple of days, and this news about DS Perry was yet another blow. I had barely known her but I somehow had more confidence in her than any of the other officers I had encountered. Not surprising, perhaps, when the only other one I had had much to do with was Rob Partridge.

'I'll see if I can find someone else to help you,' the clerk offered and disappeared into the back office in a disconcertingly familiar way.

I could hear him talking into a telephone, but I wasn't optimistic. A murder. Yes, I supposed that was more important than a kidnapping, if that is what it really had been.

The inner door opened just as I was reconciling myself to another fruitless wait. Rob Partridge, in uniform but without his helmet, greeted me with an uncertain smile, and ushered me into the bleak little ground-floor interview room. 'I just called you at the hospital,' he said. 'Sorry I didn't get back to you yesterday.'

'Look, I want to see my husband,' I said. 'I want to see Carl.' For the first time in almost seven years I was somehow starkly aware that Carl wasn't my husband. But old habits die hard.

'He's on remand in Exeter,' said Rob Partridge. 'Surely you knew that?'

I didn't. I knew absolutely nothing about police or court procedure and little more about the case I was actively involved in. I had been more or less semi-conscious in hospital for two weeks. I didn't have a clue what had happened to Carl following his arrest and my admission to the hospital. In a simplistic way I suppose I expected him to be locked in a cell somewhere in the bowels of St Ives police station.

'I thought he would be here,' I murmured lamely.

Rob shook his head. 'This is a small district police station,' he told me. 'We don't keep prisoners here. You can visit him at the Devon County Prison at Exeter whenever you like, just about. As he's on remand you have pretty free access.'

The Devon County Prison. I repeated it inside my head. The very sound of the words was chilling.

'But I need to talk to somebody first. DS Perry mentioned something that happened in America. I need to know what's going on before I see him,' I mumbled.

Partridge and I were both standing in the interview room. He gestured me to one chair and, sitting down in the other, took a packet of cigarettes from his pocket and lit up. He offered me one, which I declined, then he drew deeply on his own. The windowless little room filled with smoke. I hoped I wouldn't start coughing again. My chest still hurt.

'We searched your cottage after we arrested Carl,' he began. 'Standard procedure when you've arrested somebody on a serious charge. We found some

215

photographs and an out-of-date American passport in another name. His picture, though. It was pretty simple to check out with the States. Your Carl was really called Harry Mendleson and he had good reason to be using a false name all right. Seems he makes a habit of trying to abduct his wives.'

I waited. I felt very cold. Rob Partridge smiled almost triumphantly, only to me it looked more like a leer. He was another one who could never resist showing off superior knowledge. Something made me think he shouldn't be telling me all this, but he seemed to be in full flight.

'Only the last time it all went badly wrong. His wife was going to leave him. He wouldn't have it. Tried to prevent her getting away. Drugs were involved that time too. Apparently there was a kid, a daughter, who died of an overdose. Only five or six, she was, too. He's wanted on a manslaughter charge . . .'

I was shocked to the core. It seemed unreal. Carl was wanted on a manslaughter charge? He had drugged his daughter? Killed her? I hadn't even known he'd had a daughter. I began to shake again. I didn't know whether it was the impact of the news I had just heard or the residue of my illness. A bit of both probably. 'What happened?' I cried. 'I can't believe he killed his own daughter. How? Why? Please tell me.'

Rob Partridge looked uncomfortable at my reaction, as if he regretted telling me all that he had. He ran a hand through his spiky orange hair. 'Look, I don't know the details, it's not even my case. I only know as much as I do because I was involved in the arrest and then the search. It's CID. Detective Sergeant Perry was in charge, you know that.'

I nodded. 'But she's not here,' I said lamely.

'No, the case has been handed over to DC Carter in Penzance. That's who you should be talking to now.'

I wasn't giving up that easily. 'The photographs, the old passport. Where did you find them? I've never seen them. Carl and I didn't hide things from each other . . .'

'He hid that lot all right. We found them in the box he keeps his paints and brushes in. There's a false compartment at the bottom.'

Yes, I thought morosely, that made a dreadful kind of sense. I never touched Carl's paints and brushes, never went near his special mahogany box because he was so fussy about his painting equipment.

Partridge had begun to speak again, once more parading his superior knowledge. 'That's the thing about people living under a false identity,' he said in a self-important tone of voice. 'Getting the new identity is no problem. A doddle, that is, if you know how. The old *Day of the Jackal* trick still works. You just take a name and birth date off the gravestone of someone about the same age as yourself, apply for a new birth certificate and bingo. Everything else you need is easy once you've got a birth certificate. The problem people have is walking away from the past. They nearly always keep something, just like Carl did. It's not being able to let go of the past that catches 'em out.' He paused. 'The photographs were of the daughter he killed,' Partridge continued conversationally. 'Typical, that, really . . .'

Suddenly it was all too much for me. I could barely take in what he was saying. Tears were welling up in my eyes and I couldn't hold them back. I began to sob quietly.

217

Rob Partridge didn't seem to know what to do then. His air of self-importance vanished abruptly. 'Look, don't upset yourself. I'll see if I can get DC Carter on the phone,' he said, in a manner that suggested that the detective would be able to solve all my problems. He took his mobile from his pocket and punched in a number. Maybe it was just that Rob Partridge knew his way around a police station or maybe he was luckier than me. Most people were, I was beginning to think. Either way, he seemed to get through to the Penzance CID man straight away.

'DC Carter can see you at Penzance police station at nine o'clock tomorrow morning,' he told me after a brief conversation, still holding the telephone to his ear, with one hand over the mouthpiece.

'In Penzance?' I repeated through my snuffles. 'But I want to see Carl and he's in Exeter.'

'You can pick up the main-line train from there, straight on to Exeter. We'll fix it with the prison,' said Partridge.

I couldn't think straight and I was so used to doing what people told me to, falling in with what others said, that I meekly nodded my agreement. Tomorrow morning seemed a long way away, but I was still feeling distinctly unwell. I hoped that I might perhaps be stronger both mentally and physically by then and, in any case, I certainly did not have the energy at that moment to demand an earlier meeting.

Partridge spoke into the receiver again, relaying my assent. Then he showed me the door. 'Ray Carter'll see you right,' he promised. 'Good man, Ray.'

But I knew all he was really doing was getting rid of me.

By then, however, I didn't mind very much. The

tight feeling in my chest was quite extreme and I just wanted to lie down and go to sleep. I was suddenly quite glad that I didn't have to rush off to Penzance or Exeter, or anywhere at all.

I left the station and set off up the hill towards Rose Cottage. The climb seemed steeper than ever before. I was wheezing by the time I reached the cottage and it wasn't until I was standing outside the now dark-blue front door that I remembered I didn't have a key.

For a moment or two I dithered miserably. Then I recalled that Carl climbed over the wall of the cottage next door into our backyard when we had locked ourselves out once, and we had never got around to fixing the dodgy kitchen window.

The next-door cottage had access into its own small garden through a little gate at the front and a narrow alleyway between the two houses. I had my hand on the gate, ready to open it, before I thought that I had better not do so without knocking on the front door first. In any case, although I vaguely remembered Carl vaulting over the wall easily enough, I didn't think I could manage it without a ladder or something similar.

Our neighbour Mrs Jackson's wide smile of welcome turned into an expression of surprised uncertainty when she saw me standing there. 'Suzanne!' she exclaimed, her eyes widening and her mouth remaining slackly open as if I had grown antennae.

I smiled weakly.

Her face softened. She was a kind woman, Mrs Jackson, albeit prone to verbal diarrhoea. 'Oh, come in, come in,' she urged. I allowed myself to be ushered into her cosy kitchen.

I could see that she didn't know quite what to say next, very unusual for Mrs Jackson. Seeking, perhaps, words of reassurance what she eventually came up with was: 'Oh my God, Suzanne, you look terrible.'

'I expect I do. I've had pneumonia,' I told her flatly.

'I know, my dear, I've heard all about it and what he did to you, I can't believe it you know, not your lovely Carl, just can't believe it, and him a murderer too, and his own daughter . . .'

I couldn't believe it either. It seemed the whole town knew about the allegations against Carl and had done so long before I did. I summoned up the energy to interrupt Mrs Jackson's babbling. 'Manslaughter,' I said.

'Pardon?' Mrs Jackson looked startled again. It was an expression that somehow suited her plump-cheeked face rather well.

'Manslaughter,' I repeated. 'He's wanted in the States on a manslaughter charge. As far as I know . . .'

I was aware of my last few words tailing off pathetically.

They were quite enough to set Mrs J. off again: 'No, of course, you wouldn't know. Nice young girl like you, you'd never live with a murderer. I said the same to Mr Nichols in the butcher's, only yesterday I said. "Fancy an innocent young girl like her taken in by a man like that," I said. And him not even using his own name, pretending to be somebody else. Defies belief it does . . .'

Suddenly I realised that I couldn't take any more of this. 'Mrs Jackson,' I interrupted surprisingly firmly. 'I'm afraid I'm locked out of the house. I wondered if

I could borrow your ladder and climb over the garden wall.'

'Of course you can, my dear. Still haven't fixed that kitchen window, aye?' She didn't wait for me to respond. 'Good thing, apparently. The police have been, I expect you know that, but they had a key.'

They would have used Carl's key, I assumed. I should have thought of that when I was in the police station, I reflected. I turned my attention back to the present.

Mrs Jackson was still talking. 'Anyway, m'dear, 'course you can go in over my wall, but first I want you to sit down with me and have a nice cup of tea. Goodness knows you look as if you could do with one. Then tell me all about it. Helps to talk, you know, that's what they say . . .'

The very idea filled me with almost as much horror as had any of the events of the last week. 'I'm sorry Mrs J.,' I interrupted quickly. 'I really do feel lousy. I just want to get indoors and go to bed, please.'

She nodded understandingly, the kind of woman whose gravestone would bear the legend 'she meant well', I had often thought, and it would be absolutely the truth. She did mean well, excruciatingly so. 'Of course, my dear.'

She found the ladder and together we propped it against the dividing wall, which was about seven foot high. Mrs Jackson expressed concern about my ability to climb up it safely, and, to be honest, I felt so weak that I wasn't too sure myself. I managed OK, though, and at the top I hung on with my hands and arms, dangled my feet and legs down the other side, and dropped the two or three feet, landing safely in our little cobbled backyard.

'I'm fine, Mrs J.,' I called back in answer to her anxious enquiries. 'Yes, I'm sure I can get through the window. Yes, I'll yell if I need anything.'

I pushed the kitchen window and it opened immediately – the catch had been broken ever since we moved in. I propped a couple of breeze blocks beneath it to help give me a leg up and wriggled through on to the worktop without incident.

It was so strange to be in our little home again. In spite of the police search the place looked much the same as it had on the fateful morning when Carl had bundled me into the van and carried me off to his dreadful hideaway. And that didn't seem right. In the downstairs room I straightened a picture on a wall and replaced a vase, which had been moved from its usual place, and that was about it. I felt in some strange way that the cottage should look different now, now that everything had changed. It didn't. It felt different, though.

Rose Cottage had always seemed so cosy and safe. On that day it felt cold and empty. No Carl. No Carl and Suzanne. That was over, I felt in my bones. The silence in the cottage was deafening. I had always thought that was a daft expression, but suddenly it made sense. You have to experience it to understand. It comes, I think, from being somewhere that has lost all the life it once had, the life that gives it its reason for being. A once grand theatre that has been closed down, a school playground during the holidays, a ruined old building, a forgotten, overgrown garden – these are all places where you can be deafened by silence. I suppose there can be a certain romantic melancholy to it. In Rose Cottage such a silence was simply unbearable.

I rushed upstairs and switched on the radio, which turned out be tuned to Classic FM, just as I had left it. The bed was as I had left it too, the duvet and pillows untidily strewn across it, waiting to be returned to its daytime sofa mode. Carl and I had always been quite meticulous about folding up our bed. It seemed strange to come back to the room and find it like this, numbing, almost.

I glanced at my watch. It wasn't yet eleven o'clock. I had twenty-two hours to wait before I would learn the worst at Penzance police station and be able to travel on to Exeter to see Carl. I thought maybe I should eat and drink something, although I wasn't remotely hungry. I hadn't eaten since nibbling at an uninspiring hospital supper the previous evening and I realised that I should at least attempt to build up my strength. Shivering slightly, I wandered down to the kitchen. I wasn't sure whether the cottage was particularly chilly or if it was me. I thought a cup of tea might indeed help, as long as it wasn't accompanied by Mrs Jackson, and had boiled the kettle before it dawned on me that there wouldn't be any milk. I opened the fridge door and there was one half-empty bottle there. I picked it up and shook it gently. As I had expected, the milk did not move. When I attempted to pour it down the sink I had to prod at it with the handle of a wooden spoon to make it disappear and the sour smell spread instantly throughout the entire cottage. I made the tea and began to drink it black. Then I dug around for anything edible. Carl and I had no deep freeze and normally bought fresh food almost every day. About all I could find that wasn't thoroughly disgusting were a few not too soggy digestive biscuits in a tin. They would have to do. I certainly had neither the inclination nor the energy to go shopping.

I nibbled at a biscuit without much interest and made myself sip the tea. It was no good. I just couldn't be bothered. My chest and head really hurt now. I was beginning to wonder how big a mistake I had made in leaving hospital prematurely. Maybe sleep would help, if anything could.

I dragged myself upstairs, switched on the electric fire to full blast, then half fell on to the bed and buried myself in the duvet.

Almost at once I was overwhelmed by oblivion.

The next thing to enter my consciousness was the sound of a loud banging on the front door. 'Carl,' I thought at once as I sat up groggily. I was wet with sweat. The room now felt stiflingly hot.

It was a second or two before the remains of my brain told me that my first reaction was wrong. He was locked up in the Devon County Prison at Exeter. It could not be Carl.

Anxiously I clambered out of bed, still fully clothed, and hurried down the stairs, eager to see who was outside, but afraid.

I am not really sure who or what I feared at that instant, but it was both a relief and a surprise to see Mariette standing in the alleyway clutching two bulging supermarket carrier bags.

'I phoned the hospital to see how you were. They said you'd discharged yourself. I would have come to pick you up. You should have called . . .'

I nodded apologetically. It had not occurred to me to call Mariette or anyone else. Without Carl I considered myself to be quite alone.

'I've brought some shopping,' explained Mariette unnecessarily, lifting her carrier bags a couple of inches towards me. 'Come on, then, aren't you going to invite me in.'

I stood aside and she bustled past me. She had never been in our house before although I had been to hers several times. Carl and I had not encouraged visitors, except Will with his cheques.

I watched Mariette take in the small, dark dining room and the way Carl and I had tried to brighten it with pictures and candles.

'Shall I put all this in the kitchen?' she enquired and was halfway through the kitchen door before I had chance to reply.

I followed her meekly. She at once opened the fridge. There was nothing inside at all except a few dubious-looking jars of unknown vintage.

'Thought so,' announced Mariette triumphantly. 'You look like you could do with this lot.'

She waved a hand at her bags of groceries and began to unpack while I just stood there watching.

'What time is it?' I asked vaguely.

'Just gone five,' said Mariette. 'I managed to get away early.'

Five in the afternoon. I had slept for nearly six hours. As I began to wake up more I thought that maybe I did feel a little better. Well enough, anyway, to take some notice at least of the provisions Mariette was piling on the worktop. There were all the basics – milk, bread, butter, cheese and eggs, and there was also pasta, chicken, mushrooms, an assortment of other vegetables, some fruit and two bottles of wine – one white and one red.

'We'll start with this,' said Marietta, lightly touching the bottle of white and sounding quite masterful. 'It's cold. Where's the corkscrew?'

I gestured to the cutlery drawer. I was pretty sure there was a corkscrew there even though I could hardly remember when it had last been used. Carl and I only drank wine at home at Christmas, or maybe on our birthdays if we couldn't afford to go out for a celebration meal. Mariette had the bottle open in no time and even found two glasses without asking me where to look. I felt rooted to the spot, completely unable to contribute.

'Right then, let's get stuck in,' she said, in a tone of voice that indicated that she would countenance no argument.

Clutching bottle and glasses, she headed for the chairs around the dining-room table.

'No, let's go upstairs,' I said, coming to life again just a little bit.

She followed me up the rickety staircase and let out a gasp of admiration as she saw the view across the bay from our picture window. The room really was very hot, though.

'No wonder you're sweating,' said Mariette, gesturing towards the glowing electric fire. 'It is the end of April you know, and we are in Cornwall.'

She should have been in that dreadful old damp hut with me, I thought, but she was right about the temperature.

Hastily I switched off the fire and began the familiar transformation of bed into sofa. Mariette put down the bottle and glasses on the little table by the window and came to help me, glancing back over her shoulder as if reluctant to turn away from the view.

The lights were just starting to go on in the town below. The effect was rather wonderful. We were so far above the harbour, which you could glimpse only over and through the convoluted shapes of dozens of rooftops. I always thought it had an unreality about it, particularly at night, like a kind of toy town.

'Stunning room,' said Mariette.

'Yes, Carl and I more or less live up here,' I agreed quickly and without thinking. 'Lived, I should say,' I added more quietly.

Mariette put a hand on my arm, but didn't say anything.

'You know what he's supposed to have done in America, don't you?' I said. 'You know about the manslaughter charge?'

She nodded. 'I heard some garbled account, but I'd hoped maybe it was just a rumour . . .' She didn't finish the sentence.

I shook my head. 'No, I'm afraid it's true. At least that's what the police say. I'll know when I see him, I'm sure of that.'

I was too. I told her how I planned to go to Exeter in the morning, after seeing DC Carter.

'Good, that's exactly what you should do,' she said. Then she poured the wine while, almost automatically, I folded up the duvet and sheet.

'Let's get drunk.' She passed me a brimming glass.

I took a deep drink and thought she could turn out to be an exceptionally good friend.

When we had more or less polished off the bottle Mariette announced that she was cooking me supper. I protested weakly and she ignored me, which was probably all for the best because my head was already beginning to spin a little, the combined effect, no

227

doubt, of half a bottle of wine and not having eaten all day.

'If you don't eat you're really going to get ill,' she said.

'I have really been ill.'

'And now you're going to get better,' she told me, again in a tone of voice with which I was not inclined to argue.

She busied herself in the kitchen and I laid the table and lit the candles. She poked her head through the door and mumbled approvingly. 'Amazing what candlelight hides, isn't it,' she remarked.

'Thanks very much,' I said.

'Oh, you know what I mean,' she added cheerily.

She turned out to be what Gran would have referred to as an excellent plain cook; perfectly grilled chicken, well seasoned and enlivened with just a little garlic and rosemary, was accompanied by potatoes sautéed with onions and crisply cooked green beans. She was quick too, carrying in a tray laden with food in what seemed like no time at all.

We spoke very little about Carl or any of what had happened. Unlike the oppressive Mrs Jackson, Mariette did not try to push me into talking about it and I found I just didn't want to. There wasn't a lot to say, really. All I wanted to do was get through the time before I could see him, meet him face-to-face and ask him to tell me the truth. And the wine certainly helped with that. Mariette swiftly opened the second bottle and by the time we were halfway through it I was beginning to forget about time entirely. I was not used to so much alcohol. I had never thought about it before, but when Carl and I occasionally shared a bottle of wine he always drank the greater part of it.

That evening was my first experience of the therapy of a good relaxed friendship mingled with plenty of alcohol. It was just what I had needed and Mariette, bless her, had instinctively realised it.

Typically, she offered to drive me to Penzance in the morning, but did not press the point when I declined. I told her she had a job to go to, one she enjoyed, that she'd already done enough for me and I could get the train. She did not argue, but instead conjured up yet another of her seemingly endless stories of adventure in love – or in her case perhaps lust was more accurate. This one centred around one of the fitness instructors at the gym she had recently started attending, his cycling shorts and whether or not he stuffed a sock down his lunchbox which, amazingly enough, she had yet to know for certain but felt sure she would be able to reveal from first-hand experience shortly.

Mindless chit-chat may not seem much of a solace to a woman whose life has just fallen apart, but sometimes it's not a bad diversion. By the time we had reached the cheese and fruit stage Mariette actually had me laughing. Quite an achievement in the circumstances.

Mariette, bless her, played nursemaid and insisted on ensuring I was safely tucked up in bed before she left. Almost immediately, and perhaps unsurprisingly after all I had drunk, I sank mercifully into oblivion again.

But I woke not long after four, the wine having done its best before losing its power over me, and tossed and turned for another hour and a half before giving in to wakefulness, getting up and making tea. My head was a bit fuzzy but I did not feel nearly as bad as I probably deserved to. In fact, I was definitely considerably stronger than I had been the previous day.

Just as I was leaving the house to catch the 7.30 train, having located the spare key in its usual place tucked under the edge of the carpet, Will arrived. I opened the front door and he was standing on the doorstep with one hand raised as if about to knock. It was a clumsy meeting. We almost bumped into each other.

He spoke first. 'I went to the hospital last night, I didn't know you'd left . . .'

'I'm sorry,' I said, not really meaning it. I wasn't much concerned with anyone except me and Carl right then. 'I should have let you know . . .'

'No. No. Of course not. It's just that I've got something for you, the rest of what I owe you . . .'

He produced one of those familiar brown envelopes. As ever, the practicalities of life were eluding me. I had not given money matters a thought, beyond being able to get myself to Exeter to see Carl. The sight of the brown envelope concentrated my mind. I realised suddenly how welcome it was. Presumably soon there would be rent to pay and other bills.

I took the envelope from him and studied it almost curiously.

'There's just over £500, I've had a really good run,' he said. 'Sold two of his big abstracts and another couple of the little watercolours as well.'

He sounded almost eager.

'Thank you,' I said, stuffing the envelope in my pocket. There was not time to tuck away the cash in its usual hiding place. And in any case it was a matter of habit not to allow visitors, rare as they had always been, to become aware of our secret cellar.

I was still hovering in the doorway and Will remained on the doorstep directly in front of me. He made no attempt to move. I stepped forward, pulling the door shut behind me and only then, with great reluctance it seemed, did he shift back out of the way.

As I was locking the door he began to talk again. 'I just wondered if I could do anything to help. There must be something . . .'

Yes, there was. I wanted him out of the way, so that I could get to Carl. 'No, Will, there isn't,' I said. 'Now please, you're just going to have to excuse me.' I spoke a little more curtly than I had meant to, but I was in a hurry.

Will looked quite crestfallen. 'Oh, yes, of course,' he muttered in a bleak sort of way.

I had neither time nor inclination to worry about his sensibilities.

He still did not move and I simply sidled my way round him.

'Goodbye, then,' he said.

I think I called a goodbye or something similar to him over my shoulder but, to be honest, I can't really remember.

I was intent upon my journey, hurrying, even though I didn't need to, as I rounded the corner at the end of our alleyway and began to make my way down the hill towards Porthminster and the railway station, leaving Will still hovering outside Rose Cottage.

Luckily the train was punctual and I arrived in the centre of Penzance half an hour or so later with plenty of time to have a cup of coffee on my way to the police station.

DC Carter was older than I had expected. He had a pleasant enough manner but somehow gave me the impression that he was not terribly well prepared about Carl's case.

He was small for a policeman, with hair so dark that I wondered if it were dyed. He had a crumpled look about him and bore a more than fleeting resemblance to the American TV detective Columbo. However, the resemblance stopped sharply at physical appearance. Ray Carter showed no sign whatsoever of Columbo's intelligence.

He kept me waiting for several minutes, sitting on a plastic chair in the reception area of the modern purpose-built police station which was nothing special but something of a palace compared with St Ives, before taking me to his first-floor office.

There he shuffled papers on his desk and did his best to tell me as little as possible.

'As you know, your husband has been charged with abducting you and he will be committed for trial here at Penzance,' he recited unhelpfully. 'We haven't got a date fixed yet, but in any case the committal will be just a formality. You won't need to be there.'

I hadn't thought that far ahead. A trial – me giving evidence against Carl. It didn't seem possible. In spite of everything I still wasn't sure that was what I wanted, or even that I could cope with it. I suppose I was still hoping that when I saw Carl he would put things right, just as he had always done, that he would in some way be able to tell me it was all one big mistake.

'I'm not sure that I want to go ahead with it. Maybe I should withdraw the charge. Can I do that?' I was still feeling far from my best. I stumbled over my words in confusion.

'No, you can't, Mrs Peters,' he said. Everybody still called me that, even though it had turned out to be a much greater lie than I had ever suspected.

'Your husband is accused of a criminal offence. The crown is prosecuting him, not you.'

Carter's voice was weary. He was certainly a very different prospect from either Rob Partridge or DS Perry. I didn't think I was going to get very far with him, but I tried. 'What about the American charge?' I asked. 'I need you to tell me about what Carl did over there, about his daughter and him being wanted for manslaughter.'

Carter sighed and rubbed the back of one hand across his forehead. 'You know about that, do you? And I bet I know who gave you all the inside info, too.'

'The whole of St Ives knows about it as far as I can gather,' I countered, finding just a little bit of spirit.

Carter managed a tight-lipped smile. 'I expect they do, too. Look, I doubt very much that I can tell you any more than you know already. He's a wanted man in America all right and that means the American government can apply for a warrant for extradition. That's really as much as I can say until we know exactly what is going to happen.'

He didn't actually use the phrase 'it's more than my job's worth' but you knew that was what he meant. Ray Carter was the kind of policeman who went strictly by the book.

I made one or two more attempts to extract information from him, but eventually gave up. In any case I didn't have a lot of time to spare. I wanted to catch the 10.04 train to Exeter to see Carl.

As I got up to leave I said softly, more to myself than anything else: 'I didn't even know he had a daughter . . .'

Ray Carter's face softened. 'C'mon, I'll run you down to the station. I know you're off to the prison. It's all fixed, by the way.'

Rob Partridge was probably right. Just because he had probably neither shown any initiative nor taken any kind of risk in his whole life didn't mean DC Carter wasn't a nice man.

The main railway line out of Penzance runs through the heart of Cornwall and then, after Plymouth, meanders along the South Devon coast via Dawlish Warren. Much of the scenery along this tortuous route is quite spectacular, but I wasn't in the mood for sightseeing. I just wished the bloody train would go a bit faster. You can travel the 200-plus miles from Exeter to London in two hours and eight minutes by train. Exeter is only just over 100 miles from Penzance, yet the rail journey takes an extraordinary three hours. That's Devon and Cornwall for you, I thought glumly as we finally chugged into the old county town.

My ticket, the cheapest going, had cost twenty-six pounds. I had less than ten pounds of Will's original forty left. Grateful, suddenly, for his last-minute visit and the brown envelope tucked snugly in my pocket, I took a taxi from St David's Station to the County Prison, a forbidding Victorian building prominently situated high on a hill overlooking the rest of the city. It was a chilling sight and I dreaded to think of Carl locked up inside. For a history enthusiast like myself it was all too easy to imagine a gallows set up before the enormous double gates and a crowd, baying for blood, gathered for a public execution.

Between them, PC Partridge and DC Carter had made all the promised arrangements. I was expected and I gained entry easily enough. I was searched and asked if I had brought anything to give to Carl. I hadn't. To be honest I hadn't even thought about it. I was taken to a room in which other prisoners were already seated at tables talking to visitors.

I sat down as instructed and waited. A drawn and haggard-looking man was led into the room. It was Carl. I know it sounds crazy, but the change in him in such a short time was so dramatic that I barely recognised him. He looked broken.

In spite of everything I felt the tears come to my eyes. I was torn between my belief in the love we had shared and the awful things Carl had apparently done in his life, things that I still found hard to believe. He had held me prisoner, there was certainly no doubt about that, and in such conditions that I had nearly died of pneumonia. I tried to harden my heart against him, but I still could not equate all that I had discovered about Carl with the gentle, loving man I thought I had known so well and the feelings I had had for him for so many years.

He seemed to shuffle rather than walk. He wasn't the same Carl at all. He couldn't have lost any substantial weight in a fortnight, surely, but I thought he was thinner than when I had last seen him, gaunt almost. There was a nervous twitch at the corner of his mouth, which I had not noticed before. Maybe it had not been there. And yet, when he looked at me, his face lit up the way it always did.

He walked straight up to me and wrapped his arms

round me. 'God, I'm glad to see you, Suzanne,' he said.

The prisoner officer standing nearby let him hold me and kiss me for a moment before he stepped forward and gestured for both of us to sit down opposite each other, separated by a table.

Carl leaned forward and grasped my hands. 'I've missed you so much, sweetheart.'

It was weird, almost surreal. He was behaving practically as if the kidnap had never happened. His expression was full of the love and kindness to which I had always been accustomed. But if he knew of how ill I had been he gave no indication of it. And the memory of being kept captive by him in that terrible hut, of being tied to my bed, was too vivid for me to be won over that easily.

'Why did you do it, Carl?' I asked quietly.

At first he looked puzzled. 'I'd never have h-hurt you, not you,' he said haltingly.

I stared at him. That was no answer.

'Why did you do it?' I asked again and this time I could hear the anger in my own voice.

'I wanted to protect you, to look after you, that's all.'

I withdrew my hands from his. Suddenly I didn't want him touching me. 'Oh, not that again, Carl,' I said sharply.

He recoiled from me as if I had hit him. Then he seemed to recover himself and carried on speaking as if he had not been interrupted at all. 'You see, you are so d-different, you were always d-different. You understood. You wanted me to look after you. You needed me to protect you, didn't you?'

The words were all too familiar, much the same as

he had used while he had been keeping me a prisoner. The nervous stammer was familiar too. I did not reply.

'Didn't you?' he asked again.

He was right, of course. I had wanted that. I nodded slightly.

'Yes, of course you did. We were made for each other, weren't we? If only I had found you first everything would have been all right, for both of us.'

I wasn't getting anywhere. I decided to concentrate on what I really wanted to know. 'Carl, you let me believe I had killed my husband. You showed me that knife covered with blood. And you knew I hadn't killed Robert, didn't you?'

He stared at me. 'You did kill him,' he said.

'No, Carl, I didn't. Nobody killed him. He died of sclerosis of the liver. There was blood, but you must have seen that he hadn't been stabbed.'

'He had been stabbed.'

'Carl, don't be so stubborn. You must have seen that . . .'

'Must I? Then why didn't you?'

Was it my imagination or was there a sly note in his voice.

'Carl, I had been badly beaten, I was in shock. You were perfectly calm.' I could still remember vividly how calm he had been, unnaturally so perhaps.

He shook his head sorrowfully. 'I showed you the knife, you saw it, you saw the blood on it.'

'Carl, that knife was never used on Robert,' I continued. 'For all I know you may even have put the blood on the blade.'

His face turned even paler. 'You'd b-believe that of me?'

I didn't reply. I wasn't going to fall for emotional blackmail, not any more.

'I'd never do anything to hurt you,' he said again. It seemed about all he had to say.

'You have hurt me, Carl, you've hurt me beyond measure.'

'I wanted to hide you away, that's all . . .' he whispered, the same mindless babbling, it seemed to me. 'I wanted you always to be mine. I had to keep you safe. Maybe I can explain. There are things I should tell you, if I can find the words after all this time . . .'

'I'm sure there are,' I said, still feeling angry. 'What happened in America, Carl? You're wanted on a manslaughter charge. Is it true that you killed your daughter?'

'Is that what they told you?'

I nodded.

'Then you know, you know what happened.'

I shook my head. 'Carl, I want to hear it from you. I wasn't even aware that you had a daughter, remember?'

He smiled bleakly. 'I haven't,' he said in a dead tone of voice. Then he was silent.

'Carl, just tell me what happened. Please.'

In spite of everything I still wanted him to say there had been a dreadful mistake.

He looked up and I could see the pain in his eyes. 'I wanted our d-dream to last for ever. I just c-couldn't bear it to end. But I knew it was going to. I could feel it h-happening all over again. The one I loved most, the one I most wanted to protect. It was going to go wrong again and I c-c-couldn't let it. You must see that?'

I didn't see anything at all. He was babbling and talking gibberish as far as I was concerned. And he was stammering badly by then. 'Of course I do,' I lied. 'Just tell me, I have to know, did you kill your daughter?' I kept on staring at him. Silent. Waiting.

'Oh yes, I k-killed her, I killed her all right,' he said eventually. His voice was very soft.

I swallowed hard, fighting to keep control. 'Tell me what happened.'

He was looking into the middle distance now, unseeing, unaware I thought, even of where he was. 'My wife never understood, you see. I d-did every-thing for her. I was so proud when she had our child. I worked hard. She wanted for nothing. But it wasn't enough. She always had to have other people around and she shouldn't have n-needed them, that's how the problems started . . .' There were tears in his eyes.

'What happened, Carl?' I asked. 'You must tell me.'

'She said she was leaving me and taking our daughter with her.' He sounded so strange, slightly hysterical almost. 'She said she'd had enough of being shut away with me. That she wanted to live. That she couldn't bear to be with me any more.' He shrugged his shoulders. 'Well, I c-couldn't let her go, could I? I couldn't lose them. They w-were everything to me. Like you. To begin with I thought she was like you, but she wasn't.' His eyes opened wide as if he was surprised by what he was saying. 'I just wanted her to stay, wanted them both to stay . . .' He put his head in his hands.

'So you used drugs, didn't you, Carl? Drugs to subdue your own family, to keep them with you, just like you tried to do with me.'

239

He raised his head slightly. He had started to cry. Tears trickled down his face. 'What do you th-think I am, Suzanne?' he asked.

'I don't know any more, Carl. I really don't.'

'If you have stopped believing in me, Suzanne, there is no point in anything any more,' he said flatly.

'Carl, you drugged me, the woman you are supposed to love more than anything.'

He reached across the table in an attempt to grasp my hands again. I pulled away from him.

'I do love you and I didn't drug you, Suzanne, not really. It was just something to make you sleep.'

That was what he had told me in the dreadful hut. It wasn't the way I saw it, nor the police. Suddenly my anger overwhelmed me. 'Is that what you gave them, your wife and five-year-old child, for God's sake? Just something to make them sleep? I'm sick of your lies, Carl. Even your name is a bloody lie. Tell me, Carl, tell me the truth, damn you, you bastard,' I virtually screamed at him.

Carl more or less cowered in his chair. I don't suppose I had ever yelled at him before. I had certainly never sworn at him like that, not in all our years together. Several other prisoners and their visitors turned to look at us. One of the prison officers took a step forward as if considering intervening, but he retreated again.

Carl merely stared at me in shocked silence.

When I spoke again I managed to do so in a more or less normal tone: 'Just tell me. Did your daughter overdose on drugs you had given her, is that true?'

'The drugs were for her mother, not her.' Carl's voice seemed to come from a long way away.

'Oh, that's all right then,' I snapped at him. 'You

240

didn't mean to drug your child, only her mother, is that it? For God's sake, just tell me, Carl, did your daughter overdose?'

'Oh yes,' he moaned, still cowering in his chair. 'She overdosed . . .'

'And she died,' I said flatly.

'Yes, she died,' he repeated. He was sobbing quite loudly by then. 'I killed her. That's what you came here to hear, isn't it. It's true. It was all my fault. And I've never f-forgiven myself, never . . . I couldn't let it happen again, I just couldn't. I couldn't lose you as well.'

I felt as if I had been kicked in the stomach. Somehow I had expected Carl to deny it, to have some kind of an explanation. Even after what he had done to me I could not really believe that he had killed his own child. Now I had to. He had told me so himself. He was still babbling on. It was a kind of torture to listen to him.

He put his head in his hands. 'I c-couldn't let them leave me. As long as I kept them close to me they would have been safe, you see. I just wanted to keep everyone s-safe, all of them, like I did you . . .'

'Safe from what, Carl?'

Abruptly he stopped crying and stared at me, as if uncomprehending. 'I guess I'm pretty mixed up, but . . .'

I'd had enough. I certainly didn't want any more of his excuses. I had heard all I wanted to hear. 'No, Carl,' I told him firmly. 'I'm not going to listen to any more of this.' I stood up. 'I will never forgive you,' I said. 'And I never want to see you again as long as I live.'

I turned my back on him and headed for the door.

I heard him cry out in anguish but I didn't look round. I half ran out of the room and the tears were running down my face.

I wasn't crying for Carl. And at that moment I could already feel my love for him turning to hate. I was crying for my own lost life, for all those years he had stolen from me.

Fifteen

I returned to the cottage. After all, where else did I have to go? I arrived there just before 9 p.m., having caught the 5.22 from Exeter, and treated myself to a taxi home from Penzance.

I was exhausted and very hungry. There had been a buffet car on the train but I had not had any appetite for a while after seeing Carl and by the time I arrived in St Ives my stomach had begun to send serious messages to remind me that it had not received any food all day. I made tea and toast, and scrambled a couple of eggs. After I'd eaten I lay down on the sofa. I didn't even have the energy to make it into a bed again.

I think sleep could have been my body's way of providing me with a kind of therapy. Had I been bothering to think about it logically I might have worried about being unable to sleep, but instead the oblivion descended almost as soon as I put my head on the pillows.

Once more I was woken by a hammering on the door.

I peered out of the window. At first I couldn't see anybody, but then, illuminated by the street light on the corner, I watched the tall, bulky figure of Will step back from the porch and tip his face towards me, peering at the upstairs window. The last thing I felt able to cope with was a visitor, so I ducked away. I didn't want him to see me. I waited almost a minute before I looked out of the window again. Mercifully Will seemed to have gone.

I looked at my watch. It was almost 10.30, a bit late to come calling, I thought vaguely. Then I slumped on to the sofa again and tried to recapture the oblivion I had achieved before he turned up on the doorstep, but without success at first. At some time during the night I found the energy to turn the sofa into a proper bed and maybe that helped me eventually to fall into a deep sleep.

I was awoken by another loud knocking on the door. But this time it was broad daylight outside. Morning had presumably arrived. I reckoned the caller could reasonably be one of three people – Will again, Mrs Jackson, or Mariette – and it made little difference to me which. I didn't want to see anybody, not even Mariette – in spite of the undoubted success of our last evening together. I did not even look out of the window but waited quietly for the caller to go away.

After a moment or two I heard Mariette's voice calling through the letter box. 'Are you there, Suzanne? It's me. Are you all right?'

I continued to ignore her. After a bit she went away.

I had no intention of even trying to face the world. I just wanted to stay hidden away in my bed. I buried my head in the pillow and ultimately cried myself to sleep.

It was different, you see. Until confronting Carl face-to-face in jail I had been kidding myself, I suppose. But Carl had not been able to tell me that the

American allegation was all a dreadful mistake. Indeed, he had admitted to me that he had killed his daughter. I was devastated.

I had to accept that I had been quite wrong about him all those years. And to face the strong likelihood that he had known that I was not a murderer, that he had let me suffer those awful nightmares for six long years without telling me the only thing that could have made it all stop – and all so that he could have control over me. So that I would be dependent on him.

The letters were part of the way in which he kept me dependent. That made such a dreadful kind of sense.

Even so, in spite of what I had told him in his cell – that he had stolen my life from me – it wasn't really true. Carl had turned me into a fugitive, Carl had taken my freedom from me, but I had to take some responsibility for that too. I had wanted to run away with him and he had not made me unhappy. He had given me a life, a curiously good kind of life, I had to admit. He had promised so long ago when we met in Richmond Park that he would make me happy and at times he had made me quite blissfully happy. I accepted totally that he had loved me – obsessively perhaps, but truly too, there was no doubt about that.

I could even half forgive him the kidnap. Back at home in the comfort of the little house I had shared so contentedly with him it was hard to recall that I had not long ago been frightened of him. It still didn't seem real, somehow. I was so confused.

Maybe I could eventually forgive him for sending the threatening letters, but what I could not live with, could never forgive or forget, was what he had done before he met me. He had killed his own child – and all through his total inability to let go of anyone he loved. I had suffered enough with guilt because I thought I had killed a violent, drunken monster of a man. Carl had been responsible for the death of an innocent child. He had assumed a different personality and invaded my life, and all the time kept his past, even his real name, a secret from me.

I wondered how he had managed to do that for all those years. We had been so close. At least I thought we had been so close.

I slumped into a kind of trance, reliving my years with Carl, going over and over all that I had learned, all that had happened. I lost track of how long I stayed like that, but I suppose I knew that several days must have passed. Physically I felt lethargic and washed out, but there were no signs that the pneumonia threatened to return.

I ate everything that Mariette had brought, all the eggs and milk and cheese, the potatoes and the other vegetables, and all the fruit plus the stale digestive biscuits and a tin of sardines I found lurking in a corner of the cupboard. I wasn't hungry and had no interest whatsoever in food. I ate automatically and for comfort in the same way that I slept, welcoming oblivion again and again.

But when the food ran out I did not consider shopping for more provisions.

I had little concept of night and day. I kept the curtains drawn all the time. I cocooned myself in my own misery.

At some stage a letter arrived from Carl:

My darling Suzanne,

I know I have hurt you but all I wanted to do was to look after you. Please come to see me again and I will try to explain everything to you. I love you so much. I had to keep you safe . . .

There was more of the same but I was no longer impressed by it. He did not mention his daughter once. In fact, the letter only increased my anger and sense of betrayal. I tore it into small pieces and flushed it down the lavatory.

Intermittently, somebody or other knocked on the front door. The days passed. In a way they were endless, it was as if time had stopped. I continued to ignore callers. Mariette always shouted through the letter box. She began to sound increasingly anxious. I don't know why I couldn't bring myself at least to speak to her. But I just didn't want to be bothered.

Eventually, early one evening, I heard a particularly loud, authoritative knock on the door, followed by Mariette's voice through the letter box: 'Suzanne, please, please open the door. I've been so worried about you.'

Again I did not respond.

Then I heard a man's voice. 'Mrs Peters, are you there? This is the police. Constable Brownly. Please open the door.' He repeated the request several times. Then he said: 'Mrs Peters, I'm concerned about your safety and your health. I should warn you that if you don't answer the door I'm going to break in. If you're there, please answer.'

I had been sitting at the top of the stairs, hugging my knees to my chin. Almost grateful that a kind of deadlock had been broken, I got to my feet and stumbled downstairs. My movements seemed clumsy. I knew that once more I was barely functioning.

I opened the front door. Constable Brownly, a very young uniformed officer, looked relieved and as if he didn't know what to do or say next.

Mariette's face, breaking into a smile as I pulled the door towards me, changed to an expression of shock when she saw me.

I hadn't washed or changed my clothes in the time I had shut myself away in the cottage. And I had not even really thought about it until this moment. There were dirty dishes all over the place. My usually immaculate little home was a mess and so was I. That would never have been allowed were Carl still in residence, I reflected obliquely, and just thinking about Carl cut into me again.

I didn't speak. I couldn't find words. All I could feel was a dreadful blankness.

Mariette didn't say anything either. She just stepped towards me and hugged me.

I started to cry again then. And I just couldn't stop.

Mariette took me home and, with remarkable fortitude, her mother agreed that I could stay, even though the cottage was so small and had only two bedrooms. Mariette insisted on giving up her own pretty room at the back of the house for me and said she would be quite comfortable on the sofa bed in the brass-ornamented front room downstairs.

I had neither the grace nor the energy to protest. She undressed me, washed me, lent me a nightie and tucked me up in the little single bed. Still I could not stop crying.

'Mum's called the doctor,' she said.

I began to protest.

'No, you need help. Something to calm you down, maybe.'

I protested more loudly. 'No,' I more or less shouted. 'No, no more drugs.'

'All right, shush,' said Mariette, who was proving to be extremely stoical. 'Whatever you say. Nobody's going to make you do anything you don't want to ever again. I won't let the doctor bully you, don't worry about that.'

I gave in. She was probably right. I did need help.

The doctor turned out to be a young blond woman with old eyes. She introduced herself as Mavis Tompkins and in spite of her age was one of those people who instantly inspired confidence. Quite a bonus for a doctor, I thought. You almost felt better just for seeing her. We talked about therapy and victim support more than drugs, and, although her manner could not have been further from any kind of bullying, I did allow myself to be coaxed into agreeing to virtually all her suggestions.

'Not yet, though, not yet,' I said anxiously, after saying, yes, I would see a therapist.

'All right, not yet,' she acceded perhaps reluctantly, as I buried myself yet again in the dark warmth of Mariette's bed.

I stayed with Mariette for almost three weeks, regaining mental and physical strength, and I shall always be grateful for the patience and support she and her mother unstintingly gave me.

During that time I made no attempt to enquire about Carl and what was happening to him, and I heard nothing further from the police. DS Perry was still in Plymouth, more than likely, and DC Carter was not the kind of man who would make contact if he could avoid doing so. He wouldn't want to risk stirring up trouble for himself unnecessarily.

I told myself I didn't care what happened to Carl, as long as I never had to see him again.

I suppose I had a kind of breakdown. Not surprising when you considered all I had been through. I blocked everything out. Most important of all was to block Carl out.

And that might have been the way it would remain, had it not been for the intervention of Will Jones.

My time with Mariette and her mother was actually surprisingly peaceful, in spite of my distressed state of mind, but after three weeks I knew I must be overstaying my welcome. The sofa bed in the front room couldn't be that comfortable, and Mariette continued to insist that I remained in her bedroom until I was both mentally and physically stronger. However, when I eventually expressed a desire to return to Rose Cottage both Mariette and her mother were worried that the house itself might upset me and suggested I looked for somewhere else to rent.

Perhaps stubbornly, I insisted on going back to the cottage. More than anything else I wanted at least to try to bury the demons that lurked there. I felt it was something I had to do alone, so I made my own way up the hill, carrying the small bag containing the few clothes and books Mariette had collected for me.

I had not been back since the night she and the policeman had knocked so forcefully on the front door. I remembered clearly enough that we had left the place in a fearful mess, complete with all those dirty dishes piled in the kitchen sink. I just hoped no mice or even rats had been attracted.

But when I unlocked the front door a pleasant surprise awaited me. The place looked and smelled fresh and clean, there were newly cut flowers in a vase on the table and not a dirty dish anywhere to be seen.

'Bless you, Mariette,' I said to myself with feeling.

She had been back to collect one or two things for me and to pick up the mail occasionally, and must have worked her magic on the cottage then. There had been no further letters from Carl. Maybe he had accepted that I wanted nothing more to do with him.

Rose Cottage was a wonderful surprise. I spent the day pottering around and realised that I must be beginning to cope. At any rate I was functioning after a fashion. I walked down to the town to do some shopping. I was still conscious of curious stares and had yet to venture back into any of the hostelries Carl and I had frequented. Nonetheless I didn't find the exercise too difficult.

Steve, the matinée idol fishmonger, fussed over me charmingly and insisted on giving me a small, beautifully dressed fresh crab as a present. 'Good to see you back, Suzanne,' he said. 'I've got some first-class fresh halibut coming in in a couple of days. I'll save you a piece.'

I had smiled wanly. Halibut, Carl's favourite. The king of fish, he called it. How the memories flooded back.

At home that evening I blessed Steve for his crab, not least because it meant I barely had to cook. I boiled some rice to eat with the crab and made a little green salad. The crabmeat was rich and sweet and, as ever, the plain boiled rice brought out its flavour beautifully – that was something, one of so many things, Carl had taught me. As I ate I realised I had not enjoyed a meal in a long time, probably not since before it all happened.

Afterwards I settled mindlessly in front of the TV for a couple of hours. I went to bed before midnight and slept surprisingly well – no more nightmares, not of any kind.

In the morning I made a concentrated effort to think about my future: what I was going to do next. I needed to work, I understood that. I had no money and no apparent way of acquiring any. It was hard to imagine what kind of work I could do, Carl had certainly been right about that. The library job had long been filled and, in any case, I still doubted that I would ever have been regarded as suitably qualified.

Mariette and her mother had kindly allowed me to stay with them free of charge but there had been rent to pay on the cottage and other bills to settle, and there was not a lot left of the £500 Will had given me – certainly not enough to pay for the next month's rent, which would soon be due.

I counted the remaining notes and coins, still in the original envelope over and over again. Each time it came to the same amount: £110 25p. An electricity bill for almost £100 had come in the post that morning. That effectively took care of that. Suddenly I began to feel quite desperate. How was I going to live?

Strange for me to be worrying about money after a lifetime of having someone else to take care of such matters. It was actually quite frightening and was one bit of independence I could still do without, I thought wryly.

Then I had an idea. I wondered if Carl might have left any cash in our usual hiding place. I thought it unlikely, I assumed he would have taken whatever money he had with him when he rushed me off to that awful damp shed in the middle of nowhere, but you never knew.

On the off chance I decided to have a look in the cellar. I rolled back the linoleum floor covering and found the crowbar under the sink. I had never prised up the flagstone that served as a trapdoor on my own before and it did not prove to be an easy task. I had to lean on the iron bar with all my weight in order to budge the stone at one side. Then I wedged a piece of wood under the open end, did the same trick with the crowbar on the other side and somehow managed to slide the stone to one side. I fetched the small ladder that lived under the stairs and lowered it down through the hole.

First putting a torch in my pocket, I climbed carefully down. Although I had been as tickled as Carl when he discovered the cellar, I did not much like being in it and certainly not alone.

Resolutely I switched on the torch and felt behind the pile of Carl's paintings, which were neatly stacked in one corner. There was no sign of the leather document case.

'Damn!' I said out loud. I wondered if the police had found it in the shed or in Carl's van, and if it was at the police station now. I had not thought to ask. But even if it were there, I doubted they would hand it over to me. After all, it was Carl's property, I supposed.

I shone my torch over the paintings. There were five of them, all abstracts. Will would take any number of the chocolate box landscapes, but never more than two or three of the abstracts at a time. There was a very limited market and he just didn't have the wall space. In spite of various attempts, Carl had not found any other gallery in St Ives prepared to take his abstracts at all. Still, they were worth as much as £200 or £300 each on a good day. I decided to get them out of the cellar and see if I could at least get them displayed somewhere. Maybe I could play the sympathy ticket.

I carried the five paintings to the foot of the ladder, then climbed up a couple of rungs reaching down to pick them up one by one, lift them as high as I could and push them out on to the kitchen floor. As I did so I reflected that any revenue from their sale would surely technically belong to Carl, but I thought I might be able to persuade Will at any rate to bend the rules. He had already done so once, after all.

When I had successfully manhandled the paintings out of the cellar I carried them into the dining room and propped them up around the walls. They were good, no question about that. Whatever else he had done in his life, Carl could certainly paint. For just a fleeting moment I experienced a flash of nostalgia for what might have been. But I knew all I could do now was concentrate on the present. Carl was in jail. Our life together was over.

I decided to have a final look in the cellar to check that there was nothing else down there of value. There wasn't. I shone the torch carefully into every nook and cranny revealing only some cans of paint, sidelined from Carl's studio, a box of scrubby brushes, several packets of short stubby crayon ends and a number of used sketch pads, all arranged in tidy piles. Carl didn't like throwing things away, just in case he might ever need them again one day. There were also a couple of cardboard boxes, one containing Christmas decorations and the other some candles and some old magazines. I thought I might at least make use of the candles and dragged the box over to the ladder.

Then I heard a knock on the front door.

I had promised Mariette faithfully that whatever happened I would never repeat my performance of locking myself in the house and ignoring callers. So dutifully I clambered up the ladder, switched off my torch and put it on the kitchen worktop, shouting 'just a minute'. I shut the kitchen door firmly behind me and hurried to open the front door.

Will Jones stood on the doorstep smiling broadly. He was carrying a large bunch of roses. 'Welcome home,' he said and thrust the flowers into my hand.

I smiled my appreciation. I knew that Will had enquired regularly after my welfare during the time that I had stayed with Mariette, and that she had relayed to him my thanks and explained that I really did not want to see anyone for a bit. I simply hadn't been able to face visitors. I still didn't exactly relish the prospect, but Will just might have another of those welcome brown envelopes on his person. 'I was just thinking about you, Will, come on in,' I invited. Well, it was true in a way, albeit not quite the way he seemed to take it.

His face positively lit up. 'I thought you could do with a man about the place.' He beamed at me. It seemed a very strange thing to say in the circumstances.

I couldn't think of any reply, really. He followed

me into the dining room and I gestured to the paintings all around us. 'I was hoping you might be able to find a place for a couple of these, and bend the rules a bit about payment,' I said. 'I could certainly do with the money . . .'

Will didn't even glance at the paintings. He just stood there in the middle of the room staring at me. 'You look prettier than ever,' he said.

I glanced at him curiously. 'Go on upstairs and I'll bring up some coffee,' I instructed, slightly thrown by his rather bizarre compliment.

In the kitchen I didn't bother to put the stone back over the cellar. Will would have heard me and wanted to help, and Carl and I had always been strict about keeping our hiding place a secret. In any case I was fairly used to dodging around it, and I quickly made coffee and carried a tray upstairs to join Will.

He was as avuncular as ever, but I had even more difficulty than usual making small talk.

I sat on the sofa next to him and found myself noticing how often he touched me as we chatted. He'd always done so, of course, but it hadn't seemed to matter when Carl was around.

Suddenly he leaned very close to me and put his arm round me. He had often done that before too, but I instinctively knew that this time was different. 'You miss Carl, Suzanne, don't you?'

'Yes,' I responded truthfully.

'The two of you were so perfect together.' There was something in Will's voice that I couldn't quite identify, something not very pleasant.

I studied him more closely, perhaps seeing him for the first time, this man I had both liked and trusted. I suppose I had never really looked beyond the flamboyant exterior before, never seen beyond the showman. His silver bouffant hairdo no longer looked attractively eccentric – just rather pathetic. He had always been a kind of parody of himself. His eyes were red-rimmed. He was definitely under some sort of strain.

'You never did understand,' he went on. 'That was the problem. And I could never tell you . . . never find the words, you see . . .'

He pulled me even nearer to him and I realised suddenly that his hand had dropped down so that he was lightly stroking my breast. Curiously, perhaps, it was still the last thing I had anticipated.

'You miss Carl in every way, I expect . . .'

His voice was very low. Suggestive.

I wrenched myself away from him and stood up. 'Don't be silly, Will,' I said, trying hard not to make too much of it.

But I had said the wrong thing. There was anger in his voice when he spoke again. 'Don't be silly, Will,' he repeated, his voice mocking mine. 'That's how you think of me, that's how you've both always thought of me, isn't it? Silly Willy, we can treat him how we like, he'll still come running, still knock himself out trying to flog Carl's bloody awful paintings.'

I was stunned by his sudden outburst. He was speaking in a kind of bitter whine. 'What on earth's the matter with you, Will?' I asked. 'You've always admired Carl's painting, haven't you? And I thought we were friends.'

'Pah,' snarled Will. 'He's no better than any of the others, just very very average. But he had you, didn't he? And together you were . . .' his voice softened '. . . so special.'

257

Was that it then? Will was jealous of Carl and me?
I couldn't believe my ears. It had never occurred to
me. Not to either of us.

'I was your friend all right, oh yes, I was such a
good friend,' he went on. 'But you two, you barely
noticed me, did you? If it didn't suit you, you turned
me away. Remember the night I brought you the pink
champagne? It made no difference, did it? I could
have brought diamonds. You two wanted to be alone
together. Nothing else mattered. You just turned me
away . . .'

He paused. I didn't speak. Merely calling him silly
had brought on this outburst? All sorts of jumbled
thoughts were beginning to occur to me.

Meanwhile the tirade continued. It was as if, once
he had started, he couldn't stop. 'You never took me
seriously, did you? You had no idea about my
feelings. Not either of you. And you, Suzanne, you're
so soft and lovely, I always liked so much just to touch
you . . .'

I shivered, thinking of how often he had done that.
But in such a way that I had never really minded and
neither had Carl. He was quite an actor, was Will, but
then, we had always thought that.

'I knew there was no hope, of course, there was only
ever Carl for you. So I was prepared to accept that.
Just to be near you. I tried to tell you how it was, I
really did. I was prepared to settle for friendship. But
you kept shutting me out, didn't you? Both of you.
Making a joke of my feelings. It was so unfair . . .'

His voice was wheedling and yet very hard. He
really was beginning to scare me.

Sometimes things are suddenly very clear and you
wonder how you missed them before. How could

Carl and I have been so blind? But then, we had always been so totally wrapped up in each other. Will was right about that.

I thought of the time he had come to dinner and told us how he envied us, how we had so much, how he would have swapped his gallery, his car, everything he had for what we had. And yes, Carl had made a joke of it, as he usually did. How Will must have hated that. 'Why are you telling me all this?' I asked.

'I thought you might have known already.'

I had known nothing. But I was beginning to realise a lot. I had a feeling I had made an awful error of judgement, that I had got something horribly wrong.

I took a deep breath. 'Did you threaten us, did you send the letters, Will?' I asked. I spoke very softly, trying to keep my voice expressionless.

He looked for a moment as if he were going to deny it. Then he turned on me. 'Of course I did,' he shouted. 'And you never suspected for a bloody moment, did you. Not Silly Willy, whom you could treat like dirt and I'd still ask for more.' He laughed. It was not a pretty sound.

'Why, for Christ's sake?' I asked, really scared now. 'Why did you do it?'

'I've just told you,' he said. 'It was the way you treated me, both of you. And if I couldn't have you I was going to hurt you, Suzanne, you and him. I wanted to give that perfect . . .' he spat out the word then continued '. . . that perfect life of yours a shaking.'

'You tortured us,' I yelled at him. 'We did nothing to deserve that.'

'I was the one who was tortured.'

Will's red-rimmed eyes burned into me. My legs felt like jelly.

'I thought Carl had sent the letters, done it all, I really believed that.' I was thinking aloud really.

Will leered at me. 'Carl?' he repeated wonderingly. 'That was a bonus for me, wasn't it? I never expected that.'

I wanted to hit him, but I didn't have the courage. I couldn't believe that this evil, poisonous side of Will had been lurking all this time and neither Carl nor I had seen it. But, of course, we had rarely seen anything much except each other.

Then Will stood up and I became disconcertingly aware of how big he was. We were quite alone and the walls of Rose Cottage were three and a half feet thick. Carl and I had never heard the neighbours, nor they us as far as I knew. I began to wonder what Will had really come to the cottage for. It was hard to believe that he would have confessed all this on the spur of the moment. Could he be that uncontrolled? What was he intending to do now?

He began to speak again. 'I could have given you so much more than he ever did, you know, in every way . . .'

I didn't want to hear any more. I just wanted the man out of my house. 'You'd better go, Will,' I said, struggling to stay calm.

'Really? Yes, and every time before I've always gone, haven't I? Meekly left you and that pretentious American bastard alone whenever you wanted me to. Or that's what you thought, wasn't it?'

He took a menacing step towards me. I began to think that I might be in real danger.

'I've stood outside, you know, late at night, listening to you having sex. Listening to your cries, Suzanne.'

260

I cringed, feeling slightly sick. Was it true, I wondered? It could have been. Carl and I had almost always slept with the window open a little. We'd never given it a thought. I shuddered involuntarily.

'C'mon, why don't you give me just one chance,' he said. 'Let me have you. Let me give it to you, show you what it can really be like. Were you crying out because you were satisfied, Suzanne, or because you needed more? I doubt that pathetic bastard ever fucked you properly, did he? I doubt he had it in him . . .'

My instinct was to cower away from him. That had always been my instinct when faced with a threat. But not this time. Instead of taking a step backwards I made myself take a step forward towards Will. He towered over me. I refused to allow myself to be daunted. 'Will, I despise you,' I told him. 'The only way you are ever going to have me is to rape me. Is that what you want? Is that what you are, as well as everything else, a rapist?'

Something flickered across his eyes.

He reached out with one hand, thrust it between my legs and pushed hard upwards, so hard that it hurt, which was no doubt his intention.

I tried not to flinch.

For what seemed like for ever he stood in front of me staring at me, his hand thrust against my crutch, his long bony fingers digging into me. I returned his stare as levelly as I could.

Eventually and abruptly he removed his hand and spoke. 'You're not worth it, are you? I've come almost to hate you, you know. That's what happens if you keep rejecting someone.'

He stepped back. 'Carl murdered his daughter, he

261

kidnapped and drugged you, Suzanne,' he said calmly enough. 'You can't still feel anything for him, surely?'

He didn't wait for a reply. He turned on his heel, ran down the stairs and left the cottage through the front door.

I felt sick. I half fell on to the sofa bed, put my head in my hands and wept.

Sixteen

I remained crouched on the edge of the sofa bed, crying, for several minutes after Will had gone. Then very suddenly I realised what I must do next. I had to see Carl. I had to tell him what Will had been doing to us. Will's confession changed so much. Carl had not been responsible for any of the threats, not sent the letters. And, just maybe, neither had he deliberately deceived me all those years about the way Robert had died. I had to tell Carl that I had done him a big injustice. This time I had to get to the bottom of it all.

I jumped to my feet, grabbed my coat, shoved all my money in my pocket and headed down to the town. I stopped at the first call box on the way to phone Penzance police station and for once got almost straight through to the police officer I wanted to speak to. 'I want to see my husband,' I told DC Carter. 'Can you arrange it for me?'

'No problem,' he replied. 'He's on remand and you can visit more or less when you like, we've already told you that. When do you want to go?'

'Today – as soon as I can.' I planned to catch the next train out of St Ives and then pick up the first available Intercity Service at either St Erth or Penzance.

'Ah, that is a problem,' said Carter. 'He's due to

appear at the Magistrates Court in Penzance this afternoon. It's his committal . . .'

'Penzance!' Just half an hour or so's journey by train. Maybe I didn't need to travel all the way to Exeter after all. 'I'll come to Penzance, then . . .'

'Whoa,' said DC Carter. 'Hang on a minute. He's only being brought in for committal proceedings. It's a formality. He won't be allowed visitors here. Then straight back to Exeter. You won't be able to see him.'

I wasn't really listening. If Carl was going to be in Penzance later that day then so was I. I barely said goodbye to DC Carter, who was still chuntering away at the other end of the line when I hung up. I ran most of the way to the little station out at Porthminster Beach. I wasn't sure of the train times and was terrified of just missing one, and then maybe just missing Carl.

In the end I had to wait half an hour for the next train. It was a very lovely day and the first part of the track runs right along the coast but I was too distracted to admire the beauty of the Cornish countryside. By the time I got to Penzance I could hardly contain myself. It wasn't far from the station to St John's Hall, the old Victorian building opposite the police station which I knew housed Penwith Magistrates Court, but this time I didn't walk. I felt as if I couldn't afford to waste a minute so, my financial considerations of earlier that day now paling into insignificance, I took a taxi.

As soon as I came close to St John's Hall I realised something was amiss. There seemed to be police everywhere. The traffic slowed to a halt, and I jumped out of the cab and paid off the driver. A patrol car, lights flashing, and siren in full song, came out of the police station yard so fast as I crossed the road towards the court that I only narrowly avoided being run over.

Both the entrances to St John's Hall, which had once been home to Penzance Assizes and the old hanging judges, were cordoned off and uniformed constables stood on sentry duty.

I kept walking, desperate to see Carl and trying to look as if I was in some way involved in official business, even though I hardly looked the part in my jeans and sweater. I had no success. I was stopped at once by one of the policemen sentries. 'I am afraid you can't go in, madam,' he said.

'I have to,' was all I could manage.

'Sorry, madam,' replied the officer in tones that brooked no dissent. 'We have an escaped prisoner situation and nobody is allowed to enter or leave the vicinity.'

'But I have to see my husband,' I insisted, hardly hearing what he was saying, just aware that he was preventing me from fulfilling my purpose.

I half tried to push past him.

He put a restraining hand on my arm and positioned himself more solidly in front of me.

'Well, you can't go in there to see him, that's for certain. Who is your husband anyway?'

'Carl Peters, he's appearing in the Magistrates Court today. He's been in jail in Exeter. If I could just see him for a few minutes . . .'

I saw the startled expression on the young constable's face. 'But, but, that's . . .' He stopped speaking abruptly, as if suddenly aware that he was about to give away something he shouldn't. At that moment I knew with devastating clarity who had escaped that morning from Penwith Magistrates Court.

'Oh, my God,' I said. 'It's Carl, isn't it, Carl who has gone . . .'

'I really can't say, madam,' said the constable, his head swivelling in all directions as if he were desperately seeking rescue from a situation he had no idea how to handle. 'But I think maybe I should get someone to talk to you . . .'

An expression of some relief crossed his youthful features as he half turned away from me and, still with a hand on my arm, called to a uniformed sergeant walking across the car park. The sergeant came over. The constable released his grip on my arm, asked if I would wait a moment, and he and the sergeant went into a huddle.

I could only catch the odd word.

'Mrs Peters . . .' 'Here to see her husband . . .' and finally, from the sergeant: '. . . fetch DC Carter.'

The sergeant asked me to wait just a moment and made it clear he was not going to engage in any further conversation. I protested fruitlessly while the constable retreated in the direction of the court room, but fortunately reappeared swiftly with a harassed-looking DC Carter.

'Mrs Peters,' said Carter in a voice even wearier than the one he had adopted the first time I met him. 'I wonder if you'd mind coming across to the station with me. I think you and I had better have a chat.'

It seemed that Carl had been transported from Exeter along with several other prisoners by the private security agency now employed by the Devon and Cornwall Constabulary.

'But how on earth did he get away?' I stuttered. 'Carl wouldn't know how to plan an escape. He's no jail breaker.'

'Don't bloody need to be nowadays,' muttered DC Carter grumpily. 'Grasped his opportunity, didn't he. Over the road waiting to be called, realised there wasn't a lot to keep him there. So off he trots . . .'

Carter looked as depressed as I felt but not at all surprised. We were talking in his first-floor office. He rummaged in a trouser pocket and produced a crumpled packet of cigarettes. 'Smoke?' he enquired. I shook my head. He nodded his. 'Horrible filthy habit,' he said just as grumpily. 'Bloody private security,' he went on. 'Ever since Centurion took over transporting prisoners it's been bloody chaos.'

His vocabulary might have been limited but he was being much more communicative than previously and even in the state I was in I noticed that he was being uncharacteristically indiscreet. He was angry, I could see. I did not speak. I did not want to break the spell.

'Half the time there's no police presence at all over there on court days,' he said, gesturing vaguely through the window in the direction of St John's Hall. 'Everything's about saving bloody money, isn't it? And Centurion operate on minimum staff. We've had people being given custodial sentences and asked to wait at the back of the court till a security officer can be found to cart them off somewhere. They just bloody walk out, don't they? Bloody madness.' He shook his head woefully. 'Six months I've got left of my thirty years, then I'm on my toes. And now this has happened. I'm supposed to be winding down gently, I am. Some bloody hopes . . .'

His mood had its uses. But I was beginning to have had enough. 'Is Sergeant Perry back in Cornwall yet?' I asked hopefully.

'No such bloody luck.'

We both felt the same about that, then.

'Look. I still can't understand how Carl got away. He was already in custody, wasn't he? Surely he would have been in a cell.'

'Yeah.' Carter spat out the word. 'In a cell with the bloody key left in the lock. Stupid bastards deny it, of course, but this isn't the first time. All Johnny has to do is put his hand through the hatch in the door, turn the key, then leg it up the steps out into the car park. There's only a Yale lock on that outer door. Dead easy. 'E's away and those buggers from Centurion don't even know it, dozy lot of bastards . . .'

DS Carter took a long, slow drag on his cigarette. Maybe the nicotine jerked his brain into action. 'Right Mrs Peters, now you know,' he said, trying, although not succeeding very well, to sound brisk and efficient. 'And it's me supposed to be doing the interviewing. So let's have some answers from you, shall we?'

I only wished I had some answers to give.

'Have you any idea where your husband might have gone?'

I shook my head. I did not even know why he had run. Surely he couldn't think he would get away for good. But if he hadn't planned it, just grasped an unexpected opportunity in the way DC Carter had described, well, that did make a kind of sense. After all, I knew only too well that it was in Carl's nature to run away from things, to try to hide rather than to face reality.

'Might he be trying to find you?' Carter asked.

I thought about it. I considered it quite likely. I had not had any contact with him since that one visit at Exeter. I had not answered his only letter and that would have hurt him deeply. He knew that I had lost all trust in him and for a time had believed him capable of almost anything. Yet I did not doubt that Carl would still love me, still want me. That was the kind of man he was.

'Maybe,' I replied. 'I just don't know. I'm stunned, you see. Whatever I expected it wasn't this. Never this. I didn't even imagine someone like Carl could escape . . .'

I was indeed bewildered.

'Why did you want to see him so desperately today, anyway?' Carter's voice was sharper now and it made me concentrate, or at least attempt to focus properly upon the events of the day.

'I found out that Carl wasn't behind any of the threats. It changes things. I'm not sure quite how much, but I need to know . . .' I heard my own voice trailing off.

'What threats?' asked DC Carter.

In spite, or maybe because, of my distress I was suddenly irritated. It had been like this ever since DS Perry had been shipped off to Plymouth. Carter had never appeared to get to grips with the case. I suppose the whole thing had already seemed like a mere formality to him. All he had to do was tie the final knots. It was rather more than that to me and, of course, to Carl. Maybe if Carter had had his finger properly on the pulse, things would not have gone as far as they had. I had no real reason for thinking that, I just didn't know what to think any more.

'The threatening letters we received, the damage to our van, the writing on our door,' I recited as patiently as I could manage.

He looked blank.

This time I could not keep the irritation out of my voice. 'Horrible messages which frightened me so much I went to the police. It was what started everything. Otherwise there wouldn't be a kidnap charge against Carl . . .'

'Oh yes, I remember,' said Carter, but I wasn't sure whether he did or not. 'He'd still be wanted on a manslaughter charge in the States, though, wouldn't he?'

My patience was running out. 'That's got nothing to do with it,' I snapped, although I knew what I was saying could not be true.

'And the man did kidnap you and drug you. Whatever brought it about, he had the capacity to do that. Nothing alters that.'

He was right, of course. But the fact remained that if Will Jones hadn't launched his hate campaign against us it was highly possible that none of this would have happened. Perhaps Carl and I would still be living our quiet, contented, obsessively close lives in Rose Cottage. Is that what I wished for? I had come to believe that Carl had deceived me terribly throughout our time together, but maybe that wasn't so, after all. Not entirely, anyway. I wasn't sure of anything except that I was desperate to know the whole truth. I had changed in the last few weeks. I didn't want to be an ostrich any more. I didn't want to hide my head, or any other part of me, come to that, in the sand for the rest of my life.

'So, these letters and the rest of it, do you know who was responsible?'

'Yes.'

'Well, who was it?'

'It doesn't matter,' I replied and in a way it didn't. Carl was not responsible, which was all that mattered.

'Whoever did so has almost certainly committed an offence and could be prosecuted for harassment,' continued DC Carter in a flat monotone.

I knew that and I didn't want it to happen. There would be another trial. I would have to give evidence. I was afraid of Will, after all that he had said and done, but I told myself that he was no longer a threat and that reporting him to the police could make him more of a danger rather than less.

'More importantly, maybe Carl will go after him,' DS Carter went on.

It seemed extraordinary to hear Carl described in these terms. In spite of everything it just wasn't the way I saw him. 'Carl doesn't even know who did it.'

'Indeed, and it must be driving him mad not knowing, mustn't it. Not knowing who destroyed his life. Perhaps he is trying to find out right now and what will he do when he does, I wonder?' Carter's words were ominous.

I was startled. 'What do you mean?'

'The man you call your husband is a kidnapper,

wanted in America on a manslaughter charge, Mrs Peters. What the hell do you think I mean?'

I just stared at him. I knew all of that was true, but I still just could not relate any of it to the gentle man I had shared my life with, the man who had rescued me from another kind of hell. I had lived with violence. I knew it inside out. Carl didn't fit the bill and yet his record did. I gave in to the pressure. 'Will Jones,' I said. 'He runs the Logan Gallery in St Ives.'

Carter then questioned me for a few minutes about why Will had made the threats, what they had said, what they meant and how many there had been. Some of it was old ground, some of it wasn't. I told him everything I could.

Eventually the detective constable nodded in a vaguely approving way. 'Good,' he said. 'Now we're getting somewhere at last. I'll send a team round straight away, as much for the sad bastard's own safety as anything else.'

Again the chilling inference.

'Right, now what to do about you,' said Carter, thumping the table. 'It's back to St Ives, I reckon.'

I nodded. 'Yes, I'll go home, I'll get the train . . .'

Maybe Carl would try to contact me. After what Carter had said I didn't know whether I hoped he would or not. My emotions were so mixed now.

'You're joking,' said Carter. 'He could be waiting for you. I'll drive you over. He's not there yet, we know that much. Uniform are already watching the place. Just give me one moment.'

He left me alone in his office for no more than a couple of minutes before returning with a uniformed woman constable whom he introduced as WPC Carol Braintree. 'She's coming with us,' he said. By the book, I assumed. I felt as if I was getting to know DC Carter,

As he led the way through the station towards the front reception I became very aware that all around was the bustle of a major manhunt. The terrible reality of it was only just beginning to hit me. Carter briefly opened a door of a room where a number of police officers were manning phones, studying wall charts and checking information on computers.

'Taking Mrs Peters back, boss,' he shouted to an officer wearing a uniform that even to my inexperienced eye indicated a very senior rank.

There was a brief exchange concerning whether or not Rose Cottage had yet been searched.

'He can't be there, boss, but we'll check the place out now just to make sure,' said Carter.

I heard mention of roadblocks and railway checks. I tried to focus on the wall chart at the far end of the room. I wasn't given long enough.

'Right, c'mon then,' said Carter, propelling me along. WPC Braintree kept very close to me as if she suspected that at any moment I might try to join Carl on the run. I looked back over my shoulder at the bustling room. It seemed extraordinary that Carl was the cause of all that activity.

Carter smiled grimly. 'We're closing off Cornwall,' he said. 'He won't get far, your Carl. It's one of the advantages of being stuck on the end of England. One road and one railway line, and that's about your lot. We can shut the county down just like that . . .' He snapped his fingers. I couldn't believe any of it was happening.

In the car – Carter's own private vehicle, I thought – the radio came on as he switched on the ignition.

Within minutes there was a news bulletin. 'A man has escaped from police custody in Penzance' I heard. There followed a brief description of Carl and what he had been charged with, and then the words which perhaps hit me harder than anything at all. 'Police advise that this man is dangerous and on no account should be approached. If you see anyone answering to his description contact any police station . . .'

Seventeen

Rob Partridge, in jeans and sweater, was leaning against the wall at the end of Rose Lane trying desperately to look inconspicuous. Difficult when you have bright-orange hair. And not only did the hair not help, but he was so well known in St Ives that half the town would have recognised him at once, with or without his uniform, and assumed from his behaviour that he was on some kind of watching brief. Including Carl, I reflected wryly.

We had to drive past at first because Carter could not find a parking space. Rob waved in a resigned sort of way. Eventually the detective managed to park, several hundred yards up the hill. He and WPC Braintree walked on either side of me as we made our way back down to the alleyway.

'No sign of him, then?' remarked Carter, rather unnecessarily, I thought.

Surely not even Rob Partridge would have remained standing around like a spare one if he had spotted the man who appeared suddenly to have become the most wanted criminal in England – well, the west of England, anyway.

Rob shook his head.

'Right,' said Carter. 'Time to search the place.'

Rob spread his hands in front of him. 'He's not in there, Ray. There's only one way in, and I've been here ever since I got the alert. He couldn't have arrived before me . . .'

I knew, of course, that you could get in over Mrs Jenkins's wall at the back, but I couldn't be bothered to mention it. In any case, Carl would still have had to go through Mrs Jenkins's front gate and make his way along the path between the two houses to get into her back garden, which was, apart from the climbable wall into our place, completely surrounded by other tall buildings.

Carter grunted. 'I'm doing this one by the book, Rob,' he said. 'Six months I've got to go. Six flaming months. If anything goes wrong with this can of worms I'm not going to be carrying it.'

I thought I knew what he meant. Rob grinned amiably. WPC Braintree remained silent. She didn't say a lot. For a fleeting moment I thought I half caught her rolling her eyes to heaven. If she had done so neither Carter nor Partridge spotted it.

'Stay watching, Rob,' said Carter. The orange-haired policeman shrugged indifferently. He had always seemed like the kind of man who would prefer to be told what to do rather than have to make decisions.

I used my key to unlock the front door and led the way inside the cottage. If I had any doubts at all that Carl might have sneaked his way past the police guard outside – however dubious it might be – I knew straight away that it hadn't happened. He wasn't there. He hadn't been there. Difficult to explain how I was so sure, but this was my house and he was my man. I knew.

Carter didn't think Carl was there either, I suspected, but he went through the motions. By the book, like he said.

WPC Braintree was despatched upstairs. Carter looked carefully around the dining room and made something of a show of peering under the table. I pulled one of the chairs back from the old table and sat down to wait. It wouldn't take long to search Rose Cottage, that was for certain.

Carter began to head for the kitchen. Just in time I remembered that I had not replaced the flagstone. 'Careful,' I warned. 'The cellar's open.'

'What's down there anyway?' he asked.

I explained about the old forgotten cellar, which Carl and I had discovered and which we used as a store-room.

'Right, better have a gander, then.' I could see him through the kitchen door bending over looking down into the hole in the floor. 'Can't see a darned thing; pitch black down there. Gotta torch?' he called.

I joined him in the kitchen, picked up the torch, still sitting quite obviously where I had left it on the worktop as it happened, and passed it to him. He climbed down the ladder and shone it meticulously into every corner. Completely unnecessary. It was, after all, very small and all that was left in it were the few discarded bits and pieces from Carl's studio and our old Christmas decorations. Clearly, there was nowhere for anyone to hide.

After emerging up the ladder, he made his way out into the backyard, He asked for a key to Carl's studio, which I gave him even though you could actually see into it well enough from outside through the big windows that ran along its entire length.

Eventually he seemed satisfied and WPC Braintree had by then come down from upstairs to announce, predictably, that there was no one up there either, nor anything of any interest.

'Right,' said DC Carter. 'I don't think you should stay here, Mrs Peters.'

'Why ever not?' I asked.

Carter sighed. 'Because your husband is a dangerous man. He has already held you in captivity. He could well be intending to harm you.'

I still could not get my head around it. I listened in amazement.

'Have you anywhere you could go?' asked WPC Braintree.

I could only think of one place: poor Mariette and her mother. They really didn't deserve to be lumbered with me again and in any case I wasn't at all sure that was what I wanted, either. 'I'd much rather stay here,' I said. 'I'm sure Carl won't hurt me. Anyway, I doubt he'll even try to come back to the cottage. He must know that you'd be looking here . . .'

'Mrs Peters, if there's one thing I've learned in thirty years of policing it is that birds always come home to roost.' DC Carter sounded weary.

'Pardon?' I said.

Carter sighed again. 'People escape, build a new identity, all of that, but they can't shrug off the past.' He was echoing Rob Partridge and, whatever my reservations about both policemen, I had to accept that they presumably had some experience of the situation I had suddenly found myself in. I had none.

Carter was still talking. '. . . You put people on witness protection schemes, resettle them with a new name, new history, new home, the lot. All they want to do is go back where they came from. They know it's bloody dangerous but they don't seem able to stop themselves. You'd be surprised how often they take themselves off back to their old stamping grounds. Happens all the time.'

'Look, I'll be fine . . .' I suddenly longed to be alone.

'Mrs Peters, I don't think you quite understand. I'm not asking you, I'm telling you. I can't take responsibility for your safety if you stay here.'

It was my turn to sigh. 'All right, all right,' I said.

'Now, is there someone you'd like to call?'

I nodded dumbly. He passed me his mobile phone. I called Mariette.

She had been in the library all day and had not heard the news. 'I just don't believe it, Suzanne,' she exclaimed. 'Are you all right?'

'Of course I'm all right,' I said. 'It's just that the police won't let me stay here. They think Carl's dangerous. It's nonsense, of course . . .'

'I don't think it's nonsense,' said Mariette. 'He *is* dangerous. He kidnapped you, tied you up and drugged you, for God's sake. He killed his own daughter, didn't he?'

Why did everybody have to keep telling me these things? Did they think I didn't know?

'Of course you must come to us. I'll call Mum, and I'll meet you there.' Mariette hung up before I could make polite noises about not having to leave work early for me.

'Right,' said Carter. 'Pack what you want, only be quick.'

I nodded glumly.

'I'll close that trapdoor up for you,' he added.

I began to climb the stairs and could hear him in the kitchen dragging the ladder up from the cellar.

Then his mobile telephone rang.

'Right,' he said. His favourite word, it seemed. I heard his footsteps clumping through the dining room. 'Sorry, Mrs Peters, we've got to go right away,' he shouted up the stairs. 'Can't wait for you to pack any more.'

I had got as far as picking up a small bag and throwing my nightclothes into it. Obediently I trotted downstairs carrying just that. 'What's happened?' I asked.

Carter and WPC Braintree had gone into a huddle in a corner of the dining room. They ignored me at first.

'Tell me, for goodness' sake,' I shouted. I knew that I sounded hysterical, I was beginning to feel hysterical.

Carter turned to face me. 'Mrs Peters, please . . . calm down.'

'Just tell me what's going on, then I'll calm down.'

Carter appeared to decide to take the route of least resistance. Something that came fairly naturally to him, I reckoned.

'It's your husband. A lorry driver reckons he picked him up and took him to Plymouth, just before we got the roadblocks set up. Must have moved damned fast. Trucker reported it to Plymouth nick when he heard the news and Carl's description on the radio . . .'

They drove me down the hill to Mariette's house in Fore Street. All along the way I pleaded with them to take me to Plymouth.

DC Carter had had about enough of me, I think. 'What earthly good would that do?'

'If Carl's there I'd find him, I know I would,' I said,

although I knew I was being ridiculous.

Brenda Powell was waiting for us. She must have been looking out of the window because she opened the front door as soon as our car drew to a halt outside her house. Why did I never seem to be allowed to make my own choices, I wondered, and was immediately ashamed of myself because both she and her daughter had been so kind to me.

Carter did not budge from the driver's seat when I got out of the car. Neither did he shut down the engine. Carol Braintree, who had been sitting in the back, quickly clambered out and installed herself in the front passenger seat as soon as I vacated it.

'C'mon, my luvver,' said Mariette's mum. Then she stepped forward and wrapped her arms round me. Not for the first time I wondered what it must be like to have a mother like Brenda Powell. I had been loved, no question of that, but I was only just beginning to realise that both the people who had loved me so much, Gran and Carl, had also wanted to control me. Did Mrs Powell want to control her daughter, or even me? I didn't think so. I was just finding any kind of concern for my well-being oppressive.

'Don't worry, I'll look after her,' Mrs Powell called after the two police officers, who seemed to consider their duty done as far as I was concerned, and had already roared off up the hill before Mariette's mum and I had even begun to retreat inside the house.

'Please let me know what happens,' I shouted at the top of my voice. But I doubt they even heard me.

When Mariette came home from the library I told her the whole sorry story. About Will. Everything. She listened carefully. 'It doesn't alter what Carl did to you in the end, though, or what he did in America, does it?' she said eventually.

'I s-suppose not,' I agreed falteringly.

'And now he's done a runner,' she added. 'I think he's barking, that's what I think.'

I didn't know how to argue with that. Although in my heart it still didn't add up, still didn't equate with the Carl I knew.

'Look, you've told me yourself it's over with Carl,' she went on. 'What you need to do now is build yourself a new life.'

'You can't go back to that house until they catch the devil, that's for certain,' Mrs Powell volunteered.

I would have laughed if I had had any sense of humour left. I was having difficulty regarding Carl as a fugitive at all, let alone as some kind of devil.

Sometimes in the morning things seem better. The morning after Carl's escape everything seemed worse.

I had to face up to a few things. Carl was on the run. Maybe Mrs Powell was right, maybe he was a devil, perhaps in a way every bit as much of a monster as Robert Foster. And maybe I had to accept that before I could move forward, which I had to do somehow or other.

Mariette's mother walked with me to Rose Cottage so that I could pick up some things, which I had not been given time to do the previous day. I didn't really want to go. The cottage was beginning to represent too many bad things. My life there with Carl just seemed like a lie now. And it was also where Will Jones had confessed that he too had deceived me.

Rob Partridge was no longer propping up the wall

on the corner to Rose Lane, but another officer – one I didn't recognise, just as conspicuously obvious in spite of his unremarkable casual clothing – was on duty.

He stepped forward as we were unlocking the door and I had to explain who we were and what we were doing there.

He glanced into the cottage over my shoulder. You could feel the silent emptiness of the place. 'I'll be right outside if you want me,' he said.

I thanked him, but I could not imagine what Brenda Powell or I could possibly want him for.

There was a coldness about the cottage that I had not noticed before. Also the way that Carl and I had lived – turning the upstairs room into a bed-sitting room because of the view, lighting the dingy dining room only with candles so that you could not see the ugliness of it, shutting ourselves off, except in the most superficial ways, from the outside world – now seemed like an absurdity.

I climbed the stairs with reluctance and began to sort out enough clothes to keep me going for as long as Mariette and her mother would have me. Downstairs I could hear Mrs Powell bustling about. She had volunteered to clear the fridge and make sure nothing perishable was left in the kitchen. I didn't care, really, but she was that sort of person. I could hear her muttering to herself.

After a bit she called out to me. 'Suzanne, will you come down and give me a hand with this flagstone out yer. One of us is going to fall down that hole in a minute.'

I thought for a moment whether there was anything else I wanted to retrieve from the cellar before we sealed it up, but I knew there wasn't. In any case, I really didn't want to go down there again. Together we tried to manoeuvre the stone until Brenda Powell gave a little cry and stood up straight clutching her back.

'Don't hurt yourself,' I said. 'Let me try on my own. I know there's an easy way to do this. I've seen Carl do it often enough.'

He used to pivot the stone on a raised bit of the uneven floor and just use the crowbar to ease it back into place. I imitated what I had seen him do so many times and with surprising smoothness the flagstone slotted snugly back into the black hole, which was all you could see of the cellar below. I unrolled the vinyl floor covering over it and stood up to await further instructions. I still wasn't capable of doing much thinking for myself.

'Something else we won't fall over now,' said Mariette's mum.

Only when the cottage was 'in apple pie order' – her words not mine – did she consent to leave.

Apart from the fact that the Powell home was so small – although I had insisted that I take the sofa bed in the front room this time – there were a number of other reasons why I couldn't stay with Mariette and her mother for ever. Some of them were completely selfish. It was wrong to be irritated by Mrs Powell, because she was a kind woman. Nonetheless I reckoned she would drive me quite barking if I spent too much time with her.

Mrs Powell and Mariette were probably right, though. My life at Rose Cottage was over. I still didn't really feel in danger from Carl, but neither did I think that the cottage could ever be my home again. I needed to work, to earn money, to discover whether I was even employable, in any capacity.

My most immediate concern, however, was to find out what had happened to Carl. He hadn't returned to Rose Cottage, so where had he gone?

Back at the Powell house I paced the floors waiting for news. Several times I called Penzance police station, but DC Carter was never available. Eventually, I think maybe because those answering the phone became so fed up with me, I was given the detective's mobile phone number.

He didn't seem all that overjoyed to hear from me but at least he answered my questions. He was, it transpired, still in Plymouth. 'We're pretty sure it was Carl here,' he said. 'The lorry driver couldn't identify him for certain from the photograph we showed him because he said the man he picked up was wearing an anorak-type jacket with a hood, which he kept over his head all the time, and didn't seem to want to look at him. But that was the kind of coat Carl had on when he was taken to Penzance and there's been a robbery here in Plymouth . . .'

I felt the by now all too familiar tightening of my stomach muscles. 'But, but, you haven't caught him then, you don't know for sure . . .'

'We haven't caught him, that's right enough.'

'And the robbery? Why do you think it was Carl?' A terrible thought occurred to me. 'Nobody was hurt, were they?'

'No, not unless you count the old lady he half frightened to death pushing past her, in such a hurry to get away. She's our witness. Same thing. Man with his anorak hood over his head. Right height and build.'

'Is that all?'

'That and what was taken,' replied DC Carter tetchily.

I waited.

'The robbery was in one of those luxury blocks of flats up on the Hoe . . . some cash, jewellery, a few easy to sell knick-knacks – and a passport.'

Carter paused triumphantly.

I could see what he was driving at. Carl needed money and the means to get away. He needed a passport. The police had his old out-of-date American one. If he had a new one in either of his names, I had never seen it. I didn't think Carl was likely to be the only person in Devon or Cornwall who might have a use for someone else's passport, but I supposed the circumstantial evidence did point to him.

'And the timing,' DC Carter continued. 'The timing's spot on. The robbery happened about two hours after the lorry driver reckoned he dropped him off. Carl would have had just one aim once he'd got out of Cornwall – money and the means to get abroad if he wanted to.'

'But how could he get away with someone else's passport, what good would that do?'

'Flown out of Heathrow lately?'

That was a laugh. I had never been out of the country.

Carter didn't wait for an answer. 'Half the time they don't even ask you to open up a British passport any more. But I doubt he'd risk that. Across to Europe from any channel port would be a better bet. More often than not the checks are little more than a joke. And your man's an expert, too, don't forget.'

I was startled. 'What do you mean?'

'Done it before, hasn't he? Came to the UK from the States and built himself a whole new identity. Stayed hidden all that time, too. Might have got away with it for ever if it hadn't been for you and those threats. Knows what he's about, doesn't he?'

I was deeply depressed when I hung up the phone. It wasn't just DC Carter who regarded Carl as a common criminal – or maybe an uncommon one; they seemed to think of him capable of a kind of cunning I had never seen in him – I supposed every police officer involved did now.

I wondered where Carl would go. It seemed increasingly unlikely that he would return to St Ives. If he really was planning to leave the country would he go back to America?

I assumed not. After all, he was wanted on a manslaughter charge there. Out of the frying pan into the fire, surely. Although I remembered what DC Carter had said about the urge to return – 'birds always come home to roost'.

During the next couple of weeks I began to feel anger more than anything else. And I didn't know what to do at all. Mariette suggested I gave notice on Rose Cottage. At least that would save some cash and I wasn't going back was I?

She and a friend with a transit van – Mariette seemed to have a supply of very useful friends – moved my belongings out of the cottage, including my bike, which had been carefully mothballed at one end of Carl's studio, the steeply sloping, sometimes almost vertical streets of St Ives being ill suited to cycling. And it was arranged for me to store the stuff in another useful friend's garage until I had sorted myself out. Although I wondered sometimes if I would ever sort myself out.

I really did go through a very angry period again. I was quite ruthless with Carl's possessions. I threw away his Leonard Cohen records. All of them. I can't believe now that I did that. The records went off in the Penwith District Council dustcart. I was quite convinced that I would never want to hear Leonard Cohen sing again.

I gathered up all Carl's paintings that were around the place, not just the ones that had been in the cellar but also the various ones we had hung on the cottage walls in better days, and asked Mariette if she would take them around to Will Jones's gallery. At the last moment I kept back only one, *Pumpkin Soup*. In spite of everything I just could not quite bring myself to part with it.

Mariette knew well enough why I didn't want to take the paintings round to the Logan Gallery myself, but I was beginning to understand money a little and its importance. I thought Will would take them. He almost wouldn't dare not to, I reckoned, although the fact that I had seen him walk past Mariette's house many more times than could be just chance made me nervous.

Goodness knows how he knew I was living there, but it wouldn't have been difficult in St Ives, of course. Mrs Jackson could have told him, or almost anybody popping into the gallery. And it was the second time I had taken refuge with Mariette and her mother.

Sixteen days after Carl's disappearance I received a phone call at Mariette's house from Detective

Sergeant Julie Perry. She was back in St Ives at last and wanted to see me. 'I'll call round if you like,' she said. 'I've got some news for you.'

The stomach muscles knotted again. 'C-Carl,' I stammered.

'No,' she said. 'Nothing on him. Something different – and well, it's a bit of good news, really.'

She rang off, leaving me wondering what on earth she could be going on about.

I watched for her out of the window and rushed to open the door when a little under an hour later, I saw her approaching.

I led her into the little front room.

'I'm sorry I left you in the lurch. I didn't have any choice,' she said.

'I had DC Carter,' I remarked expressionlessly.

'Yes,' she said, equally expressionlessly.

'Anyway, I don't suppose it made any difference in the long run. It just felt as if I didn't know what was going on, that's all. Still feels a bit like that, really . . .'

She nodded. 'I'll try to help now I'm back; I did know more about the case than anyone else. But first of all, the news. It seems your husband left you rather a lot of money.'

I was bewildered. In my mind Carl was still my husband. What did she mean, 'left' me money? He didn't have any, as far as I knew. And he wasn't dead. Then, like a flash, it hit me. My husband. Robert Foster.

'Good God,' I said.

'Maybe,' said DS Perry. 'I've never been too sure myself.'

Preoccupied as I was, I couldn't help smiling.

I hadn't even invited her to sit down – well, it

wasn't my house. She did so anyway, on the sofa by the window, which also served as my bed. I sat in an easy chair opposite, and looked at her expectantly.

'There's a solicitor in Hounslow wants to get in touch with you,' she went on. 'Apparently you're the sole beneficiary of your husband's will.'

'Good God,' I said again.

This time she just carried on as if I hadn't spoken. 'The solicitor's only just found out you're alive. In the nick of time, I understand. After seven years you could have been declared legally dead. When they were making enquiries after you told us you'd killed Robert Foster the Met contacted what was left of Foster's family, just a cousin, I think, and he wasn't exactly delighted to hear about your resurrection. He was next in line, you see. Apparently made some enquiries about the seven-year limit in such a way that the solicitor's suspicions were aroused. He started digging, and contacted the police. I wasn't quite sure where they should write to you. So I thought I'd pop round. Here's his address and phone number.'

She passed me a piece of paper. James Fisher, Fisher, Hall and Partners, High Street, Hounslow. As I studied it I began to think about Robert and what assets he might have had. We had lived in a manse owned by the chapel and I couldn't imagine he had been paid very much. Surely he couldn't have left a lot. Yet as I pondered I remembered Gran's money. I didn't think she would have had much in the bank either, but she had owned her own home. That must have been worth a bit.

'Do you know how much?' I asked.

'They didn't confide. Let's hope it's enough to help

you build a new life.'

I nodded. 'Thanks. I'll call him.'

'Do that.'

Money had never meant a great deal to me before and of course I had never handled it, but I was changing. I appreciated instantly the difference this legacy could make to the new life everyone seemed determined that I should build.

Meanwhile, though, the old life still loomed pretty large. 'I wish I knew what had happened to Carl and where he is now.'

'Ray Carter is quite convinced he's done a runner back home to the US. Certainly we've not had a sniff of him since that Plymouth business. He's just disappeared. Maybe Ray's right.' Julie Perry paused. 'For once.'

'I know,' I said. 'He told me his theory about birds coming home to roost and all that. But Carl is wanted on a more serious charge there than he is here. Manslaughter, for goodness' sake. He killed his daughter.'

'Well, yes, but it was in a road accident. He is still wanted on a manslaughter rap for it, but they're hardly going to launch a major manhunt . . .'

'What?' I barked out the word. I was pole-axed. 'Road accident? Nobody told me anything about a road accident. I thought the little girl died because Carl had drugged her.'

'Oh, bloody hell.' Julie Perry closed both her eyes for a couple of seconds and tapped her forehead lightly with the fingers of one hand. 'Didn't anybody explain what happened?'

I shook my head. 'Rob Partridge told me his version, but he just said that Carl had killed his daughter. With drugs, I'm sure that's what he said. And DC Carter wouldn't tell me anything. Said there could be an extradition warrant . . .'

My voiced tailed off. I was still stunned, unable quite to take in the enormity of what I was learning.

'Bloody typical,' responded DS Perry. She sounded exasperated, partly at herself I somehow thought. 'An extradition warrant for a motoring charge, albeit manslaughter, when we already had him banged up for abduction. I don't think so.' She shook her head. 'Sorry, Suzanne,' she repeated. 'I knew I should have stayed in touch, kept my eye on the ball. It's not easy, though, when you get plunged into a murder. Every minute in the day . . .'

I interrupted her then. My brain had started to work. I leaned forward in my chair. 'Please tell me everything,' I asked. 'Please.'

'Yes, of course. Everything I know, anyway. You are obviously aware that Carl is really Harry Mendleson from Florida and that his troubles with the law started when his wife threatened to leave him?'

I nodded.

'He's an exceptionally possessive, protective man, isn't he?' she went on. 'He likes to keep the people he loves very close, too close sometimes. But you know that . . .'

I nodded again. I knew that all too well.

'Well, he overdid it, didn't he? Makes a habit of that, it seems. Wife couldn't take it. Told him she was leaving and taking the child with her. I understand there was another man involved. There was a terrific row. Carl locked all the doors of the house and told her he wasn't going to let her go. The wife was on

Valium – not surprising, really. While they were fighting the child got into the bathroom and took some of her mother's pills. She was only five, she was frightened, wanted attention, I suppose, wanted her parents to stop rowing. Didn't know what she was doing. Who can tell? Anyway, when the child collapsed Mendleson and his wife realised what had happened, bundled her in the car and took off for the hospital.'

That was very different from the way it had been put to me, from what I had imagined had happened. 'I thought he had deliberately drugged them both, and that the child had overdosed. I'm sure that's what Rob Partridge told me.'

Julie Perry grunted. 'No doubt he did. The man deliberately drugged you, so if Partridge had heard of the drug involvement in the previous case, which obviously he had, that meant he'd done it before too. Standard police thinking, villains running true to form. Standard for the PC Partridges of this world, anyway. He wouldn't have checked it out, it wasn't his case, just passed it on as if it were gospel.'

She paused. Her turn to have said something she shouldn't, perhaps.

'The girl overdosed all right,' she continued with a small sigh. 'But there was no question of Mendleson being responsible for that. He was ultimately responsible for her death, but it was actually a tragic accident. He panicked and took off, driving like a lunatic. Just a block or so away from the hospital he crashed his car. Turned off the main drag too fast and rolled the thing. He and his wife escaped virtually unscathed, they were belted in the front, but they'd laid the little girl down on the back seat. She was killed outright. And it wasn't pretty. She was decapitated.'

I shivered. An horrific picture had instantly presented itself. Then I thought about my one visit to Carl following his arrest. 'But he told me he killed her. I asked him. "Is it true that you killed your daughter?" He said yes. That's all. None of the rest of it. Only yes.'

DS Perry nodded. 'That's how he sees it, I suppose. And, indeed, he did kill her in a way. But not deliberately – he was trying to save her.'

'So why didn't he explain? I accused him of drugging his wife and child. He denied it, yet in such a way that I didn't believe him – couldn't believe him. He barely protested. He seemed to accept everything I said to him. He just went along with it. Why, oh why?'

The words came tumbling out.

Julie Perry shrugged but did not attempt to answer. How could she? I suppose I knew the answer, though, even then: 'If you have stopped believing in me, Suzanne, there's no point in anything any more,' he had told me.

Eighteen

I sank into one of my trances after DS Perry left. She had absolutely staggered me. I might be rich. Or at least solvent. That would have been enough to bowl me over. But what she had told me about Carl changed everything. First of all I had discovered that he had not sent me the threatening letters, then that he had not intended to harm his daughter, indeed not tried to harm her at all and certainly not forced drugs on either the child or her mother.

Where did that leave him? Where did that leave us? I wasn't sure. I was beginning to think again that perhaps he wasn't really such an evil man after all, that maybe my initial judgement of him had not been so far off the mark.

I reminded myself that he had been so intent on keeping me under his control that he had held me a prisoner against my will. For all those years I had believed that I had killed my husband. I still had no way of knowing whether or not Carl had been aware that I had not done so. I could hardly credit that he would have deceived me so cruelly for so long. But there was no doubt that the life of hiding apparently forced upon us suited Carl only too well. I had been totally dependent on him, and that, of course, was exactly how he liked it.

At best, Carl was a sick man, only I had never known that. At worst? I didn't know whether I could ever forgive him, but I did know that I wanted to find him, to confront him with my new knowledge and demand that he talk to me properly about his past. I felt I could not get on with my life, with or without Carl, until I had done so. I would search for him all over the world if necessary.

The money I had apparently inherited suddenly took on a whole new importance. Money climbed mountains, I was beginning to learn that. I had never travelled anywhere on my own. I had never been out of the UK. I had never been in an aircraft in my life. I had no passport. If I had money then none of this was an obstacle.

I glanced at my watch. It was two in the afternoon. I rushed to the telephone and called Hall, Fisher and Partners in Hounslow. James Fisher was out at lunch. I left a message asking him to call me back. It was almost three thirty before he did so, by which time I was pacing the floor again.

He confirmed that I was the sole beneficiary of Robert Foster's will.

'Am I really?' I asked unnecessarily.

'You sound surprised, Mrs Foster.'

It was a very long time since anybody had called me that.

'In view of the way he treated me, yes, I am a bit.' I couldn't help but tell the truth.

'I have heard something of that from the police. They did investigate your disappearance at the time, you know. A number of people, neighbours and even one or two of his congregation, suspected that Foster had been beating you.'

'But nobody did anything about it.'

'No. And when you disappeared after his death it

didn't really make sense to anyone. I know now what happened more or less, of course. Extraordinary story.'

'Yes.'

Fisher's telephone manner was relaxed and friendly. He spoke softly, with just the trace of a Scottish accent. He was very chatty, but he hadn't told me what I wanted to know yet.

'How much money is there?' I asked bluntly.

'It's around £130,000.'

I drew in my breath quickly. To me that was a fortune. 'When can I have it?'

'Ah.' It was the solicitor's turn to sound surprised.

But then he didn't know what I wanted the money for, how important it was for me suddenly to find Carl. Harry Mendleson might be the name he was born with. To me he would always be Carl.

'Well, your husband's will was quite straight-forward, Mrs Foster . . .'

Each time he used that name it gave me a jolt. I might not be Mrs Peters but I certainly no longer thought of myself as Mrs Foster. I suppose I had never truly considered myself to be Robert's wife. More his victim, really.

James Fisher was still talking. I made myself concentrate. I had to take control now, to manage things for myself. There was no one left to do that for me and in any case for the first time in my life I did not want anyone to.

'. . . and the Reverand Foster had made me his executor, which simplified things. I took out probate quite soon after he died and the funds have been invested on behalf of the will's beneficiaries. In this case yourself. They are almost immediately releasable once the appropriate papers have been signed and I am satisfied of your identity, of course.'

'Of course.' I hoped that wouldn't be a problem. I didn't have that much with which to identify myself. I wasn't even always sure what my identity was, to be honest.

'It would be simplest if you could travel up to Hounslow to our offices here. I am sure we could sort everything out quickly then.'

'To Hounslow?'

The place seemed like another world to me now and not one I had ever wished to return to. I reflected for a moment. Maybe I could lay a few ghosts to rest while I was there. A thought occurred to me. Could Carl have returned to west London, to his first refuge in England, perhaps even to the place where he and I had met?

'It would be simplest, Mrs Foster . . .'

I was off in my own world. Thinking back. Thinking forward.

'. . . Mrs Foster? Are you still there, Mrs Foster . . .'

I said I was there all right, just wondering how quickly I could get to Hounslow.

He suggested two days hence. I agreed with alacrity.

Only after I had put down the phone did I reflect that it was all very well inheriting £130,000, but the only cash I actually had in the world right then was about £150.

That night Mariette gave me the solution to the immediate practical problems. First of all I told her about the will. 'I can't believe it,' I said. 'Just as I was wondering where the next penny was going to come from all this has fallen into my lap.'

'I wouldn't put it like that, exactly,' she said. 'Most of it probably came from your gran in the first place. Foster stole it from you.'

'We were married, Mariette.'

'Huh! Some marriage.'

'Legal, though, which has worked to my good fortune in the end, I suppose. Robert treated me as if he hated me, yet he so carefully left all his money to me. Bizarre!'

'Guilt, I'd say. Anyway, you were married to him so you'd almost certainly have inherited with or without the will.'

I grinned. 'Maybe. Anyway I have to go to Hounslow the day after tomorrow. I need to catch the earliest train. How much do you think it will cost?'

'You'll have to get the Golden Hind and saver tickets aren't valid. It'll be well over £100.'

'That'll nearly clean me out. And I have to get out to Hounslow . . .'

Mariette rummaged in her bag and passed me an envelope. 'Will Jones', she said with a chuckle, 'took all the paintings and offered you £600 in advance. I didn't even have to ask. Perhaps he has got a conscience after all.'

I remembered Will's unpleasant sexual approach to me in Rose Cottage. The thought of it made my flesh crawl. 'Wouldn't bet on it,' I replied. 'Amazing the way everyone's throwing cash at me, all of a sudden, though.'

'Don't knock it, maybe some of it will rub off on me,' said Mariette.

She phoned Great Western Railways and used her own credit card to reserve me a seat on the Golden Hind leaving Penzance at 5.15 a.m. She also nobly offered to drive me there from St Ives.

In spite of the mind-numbingly early start I quite enjoyed the journey to London. I was beginning to appreciate what independence meant – freedom, really. And it's a sad fact of life that no one can be free in the modern world without financial independence. I treated myself to breakfast – the full fry-up including potatoes, although I did draw the line at black pudding. I had never eaten a meal on a train before and I reckoned I could rather get to like it. At Paddington I planned to take the Underground, changing at Earl's Court from the District Line to the Piccadilly Line and on to Hounslow Central. I knew it was just three or four minutes' walk to the High Street offices of Hall, Fisher and Partners.

For once, everything worked like clockwork. The Golden Hind arrived on time at Paddington just after 10 a.m. and tube trains came along quickly for me both there and at Earl's Court. I arrived at Hounslow before 11 and my appointment was not until 11.30. I knew exactly how I wanted to spend the half-hour.

The manse where I had endured the most unhappy years of my life was only about five minutes or so further on from the Underground station than the offices of Hall, Fisher and Partners.

For some reason I was drawn to it. I felt it was important that I went to look at the place again. I suppose I thought vaguely that I had finally to confront my past in order to overcome it.

So I carried on walking until the big Victorian villa loomed, ugly as ever, before me. It had not changed much although it badly needed a coat of paint. That kind of neglect had never been allowed when Robert had been the incumbent. He had insisted on high

300

standards in almost all directions except his own behaviour, I reflected ruefully.

I stared at the house long and hard. Suddenly and quite vividly I could see Robert's face in front of me, his towering bulk dwarfing me as he approached, fists clenched, ready to attack me in the way he had done so often. For a few brief seconds it was as if I were transported back through time to the horrific existence I had endured with my monstrous husband. But, to my astonishment, I felt no fear. Inside my head I stood my ground. And, as if by magic, the dreadful image of Robert disappeared as swiftly as it had presented itself. I suppose that was the moment when I realised I had become a different kind of person. I was no longer a victim. I was quite determined that nobody, absolutely nobody, was ever going to hurt me like that again.

I turned away from the horrid old house and began to walk back to the solicitors' offices. I didn't look round. I never wanted to see the place again. That part of my life was finally over. A few ghosts had indeed been buried, I thought to myself almost triumphantly.

James Fisher was a short, plump man, nearing retirement age, I imagined, with an easy way about him. He greeted me warmly and promptly at 11.30 in his comfortable but slightly shabby office above an estate agency. And, in spite of his earlier comments about identification, he seemed pretty sure that I was who I said I was. I began to explain that I had no papers with which to identify myself, except a library card in the name of Peters, which I didn't think would be much help. He seemed unconcerned. He asked me to sign my name on a piece of paper and compared it briefly with my signature on a document that I recognised to be a copy of my marriage certificate. Then I noticed that in the file lying open on his desk there were several photographs of me, including a large wedding photograph with Robert. The unwelcome memories that returned made me inwardly cringe.

My meeting with James Fisher took little more than half an hour. Everything was, indeed, just as he had promised on the phone, quite straightforward.

'You'll have access to your money within a couple of days, Mrs Foster,' he said, after giving me a copy of Robert's will and asking me to sign various pieces of paperwork.

It occurred to me that I had never even had a bank account. I didn't think this would be a problem – not with £130,000 behind me.

I thanked him and left. I knew what I wanted to do with the remainder of my day: bury some more ghosts and begin my search for Carl.

I took the Piccadilly Line back to Hammersmith, from there caught a bus across Hammersmith Bridge to the Sheen Road, and hopped off quite close to the other old Victorian building, which had figured so largely in my life: the one that had been Carl's home when I first met him.

This time I did not hover around outside as I had done at the manse. I walked straight up to the front door and rang the bell to flat three, the one that had once been Carl's. There was no reply. I rang the bell beneath.

A big man, wearing grubby trousers held up by a wide belt, eventually came to the door. He seemed to be short-sighted. He leaned forward and peered at me. His breath smelled. 'Yes?' he enquired.

'I'm looking for Carl Peters, he used to live here,' I said.

'He did indeed,' replied the man in a weary sort of voice.

'I wondered if he'd been back. . .' My voice tailed off. It sounded a strange sort of query even to me.

'No, unfortunately,' said the man, leaning even closer. 'He left owing me rent. Years ago, now, but I still wouldn't mind finding Carl Peters myself.'

Ah. I began to retreat, thanking him for his time.

'Wait, who are you?'

'Nobody, just an old friend, I haven't seen him in years either . . .'

I hurried away. I didn't want to get involved with this unsavoury-looking landlord who somehow didn't quite match the large, doubtless very valuable property he appeared to own. He called after me again. I half ran down the road, looking over my shoulder. He didn't follow. Anyway, with his bulk it didn't seem likely that he would be able to move very fast.

Safely out of sight I found a bus stop and waited for a bus that would take me into Richmond. There I picked up a taxi – a rare extravagance for me, but I believed I could afford those kinds of extravagances now. I asked the driver to take me to the car park by the Isabella Garden and to pick me up two hours later. It was still quite early in the afternoon, not quite three, and I had plenty of time before I needed to make my way back to Paddington to catch the last train to Cornwall at 6.35. I walked down the rough path to the Isabella, through the iron gates and into the gardens. There could not have been a much greater contrast to the bleakness of the grey winter day when I had first met Carl. This was a beautifully sunny afternoon during early June and the Isabella was ablaze with colour. The late azaleas and rhododendrons and all the other shrubs of spring and early summer were in full bloom, and the scent of them alone was quite overwhelming.

My heart soared as it always had done in the Isabella at this special time of year. Indeed, until I reached the secluded corner where I had so fatefully encountered Carl I felt almost happy. But as I sat on the same old fallen tree trunk, suddenly it hit me. More of the trunk had crumbled away and the moss covering it was much thicker than before, I fancied, but it was so familiar and so special to me. I half imagined I could feel Carl's presence. I kept expecting him to step out from behind a bush and comfort me again, to tell me how sorry he was about all that had happened, to tell me, as he had done so often, how all he wanted was to look after me.

Being protected was not what I wanted any more, but I did want to see Carl again. I couldn't help myself. I wanted to hear the full story in his words and I wasn't going to settle for less. Not again.

The two hours passed very quickly and it was a wrench to drag myself away, both from the beauty of the Isabella on a sunny June day, and from the crazy feeling that if I waited there long enough Carl would appear. Maybe a part of me really had expected him to be waiting for me to turn up at the Isabella, just like he had all those years before.

But it wasn't to be. I had been kidding myself. I plodded up the path to the car park where my taxi was already waiting and asked the driver to take me to Richmond station where I took the underground

304

again, and easily made it to Paddington with half an hour to spare. I remembered I was hungry and I was also beginning to feel very tired. I nipped into the station buffet and ordered myself an all-day breakfast, my second of the day, it occurred to me only later, then, full of comfort food, I dozed through much of the journey home. But my every waking moment was overtaken with the riddle of where Carl had gone.

I went over everything again and again in my mind and got nowhere. I made a mental list of things I could do. I ought to get myself a passport. I had no way of knowing where Carl might be, but I wanted to be ready to follow the slightest lead. Maybe he had somehow got himself to the States, maybe he had gone back to his past as DC Carter suspected. If so I would go there. I would seek him out.

Meanwhile I would put advertisements in all the major newspapers asking him to contact me, telling him I wanted to see him. I had seen those sad pleas so often, begging missing persons to come home or get in touch, and never imagined myself searching for someone in this way. I told myself that surely he wouldn't ignore me if he knew I was looking for him. I wasn't sure of anything except that I had to find Carl.

It occurred to me that my desire to find him could become as obsessive as had been his desire to keep me.

Nineteen

The train trundled into Penzance at half past midnight. Mariette was waiting at the station for me as she had promised, in spite of the hour.

Robert Foster's money, I assured her, was all mine.

'How about a celebration, then?' she enquired typically. Never one to miss out on a party, was Mariette.

I grinned. 'When I find Carl,' I said.

She shook her head doubtfully. 'I still think you're better off without him.'

'You may be right,' I admitted. 'I just feel I can't even decide that until I've seen him again, talked to him . . .'

'But where do you start looking?'

I told her I had already started, that I'd checked out Carl's old flat in Sheen. 'I kind of believe what DC Carter says, about people on the run having the urge to go back, to go home, or whatever passes for it . . .'

'From what you've told me about him I can't imagine DC Carter ever being right about anything,' said Mariette tetchily.

I shrugged. 'I just have this feeling that something will tell me where I should go to look for Carl, and that if I ever get close to him, I'll know.' I paused. 'I'd like to get a passport as quickly as possible.'

Mariette was a very practical person. Her reply did

not surprise me. 'There's a man who comes in to the library who knows someone in the Passport Office,' she said. 'He sorted things out when Mum was going on holiday to Tenerife once and discovered at the last moment that her passport had run out. I'll get on to him.'

'You're a marvel, Mariette,' I said. And to me she was. Nothing ever seemed to be problem to her.

'But why do you want one so fast anyway? You're not going to run away too, are you?'

I grinned. 'I don't think so,' I replied. 'I may want to go to America to find Carl, though. Maybe he has found his way back there, that's what DC Carter thinks.'

'Man doesn't have a clue, if you ask me. First of all he thought Carl would come to you, didn't he? He hasn't done. Yet. Maybe he still will. Shouldn't you just stay where you are, wait here?'

'I'm not sure I can,' I said. 'I feel I have to do something. In any case, if Carl were planning to come back to St Ives to find me I reckon he would already have done so. I imagine that he feels rejected by me. I made it quite clear that I wanted nothing more to do with him when I saw him in jail and then I didn't answer his letter . . .'

My voice caught in my throat.

'You really are sure you want to find him, aren't you,' muttered Mariette resignedly.

I assured her I was.

She sighed. 'Men,' she said. 'Nothing but trouble.'

'Is that why you have nothing to do with them?' I asked sweetly.

'Maybe that's what it will come to.'

'And pigs might fly,' I replied.

307

'As a matter of fact there are days when I just can't wait to get old and past it.'

I could only grin. There she was, radiating vitality as usual, perfect skin, shiny black hair, a woman born to drive men mad if they weren't already.

But my mind was still on more serious matters. 'Mariette,' I said hesitantly, after a short pause. 'If I did decide to go to America . . . would you come with me? . . . I mean, I'm not sure I could manage on my own and I have the money to pay for both of us . . . and we could try to make a holiday of it . . .'

I wasn't sure there was actually much chance of that in my frame of mind, but if Mariette suspected as much she did not let on. 'I thought you'd never ask,' she said.

Over the next couple of weeks we prepared for our trip. I took myself off to Penzance to buy some much needed new clothes. This time I travelled alone and I bought garments that suited me, not Mariette, fond as I had become of her. Carl had probably been right about the tarty orange suit episode. I had attempted to turn myself into somebody I wasn't. That was another thing that was never going to happen again.

We also had to sort out passports and tickets, and car hire. Yet another of Mariette's many friends, who lived in London, obtained a copy of my birth certificate. I decided that my passport would be in my maiden name. It was simplest and in any case I no longer desired to be either Mrs Foster or Mrs Peters.

I became Jane Adams again, the name I was christened with. At least, according to my brand new passport I did.

Mariette was pensive as she fingered the pristine

document. 'You know, you're still Suzanne to me. I can't imagine calling you anything else . . .'

I smiled. 'That's all right,' I said. 'I guess I'm still Suzanne to myself too.'

Official documents were one thing, but I could never really be Jane again, not inside my head. Too much had happened. And, in fact, the memory of the night when Carl had given me my new name, although tainted by the lies we had lived, remained too vivid. I could not easily discard my name, even though I had thrown away Carl's records and CDs of the Cohen song from which it had been taken. And, to be honest, I was already beginning to regret that.

Before we left for America I made a final call to DS Perry to make sure that there was no further news of Carl. She had earlier supplied me with all the information she had from the Florida police about Carl and the death of his daughter, including the name of the man who had been the investigating officer at Key Largo when he had been charged with manslaughter.

'I don't know exactly what you're expecting to find over there, but don't build your hopes up, will you?' Julie Perry cautioned.

'I'm expecting nothing but you know what I'm hoping for, I'm hoping I might find Carl, or at least discover more about him,' I said.

'As long as you don't end up wishing you hadn't . . .'

She didn't seem quite to finish the sentence, but I thought I knew what she meant.

Mariette and I flew out of Heathrow en route to Miami just fifteen days after my journey to Hounslow. I had a suitcase full of new clothes, a chequebook, a Barclays Premier gold card and, of course, a passport. I thought that was pretty good going. And I must confess that even in my distress my new-found independence gave me considerable satisfaction. In spite of my extraordinarily sheltered past I found that I took to it with surprising ease – although I realised I would not have managed such a big trip so effortlessly without Mariette. Her only previous trip to the States had been a package tour to Disneyworld at Orlando, but she seemed totally confident that this prepared her for almost anything America could throw at her. Nothing much fazed Mariette.

Any notions I had about transatlantic travel being glamorous were well and truly scotched by nine hours in Virgin economy class. I am not particularly tall, about five foot six, but I felt as if I had been wedged in to my seat with a shoehorn. By the time we reached our destination the circulation in my legs seemed to have disappeared and I couldn't help thinking about the newspaper articles I had read claiming that being cramped on aircraft can cause blood clots and kill.

'If we were animals,' remarked Mariette crustily, 'there would be animal rights protesters, waving bloody great banners, waiting for us on the tarmac.' I managed half a smile.

As we battled our way through Immigration I became increasingly glad that we'd decided not to go further than the airport Hilton that night. I had heard about jet lag but nothing had prepared me for it. I had never been so tired in my life.

We had a huge room in the Hilton overlooking a runway – almost on top of one, it seemed – and yet we could hear very little aircraft noise through the triple glazing. We both crashed out instantly and woke very early with the morning light. Then we sorted out our prebooked hire car – something the Americans called a compact. It seemed like a limousine to me, but then about the sum total of my previous motoring experience had consisted of travelling around in Carl's elderly van, which we had never quite afforded to change and every year had nursed painstakingly through its MOT.

Mariette had to do all the driving but the distances we expected to travel were not great – Key West, our furthest destination at the southernmost tip of the Keys, being less than 200 miles from the airport – and she said she was quite looking forward to it. We were on our way before 8 a.m.

Refreshed by sleep and in bright sunshine we navigated ourselves out of Miami without too much difficulty and headed down Highway 1 to Key Largo where Mariette, using an already much thumbed tourist guide, had booked us into a little bayside motel called Neptune's Hideaway.

For forty-five dollars we rented a spotlessly clean room, which I gathered was small by American standards, but boasted a seven-foot-wide, king-sized bed around which we had to walk sideways while also negotiating the obligatory fridge and TV. I sat on the bed with my feet on my suitcase while I phoned the police station and asked for Detective Theodore Grant. I was told he had retired but the officer I spoke to was helpful and informed me that Theo Grant ran a boat charter company a couple of miles down the coast. I was all for taking off there right away, but Mariette said she wasn't going anywhere until she had had something to eat.

I allowed her to tempt me into the Sundowners bar and restaurant next door, where we sat on a wooden terrace overlooking the bay while I discovered for the first time what a sandwich means in America.

By the time we had ploughed our way through a mountain of food, which would probably have been presented in the UK as a three-course dinner, I realised I had managed to get myself mildly sunburned. The weather in Florida at the end of June and beginning of July can be stiflingly hot, I had been warned, and the sun very dangerous, but in the Keys a deceptively refreshing breeze blows almost all the time. After we had eaten Mariette consented to drive to Theodore Grant's boatyard.

Grant was a heavily built man with a head of thinning white hair and a wary look in his eyes, which probably came from years in the police force.

When I explained who I was and why I was there he didn't seem very happy about it. 'Messy case. I'd hoped it was ancient history,' he muttered. But he invited us into a room full of rusting filing cabinets, which apparently served as his office, and even offered us a beer. We sat by a window overlooking the bay and he talked freely enough.

'One of the nastiest motor accidents we've had around here. They found the girl's body half in and half out of the car,' he told us, taking a long pull at his bottle of Budweiser. 'But her head was twenty yards away on the grass verge. Harry was sitting next to it stroking the hair. It took our boys several minutes to get him to leave it and let the medics cart it away along with the rest of her.'

Grant shuddered and had another drink of beer.

'The accident was completely his fault. That was

the worst of it for him, I think,' he went on. 'No other car involved, simply going too fast, driving like a madman. Harry blamed himself totally, from the start, but actually being charged with manslaughter was the final straw, I suppose. He took off right after we charged him. I got a lot of shit because I'd not impounded his passport. Tell the truth, it didn't occur to me Harry would do a runner. I'd known him for years. We were buddies . . . well, till almost the end, that is . . .'

He stopped, but I got the feeling that he hadn't finished what he had intended to say. I waited for him to continue. He didn't.

'What kind of a man was Harry Mendleson?' I asked.

He looked at me curiously. I had told him I had lived with Carl for many years in England. It must have seemed like a strange question. But this was the first person I had ever met who had known Carl before I did, who may even have been close to him.

After a moment or two Grant shrugged his big shoulders. 'Mixed up, like the rest of us in this Goddamn country,' he said. 'Likeable and weak, that's the kind of man he was.'

And I'd always thought he was so strong. Strange really.

'His wife didn't find him likeable, though. He drove her round the bend. That's why . . .'

His voice trailed off.

'She had an affair, didn't she?' I prompted him. 'There was someone else. That's why she wanted to leave him.'

'That's not the only reason.'

He didn't seem inclined to say any more, in spite of

Mariette and me both encouraging him to.

'Harry was always, you know . . .' He paused again, as if searching for words. 'Harry was always . . . different, always a bit of a strange one. After the accident he completely lost it. Still, none of us round here did much to help, that was for sure.'

His tone of voice surprised me. He sounded more than concerned, almost as if he felt guilty. The caring side of the Florida police department or something more? I had no way of telling. It was just that I had begun to question everything in my mind, to look beneath the surface all the time: a new way of thinking for me.

'Where's his wife now?' I asked.

'Islamarada. Remarried. Wexford Barrymore, a hotel keeper.' Grant sighed. 'Loaded, of course. Makes more in a year than I will in my lifetime, I reckon.'

I couldn't quite see the relevance. I waited patiently until he continued to speak.

'She's had Harry declared legally dead. She won't be too happy about his resurrection, our Claire, you can be certain of that. Wouldn't be too pleased to see you two, either.'

Like you, I thought. You're not pleased to see us. None the less I persuaded him to give us the name of the hotel – the Bay Point. Mariette and I checked the mile marker on our map. It was about half an hour's drive away we reckoned.

We decided to call in there the next day on our way down to Key West.

From the moment we arrived at the Bay Point I could see what Theo Grant meant about its owner being

314

loaded. The hotel was set in extensive, beautifully tended grounds with its own golf course and tennis courts. Accommodation was in a series of individual luxury bungalows and it took us a while to locate reception. Anything as common as an office obviously had to be camouflaged. The place just oozed wealth and I felt ridiculously nervous when we eventually approached the front desk.

If Mariette felt the same way, she did not show it. She strode forward boldly and with apparent confidence addressed a young woman receptionist who was so perfectly made-up and so extraordinarily even-featured that I did not think she could be quite real.

'We'd like to speak to Mrs Barrymore, please,' said Mariette in much more cut-glass English tones than she normally used. 'We have a mutual acquaintance in the UK who asked if we would look her up.'

As the receptionist obediently picked up the phone I stared at Mariette in amazement.

'Well, it's almost true,' she hissed under her breath. 'A shared husband or as near as damn it has to qualify as a mutual acquaintance, surely.'

I said nothing. The receptionist told us that Mrs Barrymore would be out directly and asked us to take a seat.

My first sight of the woman who was probably still Carl's legal wife shook me rigid. I was aware of Mariette stiffening by my side. Claire Mendleson Barrymore was dressed in a cream silk trouser suit straight off the pages of *Vogue*, and radiated elegance and sophistication. She was smiling when she strode confidently towards us, but the smile slipped when she saw me. Not surprising.

We were so alike we could have been doubles. Even

her elaborately coiffured hair, with its shimmering reddish tint, and so many layers of immaculate make-up that they paled the receptionist's efforts into insignificance, could not disguise how alike we were.

I falteringly introduced myself, although something told me I didn't need to. Neither of us commented on our tremendous physical similarity, either then or later, but it was breathtakingly obvious. Only the window dressing differentiated us. I fancied that the receptionist was studying us curiously, too.

'I was with Harry in the UK,' I said ambiguously. 'Something happened there. I don't know if you know anything about it . . .'

She interrupted me sharply. 'More than I want to. You'd better come into the office.'

Grant had been quite right. She was no longer smiling and was clearly not pleased to see us. Neither was she going to discuss her private business in a public area of the hotel. She led us to the privacy of a small computer-filled room at the back of the reception area and closed the door firmly behind us before speaking again.

'I really had hoped he was dead.' Anger bursting from her, she almost spat out the words.

I flinched. Mariette put a hand on my arm. I still didn't speak.

'What do you want with me anyway?' asked Carl's wife.

'I wondered if Carl, I mean Harry, had been here, been in touch with you,' I replied, and realised as I spoke how feeble I sounded.

'No, thank God,' she said. But she didn't sound angry any more. Just weary. And sad. I could identify with that well enough.

316

'The cops have been on to me, of course. Wanted to know that too,' she went on. 'I can't believe he'd dare face me ever again. And you? I know what he did to you. Surely you haven't come here looking for him, have you?'

I nodded, if a little tentatively.

'You must be out of your mind. I never want to set eyes on the son of a bitch again. He killed my daughter and he's still doing his best to wreck my life.'

I could understand her feelings. Not only had she lost a child, in horrific circumstances, but she thought she had escaped from her past. I was beginning to realise that nobody ever can. She had thought she was Mrs Wexford Barrymore. Now she wasn't so sure any more. The Florida police had notified her when it had been discovered who Carl really was after his arrest in Cornwall, and contacted her again when he had escaped from custody it appeared. All of it had been seriously bad news for her, the very worst.

'I have a new husband, two young sons and a new life,' she went on. 'I will never ever forget the daughter I lost, nor how I lost her . . . but . . . life goes on . . .'

There was a catch in her voice. She paused as if unable to continue for a moment. When she spoke again she did so quite calmly and deliberately. 'Harry was a raving lunatic. I didn't know it when I married him. You didn't know it either, did you? We both found out, though.'

Theodore Grant had hinted at her being mercenary and perhaps self-seeking. Well, who could blame her? She had built a new life out of the wreckage of one she wanted only to forget and she didn't want it spoiled. She had tried to bury the terrible hurt of her previous life. I could relate to that. I studied her for a moment before we left. There was genuine pain in her eyes. She may not have been the kind of person I would choose for a friend, she did not exactly ooze warmth, but then, why should she to Mariette and me? She was another very American painted lady, but beneath the overdone layers of apparently obligatory make-up she was, more than likely, a perfectly ordinary, probably perfectly nice woman. And she had suffered. There was no doubt about that.

I didn't like her, though, for all that. But then, I suppose I wouldn't, would I?

I had just one request to make before we left. 'If you do ever hear anything from him, would you let me know?'

She laughed humourlessly. 'He really got you under his spell, didn't he?' she remarked. 'He did it to me once too . . .'

She was right, of course. I had been under Carl's spell. He was that kind of man.

'Look, Suzanne Adams, or whatever you call yourself, if the bastard ever walked into my life again I don't know what I would do. And that's the honest truth of it. I'll tell you one thing, though, he's wrecked my life once. I'm not going to let him do it again . . .'

Her words were strangely chilling. Her façade of sophistication could not mask the turmoil she was so patently experiencing. There was desperation in her voice. Her eyes glazed over as she spoke. I wasn't sure at all what she meant and suspected it might be better for my peace of mind that way. Certainly, I found myself hoping that if Carl was in America he would not try to contact his real wife.

Desperation can make people dangerous, as I knew only too well. Carl had been desperate when he had forced me to hide away with him back in Cornwall, and kept me locked up in that dreadful hut. I had considerable sympathy for the painted lady and all she had suffered, but I couldn't help wondering how far she would go to protect her new life.

There was no sense in hanging around at Bay Point. Even with my inheritance we couldn't begin to afford a room there and it didn't seem very likely that the management would invite us to stay as their guests. We climbed back into the hire car and headed on down to Key West.

'Wow,' said Mariette. 'I couldn't believe how much that woman looks like you. You saw it, didn't you. I know you did. You couldn't miss it . . .'

Uneasily I muttered my agreement.

'They say men always do that, marry the same woman over and over again. Looks are the only thing you have in common, though, I reckon, thank God. She's a bit of a hard case, isn't she?'

I smiled grimly. 'After what she's been through, what do you expect?'

I was, however, deeply disturbed by my meeting with the woman with whom Carl had shared years of his life, the woman who had given birth to his child. I suppose that was natural enough, but my feelings went way beyond jealousy or resentment or anything like that.

'There's something nobody's telling us, I'm sure of it,' I said. 'Something that has caused Carl to be the way he is.'

We had called ahead to Key West and booked into

the Artists House, home of the painter who had played such a part in Carl's childhood. Mariette insisted that I needed to calm down and relax. She was probably right. The Bay Point experience had made me very tense indeed.

She drove in a leisurely fashion and managed to find a wonderful roadside fish restaurant for lunch, which someone back home in Cornwall had recommended. Even if you knew the mile marker it was hard to spot Monte's, little more than a shack by the roadside, but as I tucked into fresh prawns and deep-fried soft-shelled crabs I was very glad we had managed to find it. I had learned to enjoy fresh seafood in St Ives, but had never eaten stuff like this – and out of cardboard cartons with a plastic knife and fork.

We arrived at Key West around midday. Mariette manoeuvred the car efficiently enough through the narrow streets of the island that forms the furthermost tip of America and even managed to find a parking space not far from the centrally positioned Artists House.

The man in charge, Jim, bade us welcome and showed us to a room, which I thought was stunningly beautiful. It had once been Eugene Otto's studio. The furniture was old and solid. I had never been in so beautiful a room. Mariette and I were both bowled over.

Even the house cat, Boots, was a stunner: big, black and sleek.

I mentioned Carl's name to Jim, his real name, Harry Mendleson.

Jim looked blank. 'We've only had the house a couple of years,' he said, when I told him how Carl had been brought up in Key West and had spent many hours in the very studio room we were renting watching Gene Otto paint. 'I'll ask around. There's sure to be somebody who knows.'

That evening we walked down to Mallory Dock in time for the sunset. We ordered margaritas out on the pier and sat on high stools gazing west. The waiters and waitresses wore big smiles that said 'Please tip me', and kept wishing everyone a nice day. There was a carnival atmosphere. It was one of the perfect sunsets the island is famous for. The sun was a blazing amber ball when it sank into the sea and everybody cheered. I fell very silent. It was exactly the way Carl had described it to me and precisely how I had imagined it. Except for one thing. Carl was not there with me.

I drank in the atmosphere and made myself concentrate. Could he be here somewhere, drinking in a bar, walking along the beach, just a stone's throw away from me?

'Birds come home to roost . . . people always want to go back, they can't stop themselves.' DC Carter's words haunted me. I knew by then that nobody much had a very high opinion of the man or his ability as a detective, but his theory was convincing and, as he had told me, based on long experience.

We walked back up Duval Street taking in the sights and found a rather good hamburger joint where we gorged ourselves on burgers and fries. On the way back to the Artists House we called at a couple of bars. Everywhere we went I asked after Harry Mendleson but drew a blank. I suppose it wasn't surprising. As far as I knew he had left Key West more than twenty years previously, had only rarely returned and had left America a good fifteen years ago. The Key is inclined to have a transient population. People come there to work in the tourist industry or just bum about for a time before relaunching themselves into real life – and nothing much about Key West was very real, I was already beginning to discover.

There must be some people in Key West who had lived there all their lives and maybe generations of their families before them, but on that first night we never came close to finding any. Maybe they had more sense than to hang out in the bars of Duval Street.

In the morning when we wandered into the kitchen at the Artists House where Jim was serving a casual buffet breakfast, he had encouraging news. 'Frank Harvey,' he said. 'That's who you want to speak to, apparently. He's a retired doctor. Lived here all his life and treated half the town. You'll find him in Ezra's bar out by the southernmost point almost every night, they say.'

'Who told you? Was it someone who knew Carl . . . I mean Harry.'

'I don't think so,' said Jim. 'I was just told Frank Harvey is the man who definitely knew him, knew the family. There's a story . . .'

He paused.

'Go on,' I coaxed.

Jim looked uncertain. 'No,' he said eventually. 'You should get it from the horse's mouth, I reckon.'

Frank Harvey looked more like a retired farmer than a doctor. And one who had led a pretty hard life at that. He was very tall and thin, and had a weathered, leathery brown face, framed by wisps of white hair, from which shone the brightest of blue eyes. It was difficult to guess his age but I thought he must be well over seventy.

He had not been difficult to find. The barman pointed him out at once. He was sitting on a bar stool with a bottle of beer and a newspaper in front of him.

I introduced myself as Suzanne Adams. He put down his bottle of beer and peered at me curiously.

'Would you like another?' I enquired.

He nodded. 'English?'

I confirmed that both Mariette and I were.

'Where ya from?'

I told him St Ives. He asked where that was.

'Cornwall.'

'Anywhere near a place called Penzance?'

'About seven miles.'

He nodded, removed the pair of heavy framed spectacles he was wearing. 'Can't see to read without these danged things on but can't see beyond a yard when I got 'em on either.' He stopped abruptly. 'I should have known it,' he murmured.

'Known what?' I asked.

'No, you first.'

'I'm looking for someone,' I said. 'His name's Harry Mendleson . . . I think you knew him once.'

Frank Harvey nodded, almost as if this was what he had expected to hear. 'So you're Suzanne,' he murmured, still staring at me. 'Why isn't he with you?'

I was startled. 'What do you mean?' I asked.

Frank Harvey took a long pull at the neck of his beer bottle. 'I had a letter from him a few weeks back, first thing I've heard in fifteen years. Said he wanted to get in touch again, maybe wanted to come back here. And there was someone he wanted to bring, someone he loved, someone called Suzanne . . .'

My heart lurched. I hadn't expected anything like this, not so soon, anyway, and with so little detective work. Thank you, DC Carter, I said to myself, you *were* right. Maybe, just maybe, Carl was actually here in Key West. 'But you haven't seen him? Or have you? Have you seen him, Doctor Harvey? Please tell me.' I was falling over my words.

The old man was too slow for me. 'Not in fifteen years.' he said. 'Not since it all happened and he went away. He telephoned me then, from Miami airport, to say goodbye. Then I never heard a thing, not until this letter. I was fond of Harry . . .'

'I have to find him,' I blurted out. 'He's gone missing. I-I don't think he's well. Can you tell me anything that might help me find him.'

The doctor seemed to consider my words carefully. But he did not speak.

I realised I had no choice if I was going to get him to trust me, so I filled the silence by telling him, as briefly as I thought I could get away with, about how I had met Carl, about Robert's death, about how Carl came to be charged with abduction and how, finally, he had escaped from the court jail in Penzance.

Frank Harvey looked sad but not all that surprised. 'Still running, then,' he murmured. He leaned closer to me. 'The years you were together, were they good years?'

'Well, yes, mostly, sort of . . .' I mumbled.

'Mostly, sort of,' he repeated. 'That sounds like Harry. Don't suppose he ever let you out of his sight, did he?'

I had to agree that was so, more or less. But I was somehow instantly defensive. 'I know what happened in Key Largo. I know why he had to leave the States. We've been to Largo, talked to Claire and to the policeman, Theodore Grant, who investigated the case. But I am convinced there must be something more that they weren't telling me.'

'Are you indeed? Well, you might be right, young lady. I don't suppose either of them told you that Claire Mendleson's affair was with Theodore Grant and that he was Harry's closest friend, did they?'

I turned to Mariette. 'There, I knew there was more. No wonder Carl, I mean Harry, went off the rails.'

Mariette didn't look impressed. 'If every man whose wife had an affair with his best friend started locking her up there'd be a lot fewer people walking the streets, that's for sure,' she said.

I frowned at her. But Frank Harvey had started to talk again. He sounded tired. 'Claire once complained to me that Harry used to call up the stores when she went shopping to check she was where she was supposed to be. Couldn't have been easy for a woman like that. Maybe you can't blame her for turning against him.' He sighed deeply. 'Harry was always off the rails, I guess, Suzanne. I was fond of him, still am. He's not a bad man, is Harry. Too much history, that's all . . .'

I waited expectantly.

Frank Harvey was staring into my eyes. 'You don't know do you?'

'Know what?'

What happened here in Key West when Harry was just a teenager, the baggage he's always had to carry with him?'

325

He started talking then about the old days, about Carl's father, Billy Mendleson and how he had never had the talent as a painter that he thought he had and how he had taken to drowning his sorrows in drink and drugs. 'Bit like we're all inclined to do in Key West,' the doctor muttered ruefully, lifting his bottle again.

I was almost impatient at first because he talked so slowly and much of this I knew already. Not all of it, though. Not by a long way, as it turned out.

'Billy took to knocking young Harry's mother around in the end,' he related. 'She denied it for years, of course. Why do women always try to hide it?'

He shook his head sorrowfully. I didn't know the answer, but I knew he was right. I always used to try to hide what Robert Foster did to me. He had expected me to and I did my best to do so. I began to realise why Carl had been so exceptionally moved when he discovered how badly Robert had beaten me.

Frank Harvey was still speaking. 'Harry had an awful childhood. His father ignored him most of the time, gave him the odd clout too, I shouldn't wonder, and his mother was too caught up with coping with his father to take much notice of him. They both took solace in drugs. Harry used to try and help his mother; from when he was a little lad, he did what he could. But I never thought she wanted helping.

'Harry was a bright kid, though, and a much more talented artist than his father was ever going to be. Billy wouldn't admit it, of course. True, though. There was a schoolteacher who encouraged the boy and, right against the odds, Harry won a place at a top art school in Miami.

'He did well there and he didn't come home for almost a year. Can't say I blamed him. Then he got a call from his mother begging him to come back and talk to his father. The beatings were getting worse, that was the truth of it, but she told Harry she wanted his help to get his father off the drugs, to get him to seek help.

'Harry came home all right. But he took one look at his father and saw an even more hopeless case than he remembered. He told his mother she had to leave. Harry was still only eighteen, but he'd had to grow up fast. He wanted his mother to go back to Miami with him. He was selling paintings and he had a grant. He had a two-roomed flat and they'd manage, he told her. She'd always hung on to Billy like a limpet in spite of everything, but she agreed in the end. Harry wanted them to take off without telling anyone, but Jeana said she had to tell Billy. Couldn't just leave him. Couldn't live with herself if she did that.

'She sent Harry out. Said she wanted to tackle Billy alone. Harry walked the streets, had a beer or two, stayed away like his mother asked him for two hours or more before he returned to their little house out the back of town.'

Frank Harvey paused and took an even longer drag of his beer. He might start off slowly, but he was a grand story-teller. If he was deliberately trying to build up dramatic effect then he succeeded admirably, and the finale to his tale was no anticlimax. 'Everything was quiet. Harry assumed his father had taken off on a bar crawl, or had simply drugged himself to oblivion. The kitchen door was unlocked and he stepped inside. There were no lights on. He slid on something slippery. He fumbled for the light switch and turned it on.

'His mother was lying on the floor at his feet in a pool of blood. Her throat had been cut and her head very nearly severed from her body.

'Behind her in the open doorway Harry could see a pair of feet and legs dangling. Later, much later, he said he knew what he was going to see before he got there. His father had hanged himself from the banisters.'

I don't know what I had expected. Nothing like this. I gripped the edge of the bar so tightly that my fingertips turned white.

I heard Mariette say, 'Oh, my God!'

Frank Harvey was watching me closely. 'Do you want me to go on?' he asked evenly.

I nodded. It was all I could manage.

He began to speak again. 'At the time, Harry didn't have anything to say. I was the police doctor then, as well as being the family doctor. It was some crime scene, I can tell you. And young Harry just couldn't find any words.

'In fact, the boy went into severe shock. He didn't speak for three months. He blamed himself, you see, always blamed himself for not making his mother run off with him.' Frank Harvey sighed deeply. 'Way I see it, young Harry's been running from something or other ever since.'

Twenty

Carl had never told me any of it. I found that hard to take. In a peculiar way I felt a certain sense of guilt, too. I had always been so wrapped up in my own problems, my own past. Maybe it was because of this that Carl had never felt he could confide in me.

It was a truly horrific story and explained so much about Carl. I dreaded to think what he must have gone through when he found Robert lying in a pool of blood – exactly the way he had found his own mother. Then there was his daughter's horrific death, in an accident for which he was responsible.

I bought Frank Harvey another beer and he carried on with the story.

It seemed that Doctor Harvey was actually a qualified clinical psychiatrist but he just hadn't been cut out for a big-time specialisation. 'Too much Key West in my blood,' he said with a chuckle rasping hoarse from the effects of years of cigarette smoking, I reckoned. He accepted a bourbon chaser, lit up another Marlboro, passed one to Mariette, coughed some more and carried on talking, telling us how something unfightable had drawn him back to practise general medicine in his home town.

'Guess I'm just another Keys bar bum. Only difference between me and all the others is that I used to keep the old doctor's bag behind the bar.'

I reckoned he was probably not doing himself

justice. Through the haze of cigarette smoke his eyes blazed clever and clear, perhaps surprisingly so in view of his obvious love of beer and whiskey.

The case of Harry Mendleson, my Carl, had fascinated him, he explained. 'Guess I sometimes used to hanker after what might have been. Trying to sort young Harry out did me as much good as it did him, I reckon, maybe more. I became his therapist, unofficially, but that's what it was. Mind you, if Harry had heard it called that he'd probably have refused to have anything to do with me.

'He abandoned his art college, simply didn't go back, wouldn't talk about it, wouldn't talk at all. He was sick, no doubt about that. I took him under my wing, I suppose, even put him up for a bit. The house his parents lived in was rented, of course, and he couldn't afford the rent. About a fortnight after the tragedy I went round there and the landlord had had him out already. Took me two days to find the boy. He was sleeping rough under the pier. Didn't look like he'd eaten or drunk a thing in days. I took him home with me, fed him chicken and fries, and he bolted it down like he was starving. Still didn't speak, though. I installed him in the spare room, got my books out and went to work. Every spare minute I had I talked to him, but it was three months before I coaxed a word out of him.'

I was moved by the image of Carl being shocked into silence. After all, the same thing had happened to me as a child, although I had been so young that I did not remember it, only what Gran had later told me.

'Now three months doesn't sound much, but it's some long time for a man not to speak, believe me,' Frank Harvey continued. 'Then, when he did start to talk, well, it was like unstopping a blocked pipe in your sink. The words gushed out. Guilt and blame, that was the sum of it, really. The kid had nothing to be guilty about, nothing to blame himself for. He tried to do his best, took on more than any kid his age I ever knew, but he didn't see it that way. If he'd done something different, if he'd taken his mother away straight off, or if he'd told his father instead of leaving that to her, it would never have happened. He could have prevented it. That's what he kept saying.

'Took almost a year before he was halfways functioning properly again. He never did go back to college but I had this old pal who ran an ad agency up in Largo – tourist stuff for the hotels and all. He owed me. I sent him Harry. In spite of everything the boy did good and he worked there till all his other troubles started.'

Frank Harvey sighed deeply and drank deeply. I bought him another bourbon and waited.

'More than his share of troubles, no doubt about that. And him always just wanting to look after people, to protect them.'

I spoke then. 'That was it from the beginning, with me. I needed protecting and there he was, just longing to protect me.'

'It is a sickness, you know,' went on Frank Harvey. 'Carl became anankastic. I've always been quite sure of that. It's an extreme personality disorder, associated with excessive controlling behaviour. His overwhelming desire to protect those he loves is all part of it. You've probably heard of Othello syndrome, that's excessive jealousy. Then there's Oedipus, obsession with your mother, generally sexual. Those are the more high-profile conditions. If you're anankastic you probably have a bit of both of those in you too.'

I felt a shiver down my spine. I had loved Carl so and there was no doubt that he had loved me. If only I had realised how flawed he had been, maybe I would have been able to help him.

Frank Harvey continued to talk. 'An anankastic is obsessive in his personal habits as well, meticulously tidy, scrupulously clean and insisting on those standards all around him. He's a very ordered person, likes routine, always has to be the one to check the house is locked up at night, would never leave a single dish in the sink when he goes to bed. That kind of thing. And of course, he'd want to know where the person he loved was and exactly what she was doing every minute of the day and night. Does that sound like the man you knew?'

I nodded bleakly. It all flashed through my mind, from how he liked to wash himself and me after sex, to how scrupulously he kept his paintbox and catalogued his work, and above all how he had always taken over my entire life.

'In lay terms an anankastic is an extreme control freak,' Frank Harvey continued. 'His motives are nearly always good. Harry's almost certainly are. He just wants to take care of those he loves, that's how he sees it.'

Frank Harvey was suddenly sounding like a doctor. I noticed how kind his eyes were as well as everything else. I could see how Carl, who never liked to talk about himself, had been able to confide in this man. I struggled to take in the enormity of what he was telling me.

'I could forgive him everything, except letting me

live a lie all those years,' I said softly. 'I think he may have let me believe I had killed my husband. I think he may have known all along that I didn't. And that's such a cruel thing . . .'

Frank Harvey interrupted me there. 'But you're not sure that he did, are you? And in any case, self-delusion is part of his condition. Even if he did know at the beginning that you hadn't killed your husband, he almost certainly came to believe that you had as much as you did yourself. In self-defence, of course. So he had to protect you, look after you like nobody else could. He was sick, Suzanne, remember that. He is still sick.'

I had never thought about it that way round before. I was grateful to the doctor. It hurt me so much to think that Carl could have deliberately lied to me about Robert's death. I grasped at the straw, comforted to think that maybe he had been as weak and confused as me, and that he had never wanted to be cruel.

I thanked Frank Harvey for his words of solace. 'I guess I had come to understand that he must be sick, even before I met you and you told me all of this. I still feel . . . I am not sure, really, but I suppose I still love him.' I fell silent.

'He's the kind of man to inspire that sort of love; he was as a kid.' Frank Harvey sounded as if he was talking to himself not me. He was staring into his glass. When he looked up his voice was quite brisk. 'And you think he may have come here, come back to his roots?' he queried.

I nodded. 'I didn't know where else to look,' I said. 'At first I thought he'd come looking for me. I thought that might have been why he broke out of jail.

Perhaps I was just kidding myself – in any case, he didn't come to me. I waited. The police were sure he would come to me too. Then I just got this feeling that maybe he needed to return here for something. Now you've told me the dreadful story I feel all the more sure I'm right. Though I don't even know how he could have got here. He had no passport . . .'

'Plenty of initiative, Harry. Needed it, the way he was brought up,' muttered the doctor.

'So you think he could be here?'

'Key West is a village. Can't imagine he'd be here long without me getting to know. Any case, he'd want to see me, I reckon.'

'Maybe not straight way,' I said. 'Look, does it make sense to you that he would come here? That's what I want to know.'

'Yes, I guess it does.'

'So where could he be?'

The doctor shrugged. 'I'd love to help you find him, Suzanne, if I could. I've my own guilt, you see. Maybe I wasn't qualified to help Harry. Maybe I should have sent him to a place where he could get proper help. My partner back then reckoned Harry ought to have been in a hospital. I thought it would be the end of him, that I could do better. Maybe I was wrong. I never in my wildest imaginings thought Harry would ever hurt anybody.'

'But he didn't,' I said quickly; then, remembering all that had happened: 'Not really . . .'

Frank Harvey smiled sadly. 'Suzanne, his daughter got killed, he abducted you and kept you prisoner.'

'He didn't mean to hurt his daughter. He was trying to help her, wasn't he? And he didn't abduct me, that wasn't the way he saw it, he only wanted to keep me safe. He didn't mean to hurt anybody.' I blurted the words out, tears misting my eyes. It was all such a mess and I knew it even as I spoke.

'But he did hurt people. I know he didn't mean to. It's not in his nature. Harry isn't an evil man, he's never been that. He's always been a gentle, kind person. But he carries a lot of demons around with him. Maybe I didn't realise quite how many.'

'You've nothing to be guilty about, Doctor Harvey,' I said. I found I already liked and trusted this old man, who so clearly had his own flaws.

He smiled fleetingly. 'Call me Frank,' he said.

'Do you really think he believed I had killed Robert, that he came to accept it as the truth?' I asked.

'Almost certainly. It would have been intolerably cruel otherwise to have allowed you to bear that burden for so long. Harry would not deliberately be so cruel. It's just that, well, we all make ourselves believe certain things, particularly about those we love. With Harry it goes a bit deeper. He puts those he loves on a pedestal, wants them to be in a situation where only he can take care of them, and that's what he makes himself believe, that he has to protect them.'

I reached out and touched the doctor's hand. It was veined blue with age and shook slightly, the result of all that whiskey no doubt. 'Thank you, Frank,' I said and I meant it.

He understood at once, I could see that, and put his other hand on top of mine. 'You've loved a good man, Suzanne,' he murmured. 'But a good man with a terrible weakness.'

I smiled, lapping up the reassurance. I had lost a lot

335

of my belief in myself when I stopped believing in Carl. You do that, I think, if you have devoted many years of your life to something you discover might have been a lie. I had come to think this about my whole relationship with Carl. I knew now that it hadn't been a lie, I knew it with devastating clarity. I just wanted to find Carl and tell him too.

'Come and see me tomorrow at my house,' said Frank Harvey, jotting down his address on a beer mat. 'I've got something I want to show you.'

'The letter?'

'Sure. And something else besides . . .'

Mariette tucked her arm through mine as we walked back to the Artists House. It was a beautiful night. The moon cast long shadows along the streets and the stars were so bright that in patches the black sky turned almost to silvery white.

When we got back to the house Mariette ordered me to put on my bathing costume, produced a bottle of white wine from the fridge in our room and led me to the jacuzzi in the backyard. 'We need a drink and a bit of relaxing,' she said.

The water was warm and frothy, and the wine was cold and smooth. The combined effect was indeed relaxing. And although Frank Harvey's story had shocked me rigid it brought me closer to understanding Carl and what had made him into the kind of man he was more than anything that had come before.

By the time we came to go to bed I was pleasantly drowsy and I slept more soundly than I had in weeks.

In the morning I felt refreshed both in mind and body. 'He has to be here, he just has to be,' I said.

Mariette did not look convinced. 'You heard what Frank Harvey said, Key West is a village. He'd know . . .'

'Not necessarily, not if Carl did not want him too. It was fifteen years ago that anybody here last saw him. People change and Carl is very resourceful, you know.'

'Yes,' said Mariette crisply. I knew that she was still not at all sure that Carl really was worth looking for.

'I have to find him,' I told her simply.

Mariette sighed. 'I know, it's just that . . . well, all this psychobabble, it doesn't actually change the dreadful things he did, does it?'

Mariette was Cornish and down to earth. Her reaction was entirely predictable and probably very good for me.

'It does for me,' I nonetheless replied firmly.

The next morning after breakfast I left Mariette lazing in the Artists House gardens and contemplating yet another session in the jacuzzi, while I found my way to Frank Harvey's house, an attractive wood-fronted old place in a quiet tree-lined road just a block or two away from his favourite bar.

He took me into a small book-lined sitting room, slightly shabby but homely and comfortable, fed me coffee, then gave me his letter from Carl. It held no surprises. It was just as Frank Harvey had told me, but I found it quite moving to hold it in my hand and to see Carl's neat, carefully formed handwriting again.

I have a new identity and a new love in my life. Her name is Suzanne and she means everything to me. I dream of one day being able to bring her back to

337

Key West, but I do not know if it will ever be possible. I would have to live as the person I now am, not Harry Mendleson any more. Would anyone there remember me, apart from you, do you think?

Carl had included a Post Office box number in Penzance, something else I hadn't known about.

'I replied, but I've never heard any more,' said Frank Harvey.

'By the time your letter arrived in Penzance, Carl was probably already in jail,' I reflected wryly.

The doctor nodded. Then he picked up another envelope from the table beside his chair, removed a photograph from it and passed it across to me.

The picture was of a man and a woman with a small boy. I knew instinctively that the boy was Carl, even though I had never before seen any photographs of him as a child. The man looked a bit like Carl did now, only his reddish-blond hair was much longer, almost down to his shoulders, and he had a full beard.

It was the woman who was the shock. I could almost have been looking at a photograph of myself.

I gasped. 'Is that why you said "should have known it" when you first looked at me properly in the bar last night?'

Frank Harvey nodded and gestured towards the picture. 'Harry with his parents,' he remarked unnecessarily.

I studied the photograph more closely. When it was taken, Carl's mother would probably have been a little older than I was now, in her early thirties, I thought, and her hair was approaching waist length, very Seventies. But the likeness to myself was staggering. 'All three of us are alike. Claire looks just like her too,' I said quietly.

Frank Harvey nodded again. 'Yep. That worried me from the start. And Harry married her within six weeks of meeting her. I reckoned he was looking for his mother more than for a wife and Claire was never going to be that. Harry felt that he had let his mother down, not looked after her properly. I never managed to change his mind about that. It's what turned him anankastic in the first place, I'm sure of it. He kept trying to put it right, you see, I think that's how he saw it. That's what he did with Claire, and he failed. Tragically . . .

'Then you came along and he tried to do the same thing with you.'

I thought again, as I did so often, about my first meeting with Carl. So that was why he had approached me in the way he had. He had seen his own mother sitting there on that old decaying tree trunk, his mother crying those awful, desperate tears. That was why he had loved me so obsessively and why he had always been so determined to protect me. Fleetingly I wondered if that was all there had ever been behind his love for me.

'Can an anankastic be cured?' I asked suddenly.

Frank Harvey looked thoughtful. 'Probably not,' he replied. 'But his condition can be controlled. I reckon Carl managed to do that a lot of the time, from what you've told me, didn't he.'

I nodded agreement. I had nothing to say. I was shaken by just how little I had known of the man I had shared my life with.

Over the next few days I despatched Mariette to ride

the Conch Train through the city streets, visit Hemingway's house and take part in the other tourist rituals that were almost obligatory for visitors to Key West, while I looked for Carl.

This was all I wanted to do. It was what I had come to America for. And I was happiest alone. I prayed that I would catch sight of him around every street corner, in every bar I hoped to meet someone who had seen him. Most didn't even seem to grasp what I was saying, or maybe that was just the impression they gave, and appeared to regard me merely as possible pick-up material.

At night Mariette and I had dinner together and maybe visited a bar or two, while I tried desperately not to spend the entire time pumping everyone we encountered about Carl. Mariette, of course, fitted into Key West as if it were a pair of old slippers – as, indeed, to anyone born and bred in St Ives it more or less was. I truly felt there was a strange kinship between this idiosyncratic island at the southernmost tip of America and the little Cornish seaside town in which we had made our home. Those who are left of the indigenous population of Key West are a weird and wonderful lot. Curious though it may seem, I really could believe that you could swap them with the remains of the indigenous population of St Ives with not a lot of trouble. Carl had been right about that. They would fit easily into each others' environments. So strange to come halfway across the world and feel this.

Mariette, of course, denied it hotly. 'When we go back you can try asking for a margarita down the Sloop and I'll just watch,' she said, deliberately refusing to understand what I was trying to say.

I gave up, then. But I still believed I had discovered a truth.

Every evening at sunset, while Mariette drank margaritas at Mallory Dock and flirted outrageously with the waiters, something of a reflex action for her, I reckoned, I got in the habit of walking by the sea. I had a vague belief that I would find Carl on a beach somewhere at this time of day, away from the masses of people on the pier, all alone watching the sun go down.

Mariette and I had bought the cheapest air tickets available and were locked in to a flight home after ten days. Having spent eight of these in Key West, fruitlessly searching for my lost man, it was time to head back towards Miami. With a heavy heart, now, I went for my last evening beach walk. I had lost my initial optimism, my stubborn belief that Carl must be here somewhere. I was coming to have to accept that the world was a pretty big place. He could be anywhere.

As far as Key West was concerned my search had become merely automatic. I no longer believed Carl was there.

On this last night on the island I walked along the beach over by the big hotels at the back of the old town with my head down, kicking my toes in the sand, not even bothering to look around me.

I heard the music first, those familiar haunting strains wafting through the cooling evening air.

> Suzanne takes you down
> To her place near the river
> You can hear the boats go by
> You can spend the night beside her . . .

Then I saw him. He was sitting on the sand with his back to me, hunched into some kind of dark coat, silhouetted against the setting sun. I could just see the top of his head, the familiar sprouting of spiky fair hair. The music was coming from a ghetto blaster by his side.

For a second or two I stopped in my tracks. I stood absolutely still. Then I began to run, calling his name, but still he did not turn round.

By the time I reached him the tears were pouring down my face. I flung myself on to the sand in front of him and reached out my arms towards him. His head was slumped almost on to his chest. At last he looked up.

His eyes were glazed and bloodshot. His skin was filthy and covered in red blotches. His hair was actually peroxide white, black at the roots and filthy. He stank. The eyes stared, the trembling, cracked lips began to shape a parody of a smile. 'Who are you, then, sweetheart? Come to keep me warm in the night, have you?'

He swayed his body towards me. I recoiled sharply, at the same time noticing the empty syringe nearby on the sand. From the ghetto blaster I vaguely heard the voice of a disc jockey. 'And there we have it, folks, an ultimate sound of the Seventies . . .'

My arms were still outstretched. Gravity allowed them to fall to my sides. I shuffled further back from him, found my feet and started to run, the tears falling freely now.

It had not been Carl sitting on the beach waiting for me to come to him, to find him, while he played our song over and over again. Just some sad druggie giving himself a fix. Oblivious, probably, to the music being played on his radio, to the song that had shaped so much of my life.

I slowed to a walk and wiped away the worst of my tears before rejoining Mariette on the pier. Nonetheless she gave me a curious glance and the muscle-bound young man in singlet and shorts who had no doubt been chatting her up took one look at me and retreated fast.

My distress had turned to anger, and I think it showed. 'C'mon let's pack and get out of here,' I said. 'I'm done with chasing shadows.'

Twenty-One

We went to bed early and left right after breakfast, having decided to spend our last night at the Neptune Motel from which we could be at Miami airport in just over an hour and a half. I promised Mariette that the search for Carl in the Keys was over. I didn't tell her about my experience with the druggie and his radio, but she knew something had happened.

We drove the first part of the journey in silence. I had insisted that I didn't even want to talk about Carl any more and that I intended simply to enjoy our last twenty-four hours in Florida. The trouble was that when you cut Carl out of the conversation just like that, there suddenly didn't seem to be anything else to talk about.

Mariette wasn't fooled. As we crossed the bridge into Islamarada she glanced at me sideways. 'Want to check with the painted lady?' she asked.

I shook my head.

Mariette smiled. 'Liar. It won't take ten minutes. At least you may be able to satisfy yourself that Carl hasn't been to see her while we've been chasing all round Key West.'

I smiled back. 'Thanks,' I said.

Maybe I remained a dreadful judge of men, or perhaps it was just how you looked at things, but as far as finding a friend went I'd struck gold with Mariette. I was certain enough of that.

We pulled into the Bay Point's mile or so long drive just before 11 a.m. and this time were able to drive straight to reception. The plastic receptionist greeted us with the same artificial smile as before and, when we asked to see Mrs Barrymore, pushed a series of buttons on the telephone beside her with what was no doubt her customary efficiency.

Over the phone's speaker system the voice I remembered so well said simply: 'Yes.'

'I have Miss Adams and Miss Powell from the UK for you again, Mrs Barry . . .' began the girl.

She was interrupted by an angry-toned outburst: 'Sandra, didn't I say that if those two turned up again you were to tell them I was . . .'

We didn't hear the rest because Sandra promptly switched the speaker mode off. Blushing slightly she apologised to us and said that unfortunately Mrs B. was not available. It was quite reassuring to see that Sandra did have some human qualities but we obviously were going to learn no more from Claire Mendleson Barrymore.

We told Sandra we'd got the message and left.

'I wonder if she has heard from Carl,' I mused aloud as we climbed back into the hire car.

'She won't be telling us, that's for sure, not either way,' muttered Mariette.

'I can't help wondering what she might do if he did turn up here. I think she might be capable of, well anything, don't you . . .'

Mariette was ever practical and to the point. She was also beginning to lose patience, I suspected. 'What, like your Carl you mean?'

'No, of course not . . .'

She interrupted me. 'I know, I know, he never

meant to hurt anyone. If you ask me, he and the painted lady probably deserved each other.'

I decided to ignore her inferences. 'She would like nothing better than to be rid of him for ever, though, wouldn't she?' I persisted.

Mariette sighed wearily. 'Suzanne, you've been watching too many bad movies.'

I imagined she was right, as usual. But I decided to make just one last call. From the Neptune Motel I phoned Theodore Grant – I didn't feel up to any more rebuffs in the flesh – and asked him the question I had wanted to put to Claire.

'No,' he responded easily enough. 'Still no sign of him around here. But, in any case, I don't figure he'd want to seek me out . . .'

I gave him Mariette's number back home and asked if he would be good enough to call us there if he ever did see Carl or hear anything at all of him. He agreed he would, although I didn't really believe him. I didn't tell him that I had learned about the part he had played in the break-up of Carl's marriage and all that happened after Claire told him she was leaving him. There didn't seem any point.

We had dinner at the Sundowners that night, enjoying the moonlit balminess of the Keys for the last time. At least, I hoped Mariette enjoyed it. Try as I might, I remained totally preoccupied.

The next day we drove to Miami, deposited the hire car and caught our flight home, which, while torturous in every other way, as had been the outward flight, at least left and arrived on time.

I guess I had been harbouring the hope that we would return to some news of Carl. We didn't. The Devon and Cornwall Constabulary continued to have an alert out for him but nobody had seen or heard anything of him. If it had been Carl who had thumbed a lift to Plymouth from a lorry driver, he had left no further trail. And while we were away a well-known local villain had been arrested and charged with the burglary at the Plymouth flat, and the stolen passport recovered.

Carl seemed to have disappeared into thin air, and I didn't need Mariette to remind me that this wasn't the first time.

Carl had fled to England after the death of his daughter, and built a new life and a new identity for himself. I had become part of that without even knowing it. Maybe he was just doing it again. Maybe that was how he would always live.

'If you ask me he's never stopped running,' Frank Harvey had said.

Perhaps it was all Carl really knew how to do. He had certainly always been good at it. He had had a kind of sixth sense, it seemed now, for keeping us out of trouble during our time at St Ives, right until the very end.

'Getting a new identity is no problem,' Rob Partridge had told me. 'It's not being able to let go of the past which catches people out.'

That and chance, and carelessness. Driving too fast, getting burgled, getting ill. Carl had never been careless. But he couldn't have bargained for Will Jones's ridiculous jealousy, and both of us were in turn so obsessed with our own pasts that even the possibility of those threatening letters having referred to anything except the various secrets we were hiding had only fleetingly occurred to us and been swiftly dismissed.

But now, one way or another, Carl was gone.

'You have a life to live,' Mariette instructed. 'You're on your own now and you just have to accept it.'

Once again she was right, of course. And perhaps one of my problems was that I still harboured the notion that sooner or later Carl would come looking for me.

There were times when I suspected Mariette's patience was running out for good, which was fair enough really.

Mariette's mother's patience was definitely running out. I was able to pay for my keep now, of course, but I knew that she would like her front room back. In any case there was barely space for me in it along with all those pieces of brass, and even if Mrs Powell's cottage had been big enough to accommodate a lodger comfortably I would not have been a particularly attractive long-term proposition – I came with far too much mental baggage.

In the end I stayed with the Powells for another three weeks after returning from America, before finding myself a small flat to rent just off the Hale Road. It was at the top of the hill past the Porthminster Hotel, quite a steep climb up from the town, and there was no sea view, but it was clean and comfortable, and would do well enough until I had fulfilled my next aim. I wanted to buy a modest home of my own. I had just about enough cash as long as I could work – and Mariette solved that problem for me a couple of weeks later when she announced excitedly that the St Ives Archive Study Centre, housed upstairs at the library, was looking for a new researcher. The pay was a pittance but it was better than nothing and the work suited me absolutely. Carl had been right about one thing: I had no experience of being employed and I had indeed wondered what kind of a job I would ever be capable of holding down. But I'd got lucky and found something that was close to perfect for me. It meant burying my nose in books and old papers, which I had done for pleasure all my life, and although I had never used computers before, I could type, thanks to Gran, and I took to the computer age with surprising ease. I was really quite excited about the whole thing. If I failed it would not be for want of enthusiasm or effort.

Nonetheless I found my first week at work totally exhausting. I supposed I would get used to it and that nervous tension was the main part of the problem. The Centre was involved in a particularly demanding project concerning the history of the part of town where the Tate Gallery now stands and I was even asked to work on the Saturday morning. Mariette was also on duty in the library but at lunchtime I turned down her suggestion that we go for a beer and a sandwich. All I wanted to do was to get back to my flat, put my feet up and have an afternoon nap.

It was the third week in August. Almost exactly three months had passed since Carl had escaped from the court jail at Penzance, and even I was beginning to wonder if he really had gone for good and reinvented himself somewhere else.

I kept in touch with DS Perry, but she had nothing more to tell me, although she assured me that she remained in contact with the police in America and that if there was any news of Carl there she would know at once.

For once I wasn't thinking about Carl at all as I began to walk wearily home that sunny Saturday afternoon. My new job had not only proved to be both mentally and physically tiring, but had also given me plenty to occupy my mind, which was probably just what I needed. The walk was uphill all the way. There was a bit of a short cut, which I had so far avoided because it would take me straight past Rose Cottage, but I was so worn out that I decided only the fastest way home would do.

When I turned into the familiar alleyway for the first time in so long, I noticed a Dyno-Rod van on the corner and, as I walked past the cottage, out stepped Will Jones. I supposed I had realised that I would meet him sooner or later, although since returning to St Ives I had deliberately avoided anywhere close to his gallery and the two or three pubs that I knew to be his favourite haunts, but I was shocked to see him emerging from my own front door. I still thought of it that way, you see. Well, six and a half years in one little house is a long time.

I gasped. Will stepped smartly back. Then he smiled. I glowered.

'Hi, Suzanne, I've been looking out for you,' he said. I could hardly believe my ears. Had the man no shame?

'What do you mean, looking out for me?' I snapped. 'Haven't you been following me? Isn't that what you normally do?'

He assumed a hangdog expression. 'I'm sorry, I can't help caring for you.'

He made me sick, he really did. He had caused so much damage.

'I've only ever wanted to look after you,' he said. His voice was a whine.

I wanted to slap his face. In any case the last thing in the world that I wanted was anyone 'looking after' me ever again.

'What are you doing in my house?' I asked coldly.

'It's not your house any more,' he replied.

'You know what I mean,' I said.

'I'm renting it,' he told me.

I had suspected as much. The very thought gave me the creeps. Was I to be haunted by obsessions all my life? 'I don't believe it!' I said. 'How could you?'

He assumed an expression of studied innocence. 'I have no idea what you mean. I just wanted a little place in the middle of St Ives, that's all.' He smiled, only it looked more like a leer.

I didn't know whether to laugh or cry. The whole thing was absurd. Will Jones lived in a big modern clifftop bungalow off the Penzance road. The only possible interest he could have in Rose Cottage was me. I knew that. And so did he.

'You're not actually living here, are you?' I enquired.

'Of course.' He puffed up his chest a bit and stood up very straight, as if the full extent of his towering six foot five would automatically give him an advantage. Somehow he managed to look even more pathetic.

'Will, you're not right in the head,' I said. 'Why don't you go and get yourself committed.'

'What, like your Carl should have done?'

I was not as short on courage as I had once been. I took a step forward and probably would have hit him but for the man from Dyno-Rod who emerged with perhaps fortuitous timing from Rose Cottage and, apparently oblivious to the conflict between Will and me, stepped between us and began to speak.

'Damned if I knows where it's coming from, mate, I've checked the drains right through and I can't find ought wrong . . .'

'That's all very well,' said Will, turning his attention abruptly away from me. 'But you're going to have to keep looking because I just can't put up with the stink in there.'

The Dyno-Rod man retreated back into the cottage, shaking his head and scratching it at the same time.

Will turned back to face me. 'Did you and Carl have any trouble with the drains?' he asked conversationally.

My anger welled up again. 'Will, I don't give a fuck about your fucking drains,' I stormed. 'But I'll tell you this.' I jabbed a finger firmly in his chest. 'If you are following me around again, if I ever see you, if you ever come near me, then I'm warning you, I'm just not responsible for what I might do to you. I have had enough, do you hear me?'

I wasn't entirely certain, but I didn't believe I had ever used the word 'fuck' in anger before. I thought I was being pretty menacing. Will appeared to think so too. He looked stunned rigid, which had indeed been my intention. In spite of my angry reaction when he had first told me he had been responsible for all the threats, he obviously still thought of me as meek and mild Suzanne. Maybe he had put that out of his mind. He was the sort of man who went in for selective memory. After all, it came hand in hand with obsession.

'OK, OK,' he said, backing off with both hands

held high in compliance. But I was so angry he didn't move quickly enough for me. I pushed him out of the way and he must have been off balance because he fell heavily on to one knee.

'I'm sorry, you just don't understand,' he whimpered pathetically.

I brushed past him, only narrowly overcoming the urge to kick him in the teeth.

I spent Sunday reading and being lazy. The afternoon was gloriously sunny and, braving the holidaymakers who were out in force, I went for a short walk along the beach. The sun felt warm on my back. I took off my shoes and walked barefooted, the way I used to with Carl, relishing the feel of the gritty sand between my toes. The afternoon light was almost blindingly bright. It was a true St Ives day. By the time I got home and made myself some supper to eat in front of the TV I was enjoying quite a sense of well-being.

I must be getting tougher, I thought, because the confrontation with Will had not disturbed me nearly as much as it once would have done. I was more outraged than upset that he had chosen to move into the little cottage that had been my home with Carl.

I had no doubt his motivation was all part of his obsession with me and this was further indication that it was far from over. But I felt strangely confident that I could deal with it now. I had seen the shock with which he responded to my outburst and had a feeling he had realised that not only was I no longer a pushover but neither any more was I the Suzanne he claimed to have such strong feelings for. Maybe he would leave me alone. If he didn't then I would simply report him to DS Perry and insist that this time she took formal action. He had already been cautioned once, I had been informed, when I had first told DC Carter who had been persecuting Carl and me. The law was getting harder on stalkers and quite right too. I knew well enough the damage they could do.

Still tired, in spite of my lazy day, I went to bed early and felt much brighter and more alert when I woke on Monday morning. I made an instant decision that I would no longer take the long route to work. I would walk straight past Rose Cottage whenever it suited me. I certainly was not prepared to avoid anywhere in town in order not to meet up with Will Jones.

Feeling quite sprightly and rejuvenated, I began the walk down the hill to the archive centre almost lightheartedly. It was a lot easier going down than climbing back up, for one thing.

As I approached Rose Cottage I noticed there was a uniformed policeman standing outside. My first thought was that I hadn't even reported Will Jones yet. Then I became aware of quite a buzz of activity around the cottage. On the corner I could see DS Perry's car and beyond that a police squad car. As I approached, out through the front door stepped a man clad from head to toe in a white paper suit. And through the open door opened, I fancied I got a whiff of the bad drain smell Will Jones had complained of.

Suddenly it hit me – I knew. My legs started to move of their own volition and I practically threw myself past the sentry policeman into the front room of Rose Cottage. He made a desultory attempt to stop me but, propelled by the horror of my awful realisation, I was too quick for him.

I heard myself scream 'Carl, Carl' as I headed for the little kitchen, which I could see was the centre of activity.

DS Perry was standing in the doorway. 'Suzanne don't,' she cried, alarm in her eyes.

I pushed past her too. My desolation gave me both power and purpose.

I charged by another white-suited character. The flagstone trapdoor to the little cellar was cast aside as I had somehow known it would be. Just as I reached it somebody grabbed me in a kind of rugby tackle around the legs but I flung myself on to my belly, half taking whoever it was with me, so that I could see clearly down into the cellar. In fact, I allowed virtually the whole of my top half to drop through the trap. The rest of me would have followed were it not for the grip on my legs.

The cellar was brightly lit by police arc lamps. My face was just a couple of feet away from the alarmed upturned features of another paper suit, this time a woman. She was on her knees examining something spreadeagled on the floor. The stench was awful here. The something on the floor took form. It was a man. A man with virtually no face. The man with no face of my nightmares, except I knew with devastating clarity who this was. And it was not anyone who had ever wanted to hurt me, just to protect me. The decay of his flesh, the puffy black nothingness of him did not detract from my instant recognition.

'Carl, Carl, Carl,' I screamed at the top of my voice. I was quite hysterical. Utterly beyond reason. Terrible grief, total horror overwhelmed me.

I felt myself being half pulled, half dragged up out of the hole in the ground away from the putrid remains of the only man I had ever loved. I was half carried into the dining room and helped into a chair. DS Perry was beside me making soothing noises. My eyes were blinded with tears. I brushed them aside as best I could with the back of my hand and tried to focus on her. All I could see, lurking behind her, white-faced, was Will Jones.

The madness came over me once more, and with it came the power and the purpose. I threw myself forward again, hurtling at him. 'You murdering bastard,' I screamed. 'You filthy, murdering scum. You killed him. You killed Carl.'

This time strong arms were quickly round me, restraining me, but not before I had managed to reach out with one hand and rake my fingernails down Will Jones's cheek. The blood spurted instantly from a row of slashes in his flesh. Will cowered away from me and let out a little whimper like an injured puppy dog.

DS Perry was on one side of me and DC Carter on the other. But I couldn't stop myself struggling. I wanted somebody to pay for Carl's death. And I was quite certain that Will Jones must have been responsible. He wanted me for himself, after all.

DS Perry began to talk to me very clearly and slowly, staring directly into my eyes, her hands cupping my face. 'Look at me, Suzanne, and listen,' she said. 'It wasn't him. It wasn't Will Jones. He didn't kill Carl.' She spoke quietly but with authority.

I tried to calm myself.

'Just tell me,' I whispered hoarsely, my anger, all my energy, spent. 'Tell me who did?'

Julie Perry continued to stare into my eyes. 'Look, we've only just found him. We have a lot of checking to do. But, well, we don't think anybody killed him.'

I shook my head in an attempt to clear the fog that seemed to have engulfed it. I didn't say anything, merely looked at her enquiringly, more than that, pleadingly.

'There's a letter he managed to write while he was down there,' she went on. 'I'll give it to you as soon as forensic have finished with it. I think you might find it comforting. It's for you . . .'

I interrupted her. 'Suicide,' I cried. 'Oh no, oh no.'

Had Carl really taken his own life, here in the little house where we had been so happy? If so, then I had to accept that my rejection of him must have been at least partly responsible.

'No, not that either . . .' she began, then paused.

Briefly I was relieved. But only briefly. Carl was still dead.

'Go on,' I said. 'Please go on. What happened? How did he die?'

'The letter makes it clear that Carl came back here, just as everyone originally thought he would, looking for you. We think he climbed in through the kitchen window, probably the very night after he escaped from the court at Penzance. The cellar was open, wasn't it? DC Carter remembers leaving it that way. Perhaps Carl tripped over the flagstone cover. Maybe he dropped straight in. Either way, we know that he fell into the hole, hit his head, and knocked himself unconscious and broke both his ankles – the doctor's already been able to tell us his ankles are broken and that's why he couldn't get himself out of the place.'

She gestured vaguely at the woman in the white paper suit now standing at the back of the room. An awful realisation was beginning to take form inside my head.

'Then someone put the flagstone back,' Julie Perry continued. 'He's been there ever since. The place is pretty well sealed when its covered in, which is why no smell got out for so long. But he probably died of dehydration. It only takes a few days. It was just a terrible accident, Suzanne . . .'

She was still talking, but I wasn't listening any longer. I wasn't hysterical any more either. I felt very cold and very alone.

'He must have been lying down there when I put the flagstone back,' I heard myself whisper. 'I did it. I shut him in there.

'I killed Carl . . .'

Epilogue

Still when I think back to that awful day I feel the horror and the sense of guilt, and above all the terrible shock, as if it were yesterday. I have, in fact, learned to cope by thinking about it as little as possible. There is in any case nothing I can do now to change any of it.

And I have learned to accept that I was not to blame. I have had to do that in order to carry on with my life, which I have managed to do to a degree which continues to surprise me.

The letter Carl left behind was both comforting and painful. He had written as best he could with the bits of old crayon ends and used sketch pads that had been stored in the cellar, scribbling over the sketches he habitually made when he planned out his paintings. It was not easy to read – he had, after all, been badly injured and was forced to write in the dark with only very inadequate materials. The letter was in several colours. Carl had obviously used each crayon end in turn until they became totally blunted and his writing, usually so neat, was scrawled and barely legible.

My darling Suzanne [he wrote]
    I came here to find you, to tell you how much I loved you and how sorry I am for all that happened. I know I shouldn't have run away. I

seem to have spent all my life running, but when the opportunity presented itself I couldn't resist it. I was afraid I would never see you again. Now I am even more afraid of that.

I hope you can read this, my darling. There is no light in the cellar. I fell straight into it when I climbed through the kitchen window. You wouldn't think I would make a mistake like that, would you? After all, I was the one who opened up the old cellar in the first place. I suppose I didn't even consider that it might be open.

I cannot believe now that I locked you away like I did, tied you up. Sometimes I get so frightened for those I care about that I lose all control. I wanted so badly to keep you safe. Maybe it's time I tried to explain to you some things about me, some things about my past. They might help you understand me even if you never forgive me . . .

He then attempted to write down many of the things I had learned about him in America, telling me, when it was already too late, the kind of truth about himself that might have made possible a relationship that I now saw had never had a proper chance of any real normality. At least half of the letter was impossible to read. Not only was Carl having to write over his own old sketches, but also he must sometimes have been trying to use completely blunt crayons without realising that they had no lead centre left. In places all that appeared on top of the drawings already on a page was a scratchy imprint.

There was a mention of Robert Foster and the way in which he died, but sadly I couldn't decipher it. I just had to accept that I would never know for certain whether Carl had really believed I had killed Robert.

I made a decision about that even as I read the letter for the first time. I decided I would believe in Carl again. Absolutely. I had to in order to make any sense of our life together and of our love. From that moment on I accepted in my mind that, confronted not for the first time in his life with the awful spectacle of a dead body covered with blood, Carl had made the same tragic mistake as I had. He had honestly believed I had killed my husband. To believe that was, I was sure, the only way forward for me.

The image of Carl trapped down there, struggling to explain himself, still intent on declaring his love for me, made me shudder. There were odd phrases that stood out, cut into me almost as if I were being stabbed by the knife that for so long I believed I had used on Robert.

I thought you would have found me by now, my darling. I keep calling out to you, but my voice is not very strong any more and I have not heard a sound from upstairs. Maybe you are not there? I don't know how long I have lain here. My head hurts. I think I knocked myself out and I could have been here for some time before I came to. I have no sense of time. If I could stand up maybe I could move the trapdoor, but I think both my ankles are broken. I have tried to pull myself upright, but I am too weak and in too much pain.

The letter made it clear enough that Carl must indeed have knocked himself unconscious when he fell into the cellar, and did not recover consciousness until after I had replaced the flagstone and sealed him in what was to become his tomb.

That, of course, was the bit that would always haunt me.

It also seemed that he wrote the letter over a period of several days, the last days of his life, in fact. Maybe he did not have the strength to write very much at a time. He must have been in a great deal of pain from those broken ankles and growing weaker hour by hour. I imagined him crawling across the stone floor to find the sketch pads and the crayons – he would have known exactly where they were, of course, although it would have been pitch-black down there, because even in the cellar Carl had stored things in a scrupulously ordered way – and then struggling to write down his last thoughts.

The final paragraph still makes me cry every time I read it.

My mouth is very dry. I cannot call out any more. I am sure now that the house is empty. I think I keep lapsing into unconsciousness. I doubt I can survive much longer. All I can think of is you, Suzanne, and how I have let you down. I long for the chance to hold you in my arms one last time and beg your forgiveness. I am pretty sure now that chance is never going to come . . .

There was no proper goodbye. That was where the letter ended. Maybe Carl had fallen into his final unconsciousness then. Or perhaps he had never found the strength to write any more. I was sure that was not the ending he would have planned for his last message to me. But it was the only ending there was.

I keep the letter tied in ribbon in the drawer of my bedside table. I try not to look at it very often. There is no point. I have cried all the tears I can muster for Carl and for our life together. I have grieved as much as I am able.

We buried Carl in St Ives on a wet Monday morning. The rain fell softly but relentlessly all day and somehow that seemed appropriate. It tasted of salt, as it always does in St Ives, and reminded me of rain-soaked walks along empty winter beaches arm-in-arm with the man I was finally saying farewell to. His body now lies in an English churchyard in the little seaside town where I think he experienced, with me, as much happiness as he was ever capable of.

Frank Harvey came over from America and we sat together in a pew at the front of the parish church along with Mariette and her mum.

I was surprised by how many local people turned up. I had not realised they would care, particularly after knowing what Carl had done. But they had like him, of course. You couldn't help liking Carl. Or loving him . . .

Our neighbour Mrs Jackson, old Don Nash, Pete Trevellian from the Inn Plaice, Mrs Scroggins from the library, Steve the handsome fishmonger, my two colleagues at the Archive Centre, and several of the bar staff and regulars from our favourite pubs were all there. DS Perry turned up, which I had somehow expected, but so did DC Carter and PC Rob Partridge, which I had not. The biggest surprise was Fenella Austen, who not only attended the funeral but sought me out later at the graveside.

'He was right, you know. I was jealous of him, of you both,' she said.

I turned to her in surprise.

'No, not his work. I'm long past that.' She gave a small, rueful smile. 'The way he was with you, more than anything. I've never had that with a man. He was flawed, but then who isn't? It's a wonderful thing to be loved the way you were, Suzanne, and don't you forget it. Not many of us get that lucky.'

She had tossed her head in familiar fashion, sending a waft of smoke-laden whiskey fumes across the churchyard, and set off over the wet grass. But after a few steps she stopped abruptly and swung round to face me again. She was wearing a big shiny black cape instead of a raincoat. It billowed out behind her as she moved, making her appearance quite dramatic. 'Another thing,' she instructed in that familiarly centurion way of hers, one arm stretched out before her, finger pointed towards me. 'Don't let this ruin your life. That's the last thing Carl would have wanted. Rise above it, Suzanne. Have a good life. Be happy. You owe him that. After all, it's all he ever wanted for you, isn't it?' I studied her retreating back in amazement.

I continued to receive support from my friends in St Ives throughout the weeks and months that followed the funeral. I had never known that kind of support before and I had frankly not realised that I had friends, apart, of course, from Mariette and her mother. Small towns are like that. The gossip can drive you out of your mind, but the people do rally round in times of need.

I never saw Will Jones again. Apparently he left St

Ives soon after Carl's funeral – which fortunately he made no attempt to attend – and a little later 'For Sale' signs appeared in the window of the Logan Gallery and outside his bungalow. Mariette heard on the jungle drums that Fenella Austen had popped round to the gallery, along with two particularly brawny fishermen drinking pals, and had a quiet word with him.

You never know quite what to believe when it comes to local gossip, but I found I could easily imagine the scene and I doubted there had been anything very quiet about it. Fenella Austen in full flow was enough to frighten anyone off, with or without muscle-men to back her up. I was beginning to have to revise my opinion of St Ives's raddled doyenne artist.

Apart from taking a few days off after the shock of Carl's body being found in Rose Cottage and the week's holiday I arranged for the funeral – following the autopsy, which had predictably confirmed that Carl had died of dehydration – I carried on working at the Archive Centre. It kept my mind busy and gave me a small income to supplement the interest on Robert's legacy, the bulk of which, with advice from yet another friend of Mariette's, I had invested.

One way and another all that had happened in my life seemed finally to have given me a strength I did not know that I was capable of. When I look back on my time with Carl now, and the way it ended, I do not do so with the degree of distress I would expect. Instead, I remember the great love and happiness that we shared.

'Not many of us get that lucky,' Fenella Austen had said. And I knew she was right.

It has been almost a year, now, since Carl's body was discovered. DS Perry has become a friend. Nowadays I call her Julie. She is bright and down to earth, and has experienced so much. She has proven to be a terrific shoulder to lean on. Mariette remains as supportive as ever. And fun. God, how I need to have fun. Out of the blue she has become engaged to marry her fitness instructor, although there's something about the way she talks of him that makes me wonder just how serious she is.

Perhaps curiously, I never really considered leaving St Ives. I reckoned I had done enough running. And in any case, where else would I have gone?

I have bought myself a tiny terraced house not far from the flat I rented off the Hale Road. It is even smaller than Rose Cottage, but has been recently modernised to quite a high standard. The one bedroom is fully fitted in smart pale oak, and the kitchen even has a microwave and a small dishwasher. I find it quite luxurious. Again there is no sea view, I could not afford anywhere with one if I wanted to keep enough of Robert's legacy invested to give me some kind of financial security. But I am content knowing that this is my space in which I can make my own decisions.

I am learning to drive. To have both a car and a home of my own seems to me the ultimate in independence. In spite of the horrors and the great sadnesses of my past I am almost happy. I no longer have nightmares. I have learned to play tennis and I am taking swimming lessons. After work I often go to the cinema with my new friends or for a drink in the pub or to a restaurant for a meal. I am now leading the ordinary, perhaps rather dull, unexciting life I had always yearned for – but it is a normal life. And so many of the simple pleasures and pursuits that I enjoy were denied me by my various 'protectors'.

It's hard to explain what that means when you have spent a lifetime believing that all those kinds of things were always going to be impossible for you.

The only thing absent is a lover and I do miss that. But I can put up with it. I have to put up with it, because I am not yet ready to cope with that sort of intimacy. And I think it will be a long time before I am.

A single dad, unusually perhaps these days a widower rather than a divorcé, lives next door. I have been to the cinema with him once or twice and out to dinner and for a drink several times when he has been able to get a babysitter for his four-year-old daughter. He is good company and he knows what pain is, having nursed his wife through a long terminal illness. I enjoy being with him and am growing quite fond of him. Mariette teases me relentlessly and refers to him as 'your chap'.

He isn't quite that and there has certainly been nothing physical between us so far other than a few brief goodnight kisses. But I like him and I like the fact that he seems to sense that I'm not ready for anything more just yet. Perhaps he isn't either. I don't really know.

I do know that Carl is a hard act to follow and I am beginning to understand just how special our relationship was. I no longer think of it as having been founded on a lie. Our feelings were not a lie. Our love was an overwhelming truth and nothing that has happened could ever change that.

Indeed, Carl had loved me so much that it had, in

a way, been his final undoing. That was a painful legacy, but there are worse ones.

Nor do I feel guilty any more. In fact, far from it. I sometimes wonder if Carl's death was not a kind of release. I regret terribly that he died alone and such a dreadful death. But I am no longer sure how much I regret his death in itself. Sometimes I wonder if Carl could ever have coped with the real world instead of the pretend one we had built around us.

Could he ever have sufficiently conquered his obsessiveness in order to share his life with a woman who wanted more than just him, one no longer prepared to live only in his shadow? I would never have been able to go back to being the Suzanne I had been before, the Suzanne he had created. I am now quite sure of that.

Never again would I rely on one human being. Never again would I let a man or anyone else make my decisions for me, let alone run my entire life.

I could never love anyone more than I loved Carl. But now that I have tasted normality and freedom, or as close to it as any of us can get, I realise that nothing less will do.

Imagine being let out of prison. You would never want to go back, would you, however kind the jailer, however warm and pleasant the jail?

That may be a cruel analogy, but it is what my life with Carl became – not just because of his behaviour, but also because of my own belief that I needed to hide, living in fear of discovery for so long, convinced that I could never have the kind of life others enjoyed. I had been imprisoned all right, not only in that awful old shed, but throughout all my time with Carl. It had been at times an almost glorious imprisonment, but an imprisonment nonetheless. And it is only since I accepted this, that I have been able to go forward.

I can face the future now, because I have finally conquered my past. All of it. My weird, restrictive childhood, my terrible marriage and the awful violence I suffered, my years with Carl culminating in the abduction, all that is behind me now. I am no longer frightened and unsure of myself.

Carl's wonderful *Pumpkin Soup* dominates the living room of my little house, hanging in solitary splendour on a white-painted wall. It is all I have left of him, apart from my memories.

I still call myself Suzanne. Suzanne Adams. Mrs Peters no longer sounds right. But Suzanne, the name Carl gave me the night we arrived in St Ives, the night our extraordinary hidden life together began, that name I will bear for ever.

Carl's voice is already not quite so clear inside my head as it once was. But I think I will always be able to hear him, albeit more faintly as the years pass: 'You're Suzanne from now on. Suzanne, my Lady of the Harbour.'

FOR DEATH COMES SOFTLY

Fanatical love, a dangerous obsession and a
terrible deadly secret ...

DCI Rose Piper's life is in turmoil. At only thirty-five, her
marriage has collapsed and she is unsure about her future
with the police. She retreats to a remote island off the North
Devon coast to rebuild her strength. There she meets
charismatic Robin Davey, owner of the island.

When a tragic accident means that their paths cross once
more, Robin and Rose begin a passionate affair. Then the case
Rose is working on takes a sinister turn. She begins to fear
her personal life is affecting her professional performance.
She has ignored the friends who warned of secrets in Robin's
past. But the time is coming when she will have to discover
the truth about her lover ...

Praise for Hilary Bonner:

'A well-crafted thriller full of sexual tension' *Sunday Mirror*

A PASSION SO DEADLY

A man is murdered in the gardens of a Bristol hotel.

Inquiries reveal that he worked as an escort for a local agency. Rose Piper, investigating DCI, cannot trace the woman he was on his way to meet, and a different suspect enters the frame. But then another employee of Avon escorts is found dead …

In the heart of the West Country, Freddie and Constance Lange live a comfortable existence on land the family has owned for centuries. Freddie adores his wife, an ex nurse who is indispensable to the community for her solid calm and support.

But when Constance and her beloved son fall out, the Lange's idyllic family life is fractured. A darkness creeps in, culminating in tragedy. The two very different worlds of Rose Piper and Constance Lange collide in a tense story of sexual obsession and revenge.

A FANCY TO KILL FOR

'Welcome to a sharp new talent in crime writing'
Daily Express

Richard Corrington is rich, handsome and a household name.
But is he safe?

Journalist Joyce Carter is murdered only a few miles from
Richard's west country home. Richard's wife suspects he has
been having an affair with Joyce and forensics implicate him
in the killing.

But Inspector Todd Mallett believes that Joyce's murder is
part of something much more sinister and complex. There
have been other deaths; the senseless killing of a young
woman on a Cornish beach, another in a grim London
subway ...

And somewhere on the Exmoor hills a killer waits. Stalking
his prey. Ready to strike again.

THE CRUELTY OF MORNING

On a sunny Sunday in 1970, in the Devon resort of Pelham Bay, teenager Jennifer Stone discovers the corpse of a woman in the sparkling summer sea. It is an event that is to shape her destiny and that of Mark Piddle, the young reporter called to the scene, for the next twenty-five years, until the intense tragedy is resolved and a long buried mystery comes to light.

The Cruelty of Morning is a tale of dangerous obsessions, small-town secrets and a destructive, mesmerising love-affair.

Praise for Hilary Bonner:

'A compelling thriller that skilfully weaves together passion and tragedy with sinister obsession' *Company*

'I was caught on pago one by this mesmerising thriller and raced through it in a single sitting … a dark, erotic thriller. Robert Goddard with sex' Sarah Brondhurst, *The Bookseller*

JUDAS CHILD

Carol O' Connell

Sadie Gren's purple bicycle was found abandoned at the bus stop. Then her friend, Gwen, disappeared, which led the police to propose a runaway theory to the press.

But State Police Investigator Rouge Kendall wasn't convinced. On a barstool in Dame's Tavern, where Kendall spent a little too much time, he remembered his own mother, begging for the life of his twin sister, Susan.

That was fifteen years ago. And a man had been imprisoned for that murder – a priest, barely in his twenties.

Father Paul Marie continued to proclaim his innocence. And current events might prove that he was telling the truth, that someone else might be responsible for all three crimes ...

Taut, menacing, intensely felt, Carol O'Connell's fith novel reveals a total mastery of her craft.

'A heart-stopping, twist-in-the-tale novel of intelligence and suspense. True thrills don't come cheap, but they sometimes come as well-written and mesmerising as this.' Frances Fyfield, *Night & Day*

'A menacing and unsettling thriller ... more shocking surprises than a nail-biting horror film ... O'Connell is a consummate story-teller ... a unique talent who deserves to be a household name. The *Judas Child* is a scary monster of a book that should do just that.' Val McDermid, *Express*

FRIENDS IN HIGH PLACES

Donna Leon

'Crime writing of the highest order' *Guardian*

When Commissario Guido Brunetti is visited by a young bureaucrat concerned to investigate the lack of official approval for the building of his apartment years before, his first reaction, like any other Venetian, even a cop, is to think of whom he knows who might bring pressure to bear on the relevant local government department. But when the bureaucrat rings him at work, clearly scared by some information he plans to give Brunetti, and is then found dead after a fall from scaffolding, something is clearly going on that has implications rather greater than the fate of Guido's own apartment.

Brunetti's investigations take him into unfamiliar areas of Venetian life – drug abuse and loan-sharking – while the deaths of two young drug addicts and the arrest – and subsequent release – of a suspected drug-dealer, reveal, once again, what a difference it makes in Venice to have friends in high places.

'With her usual skilful plotting and perfectly judged pace ... this is Leon's best so far' *Scotland on Sunday*

'Rich entertainment' *Sunday Times*

'All donna Leon's novels are excellent ... *Friends in High Places* is, however, by far the best' *Evening Standard*

'*Friends in High Places* is a splendid read, clever and provoking' *Observer*

ALSO AVAILABLE IN PAPERBACK

☐ For Death Comes Softly	Hilary Bonner	£ 5.99
☐ A Passion So Deadly	Hilary Bonner	£ 5.99
☐ A Fancy to Kill For	Hilary Bonner	£ 5.99
☐ The Cruelty of Morning	Hilary Bonner	£ 5.99
☐ Friends in High Places	Donna Leon	£ 5.99
☐ Harm Done	Ruth Rendell	£ 5.99
☐ Judas Child	Carl O'Connell	£ 5.99

ALL ARROW BOOKS ARE AVAILABLE THROUGH MAIL ORDER OR FROM YOUR LOCAL BOOKSHOP.

PAYMENT MAY BE MADE USING ACCESS, VISA, MASTER-CARD, DINERS CLUB, SWITCH AND AMEX, OR CHEQUE, EUROCHEQUE AND POSTAL ORDER (STERLING ONLY).

EXPIRY DATE .... SWITCH ISSUE NO. ☐☐

SIGNATURE ....

PLEASE ALLOW £2.50 FOR POST AND PACKING FOR THE FIRST BOOK AND £1.00 PER BOOK THEREAFTER.

ORDER TOTAL: £................................ (INCLUDING P&P)

ALL ORDERS TO:
ARROW BOOKS, BOOKS BY POST, TBS LIMITED, THE BOOK SERVICE, COLCHESTER ROAD, FRATING GREEN, COLCHESTER, ESSEX, CO7 7 DW, UK.

TELEPHONE: (01206) 256 000
FAX: (01206) 255 914

NAME ....

ADDRESS..

....

Please allow 28 days for delivery. Please tick box if you do not wish to receive any additional information. ☐
Prices and availability subject to change without notice.